"I'm not afraid of you. If you lay a violent hand on me, I'll wait till you're asleep and shoot you. Or . . . or poison your food the next day."

At her audacious blustering, he threw back his head and gave a muffled shout of laughter. The idea of Christina boldly threatening his life delighted his sense of the ridiculous. She tried to shove him away, furious at the swaggering amusement he made no attempt to hide. He cupped her little butt with his big hands and pulled her relentlessly against him. He wanted to slide down with her into the silken cocoon of her bed and drown himself in the satiny pleasure of her body. He could spend a lifetime making love to her . . .

"My little spitfire," he murmured. "You've more strength of will than most men, sunshine. But not, I think, more than your husband."

He bent his head and covered her parted lips with his own.

Other **AVON ROMANCES**

Sunshine and Shadow

Kathleen Harrington

AVON BOOKS ◆ NEW YORK

SUNSHINE AND SHADOW is an original publication of Avon Books. This work has never before appeared in book form. This work is a novel. Any similarity to actual persons or events is purely coincidental.

AVON BOOKS
A division of
The Hearst Corporation
1350 Avenue of the Americas
New York, New York 10019

Copyright © 1993 by Kathleen Harrington
Inside cover author photograph by Debbi De Mont
Published by arrangement with the author
Library of Congress Catalog Card Number: 92-97294
ISBN: 0-380-77058-X

First Avon Books Printing: May 1993

AVON TRADEMARK REG. U.S. PAT. OFF. AND IN OTHER COUNTRIES, MARCA REGISTRADA, HECHO EN U.S.A.

Printed in the U.S.A.

RA 10 9 8 7 6 5 4 3 2 1

To my brothers,
James Patrick
Anthony Ivan
David Louis
Steven John
and Brian Matt
Persinger

my little sister,
Carol Ann Persinger Duthoy

and especially my baby sister,
Joan Helen Persinger
who as the youngest of eight
has always been our family's
golden ray of sunshine

I love you all!

How oft, when thou, my music, music play'st,
Upon that blessed wood whose motion sounds
With thy sweet fingers, when thou gently sway'st
The wiry concord that mine ear confounds,
Do I envy those jacks that nimble leap
To kiss the tender inward of thy hand,
Whilst my poor lips, which should that harvest reap,
At the wood's boldness by thee blushing stand!
To be so tickl'd, they would change their state
And situation with those dancing chips,
O'er whom thy fingers walk with gentle gait,
Making dead wood more bless'd than living lips.
  Since saucy jacks so happy are in this,
  Give them thy fingers, me thy lips to kiss.

—Shakespeare
128th Sonnet

Chapter 1

August 1762
London

Dressed in a warm brown traveling cape and matching bonnet adorned with yellow silk rosebuds, Lady Christina Berringer stood on the steps of Sanborn House and glanced around St. James's Square. The formal entry of the three-story town house faced the spacious central piazza. The east side, with its charming bay windows, looked down on Duke of York Street, where a traveling berlin and four matched grays already waited for her on the corner. The footman was just descending from his high perch at the rear of the vehicle when he saw Christina wave to him. He nodded and hurried toward her. Behind her in the entryway, her lady's maid stood with a small valise and a bandbox.

"Here, give them to me, Marie," Christina instructed. She turned and reached for her baggage. "You mustn't come out into the cool air, or you'll take a worse chill."

"You'd best hurry, miladi. The coach is already waiting," the abigail answered in a raspy voice. Clutching a faded wrapper tightly about her thin frame, Marie Boucher stood in the entry, her long fingers anxiously pressed against the brass knocker on the open front door. "I wish you'd let me come with you, mademoiselle," she scolded. "You shouldn't be traveling alone. It would be far wiser to wait for the return of Lord and Lady Sanborn, regardless of the urgency of the note."

"Nonsense! They won't be back for hours. And besides,

1

my sister is needed at home. She can't be traisping off to St. Albans with me at the drop of a hat. Don't worry, Marie. I'll be perfectly safe. Lady Muggleton's coachman will deposit me right on her doorstep. Now stay inside and explain what's happened to my family when they return."

In the northwest, black storm clouds gathered, foretelling the near arrival of autumn. Christina ignored the gloomy signs of foul weather and hurried down the town house steps. If she didn't leave at once, there was a chance that Gwen would return and try to stop her. At the very least, her calm, rational, older sister would delay her, insisting that Christina wait until Gwen's own personal maid could pack a bag and go along. As the door of Sanborn House closed behind her, Christina kicked up her heels and raced across the street like a hoyden.

The driver, who'd been gazing abstractedly at the darkening sky, tipped his hat and clambered down from the enormous height of his box seat to join the footman. The two retainers, very likely father and son, were dressed in familiar red and gold livery. They bowed to her in perfect tandem.

"Ev'ning, my lady," said the burly coachman. He smiled congenially, and the twinkle in his warm blue eyes brought a fleeting memory of her grandfather. "I wasn't expecting you for a good while yet. Does your ladyship have some trunks for me to lift up?"

She returned his friendly smile. "No. No trunks. There simply wasn't time to pack anything but a small traveling case. Here, take this and let's be off. I'm eager to arrive as soon as possible."

Barely glancing at the heraldic shield displayed on the side of the coach, she accepted his hand and nimbly hopped up. The door snapped shut, the two men scrambled to their respective places, and the conveyance leaped forward as the driver's whip snapped out over the lead's head.

Marie Boucher cracked open the tall door of Sanborn House and peered into the dusk. She smiled at the sight of the carriage bowling out of the square. Her satisfaction was short-lived. Another coach-and-four drew up to the recently vacated street corner. On the other side of Duke of

York, a woman hurried out of her fashionable residence. She was dressed in a voluminous velvet cape with a hood pulled well down over her hair and partially hiding her face.

The lady moved purposefully to the waiting vehicle and called up to the ferret-faced driver. "Here, coachman. I've two small trunks that must be fetched. You'll find my baggage just inside the hallway. My servants will help you bring them out and load them up on top."

The unliveried driver, attired in merely a nondescript tan coat, quickly doffed his cap and scrambled down. He bowed obsequiously and then hustled toward her house. In a matter of minutes the second coach departed, heading in the same direction as the first and gathering speed as it left the square.

"Mon Dieu!" Marie gasped. She flew down the steps and to the deserted corner. Despite the fact that a swath of black fabric had been deliberately draped across the coat of arms emblazoned on its door, she'd recognized the second coach. But too late.

Surprised by the jolting pace, Christina pulled back the gold silk blinds and watched the elegant homes and stylish shops of Mayfair fly by. No doubt the coachman was trying to beat the storm. With a sigh of anticipation, she removed her bonnet and slipped back against the plush red cushions piled in the corner of the seat. What would one offer an astute collector for a lute once owned by Ottaviano Petrucci? She bit her bottom lip and mentally calculated the value of such a prize.

Only that afternoon her dear friend Jacob Rothenstein had helped her acquire a zither, a timbrel, and a flute, all from the fourteenth century, and all in near-perfect condition. The wealthy merchant and banker had explained that a wily old London trader named Colley Moss had brought them to him eight days ago. Moss had purchased them from an ignorant Buckinghamshire peddler, who knew no more of their real worth than their first owner. But Colley Moss was well aware of their value. Christina had had to pay the staggering sum of nine thousand pounds for the trio of ancient instruments. Thrilled by their acquisition, she'd wondered aloud about the original owner, who'd so foolishly parted with such treasures.

Jacob's brown eyes had been serious as he'd leaned on his cane and met her gaze. "Moss claimed the peddler swore it was a nobleman who's been reduced to penury by his own father," he told her, stroking his long white beard. "Said the unhappy buck had been forced to empty his attics just to pay his younger brother's tradesmen's bills."

Propping her feet up on the velvet-covered seat opposite her, Christina now smiled to herself in delight. Her afternoon's run of good luck had continued. She'd returned home from Rothenstein's warehouse to find the note from Muggs. The fact that her maid was ill hadn't stopped Christina. She knew that she absolutely couldn't miss the opportunity to purchase an Italian lute dating back to the fifteenth century.

A distinguished white-haired butler opened the carriage door and assisted Christina down. He offered her the support of his elbow and led her through the wide oak door, which stood open to the rain, and into a magnificent baronial hall. She'd never before given any thought to what Lady Muggleton's home might look like, but somehow she'd never expected her grandmother's seventy-year-old friend to live in such historic splendor. The enormous room was downright medieval in appearance, with a tremendous shield of heraldry displayed proudly above the main portal. Against a gold background, a red dragon snorted fire, while at its sharp-clawed feet was an inscription in Latin which Christina translated with increasing wonderment: *Honor and Duty Above All.* Pike, staffs, even broadswords and claymores were stacked haphazardly in the corners of the hall, while wooden boxes, upended packing crates, and straw-filled barrels were scattered across the black and white tiled floor.

The butler indicated that he would take her cloak, bonnet, and gloves. After divesting her of these articles, he bowed. "If my lady will please follow me, I'll take you to the library. The master is expecting you."

After the ferocity of the storm, the peaceful stillness of the hallway was a comfort. Christina smiled in satisfaction as he motioned her through carved double doors into a well-furnished library. The room was as hushed as the hallway; obviously, the household had been long abed. So much for Lady Irene Muggleton staying up till all hours of the night, visiting with Mr. Noyes and awaiting her arrival.

Satin drapes were pulled across the high windows, closing out the raging gale, while inside warm wood reflected the glowing candlelight. The walls were lined with half-empty bookshelves that should have held hundreds of sleek leather volumes. Instead, much of their contents was stacked in boxes. Everywhere, open trunks and crates held piles of letters, leather-bound books, jasperware snuff boxes, scent bottles, china figurines, cut-glass vases, medicine phials, Wedgwood trinket cases, and miniature portraits—all the personal mementos and small treasures that one saves for posterity. A vague feeling of uneasiness ruffled Christina's calm poise. Hesitantly, she stepped into the room.

"Mrs. Gannet has arrived, my lord," the butler announced. Then he disappeared, closing the doors behind him.

A gentleman, somewhere in his mid-thirties, sat at a large desk at the far end of the room. He wore no wig, and his black hair was tousled as though he'd been running his fingers through it in agitation. He'd been reading what must have been a rather unpleasant document, and when he looked up, he was still frowning. The frown deepened to a ferocious scowl at the sight of her.

"Mr. Zachary Noyes?" she asked hopefully.

He rose slowly from his chair, and her head tilted upward as she followed his ascent. He was tall, broad-shouldered, and as intimidating as only an uncompromisingly masculine man can be. In a society where males were painted, powdered, bejeweled, and perfumed, he was a glaring exception. There wasn't anything soft or delicate about him. His straight nose and angular jaw gave his features a stern, autocratic cast. A jagged scar slashed wickedly through one black eyebrow and continued across his high forehead to disappear into the hairline. There'd been no attempt with cosmetics or any other artifice to soften its unnerving effect.

"You are Mr. Noyes, I take it," she repeated, suddenly breathless.

"No," he answered, "I'm not." He leaned forward and placed his palms on the desktop. The tiniest vestige of a smile flickered across his wide mouth. "Nor are you Mrs. Gannet."

"I . . . uh, who?" She swallowed and glanced around, searching for Lady Muggleton. Her initial feeling of uneasiness slid into a dark well of apprehension as something told her that not only was her hostess absent from the library, she was also nowhere else to be found on the premises. Christina's heart thumped erratically. Oh, Lord, this time her impulsiveness had really landed her in the briars.

With a casual gesture, the man shoved the chair out of his way with one foot and came around the desk. Christina, making no attempt to be so nonchalant, took a decisive step backward and reached behind her for the doorknob. He paused, apparently reading the sudden wariness in her eyes. With a start of mortification, she realized she was staring at his scar and quickly looked away.

"Colonel Roderick Fielding, at your service." He bowed with exaggerated formality. It was a mocking gesture, filled with cynicism and self-derision. Without words, he made it clear that her tactlessness hadn't surprised him. He expected a young woman of refined sensibilities to be shocked, even repulsed, by his disfigurement.

In the candlelight, his gray eyes glittered like highly polished silver—cold and hard and calculating. He wore buff knee breeches and black riding boots. A white linen shirt was open at his throat, the lacings loosened to reveal a mat of thick black hair just below the hollow of his collarbone. The sleeves had been rolled up, displaying powerful forearms and broad hands—scarred, callused hands that surely could never be trained to delicately pluck a lute or draw a bow across the strings of a violin. Here was no effete London dilettante who dabbled in antique musical instruments. Good gad, she doubted if he'd know a clavier from a pianoforte.

Still holding on to the doorknob behind her, Christina slowly turned her hand to release the latch. A crash of

thunder filled the room. Startled, she clasped her hands together in front of her and stared at the draped windows.

He took immediate advantage of her preoccupation to
move closer. A taunting smile creased his scar-ravaged
face, revealing even white teeth.

"And you are . . .?" he prompted. He inclined his head
in encouragement, as though she were a refugee from
some asylum for the feebleminded who had wandered in
from the storm and might not be expected to know her
own name without assistance.

"Lady Christina Berringer," she snapped. She favored
him with the briefest of curtsies. "I came to see Lady
Muggleton. Where is she?"

He cocked his head and glanced sideways, as if half expecting the woman to appear by magic. "You planned to
meet her here? In my library?"

"This is the Muggleton estate in St. Albans, is it not?"

"Now there you are mistaken, Lady Christina Berringer."
He grinned in perverse glee to have caught her in such a
monumental error. "You are presently in Buckinghamshire.
And this happens to be my home, which shouldn't be too
surprising, since you were brought here in my carriage by
my servants."

The barbed words sounded needlessly curt and unpleasant. Gathering her wits about her, she gestured with an
airy wave of her hand in what she hoped was her most
worldly, sophisticated manner. "And may I say you have a
lovely home, sir? Now I really should be going." She
turned to open the library door.

He reached across her shoulder and held it shut with
one large hand. "Not just yet," he said softly in her ear.
The deep chords of his baritone voice vibrated down her
spine, rich and full and resonant.

She could feel his gaze rake over her, noting every detail of her rumpled traveling dress, her damp slippers, her
disarrayed curls. She squirmed inwardly under his stare,
but valiantly squared her shoulders and turned to face him
again. He didn't have the good manners to step back, but
continued to loom over her, forcing her to look straight up
at him, as if she were part pygmy. She pressed herself flat

against the door and prepared to scream her lungs out if he made the least threatening move.

"Going back out in this weather," he went on with unruffled calm, "would be a very bad idea." His gaze descended from her disheveled hair to her tighty pursed lips. "Lady Christina Berringer," he mused softly. His eyes narrowed, as though he were turning some newfound idea over in his mind. "You really are rather appealing, my dear, though at the moment you quite resemble a bedraggled kitten." He reached over, lifted a limp curl off her shoulder, and held it insolently in his long fingers.

She batted his hand away and glared at him. She'd been raised with two older brothers. She knew that now wasn't the time to play the frightened lamb. Men respected gumption, not missish vapors. Her best strategy was to brazen it out until she could think of a better plan. "If you'll permit me to be seated?" she said. She indicated the sofa in front of the massive fireplace with a gesture of outward assurance. He stepped back to allow her just enough space to move into the center of the room, and she wondered if he knew her knees were shaking beneath her hooped skirt.

A bouquet of yellow August roses on a massive writing table filled the air with its sweet perfume. Flames crackled in the fireplace as burning logs popped and sparked, and she moved toward the marble hearth, seeking the security of its warmth. In the large mirror over the mantelpiece, she resembled a pale, frightened waif. She gathered her courage and turned to face him. She was determined to speak with all the calm conviction she could muster.

"Whoever you are, Colonel, *sir*, be so kind as to ring for your butler. I wish my things. I'm leaving immediately."

"Fielding," he offered. "Roderick." He strode to a side table, lifted a decanter of brandy, and partially filled a tulip-shaped goblet. "Leaving in this abominable weather is out of the question. You were lucky to arrive here at all. It's a wonder the carriage wasn't mired up to the wheel hubs before you reached Uxbridge. Keighly should have put you up at a comfortable inn along the way."

"Your coachman suggested it when we changed teams at the Proud Lion," Christina admitted. "And two acquaintances of mine, who chanced to meet me there, offered to share their room with me, but I refused."

"Two acquaintances of yours?" he questioned testily. "And who might they be?"

"The Countess of Ailesbury and her older sister."

"Ah, two of my nosiest neighbors. No doubt they were too polite to ask why you were traveling unattended in my berlin this evening."

Christina shrugged uncomfortably. "They were calling something to me from across the inn yard just as I was leaving, but I couldn't quite make out what they were saying." She lowered her head and tried to smooth the wrinkles from her crushed skirt. "Perhaps they didn't recognize your coach after all."

"With the Rugden dragon displayed on the door, they recognized my coach all right, as well as the distinctive red and gold livery worn by my servants. Too bad you didn't have the sense to do the same." He handed her the glass. "Here, drink this," he ordered. "You must be chilled from the ride."

Roderick poured a generous splash of brandy for himself and sat down on the settee facing the young woman. He leaned back comfortably on the cushions and raised the crystal snifter to savor the aromatic fumes. Where in the bloody hell had she come from?

He'd spent the last three weeks inventorying every single possession he'd inherited from his mother. Every set of china, every chair, every table, every painting she'd left him had been packed for shipment and eventual sale at auction in London. Then he'd waded through his father's ledgers, diaries, and correspondence, searching for some clue that would provide the answer to the overwhelming financial debacle the deceased earl had left behind. Baffled, exhausted, and in a vile humor, Roderick had been looking forward to the momentary arrival of his comely mistress. He'd planned to drown himself in Madeline Gannet's lush curves, to bed her there on the library floor with such swift, total abandon that all the worries and cares that had tormented him since his arrival in England would be driven from his mind. Instead he'd been interrupted in his painful task by a foolish little debutante who hadn't had the foresight to stay in an inn for the night or the good grace to arrive at someone else's home.

The evening's amorous consolations, which he'd contemplated with such surety, now slipped away, only to be replaced with the irksome duty of entertaining a young lady of apparently unquestionable virtue. Worse yet, she was more than likely the daughter of an old family friend. Hell, there'd be no bedtime solace tonight. He didn't need anyone to remind him of the behavior demanded of a gentleman. Or of the fact that enormous blue eyes and honey-gold hair had always been his downfall.

She had an alluring figure despite her youth. Shapely and firm and high breasted, with the promise of a beauty that would slowly ripen in the years to come, the kind of beauty that would drive a softhearted man to the brink of insanity.

How fortunate for him that he was so hardened by experience.

Christina sniffed the brandy and took a tiny sip. Two more sips, and the drink began to spread its toasty glow through her. She watched him over the rim of her glass as he continued to stare disconcertingly up at her.

"Suppose you tell me just how the devil you ended up riding about in my coach on a night like this without even a female companion?"

She relaxed a trace. If he were going to scold her about the proprieties, he surely wasn't planning to ravish her. "I came here to visit Lady Muggleton and her friend, Mr. Zachary Noyes. I was in a frantic hurry, lest he leave before I could examine an antique lute in his possession. A lute I desperately want to purchase for my collection."

He appeared to be turning that over in his mind. The look of cool speculation in those intelligent gray eyes brought her a fresh surge of misgiving. "You're one of Waldwick's daughters, aren't you?"

"You've heard of the marquess?" she questioned evasively. She rolled the brandy snifter back and forth between her hands, just as she'd seen her father do, and the amber liquid released its heady perfume. Not for the world would she admit that this was the first time she'd ever tasted it.

"We're acquainted."

"You *know* my father?" She made no attempt to hide her disbelief. "Then why don't I know you? I vow, I've never seen you before in my life."

He ignored her skepticism and replied in a tone of overstated politeness. "I apologize for the unforgivable oversight. After many years of absence, I've only recently returned to England due to the death of my father."

Comprehension dawned at last. Of course, *that* was who he was. The Earl of Rugden. And that was why the servants' livery had seemed so familiar. Christina had attended the funeral services held for Myles Fielding with her family that past spring. The old peer, despite the fact that he'd been a bruising rider, had been thrown from his hunter. He'd been a good friend of her father's, and Austin Berringer had been deeply saddened by the sudden, unexpected loss. Although Christina had never really known the deceased man well, he'd been very close to her father in their younger days.

"I'm sorry," she said, and she meant it. "Pray, forgive me. I was so confused when I first arrived, I didn't realize who you were, even after you introduced yourself. Please accept my condolences." She lowered her lids to hide her embarrassment and stared down at her glass. Then recovering her aplomb, she glanced up once again, too fascinated to hide her curiosity. "So you're Percy's older brother!" she blurted out. "The great war hero."

"Evidently my brother's been boasting about my military accomplishments ad nauseam." The earl's deep voice was filled with self-mockery. "That must have been very boring for a girl of your tender years."

"Oh, no. It's just that Percy's very proud of you." She smiled at Rugden in tolerant female understanding. "Besides, the latest war news has been all any gentleman's been able to talk about for ages. Both *The Gazette* and *The Times* have been filled with daily accounts of all the battles. Our fleet's successful blockade of the channel was practically all any male over ten wanted to discuss at every ball held last season."

He leaned an elbow on the arm of the sofa and ran the tip of one finger over his lips in quiet reflection. A twinkle of humor momentarily lit up his solemn eyes. "I take it you're not particularly impressed with military heroes."

"I didn't say that!" she protested, stung by the astute remark. "I'm as patriotic as the next woman. Why, I'm sure, I'm very grateful to all the gallant soldiers who risked their lives to fight for England."

"But you feel there are more important things in life than rape, pillage, and plunder." He rose from the sofa. "I couldn't agree with you more." Moving to the side table, he replenished his glass.

Despite his size, he had a silent, lethal grace. She would never have guessed he was related to Percy, yet she could see the strong family resemblance now that she was looking for it. The same straight black hair. The same tall, large-boned frame. But where Percy was thin and lanky and tended to slouch, the older brother was a stiff-backed army specimen of solid, well-muscled bulk. The difference went far deeper than outward appearances, however. The younger Fielding's gray eyes were warm and full of high spirits. The elder's were cold-blooded and sardonic.

Instead of returning to the settee, he rested one arm along the mantelpiece and looked down at her from his great height. Christina edged away from him. Good gad, he had to be six feet four, if he was an inch.

"Now, young lady, I think it's time you explained how you came to arrive at Rugden Court in the dead of night."

His caustic tone implied that the fault was all her own. But getting into the wrong coach had been an honest mistake. Surely anyone could have made it. There was no need for him to behave like an annoyed schoolmaster.

"And traveling alone, at that," he continued before she had a chance to defend herself. "Not really the thing for a well-behaved little miss to do, is it? Or does your father always let you careen around the countryside by yourself in strange men's coaches?"

"Hardly ever," she gritted. "I came alone because my maid was ill. I left a note for my sister and her husband, packed a small case, and entered the coach that stood waiting for me. What I don't understand is why it was *your* carriage," she added suspiciously. "And why *your* servants put me into it and drove me here."

He shrugged. "Obviously a case of mistaken identity. I can assure you that it wasn't there for your use." Rugden moved to within inches of Christina and looked down at her, his thoughtful eyes hooded. "You must be Waldwick's youngest brat; you look no more than seventeen. How can such an unfledged chick afford to buy even one rare antique, let alone possess an entire collection?"

Christina stretched herself to her full height, which wasn't much beside his imposing stature, and spoke with honeyed insincerity. "I beg to differ, my lord. I'm nineteen years old, soon to be twenty. And contrary to what you might like to believe, it isn't necessary to be the eldest male offspring in order to receive an inheritance. You're not the only person in the world to be left a fortune." She instantly regretted her words and flushed with mortification at her inexcusable bragging. But good gad, he'd goaded her into it. "Please summon a servant," she said. "I'm leaving."

"Ah, but, Little Miss Insolence, I couldn't let you leave in the middle of this storm. The coach would be mired in mud the moment you left the driveway."

Changing his tactics, the earl flashed her a wide grin in an open attempt at beguilement. Next he'd be donning the scarlet coat draped across the back of the sofa, she thought. The sight of him in his military uniform, complete with gold braided epaulets, carmine sash, and shiny buttons, could be expected to dazzle any empty-headed ingenue silly enough to land herself in the present impossible situation. Little did he realize, she'd be far more impressed if he could play the viola de gamba with the inborn talent of his younger brother. Rugden had all the finesse of a human catapult.

"How could you deny the son of an old family friend the chance to offer you his hospitality?" he protested. "We haven't even had time to get acquainted."

Christina ignored his look of insufferable complacency. There was no need for him to treat her as though she were twelve years old and a ninny to boot. "I'm afraid I've learned more about you this evening, my lord, than I could ever wish to know."

"But you really haven't see me at my most charming."

She tipped her head and favored him with a disdainful smile.

Rugden moved to the wall and pulled the bell rope. "My butler will show you to a bedchamber. The night's half gone as it is. We'll see what can be done about your predicament in the morning." He drew near again. Taking her hand, he lifted it to his lips in the effusive, practiced gesture of a court emissary. "Till morning, Lady Christina Berringer," he murmured softly.

She snatched her hand away and pushed past him to the door. There she met the butler, who waited in regal disinterest, despite being arrayed in a garish plaid flannel night robe and Moroccan slippers of embroidered red leather.

"Hawkins," Rugden instructed, not even pausing to inspect his servant's fantastic nightwear, "show Lady Christina to her room and see that she has anything she might require."

Christina recognized the common sense of his solution to her dilemma. After all, he was a noted peer of the realm, the son of an old family friend, and a renowned officer and war hero. Faith, if she couldn't trust Percy's esteemed older brother, whom could she trust? She flounced out of the library without another word. Unable to stop herself, she glanced back over her shoulder. The earl was leaning against the doorjamb. He twisted the delicate brandy snifter idly in his scarred hands as he followed her progress down the hallway. When he caught her sneaking a look at him, he lifted the crystal glass in a mock salute and smiled again. There was a cold, speculative light in his shrewd gray eyes.

On the second floor, Hawkins opened the door to a spacious bedchamber and then withdrew. Christina quickly turned the key in the lock before inspecting the room. A thick carpet covered the floor, and pale roses decorated the faded silk wallpaper. High on the ceiling, pink-bottomed cherubs flew above a large four-poster bed. An enormous armoire, with detailed floral carvings done in the French style, graced one side of the room. She opened its mahogany doors and found her traveling cape, gloves, and bonnet, along with her emptied bandbox. The one dress she'd packed in her haste was nowhere in sight.

Her small valise had been opened, and her nightgown was laid out on the coverlet. Next to that was her dressing robe. Her blue felt slippers, not nearly as exotic as the butler's, were on the floor beside the bed, while her silver hairbrush and comb rested on the bedside table. Plopping down on the edge of the soft mattress, she took off her water-stained shoes and once-white stockings. Next she removed her skirt, bodice, and taffeta petticoat, with its wide whalebone panniers. She pulled her frilled nightdress on right over her corset and knee-length chemise. Since the boned and stitched stays were laced up the back, it was impossible for her to do otherwise. She slipped beneath the warm coverlet with an exasperated sigh and propped herself up against the pillow. It was going to be an uncomfortable night—at least what was left of it.

She took down her hair and brushed it thoroughly. Despite her strange surroundings, she began to feel drowsy. Her heavy eyelids were nearly closed when she heard footsteps coming down the carpeted hallway. The long, purposeful stride could only be Rugden's. He paused briefly outside her room and then went on. In moments a nearby door shut quietly.

Christina's gaze flew to the reassuring sight of the key in the lock. It remained just as she'd left it. Suddenly aching with exhaustion, she rearranged the pillow and scooted down under the thick comforter.

How she had come to be at Rugden Court remained a mystery. But there was no doubt that the note from Lady Irene was urgent. If the storm had brought her to a standstill, it had probably delayed Zachary Noyes as well. There was still a chance, if she left early in the morning, that she could reach the Muggleton estate before Noyes left for Edinburgh.

Her thoughts drifted to the earl. She'd met his kind before. Most women fell all over themselves at the sight of a handsome man in uniform. Nowadays a military hero took it for granted that every featherbrained chit within twenty miles would swoon at the sight of his scarlet regimentals. Colonel Roderick Fielding was no different. He might have a certain rugged appeal for empty-headed females, but he was far too sure of himself for her.

You look no more than seventeen.

What a pompous ass!

If she ever met him in London, she'd have the pleasure of giving him the cut direct. The delightful picture of herself, dressed in her most alluring gown, turning a cold shoulder on him in the middle of a crowded ballroom brought a sleepy smile to her lips. A dreadful thought intruded on the pleasant scenario. Good gad, surely he'd never be so dastardly as to tell anyone she'd spent a night in his home, unchaperoned except for his servants?

Chapter 2

Christina awoke the next morning to find herself in an unfamiliar bed. She glanced around the room, recalled the events of the preceding evening, and jumped out from under the comforter. Hurrying over to a window, she pulled aside the drape and pushed back one tall shutter. It was still raining, though the downpour had slowed to a steady drizzle. The sky was dark with more black clouds rolling in from the west. She groaned aloud at the miserable weather and then moaned again at her own stiff, sore body. Her bruised rib cage felt like someone had beaten her soundly with a stick while she slept. No one should be forced to spend the night encased in whalebone stays. She glanced at the small clock on the table beside the bed. Where was the upstairs maid? One of the staff should have brought up the breakfast tray ages ago—along with a pitcher of hot water and a basin to wash in.

Determined to rouse some help, Christina padded across the rug on bare feet. When she reached the bell pull, she changed her mind. She couldn't imagine Rugden presiding over a poorly run household. He fairly exuded ironhanded authority. The poor chambermaid was probably hiding somewhere, crying her eyes out because he'd criticized her for a minor infraction. Why cause more trouble?

Yesterday's rumpled gown lay in a heap on the floor where she'd dropped it. Since she was already laced in her corset, Christina decided to finish dressing by herself. She struggled awkwardly at the chore, first pulling on the unwieldy petticoat of cream-colored taffeta with its built-in panniers. After that came the bodice and matching stom-

17

acher of brown and white figured muslin. Last on was the cocoa-brown skirt, open in front to display the underskirt and held back by dark brown satin bows.

Marie always helped her mistress with her toilette, chattering at her the whole while in a stream of raucous French. Working solo, Christina was puffing with exertion by the time she'd finished the task. She realized, too late, that she'd forgotten her shoes and stockings. Everything had to come off again so she could reach her toes. After she had again completed her dressing, she moved to a full-length mirror hanging on the wall beside the wardrobe. Her hair was a hopeless tangle. Gathering her brush, comb, and another ribbon from her case, she attempted to fasten the unruly curls on top of her head. After each try, the stubborn locks came cascading down. She gave up and tied her hair back with a large bow, then stuck her tongue out in contempt at the little girl in the looking glass.

The disgraceful rumble of her stomach reminded her that it had been hours since she'd eaten. Well, there certainly was no point in remaining upstairs and starving. She'd have breakfast and then demand that a carriage be brought around. This time she was going to brook no arguments. Prepared to greet the obstinate colonel with all the worldly sophistication she could muster in a wrinkled dress and adolescent curls, she threw back her shoulders. Ouch and damnation! Sharp pains bounced up and down her ribs like brass mallets striking the strings of a clavichord. Her sister had always warned her she'd pay dearly for her headstrong ways. Faith, Gwen was proven correct one more time.

Christina left the bedchamber and hurried down the open staircase. She could hear the soft clink of dishes coming from the first floor's main hallway. The delicious smell of hot coffee enticed her to peek inside a small informal dining room, where Hawkins stood with his back to the door, stacking china plates on a high walnut sideboard.

Rugden was seated at the center of the table. The moment he saw her, he removed his napkin from his lap, rose politely, and smiled with consummate charm. Obviously, he was still engaged in his belated campaign of dutifully entertaining the unexpected houseguest.

"Good afternoon, sleepyhead." He turned to address the servant behind him. "See there, Hawkins. The young lady is perfectly fine. All she needed was a good night's rest."

The butler pivoted to look at Christina with honest concern. "I'm sorry for the inconvenience, my lady. I'm sure you're hungry."

"I'm famished," she admitted as she entered the room.

The earl had apparently already eaten and was merely enjoying a cup of coffee. His riding coat had been flung carelessly over a nearby chair, as though he'd come in from the outdoors only moments before. She suspected he'd been up for hours, perhaps even ridden in spite of the rain. He was neatly attired in fawn-colored breeches and waistcoat, with a crisp white shirt adorned with a simple row of ruffles at the wrist. No satin and lace for this man. No cloying perfume, either. He smelled like a fresh, clean, rain-soaked forest. And still no wig. Instead, he'd ruthlessly pulled his straight hair back into a short, clubbed queue and tied it with a narrow black ribbon. He was as spartan in his dress as he'd been the evening before, but he didn't appear nearly so fierce in the daylight.

As if to prove he wasn't, he flashed her a disarming grin. "You had Hawkins worried, my dear. He suggested we pound on your door to make certain you were all right. But I wanted to be sure you'd be feeling rested this morning and not so out of sorts. You look like a ray of sunshine on this rainy day. Sit down and have something to eat." He gestured to the chair across from him.

Christina slid into the seat indicated, and he resumed his own. She looked up and met the butler's worried gaze. "Thank you for being so thoughtful, Hawkins. I appreciate your solicitude."

Why neither man hadn't simply sent up a housemaid to wake her with a breakfast tray was something she'd discover later. Right now, she just wanted to eat. With a grateful smile to Hawkins, she accepted the plate of poached eggs and toast placed in front of her, then turned to face the earl. "I'd like to continue on my way as soon as possible. I'm anxious to reach St. Albans before Mr. Noyes leaves for Edinburgh."

Rugden pushed his chair back slightly from the table

and frowned at her. "I'm afraid you'll have to wait a while longer before meeting up with the marvelous Mr. Noyes, as fascinating as he and his lute must be. There's another storm rolling in. The sky cleared for a few hours early this morning, but I felt your rest was too important to disrupt. Besides, you'd have been stranded at the Proud Lion. You're much better off here till proper arrangements can be made."

He stood to leave, and she glared up at him. "You mean I could have resumed my journey, but you thought I needed my sleep instead?" She threw her napkin on the table. "I'd have preferred to wait at the inn till the storm blew over!"

"I decided you'd be better off here." The words were spoken with the infuriating calm of an officer used to making critical decisions at a moment's notice—decisions that were never questioned by the soldiers under him. They wouldn't dare. He nodded briefly. "Now if you'll excuse me, Lady Christina, I have some business that needs my attention."

She wasn't going to be put off that easily. Trailing after him into the hallway, she pulled on his elbow. "What am I supposed to do now?"

A smile hovered at the corners of his mouth as he lifted her fingers from his sleeve and gently stroked the back of her hand with his thumb. "Why, nothing, if it please you. Or perhaps you'd prefer a game of cribbage to while away the time?"

She jerked her hand away. "Don't you realize that I can't possibly remain here without damaging my reputation?"

His tone was filled with irony. "I'm afraid, my dear, that the damage has already been done. You should have been more circumspect in your appearance at the Proud Lion, rather than chatting with Buckinghamshire's worst pair of gossips. Unless, of course, it was your intention to be seen on your way here."

"Good gad, there was nothing to be secretive about. I told them the plain truth."

"The fact that you were alone in my carriage, on the road to my estate, with my liveried servants in attendance, will carry far more weight than your incredible tale about some antique lute. If the Countess of Ailesbury is staying at the inn, then she's probably on her way to London. That means that as soon as the weather clears, the news will spread all over the city. If it was your intention to thoroughly and completely ruin your own reputation, young lady, you couldn't have done a better job."

Christina gazed at him in horror. He couldn't be right! She wasn't, in fact, *ruined*, and they both knew it. Good Lord, no one in town would believe such a vile tale about her. Certainly not when it involved a national hero of his high caliber and unsullied reputation. And although she was known among the *ton* to be too strong-willed by half for a female and given to fanciful flights at that, still, her own moral reputation was equally unblemished.

"And now, my little stray kitten," he said, "we can wait out the storm together." He glanced back over his shoulder. "Hawkins, bring Lady Christina's breakfast into the library for her."

Taking her arm, the earl led her into the cluttered room. Christina sat down at the massive writing table and allowed Hawkins, for the second time that day, to serve her breakfast. Rugden strode over to his desk, where he seated himself and began shuffling through a stack of papers. He was soon engrossed in his work, completely unconcerned with her predicament as he pored over the documents before him. What could be so blasted important compared to the trouble she'd just landed in? The man was an unfeeling boor.

Roderick tried to concentrate on the lines in front of him as he searched for some mention of the Greater London Docks Company in his father's personal papers. If Myles Fielding had been so captivated by the idea of building new wharves along the Thames that he'd sunk his entire fortune into the scheme, why wasn't it mentioned even once in a letter to a close friend or in a memorandum to his trusted steward? It didn't make any sense, and his father had been a most sensible man.

He looked up from the papers to watch the young woman, who'd finished her meal, pace restlessly back and forth across the carpet. Going to one of the windows, she stared at the landscape being soaked by yet another cloud-burst. He wondered if she was toying with the idea of walking to the closest village. Luckily, the weather had cleared for a few hours that morning, allowing him the opportunity to send the coachman's son off on horseback. Watt Keighly carried a sealed letter, which was to be delivered directly into the hands of the Marquess of Waldwick. One way or another, Austin Berringer would soon be informed of his youngest daughter's whereabouts. Roderick hoped the letter, with his assurances that he would do everything necessary to protect the girl from scandal, would reach the old gentleman before the vicious rumors did. In his saddlebags, Keighly also carried a note for Madeline Gannet.

It was unfortunate that neither of the Keighlys had ever seen Roderick's mistress, but in all the years he'd known Madeline, he'd never brought her to Rugden Court. It would have been unthinkable when his father was alive. Consequently, none of the country servants had ever laid eyes on the voluptuous Mrs. Gannet or the young damsel who unhappily came in her place.

The object of all this masculine concern roamed about the room, nimbly skirting the boxes and barrels that littered the floor. Even in her restless state, she moved with a lissome grace. She withdrew a book from an open crate, leafed idly through it, and then tossed it back on the stack, only to wander back to the window once more. The muted light coming through the wet panes fell on the unruly curls she'd tried so ineffectively to anchor down with a dark brown ribbon. The pale light seemed to cast a glow of warmth about her, as though those few weak rays were caught in the golden strands and reflected back threefold, to shimmer and beckon like sunshine on a summer's afternoon. Memories of carefree days in his childhood, when his parents would take him sailing with his younger brother, flooded over him. He shook his head. He'd been reading too many old letters.

At last she sat down on a wing back chair. She scrutinized the contents of a nearby barrel, picked up a fine porcelain music box, and dusted off the straw that clung to it. Opening its lid, she listened to the lilting melody. The corners of her lips curved in delight as she softly hummed along.

"You're familiar with the tune?" he asked.

She was unaware that he'd been watching her, and her gaze flew to meet his. Her eyes were the deep, rich color of sapphires. "It's an old English air. You don't recognize it?"

Roderick shook his head. "The trinket belonged to my grandmother, I believe. I found it in a trunk along with a lot of other useless old things."

"It isn't useless," she scolded. "It still has a lovely sound."

He shrugged. "It's certainly not very practical."

"What are you going to do with it?" She wrinkled her nose and eyed the rest of the barrel's contents with mounting suspicion.

"Sell it."

"Whatever for?"

"For as much as it will bring at auction."

"Your grandmother's music box?" Her voice cracked in surprise. She stared at him as though he were a cents per cent moneylender from the City, a callous loan merchant who gleefully profited from the foolishness of young greenhorns caught in the snare of ill luck at the gaming tables.

Christina couldn't believe her ears. Here was a heartlessness that beggared description. What gentleman would sell his family's personal memorabilia for the few insignificant pounds it would raise? Good gad, the avaricious colonel couldn't possibly be related to the kindhearted Percy!

Rugden rose from his chair. A look of amusement played on his angular features. Walking over to her, he took the music box from her hands and returned it to the barrel. Then he smiled engagingly as he clasped her fingers in his strong ones and pulled her up to stand in front of him.

"Perhaps I shan't sell it, after all," he said. His words were low and vibrant, like the bass line of a counterpoint melody. He moved closer, and his warrior hands easily spanned her waist. "You said last night that you were grateful to all the gallant men who'd risked their lives to fight for England. Haven't you some small token of gratitude to offer a poor soldier who's just come home from the war?"

"Yes," she said. "A handshake and a 'Well-done, sir.' " She lowered her lashes to avoid his perceptive eyes.

With the pad of one callused finger, he tipped her chin upward, insisting that she meet his silvery gaze. The movement was filled with an unexpected tenderness. She quivered like the plucked string of a lute beneath his touch. How could she have thought his eyes were cold? Those dark orbs burned now with some inner excitement she could only guess the meaning of. Slowly, inexorably, he brought her resisting form against his hard one, and her full skirts swished behind her in a soft rustle of taffeta.

"I'd expect that halfhearted commendation from a superior officer," he murmured, "but not from a fair English rose." His gaze drifted to her lips, and there was no mistaking the reward he sought.

Christina could feel the iron strength of the man. The aura of unconscious power he exuded seemed to surround them, cutting them off from the outside world like a rampart thrown across a battlefield. She responded to his physical presence in a way she'd never dreamed possible. Every interaction she'd had with a suitor before had been on an intellectual level. Rugden was calling to something deep and mysterious inside her. Something she didn't understand but was compelled to acknowledge. A mixture of fear and curiosity lured her onward. He met her gaze once more, and her heart bounded inside her.

"I have two brothers, my lord," she warned in a husky whisper as he bent closer. "I'm not without a large family to protect me."

"How very reassuring for you." His firm, sensual mouth came closer to her trembling one. "And if your entire family's not enough, you can always call in the militia."

He kissed her. She expected him to be rough and aggressive; he was incredibly gentle. Coaxing, teasing, tantalizing her with expert skill, he slowly drew her to him, pulling her body tighter against his large frame, lifting her up in his muscular arms. The burning excitement she'd glimpsed in his eyes now raced through her veins. She reached up, slid her arms around his neck, and shamelessly returned the beguiling pressure of his lips.

Uncounted seconds later he broke the kiss and moved backward slightly. Gradually her breathing returned to normal as she rested her forehead against the solid wall of his chest.

"That was not well done of you, sir," she rebuked in a suffocated voice.

He cocked his head in a captivating gesture. The hint of a smile danced across his lips. "Then I'll try to do better this time." He leaned over her once again.

"Oh, no!" she cried. She braced her arms against his chest and leaned away. "I think you've been recompensed quite enough for all your brave deeds. In fact, I believe you've collected all future rewards as well. What I'm convinced of now, more than ever, is that I can't stay at Rugden Court a moment longer." She slipped out of his embrace, then turned to look back at him. "Even if I have to walk to the closest farmhouse in the pouring rain, I really cannot stay here unchaperoned."

"You don't trust me?"

Flustered, she traced the edge of a cocoa satin ribbon on her skirt with the tip of one finger and answered him with complete honesty. "Perhaps I don't trust myself." She looked up and met his amused gaze. "At any rate, I've no intention of spending the rest of the day wondering whether you're going to behave in such an alarming fashion again."

His black brows snapped together. "No harm will come to you at my hands, Christina. You have my word. There's absolutely no need for you to be frightened."

"From your vantage point, my lord, I'm sure that's quite easy to say."

Rugden strode across the room to his desk, jerked open its top drawer, and removed a monstrous horse pistol. "Here," he said. "The great equalizer." He laid it casually on a stack of papers.

Christina drew closer and stared at the forbidding weapon. Guns had frightened her since early childhood, when her father's old wheel lock musket had accidentally discharged, wounding one of the family's hunting dogs.

Though she'd been no more than four years old at the time, she could still remember the deafening explosion followed by the howl of terror and pain. The beloved retriever had survived, but Christina had never overcome her inordinate fear of firearms.

"Go on," Rugden encouraged with a perfunctory jerk of his head. "Take it." It was clear that, in his total familiarity with handguns, it never occurred to him that he wasn't doing her a grand favor.

Not about to admit to a captious stranger the humiliating phobia her family and friends were all well aware of, Christina swallowed her fear and started to reach for the pistol.

"But be careful," he cautioned. "As I'm sure you can tell, it's already primed and loaded."

"Of course," she lied. How was it possible he couldn't read the truth in her terrified eyes? Faith, she'd never actually touched a gun in her life. "My brothers taught me how to shoot their flintlocks. I've practiced with them since I was young. I'm a crack shot." She picked up the great, unwieldly weapon. It wavered about unsteadily, and she had to brace the horrible thing with both hands to keep it stable.

"Then may I suggest that you point the barrel the other way, unless it's your immediate intention to blow a hole straight through me," the earl stated calmly.

"Well, don't try anything outrageous again, or that's exactly what I'll have to do," she threatened with a nervous laugh. She carefully pointed the monstrous gun at the floor.

With a gallant flourish, he placed his right hand over his heart. "Lady Christina Berringer, you have my word as a gentleman that I will behave henceforth with every possible measure of decorum. There's no need to feel uneasy about staying on at Rugden Court. I promise I shan't lay a finger on you." He paused, and for a second an unholy light sparkled in his silver eyes. "Unless I am specifically invited to do so."

Christina bit her bottom lip and scowled at him. What a dreadful situation. She stood there transfixed, shaking in her shoes and holding the enormous loaded flintlock, which she had no idea how to use. Her numb fingers gripped the handle so hard her knuckles were turning white. Dear God, what if she bumped it? Or dropped it? It could go off accidentally. She'd heard of newly invented handguns with such fine mechanisms that only a slight touch on the trigger could discharge them. The very real possibility that she might actually shoot someone rose before her, and she toyed with the idea of telling him the truth. She was frightened to death of the beastly thing. He smiled in odious anticipation of that very event, and she decided against it. Let him worry a little.

"Very well," she agreed. "I'll remain at Rugden Court for the rest of the day, at least. Now if you don't mind, I'll remove myself from the library. That way you can go about your work without being disturbed."

"You're welcome to wander wherever you choose, Christina." His polite words seemed to hold a hidden meaning. "I want you to make yourself completely at home."

She'd started to leave, but stopped. "And that's another thing," she pointed out. "I don't think you should address me in such a familiar manner. I may look young to you, but the difference in our ages is probably not all that great. Please don't address me as if I were a small child and you were an old family friend."

"I wasn't," he said simply. The unspoken words hung in the silence between them. He'd used her Christian name not with the avuncular familiarity of an elderly friend, but with the intimacy of a lover.

Christina spent the better part of the day in the spacious music room, which, she discovered, contained a fine spinet hidden under dust covers. She placed the horse pistol gingerly on the bench beside her, careful to point its lethal barrel toward an outside wall, and whiled away the rainy afternoon playing from memory some of her favorite airs and folk ballads. Becoming restless, she peeked into the drawer of a nearby side table and discovered a pile of old music books. One included a collection of well-known poems set to music. Another, worn and stained by once-frequent use, contained lessons for the viol, the cithern, and the flageolet. Stuffed beneath the front cover of a book of country dances, she found what appeared to be an original composition. The notes and musical terms were written in a precise, delicate hand. Curious, she sat back down at the spinet. The piece proved to be a sonata for harpsichord, flute, and violin with two hauntingly lovely main themes. Christina practiced the movements several times and then began to play the entire composition.

Unnoticed by the engrossed young woman, Roderick stood motionless at the door, listening to the spontaneous program with its soothing backdrop of falling rain. His heart ached at the rush of nostalgic memories that swept over him. The sight of Christina, bent in absorption over the achingly familiar music, her slim fingers moving over the keys with grace and surety, was amazingly poignant. When she completed the piece, she sat quietly in front of the keyboard, her hands folded in her lap, apparently deep in reverie.

"You play with great talent," he said. The hoarseness of his words betrayed his ragged emotions.

Christina turned to find him watching her. "Thank you, my lord. But the compliments belong to the composer. Do you know who wrote it?"

"My mother. She was a very talented musician." Rugden walked into the room to stand beside the spinet. "It is beautiful, isn't it? That particular piece was one of her favorites. I haven't heard it in over fifteen years. I hope you'll forgive the intrusion, but it brought back so many memories, I couldn't help but come to listen."

Christina looked up at the earl in genuine surprise. It was almost impossible to imagine this burly, rugged soldier as a little boy, standing near the keyboard in fascination as he listened to his mother play. She thought of the lesson books in the nearby drawer and of Percy's virtuosity on the viola da gamba. She favored Rugden with a hopeful smile. "Did you learn to play as well?"

He shook his head. "My mother tried to teach me many times, but I showed absolutely no aptitude at all for anything musical. I'm afraid Percy inherited all the family talent in that area."

"Oh." Despite the betrayal of bad manners, Christina was unable to keep the genuine regret from her voice.

Rugden's features hardened. His chin lifted imperceptibly. "If the late countess was disappointed in her elder son, she never showed it by so much as a word or gesture. But I suppose that's what the poets mean when they speak of the blind devotion of a mother's love."

Abashed, Christina reached out and straightened the sheets of paper in front of her. She searched for a proper comment, but found none. Burn it, what *could* she say? That she was certain his mother loved him anyway, despite the pathetic fact that he had absolutely no gift for music?

Thankfully, the earl didn't wait for a rejoinder, but changed the subject with smooth grace. "Perhaps you'd care to refresh yourself before dressing for supper. I do hope you'll dine with me this evening. Hawkins will be serving the meal and can spring to your assistance should the need arise."

With a show of smugness she didn't feel, she pointed to the large gun that lay beside the folds of her gown on the bench. She didn't touch the flintlock's cold metal, afraid she'd jar it with disastrous results.

"I'll be happy to join you, my lord, but I've no need of anyone leaping to my defense. I'm quite capable of protecting myself."

"Then I'll be extremely careful," Rugden promised. His gray eyes glinted with amusement. "I've instructed Hawkins to carry up some hot water for your bath."

"Oh, and send up a chambermaid to help me, please. Outside of your butler, I haven't seen a servant all day. I've always thought my grandmother was a dragon when it came to the help, but you carry the ideal of a silent, unseen staff to new heights."

Roderick stiffened as he met her guileless blue eyes. "I'm afraid I won't be able to send up a maid to assist you, Lady Christina. My staff is rather limited at the moment. Outside of my batman, the only house servant at Rugden Court is Hawkins."

"Surely you jest!" she exclaimed. "Why, a home this size must require a retinue of at least sixty."

"Seventy-three, to be exact," he said. "But almost everyone has recently been dismissed. My housekeeper, however, was in the village visiting her daughter when the storm broke. She'll be back as soon as the weather clears."

To Roderick the appalling situation was no joking matter. His childhood home was about to be sealed up, the tall shutters at every window closed and fastened, and all doors, save one leading into the basement, bolted from the inside. The entire estate would soon be left with only a groundskeeper to protect it from burglars and poachers. He'd spent the past three weeks securing positions among his personal friends for trusted employees whose families had been at Rugden Court for over three generations. It'd been one of the hardest and most humiliating tasks he'd faced since returning to England.

"Merciful heavens," Christina croaked. She stared at him, aghast. "Do you mean I've been here alone all this time with only you and two male servants? There's not so much as a cook or a scullery maid in the kitchen?"

"Don't forget the coachman and footman who brought you here," he corrected, determined to put the matter in as cheerful a light as possible. There was no point in having her panic at this late hour.

Christina stared longingly at the tub of hot water. As promised, Hawkins had carried up bucket after bucket, until the shiny brass container was filled with the wonderful, steaming stuff. The butler, before withdrawing, had thoughtfully placed a dish of French soaps and warmed linen towels next to the hideous horse pistol that lay on the bedside table close by. The green satin gown he'd removed from her valise the previous evening hung, freshly pressed, beside a cream silk petticoat and lace-trimmed chemise in the wardrobe.

Humming softly, she started to remove her wrinkled traveling dress and stopped short. Good gad, what was she thinking of? She couldn't bathe without help. There was positively no way she could climb into that inviting tub until someone unlaced her stays. She swore a blistering oath she'd learned from her two older brothers, staggered to the bed, and plopped down on the feather mattress in an ungraceful heap. Briefly she considered clambering over the receptacle's burnished edge attired in her stays and the knee-length undergarment trapped beneath. But the thought of living in a waterlogged whalebone corset for the rest of the night was simply too horrendous. She'd either have to give up the idea of a bath or solicit help from one of the house's other occupants.

Rugden was in the next room, changing for supper with the aid of his batman. The muffled sound of their voices could be heard faintly through the adjoining wall. Somewhere in the far-off region of the kitchen, Hawkins was busily preparing their evening meal.

The delicate scent of fine perfumed soap teased her. If she waited too long, the water would cool and there'd be no decision left to make. Among her family and friends, she was known for her stubborn, headstrong ways. Well, she might as well live up to her reputation right now. Leaving her room with the pistol in her hand, she marched down the hall and knocked stoutheartedly on Rugden's bedroom door.

It was opened by a little troll of a man attired in the scarlet uniform of a sergeant in the Grenadiers. Large ears stuck straight out from the sides of his small head, which was covered with a shock of wiry red hair. For a long second, he stared at her in startled perplexity.

"I need to see his lordship," she squeaked in an unnaturally high pitch. She could feel a warm flush spread across her cheeks. "At once, please."

The confusion on the batman's face disappeared. He grinned with good-natured friendliness as he called over his shoulder, "There's a wee lassie here tae palaver with ye, Colonel. And she's no in the mood tae wait."

Rugden came to the door in stocking feet. Obviously caught in the middle of changing his clothes, he was dressed in a white linen shirt and tan breeches that were fairly molded to his massive thighs.

"Yes?" he asked with a welcoming smile. He didn't seem the least bit shocked at her scandalous behavior. Lord, for a moment she thought he was going to invite her right on into his bedchamber.

She looked up at him, opened her mouth to speak, and

closed it again. Somehow, she had to find the words. "I . . . I . . . I . . ." she stammered.

Roderick stepped out into the hallway and caught hold of her elbow. She looked so distressed, he felt a sudden alarm and glanced down the corridor, half expecting to find an intruder. "Is something wrong?"

"Yes. No. Yes!" She reluctantly met his gaze, then lowered her lashes. Bright splotches of red stained her cheeks. Her graceful fingers clutched the flintlock in a death grip. He had to lean forward to catch her next words, spoken barely above a whisper. "I need some help."

He was at a complete loss. Once again, he glanced up and down the empty hallway. "Some help with what?"

"With my ba—" She gulped and stared down at his hand buried in the rows of white ruffles at her elbow. "With . . . my bath," she blurted out at last.

Chapter 3

Roderick motioned to his valet with a jerk of his head, and Angus Duncan quietly closed the door, leaving the couple alone in the corridor. Christina was so flustered, she couldn't bring herself to look at him, and the earl smothered a chuckle under the pretense of clearing his throat.

With the fringes of her long lashes fanning out across her scarlet cheeks, she addressed the hall's carpet in a rush of words. "I can't get out of my corset by myself, and I can't take a bath with it on. I slept all last night in my stays and woke up bruised and aching. If I have to sleep in the dratted thing a second time, I'll be so sore I won't be able to move in the morning."

Roderick forced himself to keep his voice cool and disinterested. "That's certainly a problem, Lady Christina, but there's no need for you to forgo your bath. I'll be happy to be of service." He hustled her into her bedchamber before she had second thoughts.

Once inside, she hurried to stand, flushed and patently ill at ease, beside the bathtub. She had fastened her hair on top of her head with a wide ribbon in anticipation of the bath. Several curls had already escaped to fall enticingly about her oval face. A shiny tendril bounced in front of one eye, and she absently shoved it back under the ribbon, while she held the horse pistol clasped tightly against her chest with the other hand. Without saying a word, she stared up at him expectantly and waited.

"You'll have to remove your dress before I can unlace your stays," he pointed out with admirable restraint. "I'm

33

afraid you're going to have to lay the pistol down for a moment."

She glanced at the weapon as though she'd forgotten she even held it. "Yes, yes, of course," she muttered. With exaggerated precision, she placed the gun on the bedside table beside the crystal soap dish. "Now turn around," she ordered. She made a circular motion with her hand. "I can't disrobe while you're looking at me."

Obediently, Roderick swung around to face the door. Behind him, he heard her sigh of relief at his ready compliance, followed by the tantalizing and unmistakable rustle of taffeta.

"All right," she whispered. "I'm ready."

He turned to find her standing with her back to him, attired in only the corset and a chemise that reached to the middle of her slim thighs. Her bodice and skirt were on the floor at her bare feet in a careless heap. She held the embroidered petticoat up in front of her in a touching gesture of girlish modesty. Her graceful head was bent forward, revealing the pure, unblemished line of her nape, where wisps of curls floated about like tiny clouds of sweet honey. The gentle slope of her creamy shoulders above the ruched lace of the cotton chemise, with its tiny capped sleeves and dainty blue ribbons, brought his heart slamming against his ribs. She was small-boned and delicate and utterly feminine. For a man who'd recently witnessed the hideous carnage of the battlefield, the sight of the partially robed maiden standing shyly beside her bath was devastating.

"I'll expect a written reference for this later," he drawled. "That way, if I'm ever forced to leave the army, I can always seek employment as a lady's maid."

He'd wanted to distract her from the undeniable intimacy of the scene, but his rusty voice betrayed him. The scent of the perfumed soap hung on the warm, humid air, making the rose-colored room as sultry and intoxicating as a Turkish bath. She turned her head to watch him over one silken shoulder. The outline of her flawless profile rekindled the memory of their kiss. Roderick stepped up behind her and felt himself grow heavy with desire.

His usually steady fingers fumbled as he untied the

stubborn knots one by one. It was little wonder she hadn't been able to loosen the stays. Her maid had fastened them with a ruthlessness bordering on the fanatic. The innumerable rows of narrow whalebones were stitched into the linen material so closely that the ribbed garment was rigid enough to stand by itself. He could imagine the sense of relief she'd experience once she was free to slide the corset off and add it to the pile of garments on the floor.

Christina could feel Rugden's warm breath caress her neck as he worked over the laces. The moment the task was finished and the ties freed, she slipped the corset off and whirled around to face him. In her haste, the stiffly boned garment struck the edge of the bedside table. The huge flintlock dropped into the bathwater with a splash and disappeared beneath the soapy bubbles.

"Oh, my God!" she cried in terror. Flinging aside the corset, she leaned forward in a frantic attempt to catch the weapon before it struck the brass bottom of the tub. She was too late. Christina cringed, waiting for the ear-splitting boom of the explosion. The only sound was a dull thud as it came to rest on the bottom.

Unperturbed, Rugden rolled up his shirtsleeve, reached into the sudsy bath, and calmly withdrew the large handgun. He held it out over the tub at arm's length. Water streamed out of the long metal barrel like a spigot.

"Is it broken?" she gasped. She clutched the side of the bathtub to steady her shaking knees.

"No, no. It's perfectly fine." Although his tone was philosophical, his gray eyes glinted with obvious satisfaction at the rescue of his prized trophy unharmed. "A little soap and water won't hurt a magnificent flintlock like this."

He grabbed one of the towels from the nearby bed table, wiped the bubbles off the smooth walnut handle and the shiny steel barrel, and then returned the weapon to its former place beside the crystal dish.

Christina had to struggle to remain upright. Her heart beat triple time while her breath caught in her constricted throat. "I thought it was going to explode," she gulped.

"It has a safety device," he assured her. "The powder will only ignite if you release the safety, cock back the lock, and pull the trigger. You seemed so familiar with guns, I took it for granted you already knew that."

His glance skidded downward, and she realized with a start that the round neck of her chemise had gaped open in her wild bid to catch the pistol. Above the ruffled edge of the undergarment, her breasts were now partially exposed to view.

"I'll leave now," Rugden added with a wolfish grin, "before you decide to release that safety." He backed slowly out of the room, as if half expecting her to take aim and fire.

The evening meal was a simple affair. Both the butler and the colonel's batman, Angus Duncan, waited on them. The knowledge that the servants remained close by made Christina feel more comfortable. She was seated beside the earl in the center of the table, and she suspected they'd been instructed to hover over her for that very reason.

Rugden was as spartan as ever in his appearance. Black breeches, black coat, white shirt and stock. And still no wig. She found him extremely attractive in a ferocious, primeval sort of way. The jagged scar on his forehead, which had startled her at first, now seemed only to enhance his aura of uncompromising masculinity. She knew, without being told, that he'd received the wound in hand-to-hand combat, perhaps from a saber or a bayonet. She'd never seen a man so unequivocally, aggressively male. Or met one who made her feel so overwhelmingly conscious of her own femininity.

From her severely limited wardrobe, the emerald gown she wore had been her only choice. She refused to be seen in the crushed brown traveling outfit a moment longer. Conscious of the low decolletage of her satin bodice, she surreptitiously glanced down at herself. On previous occasions when she'd worn that same dinner dress, she hadn't felt the least self-conscious. But this time she was without the usual corset that gave the bodice and stomacher its taut, rigid shape—a fact her attractive host was well aware of, since he'd been the one to remove the corset in the first place. The expanse of bare skin above the dark green lace seemed to draw Rugden's gaze time and again. She scowled at him repeatedly without effect. Gad, the man had no appreciation whatsoever of the delicacy of their situation.

Roderick was absolutely enchanted with his dinner guest. Somehow, regardless of the distraction presented by the velvety shadow of her cleavage in the soft candlelight, he managed to keep up a polite flow of conversation. "I trust you were properly cared for this afternoon, Lady Christina." He paused for a moment to watch Hawkins pile her plate with more delicacies. "It was my zealous batman's idea to provide the French soaps you found in your room. And, I see," Roderick added, as he surveyed the golden curls piled atop her head, "that Hawkins managed to provide you with some finer points of women's apparel."

Christina reached up to touch one of the ivory combs. "Yes, I appreciated finding them in the room I'm using temporarily."

Just about to take a sip of wine, the earl looked over the rim of his glass and frowned. "Temporarily? You want to change rooms tonight? What's wrong with the chamber you're in?"

"Nothing's wrong with it," she clarified. "By temporary, I meant until I leave in the morning."

"Then you do like the room?" he pressed.

"It's beautiful."

Apparently satisfied, Rugden changed the subject. "Tell me more about your collection of antiques, Lady Christina." He refilled her wineglass and favored her with a brilliant smile. "Did you say that someone left the musical instruments to you as an inheritance?"

"Yes. My Grandfather Hilliard was a great patron of the arts. He was quite talented on the violin himself, but as a youth he never had the opportunity to study under a master. He was forced by circumstances to support his mother at the sudden death of his father. So all his hopes of becoming a composer had to be set aside in favor of earning a living in trade. My mother inherited her father's gift for music. She fostered it in all her children, but I was the only one in the family who shared my grandfather's fascination with antique instruments."

"And he left you the wherewithal to augment the collection as you saw fit?" The earl sounded mildly incredulous.

"Oh, more than just that," she confided. She twirled the stem of her crystal goblet absently between her fingers. "During his lifetime Grandfather provided for the livelihood of several very talented composers. It was his vision to establish a home for aged and impoverished musicians. I was entrusted with Penthaven, his estate in Cornwall, and the means to fulfill his dream."

"A high-minded goal," Rugden commented dryly, "but an old man's pipe dream nevertheless. You can't begin to support all the impoverished artists in the world, Christina. It'd be like throwing money to the wind."

"I know I can't take care of the entire world," Christina replied. She laid her fork on her plate and glared up at him. "But I can at least provide a safe haven for some of Britain's most talented elderly composers. It's a shame the way they're forced to seek a nobleman's patronage, even in their old age. If a musician's wealthy patron dies, often the young heir has no interest whatsoever in continuing the support once given so generously. Or should a widowed peer remarry, who's to guarantee that the new bride will be as interested in supporting the arts as the first wife?"

"And you intend to tackle this enormous project all by yourself?" Rugden's misgivings were all too apparent. He leaned back in his chair and stared down at her in disapproval. "A nineteen-year-old girl can't possibly make the financial decisions necessary for an enterprise of that magnitude. Even more mature females aren't capable of such difficult decisions. They're not logical enough. And they're far too emotional. I'm astonished that your grandfather even considered placing such a tremendous responsibility on your inexperienced shoulders."

"As a matter of fact," she admitted tersely, "my father is guardian of my trust."

"Now that makes much more sense, my dear." The earl propped an elbow on the edge of the table and cupped his strong chin in his hand. He looked down at her with condescending approval. "You shouldn't be worrying your pretty little head about either the impoverished or the aged. Concentrate, instead, on learning how to preside over your future husband's home. That's where a woman's talents are needed most, Christina." A faint smile touched his generous mouth. "And appreciated most . . ."

In his bed. For a second she thought he was going to complete the scandalous thought she'd read in his eyes.

He leaned closer, his hooded gaze on her lips. Christina's hand closed over the handle of the pistol that rested beside her plate on the sparkling white cloth. The cavalier look on his rugged features disappeared. Rugden raised his hands above his head in mock surrender, drew back, and grinned lazily. Then he stood and politely offered his arm. In an absurdly theatrical manner, he gallantly allowed her time to pick up the weapon before escorting her from the table.

"Let's go into the music room," Roderick suggested. "I'd like to hear you play again."

Side by side, they sat on the bench before the spinet. A candlelabrum spread its glow around them, and the amber light flickered over Christina's blond curls as she bent over the keyboard.

Roderick couldn't keep his gaze off her. He turned the sheet of music and then purposely brushed his fingers across her bare forearm. She paused and their eyes met. A jolt of hunger surged through him, the kind of aching need he wouldn't have believed possible only two days before. He'd returned to England prepared to do everything within his power to retrieve his fortune. He'd been prepared to marry for the most practical of reasons, a step he'd previously vowed never to take. After Lillibeth's death, he'd sworn never to marry again.

Watching Christina in the soft candlelight, he felt like a man who'd been awaiting a death sentence and had just been given a king's reprieve. With her honey-gold locks and emerald gown, she reminded him of sunshine on a bright spring day. The door of his dark cell stood open at last, and the warm glow beckoned him to her. Perhaps it was possible, after all those long, lonely years, to love and be loved. Then he remembered his scarred body and stared down at his suddenly clenched fist.

Unnerved by the feelings that swept over her at his touch, Christina hastily resumed her playing. She'd never felt so confused in her life. His manners were abominable. He was haughty, skeptical, and overbearing. He clearly disapproved of her plan to turn Penthaven into a home for impoverished musicians and didn't even try to hide that bald fact for decency's sake. Yet she found herself fascinated by his forthright demeanor, his lack of pretension, his unconscious assumption of authority. She remembered the dandies who, only last week, had hovered around her at a country garden party. Compared to the serious military man beside her now, they were no more than mincing, painted popinjays. Given the earl's total disinterest in antique musical instruments and his rude disparagement of her future plans in Cornwall, the sooner she left Rugden Court, the better.

Christina pulled back the faded rose drapes, opened the tall wooden shutters, and looked out in delight at the scene from her window. The morning had dawned bright and crystal clear. She looked up at the blue sky and grinned. She'd soon be on her way to Hertfordshire.

She found her traveling dress hanging limply in the corner of the wardrobe and tried to shake out the wrinkles, then donned it with a grimace of distaste. Her water-stained shoes had also been returned newly polished, although they were somewhat the worse for wear. No matter. She was going to get rid of the entire outfit once she was back home. A tattered reputation wouldn't be so easy to replace, however.

Christina descended the stairs carrying the huge horse pistol resting carefully against her bent elbow in an effort to steady its cumbersome weight. She planned to return the firearm to Rugden just as soon as he ordered a carriage for her. Not that she'd ever actually considered using the beastly thing. Lord, it still gave her goose bumps each time she thought of its precipitous slide into the tub's soapy water.

The dining room was deserted. The earl had apparently breakfasted earlier. She tried the library with more success; he was sitting at his desk with a list of accounts spread out in front of him.

He rose when she entered, glanced down at her outfit,

and smiled engagingly. "For an heiress, you certainly make do with a meager wardrobe, sunshine."

"I wasn't planning on a long stay at St. Albans," she replied, suddenly annoyed that she had to appear in her present bedraggled state. He stood before her, utterly magnificent in the impeccable scarlet and gold dress uniform of the Grenadiers. "At any rate, I came to say goodbye and to return your pistol."

"Did you, indeed? And was the weapon a great comfort to you, my little armed intruder?" A wicked smile danced across his lips.

He moved from his desk to stand in front of the fireplace and rested his arm on the mantelpiece. The great gold-framed mirror behind him reflected the sight of a heart-stoppingly handsome officer and a dowdy, rumpled miss who might easily have been mistaken for a country parson's daughter.

"It made me feel quite safe to know I could blow a hole right through you, if I took the notion," she told him, irked at his ill-timed display of humor. He stood there grinning like an idiot, while she was about to return home to face down a scandal. Holding the flintlock in two shaking hands, Christina held her breath and leveled the barrel at him. "Maybe I should, just to teach you a lesson."

Rugden threw back his head and gave a whoop of laughter. "You actually believed I'd let you wander around the house with a loaded gun? And take the chance of your shooting off one of those dainty little toes?"

"It was never loaded?" she screeched. She'd carried the horrible thing around with her for two days, terrified that it might detonate at the slightest jar. And all the time, he'd been playing a prank. No matter that he'd had no idea of her deep-seated fear of firearms, she'd never forgive him. Righteous anger at his stolen kiss, his casual dismissal of her girlish dreams, and his stupid, idiotic trick boiled up inside her. She drew back her arm and hurled the pistol. It whistled by him and smashed against the mirror behind.

Over the sound of crashing glass came the shrill trumpet of a carriage horn and the crunch of a vehicle's iron wheels pulling up the driveway. In minutes, the pair in the library heard the tramping of boots in the hall, and three men rushed into the room.

The shortest intruder was at the far end of middle age and wore a white bagwig and the sumptuous clothes of a wealthy nobleman. He was flanked on both sides by two broad-shouldered young men, one dressed in a soldier's uniform and the other wearing the fashionable riding coat and breeches of a town buck. Both were armed with drawn pistols.

"Father!" shrieked Christina. Certain they were about to kill an innocent man, she waved her arms wildly in the air and raced toward them. "Don't shoot him, Francis! Here, give me your gun, Carter," she cried, wresting the heavy firearm from her oldest brother's hands and waving it in the air like a crazed woman. Her two siblings stood still in wide-eyed shock at the sight of their little sister actually touching a gun.

"Carter, for gad's sake, take that thing away from her before she blows her foot off," stated the Marquess of Waldwick, all the while coldly watching the tall man who came across the room to meet them. "By all that's holy," Waldwick thundered, "what's happened here?"

Colonel Roderick Fielding, fifth Earl of Rugden, dazzling in the dress uniform of His Majesty's Forty-third Regiment of Foot, approached the four Berringers with the calm demeanor of a polished diplomat. He casually brushed the splinters of glass from the sleeve of his scarlet coat and bowed gracefully. "Lord Waldwick," he answered smoothly, "I'd like to request the honor of your youngest daughter's hand in marriage."

Chapter 4

"Shoot him!" Christina cried. She turned to her second brother with a sob of outrage. "For God's sake, Francis, kill the lying wretch!" Horrified at the earl's callous proposal and all it implied, she evaded Carter's outstretched hand and hugged the flintlock to her midsection with justifiable resolution. In her struggle with her brawny sibling, her unruly hair came tumbling down around her shoulders, and she tossed it back with an impatient jerk of her head.

"You can't murder an unarmed man, Christy." Carter gasped. His hazel eyes were wide with apprehension at the thought that the gun might detonate accidentally. He snatched at the firearm again, and she yanked it out of his reach.

"Well, throw him a sword and then shoot him!" she exclaimed.

While their audience watched in stunned fascination, Carter continued to wrestle with his little sister for control of his own weapon, until, at last, he managed to pry it out of her stubborn clutch. With a look of total disbelief on his face, he stared at the suddenly reckless spitfire who'd refused since she was four years old even to be in the same room with a firearm.

Thwarted, Christina whirled to face the earl once more. "How dare you?" she hissed. Her breath came in short, infuriated pants. "How dare you imply with your wretched, conniving, *odious* proposal that I'm spoiled for any other man. You know very well that nothing, absolutely *nothing,* has happened here."

43

"Nothing's happened?" the marquess parroted in relief. He lifted a quizzing glass and gazed up at the earl with an expression that was positively beatific. "I knew I could count on you, young man."

Rugden's only reply was to raise his scarred eyebrow and stare at Christina in open amusement. She squirmed with humiliation under that mocking gaze.

"Well, God's truth," she admitted to her father with a shrug, "he did kiss me. But that's all."

Waldwick allowed the magnifying glass to drop, forgotten. His shaggy gray eyebrows snapped together, and he cast an anxious glance at his distraught daughter. "Egad, Christy . . ."

"That cur forced a kiss on you?" Major Francis Lord Berringer's pale eyes narrowed with disgust. Splendid in the azure uniform of the Royal Horse Guards, he moved swiftly across the glass-littered rug to stand beside his father. He glared at Rugden with open contempt and gripped the handle of his cuirass in an insulting, provocative gesture. Rocking slowly back and forth on the balls of his booted feet, the lanky, raw-boned soldier waited for the merest sign from his sire. It was clear that nothing would have pleased Francis more than to fulfill his sister's request for the blackguard's immediate execution.

Christina cleared her throat. Well, gad, she might as well tell the whole truth now and get it over with. It appeared certain that Rugden would waste no time in tattling on her like some nasty little schoolboy if she didn't.

"Actually, I *allowed* him to kiss me," she expanded with reluctance. "It was all perfectly innocent." She stared down at her wrinkled brown skirt. The searing memory of that *innocent* kiss brought the warmth of a flush to her cheeks. "So was his helping me with my bath."

"Your bath!" Francis bellowed.

Christina heard the usually imperturbable Carter, who'd remained protectively at her side, take a deep, indrawn breath of shock. Meanwhile the rambunctious young major jerked his sword from its scabbard and lurched toward Rugden. The crunch of broken glass beneath the soles of his long knee boots seemed to enrage Francis ever further.

"You bastard!" he snarled. "I'll run you through right now."

With an exasperated shake of his head, the earl turned to Waldwick. "May I suggest that the two of us discuss this matter alone, sir, without the two young hotheads in your family trying to assassinate me?"

Waldwick nodded, then addressed his youngest son. "Francis, take your sister outside. Walk her around in the fresh air till she cools down a bit. Carter can stay with me."

"Merciful heavens, Father," Christina protested. "I'm not an overheated horse." But her initial shock at the insensitive proposal had eased by now. Assuming an attitude of regal disdain, she walked over to her brother and placed her hand on his blue sleeve. "Come on, Francis. The man isn't worth the trouble his death would provoke. He's a deceitful trickster, but that's all. Let him live with his contemptible chicanery."

With their departure the silence of the room grew ominous. Carter scowled and briefly examined the fine Italian flintlock in his hand, rechecking its firing mechanism and the toe lock that held the cock in the safety position. At the obvious show of armed belligerence, his father shook his head and motioned to his heir apparent with one beringed finger.

"Wait for us just outside the library door, Carter. I'll call you if I need you. But I don't believe that'll be necessary."

Carter inclined his head and, with a warning glance at Roderick, withdrew. The double doors clicked softly shut behind him, and the two men left alone in the library turned to face each other.

"First of all," Roderick began, "I want to assure you, Lord Waldwick, that what your daughter said was true. She's as untouched now as the evening she arrived at my home."

Waldwick drew a shaky hand across his brow and walked with halting steps toward a wingback chair that had been shoved up against the wall in the confusion. He skirted the straw-filled barrel in front of it and sank down on the soft cushion with an exhausted sigh. The three Berringer men had no doubt set out from London the minute the roads were passable. They must have literally raced to the scene to arrive so early in the day.

"Now, Roderick, suppose you enlighten me as to what exactly *has* taken place at Rugden Court in the last two days. Just who's to blame for this unfortunate fiasco?"

Leaning his hips against the edge of his desk, Roderick folded his arms across his chest. "I believe, Lord Waldwick, that what's happened is no one's fault. By some marvelous mischance, your daughter inadvertently entered my carriage. She told me she was traveling alone because her maid was ill." He paused, but kept to himself his blistering opinion of the lax family discipline that would allow a nineteen-year-old girl to take such a precipitous action on her own. Damn it to hell, everyone knew how lacking in plain common sense young females in their teen years were.

"That part of the story I can't verify," Roderick continued. "But you have my word as a gentleman that she's come to no harm while she's been a guest in my home." He met the older man's gaze with total frankness. "I kissed her. I helped her out of her corset so she could bathe. That's all."

Christina's father bowed his head and covered his face with his hands. For long minutes, he sat motionless, until the quiet of the room was broken at last by the faint chiming of a hall clock. Then he gazed up at the earl and spoke with measured restraint. "Roderick, if I didn't know you ... hadn't known you since you were a child ... If your father and I hadn't been friends since we were schoolmates at Harrow together, I'd refuse to believe this incredible story. But I know you to be an honest and courageous gentleman. By God, you've an absolutely impeccable reputation. Your late father was extremely proud of you. And rightly so."

Roderick modestly inclined his head in reply to the older man's praise.

Waldwick shook his bewigged head in painful confusion. "Gossip is already rampant in town. The Countess of Ailesbury and her sister wasted no time with their imbecilic prattle. Blister 'em, the two could win a prize at a country fair for their unstoppable tongue-wagging. What's worse, when we came through Rugford earlier this morning, every inhabitant in the village was aware that your housekeeper had been there visiting her daughter while Christina was stranded here at Rugden Court, alone with only you and four male servants in attendance. The people all knew why we'd come to Buckinghamshire. They crowded round our coach, elbowing each other for a sight of the irate papa who'd come to call out his daughter's seducer. A seducer who just happened to be their own lord."

The marquess reached inside his coat pocket and withdrew an enameled snuffbox. He tapped the cameo lid with one manicured fingernail in distraction. "Following the suggestion you made in your note, Roderick, I placed an announcement in *The Gazette* stating that the secret engagement had been one of long standing. I indicated that both families had wished for it since Christina was a small child, but it'd been postponed because of the death of her mother following a long illness."

Flipping open the small gold box, Waldwick took a pinch of snuff and sneezed heartily. "That's not too far from the actual truth, my boy. Both your parents and my dear departed wife, God rest her sweet soul, would have been thrilled at the match, had you and Christina ever had the opportunity to meet each other and fall in love. Now, however, a regular courtship is out of the question. The sooner the marriage takes place, the less time for conjecture and distortion."

Roderick crossed his booted feet in front of him and nodded. "I agree with you completely, sir. When I dispatched my footman to London to find you, I also sent along a letter for the archbishop. I've taken the liberty of securing a special license. Keighly returned with it early this morning. I've also sent for our local clergyman. He should be arriving momentarily. I suggest we begin the ceremony as soon as Reverend Hotchkiss arrives."

Outside, Christina was walking on the manor's wide front porch. She held on to her brother's arm for moral support while she mentally steeled herself for the possibility of a shot ringing out. But she knew in her heart that neither her father nor her brother would kill a man in cold blood. They might challenge Rugden to a duel of honor. They'd never just shoot him down in his own library like a mad dog.

Suddenly a whisky came bowling up the graveled driveway. Brother and sister looked over in puzzlement to see a man of the cloth step down from the two-wheeled vehicle. The newcomer was tall and gaunt, with square spectacles that rested at the very end of his large, hooked nose. Helping him down the carriage step was the earl's batman. The minister, with a supercilious smile pasted across his hollow cheeks, accorded the Berringers a slight bow before he ascended the steps to the entrance, prayer book in hand. The little red-haired Scotsman favored them with an even briefer salute and followed in the clergyman's wake.

They disappeared inside, and Christina turned to her brother. "Do you suppose he came thinking there'd be a funeral?"

Francis shrugged his shoulders, as perplexed as his sister. "I swear, it's possible! But he didn't look all that gloomy. Maybe it's merely coincidental. The man might just be stopping to make a parochial visit."

"Here? In faith, you jest!" Christina gave a tremulous laugh.

At that moment, Carter appeared at the front door and motioned for them to come inside. "Father wants to speak with you alone, Christy. He's waiting for you in the front salon."

Christina entered a large drawing room to find her father standing in front of one of its towering mullioned windows. He turned at the sound of her footsteps. His lined face reflected his deep concern. He opened his arms wide, and with a smothered sob, she ran to embrace him.

"My precious little poppet," he crooned as he tenderly rocked her back and forth. "Don't worry, child. Everything's been settled."

Christina leaned back to look into his loving eyes. At the unexpected serenity she found there, a feeling of apprehension gripped her. "Did Carter run him through, then?" she asked, aghast.

Her father chuckled. "No one's going to be killed today, Christy." He slipped his arm around her waist and squeezed her comfortingly. Then he led her to a sofa, and they sat down side by side, his arm around her shoulders. "How is it, poppet, that you came here in the first place? We've been dreadfully worried about you since the evening, two nights ago, when Gwen and Sanborn came back to London to find you'd departed their home alone in a strange carriage. I've been beside myself with worry, dear."

"I'm sorry, Father," she said. "I didn't mean to upset you. I left a note for Gwen, telling her where I was going. But it was still a bad decision." She wrinkled her nose in contrition. "Lady Muggleton invited me to St. Albans to see an Italian lute. Only it wasn't her coach, after all. It was Rugden's." She frowned to herself. The story did sound implausible.

Tapping his upper lip with a polished nail, Lord Waldwick frowned. "Have you this letter with you now, Christy?"

"No, I left it in London. But I recognized the writing. Muggs is left-handed, so it's very distinctive. There's no doubt that she sent it."

Disbelief could be read in her father's troubled eyes. He drew her gently to him, kissed the top of her head, and questioned softly, "Why did you leave Gwen's home without your maid, poppet?"

"Marie was too ill to accompany me." She grasped the sleeve of his green satin coat and squeezed his arm. "Surely you don't think I'd purposely come to this place alone?"

The marquess covered her fingers with his own in reassurance. "I know that whatever happened, child, you're a blameless victim. But regardless of your innocence, the world at large won't see it in the same light as your family does. Lord Rugden has agreed to accept responsibility in this matter, though heaven knows, he really has none. A minister has already arrived. The wedding will take place this afternoon."

Christina shook her head. "Father, I can't marry Rugden! No one could be more unsuitable. Why, he's nothing but a rough, common soldier!"

The marquess patted her hand and chuckled. "He's a

soldier all right. And a good one. But common? Hardly. And, where you're concerned, I don't think he'll be anything but gentle, patient, and understanding."

"He's not what I want in a husband, Father," she declared staunchly. "I need someone who's as interested in music as I am. A sensitive, thoughtful man who can converse on more scholarly subjects than the latest war news."

Her father smiled indulgently. "And where did you think you were going to meet this male paragon of musical accomplishment, sweetie? Good Lord, at your direction, I must have turned away over a dozen suitors for your hand this past spring."

"I know the right man's out there somewhere, perhaps in Vienna, studying under a famous master at this very moment." She lifted her chin in stubborn determination. "But he could easily come to London. Famous composers often do. I'm sure I'll meet him someday. In the meantime I have a tremendous task ahead of me, just overseeing the renovation of Penthaven. You don't think I'll abandon my promise to Grandfather?"

"You don't have to give up a thing, dearest. Just set that project aside for a while. It can wait. This wedding can't."

Christina jumped to her feet and whirled to look down at her father. "Rugden has no sympathy whatsoever for my collection of antiques. And when it comes to my plans for Penthaven, he's as dense as a board and just as unfeeling."

There was an unfamiliar tightening in her chest, as though someone were trying to smother her. She'd always dreamed of meeting a man who could be her life partner in more than name only. To her, the ideal marriage meant a spiritual melding of souls, a bonding of two cultivated minds with the love of music in common. The last thing she wanted to do was rush into marriage with that great oaf of a soldier, who'd made her lose her temper and behave like a spoiled brat. Good gad, she hadn't been angry enough to throw anything in years. But something told her that, with him around, the servants had better lock up the china.

"There's no need for this, Father." Her voice shook as she spoke. "After all, it's not as though . . . as if . . . that he . . ." Unable to finish, she trailed off in agonized embarrassment.

Waldwick raised his hand to halt her tortured words. "My darling child, don't even speak of it. Rugden has assured me of your innocence. Even without his avowal, you'd always remain my precious little girl, no matter what happened. But the ceremony must take place, if only for appearances' sake. The rumors have been flying around town. I'm afraid your escapade is the latest on-dit. There'll be no smoothing over this scandal, Christy. Only a wedding will suffice to save your reputation."

"But I can't abide the man!" She braced her hands on her hooped skirt and persisted intransigently. "What if I refuse? You wouldn't force me into this horrible misalliance, would you, Father?"

The color drained from Waldwick's face. "Then, indeed, you'd break my heart, child, for you'd no longer be accepted by polite society. You'd find yourself whispered about behind the spread fans of all the tattlemongers and never once given a chance to raise your voice in your own defense."

Christina tossed her head in rebellion. "What do I care about gossip?"

"I care. And the rest of your family cares. As for myself, I couldn't bear to see you forced to lead such a life."

Despite her show of resistance, she was shaken by her father's pale, drawn looks. He withdrew his snuffbox and fidgeted with it nervously, not even attempting to open it with his shaking hands.

"Father, are you ill?" She flew across the room to kneel in front of him.

Recalling the heart-wrenching sorrow they'd both felt at the loss of her mother barely a year past, Christina knew she couldn't cause her father any more suffering. Not through her own willful behavior. She also knew he was telling the truth. He couldn't face a world in which his daughter was ostracized. The knowledge that she was being forced to choose between the dream she'd shared with her grandfather and the love she felt for her sire brought a dull ache of despair.

She had no choice but to surrender.

Tears slid down her cheeks as she pressed her face against his satin-clad knee. "Very well, I'll do as you wish." She looked up with a growing feeling of mutiny. "But with certain conditions. First of all, I'm not going to give up my plans for Penthaven. Or for the eventual display of my collection there. I intended to go to Cornwall next week to meet with the architect and discuss the necessary repairs. There's no need for me to postpone the trip just because I'm forced into a marriage I don't want. Of course, I realize that the earl will expect an heir. After a reasonable period of time for the two of us to get acquainted—perhaps six to eight months—I'll be willing to accommodate him in that respect. After all, it will be my duty as a wife."

Her father stroked her hair. "My dear . . ."

"I'll meet my obligations in this marriage," she said through clenched teeth, "in spite of my dislike for the bridegroom. In the meantime I have a great deal to accomplish in Cornwall." She wiped the tears away with stiff fingers. "And I don't intend to hand my mind over to my husband with my wedding vows like so many of the rattlebrains I've seen. Once their engagements are announced, they stare up at their fiancés in blank adoration without a thought of their own in their empty heads. I've made my own decisions while I've been living with Gwen, and I have every intention of continuing to do so. I want all this made clear to the Earl of Rugden. If he still agrees to the match, then the wedding can take place."

Austin Berringer bent down and cupped his lovely daughter's tearstained face in his hands. She'd been the pampered pet of the entire family since the day she was born. But even though he adored his youngest child, he realized that she'd grown into a shockingly headstrong female. What other girl of her age wouldn't have tumbled head over heels in love with the handsome colonel and be willing to give up all her fantastical notions of changing the world? When her grandfather left Christina with the means to accomplish a dream they'd both shared, the old gentleman had no intention of its taking precedence over the most important issue in her life. Namely, that of choosing the right husband. And the marquess was convinced that Roderick Fielding was that man.

Waldwick kissed her smooth brow in reassurance. "It'll be as you wish, my child. I'll speak to Rugden. Now off with you. Get ready for the ceremony, while I meet with the bridegroom and the minister. You'll find a trunk upstairs that your brothers and I brought with us. Take your time dressing, my dear. There's no need to hurry. Roderick and I will be going over the settlements for quite a while."

As he rose from the sofa, the marquess pulled his youngest child to her feet, hugged her compassionately, and then gently pushed her toward the door. "Trust your father's judgment on this, Christy."

"I'm only doing it for the sake of my family," she responded obstinately and flounced out of the room.

Once again, the future father-in-law and son-in-law stood alone in the library of Rugden Court. The barrels, boxes, and stacks of papers had been removed, the furniture straightened, and the rug swept clean of the glass shards and wisps of straw. A large part of the afternoon had been spent going over the financial statements of the bride and groom. At the completion of the nuptial agreements, each man had signed the document with a quill pen, throwing fine sand on the ink to blot his signature. Now, the smiles of both gentlemen reflected their mutual satisfaction.

The marquess reached out and shook the younger man's hand. "I don't need to tell you, Roderick, that I'm pleased with the arrangements we've just set forth. The monetary aspects of this alliance will benefit you both. And I appreciate your honesty about the state of your present affairs, though I find it impossible to believe that Myles would have entered into so disastrous an investment as the Greater London Docks Company. With the use of my daughter's small inheritance from her grandfather, as well as the dowry I'm settling upon her, you should be able to put your finances on an even keel in less than five years."

Waldwick had been appalled to learn of his deceased friend's terrible misfortune. When Rugden had explained the full extent of the losses, the marquess had readily agreed that Christina would have to wait awhile before launching her costly scheme for Penthaven. Even a naive little miss, with no understanding at all of the hard ways of the world, would surely realize that altruistic experiments would have to give way to the cold reality of saving her new husband's beleaguered estates.

"As for myself," Waldwick added, "I'm delighted to welcome you into our family. There's absolutely no one I'd rather have as a son-in-law." He cleared his throat and went on. "But I'm very concerned about Christina. As you're well aware, she's being forced into this marriage for appearances' sake. For my sake, as well. 'Tis most regrettable that she must enter this union with such feelings of unhappiness. Feelings, by the way, which I'm certain will change dramatically in time. On top of that, she's been coddled and spoiled by a large and overindulgent family. She'll not take easily to a husband's controlling hand. I appreciate deeply the fact that you're willing to give my daughter time to accept the marriage before you make any connubial demands upon her. For all her independent ways, she's still just a babe."

Roderick nodded in agreement. "You have my word, Lord Waldwick. I plan to give Christina time to become accustomed to the idea of being my wife before I press for my rights as a husband. I'll be as considerate and accommodating as I can possibly be."

"I knew I could count on you to act with compassion," Austin Berringer said with relief. He'd admired the young man for many years, although for the past eleven he'd seen him only briefly on the few occasions when the officer had returned to England on leave. A decorated war hero, Colonel Fielding was a man's man. Tales of his courage were legendary.

"You must use a light rein on a high-strung filly, you know," Waldwick added, unable to resist giving a bit of unsolicited marital advice. "An easy touch, a gentle coaxing, a little sugar, and the saddle's on before the skittish little gel's even aware of it. You wouldn't want to break her spirit, if you take my meaning."

Roderick laughed softly at the age-old metaphor. "Aye, I do indeed, sir."

* * *

The fifth Earl of Rugden sprawled in contented relaxation on the settee in front of his study's large fireplace, his long legs crossed in front of him. For a while, he merely stared at the signed marriage settlement in his hand, then tipped his head back against the sofa's brocade upholstery and closed his eyes. He took a deep breath of honest satisfaction. By his own choice, and in less than an hour, he was to wed a young woman he'd met only two days before.

Roderick had proposed the hasty marriage for several reasons. First, the scandal caused by the gossip would severely damage Lady Christina Berringer's reputation, despite the fact that she was completely blameless of anything other than gross bad judgment. The moment he'd learned that all of London was aware she'd been staying at his home unchaperoned, he knew he couldn't simply walk away and leave her to face the scandalized world without the protection of his name.

Second, Roderick's father had been a good friend of the Marquess of Waldwick. Even though he and Christina had never met, Roderick had known of her existence since the day she'd been born. He might have even attended her baptism, though, at fourteen, he'd have paid the affair scarce attention. She came from a fine old family and had been given the best upbringing money could buy. She'd make him a lively, intelligent countess, and his children a loving mother.

Third and most pragmatic, he needed a speedy marriage to an heiress, and this one had practically landed in his lap. Perhaps the gods of fate had decided at last to take a benevolent hand in his sorry affairs. At any rate, Roderick intended to use her inheritance—which would, of course, soon be his—to regain his family's lost fortune.

The fourth and last reason—but certainly not the least important—was that he wanted her, in a way he'd never wanted a woman before. Not his first wife, not even his present voluptuous mistress, had made him burn the way Christina did with just the touch of her lips.

When he'd first kissed her, he'd meant to give her a teasing, lighthearted buss. But his initial intentions had been sabotaged the moment she'd slipped her silken arms around his neck and leaned her soft curves against him. He'd been rocked like a man caught in the aftermath of a grenade's explosion. As long as he lived he'd never inhale the sweet fragrance of roses without remembering that devastating kiss. Only by the strength of his uncommon willpower had he refrained from slipping his tongue inside her soft mouth, or his fingers inside the bodice of her gown. Circumstances had demanded that he behave in an honorable manner, so he'd held back. He'd continue to do so for as long as it took him to coax her into his bed. He was determined that she'd come to him of her own free will. *But come she would.*

He felt the corners of his mouth turn up in a lazy smile of anticipation. How long would it take him to woo her? Her father hadn't mentioned a specific time for her period of grace, but Roderick guessed it might take as long as six or seven weeks. The marquess was right. She was a stubborn, willful little thing. Her surrender would be all the sweeter for her initial resistance.

He'd been completely honest with Waldwick about his own financial straits, explaining to the marquess that he was nearly impoverished. It was damn humiliating to come to his bride as a pauper, but Roderick hoped that in the weeks he'd spend seducing his reluctant countess, he'd also make significant progress in the investigation he planned to launch into the Greater London Docks Company. By the time he made Christina his wife in every way, he'd be able to do so and still retain his pride. In the meanwhile, he'd do his absolute best to charm his blue-eyed, golden-haired wife into falling in love with him.

To the consternation of the recently returned housekeeper, Christina chose to wear a black velvet gown to her own wedding. When she found it, along with several other dresses, in the portmanteau her father had brought with him to Rugden Court, Christina wondered in stupefaction what Marie Boucher must have had been thinking to pack a dress that had been worn during the year of mourning following her mother's death. And then the answer dawned. The maid had recognized the likelihood that one of Christina's brothers might be killed in a duel over her honor. Leave it to the persnickety Frenchwoman to think of every last detail.

For a moment Christina was so shaken at the possibility of Carter's or Francis's demise—a circumstance she'd hitherto refused even to consider—that she stumbled to the edge of her bed and sank down on the soft coverlet. She held the black dress on her lap in stunned silence. It didn't taken her long, though, to make up her mind to wear it. Ignoring the flustered Mrs. Hawkins's protestations, she steadfastly refused to consider any of the other lovely gowns that had arrived with her father.

The marriage ceremony took place in one of Rugden Court's spacious formal drawing rooms. A surge of satisfaction filled Christina at the look of surprise on Rugden's face as she entered the salon. Her selection of funeral black didn't go unnoticed by the rest of the group assembled to await her entrance, either. Carter gave a groan of dismay, but Francis seemed to have a hard time holding back a chuckle. When she looked into his twinkling blue eyes, he couldn't resist giving his sister a broad wink.

The sorrowful eyes of her father were almost her undoing. Blinking back his tears, the marquess accompanied his daughter slowly across the room's thick Turkestan carpet. Christina felt a stab of anguish at having caused him further suffering by her rebellious choice of dress.

Flanked by the bride's family and the groom's servants, the couple stood side by side in front of an enormous marble fireplace. The Reverend Hotchkiss, apprised beforehand of the hurried nature of the union, dispensed with the usual embellishments given blushing young lovers. Instead he read a short passage from the Book of Ruth and then went straight to the heart of the matter.

The bridegroom was resplendent in a coat of carmine. Standing over a head taller than the other occupants of the room, he was a striking figure. Gold satin breeches were molded over his muscular thighs, and white silk stockings showed off his strong calves. His raven hair was pulled back and tied with a narrow black ribbon. Dark, straight brows framed his piercing gray eyes. One scarred eyebrow lifted, as if in irony, as he repeated the vows. Clearly an aristocrat from his patrician features and his proud, almost menacing stance, he was a fierce, bold knight of the realm.

He was also amazingly handsome. A strong jaw and wide cheekbones accentuated his vibrant masculinity. No foppish dandy, he had the cool self-assurance of a man used to giving split-second orders on the battlefield. Beneath the satin clothing, the corded muscles of his arms, shoulders, and thighs were in blatant contrast to the lush richness of his apparel. Colonel Roderick Fielding was a human war machine.

Female heads most certainly would have turned, and feminine hearts would have fluttered, at his ferociously male appearance had his audience been more numerous with members of that softer sex. The bride, however, stood resolutely beside her imposing groom and barely deigned to glance at him.

It was with deep foreboding that Christina responded to the questions of the clergyman. Her voice shook dangerously. She could feel the tension of those around her when she paused to fight back the tears. Yet, in spite of the uneasy delay, the exchange of vows was completed in a matter of minutes.

From his coat pocket, Rugden produced an exquisite ring of diamonds and sapphires. It was very old, very delicate, and most likely a family heirloom. It was also a visible symbol that she now belonged to him. Unable to move, Christina held her breath at the sight of it.

Rugden took her trembling hand in his own steady one. His voice was sure and even as he slipped it on her finger. "With this ring, I thee wed," he said softly. "And with all my worldly goods, I thee endow."

Christina looked up from the sparkling gems to gaze into his hooded gray eyes and wondered what thoughts he kept to himself under that masterful self-control. His lips were tightly shut, his jaw so tense that a muscle twitched visibly. For only a moment, his dark head bent over her, and she thought he was going to touch her cheek in a tender caress. Then he stood back, once again in the ramrod stance of a soldier.

Reverend Hotchkiss peered dubiously at the rigid twosome before him and apparently decided to forgo the usual suggestion of a postnuptial kiss. The awkward silence of the large room was broken by her father.

"Please, pass around the wineglasses," he ordered the plump housekeeper, who'd played the role of matron of honor. "We'll drink to the health of our newlyweds."

Mrs. Hawkins, beaming cheerily in her best Sunday dress; Hawkins, in his dignified butler's uniform; Francis, who'd served as the groomsman; Carter, in his fashionable riding clothes; little Angus Duncan, his red hair shining like polished brass; and the somber Reverend Hotchkiss all held their glasses high as Lord Waldwick proclaimed the toast.

"To the Earl of Rugden and his new countess, Lady Rugden. Long life, good health, and much happiness!"

"Here, here!" came the hearty response as those around the bridal pair drank to their future. Carter and Francis embraced their sister and bussed her in turn, then offered their hands in congratulations to their new brother-in-law. Enfolded at last in her father's arms, Christina clung to him as though she'd never let go. Only his loving presence had sustained her during the tense ceremony. She gripped his hand in quiet desperation. How could such a travesty happen to her?

The small party adjourned to the festive dining room, where a banquet awaited them. In the center of the sparkling damask tablecloth was a magnificent bride's cake, and Christina wondered in confusion how Mrs. Hawkins could have prepared it all so quickly.

The bridal couple were seated together on one side of the long table, with the other members of the family and the parson grouped around them. The bride's mournful gown stood out in stark contrast to the joyous background provided by the white figured cloth, the fine linen napkins, the glittering crystal goblets, and the highly polished silverware. Christina realized belatedly that the preparations for the occasion must have begun long before her father and brothers had arrived that morning.

His wife's flagrant choice of bridal raiment didn't seem to diminish the Earl of Rugden's pleasure in his own wedding feast. He draped his arm around the back of her chair and conversed with her parent and siblings and his own minister with enough charm to enchant an entire tribe of African headhunters. As he talked he lightly caressed the nape of her bare neck with his strong fingers. She inched away and glared at him, but the earl slipped his arm around her waist and drew her back toward him with an asinine smile of contentment. Gad, the man really was as dense as a board.

The new Countess of Rugden found it difficult to concentrate on the flow of conversation around her. She picked halfheartedly at the food on her plate and tried to ignore the virile male sitting next to her. Rugden made use of every opportunity to brush against her, and her own body responded to his close proximity with an involuntary shiver of excitement. Her contradictory feelings continued to baffle her. She was incensed at his presumptuous behavior, knowing full well the promise he'd made to her father not to press his suit beyond her acquiescence. Her family seemed as oblivious to the disreputable aspects of the situation as the earl. Their lighthearted conversation encouraged an atmosphere of warm conviviality. It seemed that, now that their sister was safely married, both brothers felt everything had been dealt with in a most auspicious manner. Whatever promises Rugden had made to her father, who no doubt had reported them in turn to her brothers, his pledges appeared to have completely satisfied the three men in her family.

During the meal there were more congratulatory toasts. Afterward they gossiped about the latest happenings in London. There was even some heated discussion over the most recent purchases of horseflesh by each man at the table. The Berringer males were avid sportsmen; nothing was taken more seriously than their blooded stock. Carter promptly invited his new brother-in-law to visit the stables at Waldwick Abbey, and the earl, on his part, asked the men to view the mounts he kept at Rugden Court. Since to do so immediately, as they most certainly wished, would have left Christina sitting alone in the dining room on her wedding day, that pastime was magnanimously postponed till morning.

After receiving again the felicitations of the household staff and the parson, who received his stipend with a gracious bow and left, the family withdrew to the music room.

"Play us a song, Christy," begged Francis with a good-natured grin.

She scowled at him. "I'd rather not."

Instead of acknowledging the reason for her reluctance, her brother began to pound out a spritely tune on the spinet with little more to recommend it than its volume. Carter joined him, and the two brothers lifted their voices in one ditty after another, becoming more and more uninhibited as the evening and the drinking progressed.

At first Roderick only listened in mild surprise while Christina's brothers sang together in uproarious delight. Then, perceiving the look of angry condescension on his young bride's lovely face, he decided to join them. His own voice was deep and powerful, and he had an extensive repertoire of old camp songs. The bold, risqué lyrics were laced with double meanings. It was all he could do to keep from laughing out loud when Christina gasped in indignation at the bawdy verses. Waldwick, lost in the memories that one particular old ballad brought back, relaxed beside his daughter on the sofa and contentedly hummed along.

Only Christina refused to join in the merriment. She sat, stiff-backed and wooden, on the satin-covered cushions and tapped her foot, not in rhythm with the music, but in increasing irritation at the frivolities of her two siblings in the midst of what she viewed as a horrid farce. Finally, in desperation, she turned to her father and invited him to a game of cribbage. Refusing to watch the three choristers continue their ribald concert, she sat down with her father at a small table in a corner and resolutely turned her back on the obnoxious trio.

As a social event, the quiet card party couldn't compete with the extemporaneous musicale. Lord Waldwick played poorly that evening, his mind more on reflections of the past than on the cards in front of him. Christina's thoughts churned at the indifference of her family toward what, by now, she'd decided should be an evening ending in a funeral rather than a wedding night. She gritted her teeth as she dealt out the next hand with an irritated snap of the cards. In her imagination, the caroling bridegroom was laid out on the polished floor in preparation for his final resting place. In reality, however, he stood at the spinet, becoming, along with her two nitwit brothers, increasingly louder and more boisterous as the time went on. The sound of their merrymaking was interrupted by the clock in the hallway announcing midnight.

"Pray, excuse me, Father," she said. "It's been a most tedious day, and I'd like to retire." She rose and bent to kiss him on the cheek.

"Christy, are you going to bed so soon?" Carter asked gaily as she moved past them toward the door. "The night's young yet. Come over and join us at the keyboard. Let's hear you play some of the beautiful old melodies you do so well."

"Not tonight," she replied with glacial politeness. She included Roderick in her glance. Her eyes were as blue and cold as a shadow on snow. "I'm dreadfully tired. So I'll wish all of you pleasant dreams, and I'll see everyone in the morning."

Carter hadn't imbibed quite so freely of the brandy as Roderick had thought. Nor was the young gentleman nearly as comfortable with the situation as he'd pretended to be. He looked down with sober contemplation at her defiant face. "We understand, Christy," he replied softly. "Sweet dreams, little sister."

Francis had ceased playing and now stood beside the spinet. He caught hold of her elbow before she could move away. Not as tall as Roderick, he still stood well above Christina. Her pulled her to him with a grin, bent over, and pecked his sister on her smooth cheek. His own blue eyes were aglow with sincere affection.

"Well, at least the parson didn't come for a funeral," Francis said with a chuckle, "even if you did wear black."

"Yes, and such a shame, wasn't it?" Christina threw a challenging glance upward at her colossus of a husband, who stood towering beside her brothers. "But in the end, all villains come to their just deserts."

Rugden had the effrontery to smile at her tart response.

"Would that all villains could end their day with such a delightful dessert," he softly replied.

Enraged at his audacity, Christina started to respond, then stopped, her mouth snapping shut on her words. She was determined not to become imbroiled in an argument she might just lose. She nodded her head, pulled open one tall door before any man could reach it for her, and left the room.

Rugden pursued her. She heard his footsteps close behind and, on the second step of the wide central staircase, turned to face him. The added height allowed her to look directly into gray eyes sparkling with amusement.

"You left before I could wish you a proper good night," he said. Without warning, his strong hands encircled her waist. He lifted her off the stairs and brought her to him.

Finding herself sailing through midair, Christina reached out instinctively to brace both palms against his broad shoulders. She could feel his muscles flex and bunch beneath the scarlet coat.

He held her up in front of him with ease and lightly, gently kissed both eyelids and the tip of her nose. Then his arms slipped around her, and he brought her up against his chest. He covered her mouth with his open one. His tongue traced a sensuous, lingering path across her lips.

Christina felt again the passionate response he'd evoked once before with his touch. Her treacherous hands slid around his neck, and she returned his scorching kiss. In her compelling, irrational need, she clung to him for support.

At last Rugden broke the kiss and placed her back on the step. He lifted her trembling hand and brought it to his lips. With his tongue, he slowly followed the crease that lay across her palm in an arrogantly erotic enticement. When he looked up to meet her gaze, her breath caught in her throat at the naked hunger in his eyes.

"Good night, Lady Rugden." His voice was as soft and rich as the ebony velvet of the gown she wore. "I, for one, am delighted that it was a wedding the Reverend Hotchkiss celebrated here today and not a funeral. Especially since I'd have been the central figure at either one." He grinned at her. "By the by, I didn't get an opportunity to tell you what an enchanting bride you made. You look lovely in black. Almost as ravishing as in your dainty little chemise."

"That's something you'll never see again." She jerked her hand away and flew up the stairs.

Chapter 5

Christina skipped down the wide central staircase, hastily pulling on her favorite pair of summer gloves. It was the morning after her wedding, and she intended to waste no time in leaving Rugden Court. From the outfits Madame Boucher had thoughtfully packed, she'd chosen a carriage dress of deep lavender muslin figured with tiny white flowers. She touched the hooped skirt with satisfaction. What a wonderful change from the travel-worn brown dress. By now she'd come to detest the horrid thing. She reached up to adjust the tiny gypsy hat perched rakishly on her head. Its long plum-colored ribbons trailed behind her, tangling wildly with her unmanageable curls. Within moments, her smile of contentment disappeared. Rugden's liveried footman was carrying her trunk up the same staircase she was so happily descending.

She stopped and leaned toward the servant to speak in a guarded whisper. "Where are you going, Watt?" She pointed downward with one lavender finger. "You're heading in the wrong direction. Take my luggage back downstairs and place it on my father's coach. Quickly, please! My family will be leaving shortly."

"But . . . but, my lady," Watt Keighly sputtered in mystification. "His lordship only just this minute ordered me to carry your baggage back upstairs. And after I'd just hauled it down like you'd told me to, not ten minutes afore."

Christina had been prepared for this eventuality. She'd chosen to have hot chocolate and toast alone in her bedchamber, rather than breakfast with her father and brothers, for the sole purpose of avoiding her new bridegroom. Only the day before the marquess had assured her that she'd be able to continue with her plans to journey to Cornwall the next week. She wasn't certain Rugden would be as willing to accommodate her as her easygoing sire. At any rate she didn't plan to take any chances. She'd learned, in her nineteen cosseted years, never to ask permission to do anything unless she was prepared to accept a negative reply. It was far better to go ahead with her own plans and face whatever furor followed. After the dust had settled she'd still have accomplished what she'd initially wanted to do. Rather than risk an argument with the somewhat daunting colonel, she intended just to wave good-bye to him from the window of her father's carriage as the Berringers took off down Rugden Court's great curving driveway. The strategy had worked often enough with her own family. Why not on her unsuspecting groom?

"Oh, no, Watt, you surely misunderstood," Christina persisted with a smile of undiluted conviction. "I need both of my trunks loaded immediately. If I know my father, he'll be off before breakfast."

"Yes, my lady." Without a word of complaint, Keighly shouldered the heavy portmanteau and started back down the stairs toward the entry.

Christina followed close on his heels. As they crossed the polished tiles of the great baronial hall, she scooted past the burdened servant and slipped out of the huge oak door ahead of him. Once free of the manor house, her feet took wing. She flew to her father's commodious traveling coach, which stood waiting for his imminent departure. Soundlessly, she stole inside the vehicle and closed the door. Forgoing the plush velvet cushions, she crouched down between the seats, making certain that not even the top of her little straw bonnet was visible through the window.

From inside the hall came the dreaded explosion. Her husband had apparently caught Keighly just as he was about to cross the threshold with her trunk.

"What the hell's going on?" Rugden bellowed at the poor footman. "I told you to take this gear back up to my wife's chambers. Get these trunks upstairs at once!"

From her hiding place, Christina couldn't hear the servant's meek reply, but whatever his explanation, it brought an immediate reaction from his master. Her quickened heartbeat matched the staccato click of her husband's booted heels as he came down the stone porch stairs two at a time. The carriage door swung open with a violent jerk.

"Get out." His low voice was soft and menacing.

A curious Watt Keighly had followed Rugden to the coach. The fascinated retainer now peered over his employer's shoulder with wide-eyed amazement to see the new Countess of Rugden cowering ignominiously between the green velvet seats of her father's carriage.

Upon this humiliating exposure, Christina half stood, trying in vain to scoot to the far side of the vehicle, her voluminous lavender skirts squashed into a pear shape by the cushions.

"Whatever are you talking about?" she exclaimed with an air of affronted indignation. "I'll be leaving with my father as soon as he comes downstairs. He told me last night he was anxious to make an early start." With a hesitant smile, she peered over her husband's shoulder at the burly footman. "So, pray," she continued, "get my things loaded on the coach."

At that point Rugden reached in, lifted her bodily out of the carriage, and carried her up the manor house steps.

"Take those bloody trunks back upstairs," the earl told a bewildered Watt in passing as he carried Christina into the library. "And this time, Keighly, you'd better goddamn well leave 'em up there."

Rugden kicked the door shut and deposited a now thoroughly frightened Christina on her feet in front of him. Her brand-new bonnet had been knocked askew in the capture and hung precariously down the middle of her back on its purple satin ribbons.

He was taut with anger. Nothing in her previously coddled existence had prepared her to face anyone quite so forbidding. He'd tossed her around with the ease of a parlormaid moving a china figurine out of the way for dusting. Good gad, he wasn't even short of breath.

Although ordinarily considered plucky to a fault by her

family and friends, she took a small, involuntary step backward and fought to regain her lost composure. She felt as though the ribbon caught around her throat was going to strangle her. Or was it the sight of his tightly clenched hands that unsettled her? Steadfastly meeting his furious gray eyes, she placed her own hands behind her back to hide her trembling fingers and strove frantically to find the least damaging explanation.

Rugden was not about to allow her the time to choose the right words in leisure. "What, may I inquire, did you think you were doing out there?" He spoke in a low voice, all the more unnerving for its total control. His icy gaze pinned her, much, she suspected, as it had skewered many a perplexed first lieutenant or flustered corporal of the guard who'd failed to carry out his orders to the exact letter.

"Why . . . why," she stammered. She untied the snarled ribbon from around her throat with shaky fingers, quickly removed her hat, and gulped for air. "As you can plainly see, I'm preparing to leave with my family. Father told me last night that he'd be departing early this morning, so I hurried to be ready. I certainly planned to say good-bye." She choked on that bald-faced lie. "Uh, uh, that is, I was going to write to express my sincere appreciation for . . ." She trailed off in acute embarrassment. Writing a thank-you note to a man who'd just married her to protect her damaged reputation suddenly didn't seem like such a noble idea.

He didn't think so, either. His deep voice was filled with a scalding irony. "You intended to *thank* me? Was that why I found you skulking in your father's carriage? You little idiot, have you taken leave of what limited sense you were born with? You actually planned to ride off with your father after saying, 'Thank you, good-bye, and I appreciate your courtesy'?"

At his scathing indictment, she straightened her spine. "Lord Rugden," she retorted in haughty self-vindication, "I'm fully aware of the enormous sacrifice you've made for my family and for my own good name. A sacrifice for which I'm certain my father has already handsomely rewarded you. I do not view your actions lightly. But I can't say that I'm grateful, for I'm not. Furthermore, I must insist that you refrain from speaking to me in that objectionable tone of voice again. We may have our differences of opinion regarding this miserable little episode, but we surely don't have to behave in anything less than a civilized manner. And in my entire life, no one has ever intimated that I wanted sense." She fluttered her hand at him as if to shoo away a persistent shopkeeper. "So now, if you'll kindly stand aside as the princely fellow you profess to be, I need to find my father. And," she added with a defiant tilt of her chin, "I'm leaving Rugden Court this morning, with or without your indulgence."

After that toss of the gauntlet, Christina threw back her shoulders and made a jaunty move toward the exit.

Her husband leaned back against the door, folded his arms across his massive chest, and effectively blocked her retreat. Beneath his white linen shirt, the muscles on his upper arms bunched alarmingly. His strong jaw angled forward in graphic displeasure as he spoke through clenched teeth. "As a matter of fact, Lady Rugden, I don't intend to stand aside while you parade out this door." He had the nerve to smile at her, though the scornful amusement never quite reached his frosty eyes. "You, my dear, and your bloody things, are remaining right here where you—and they—belong. Or have you forgotten the tender promises you made only yesterday in front of your father and brothers, not to mention the churchman who pronounced us man and wife *until death us do part?*"

His insolent tone carried the dispassionate certainty of a magistrate pronouncing a sentence of life imprisonment on some hapless footpad. A clutch of fear grabbed at Christina's heart. Not for the first time since entering his elegant home did she suspect that the Earl of Rugden was unlike any man she'd ever met before. Now she knew why.

He was ruthless.

"You . . . you can't mean that." She gasped. "You can't really intend to keep me here against my wishes!"

Rugden looked at her with a sardonic grin, his silvery gaze impaling her with its freezing intensity. "Ah, but, my little wife, I can. And I will."

Their cozy tête-à-tête was interrupted by a knock on the door. Reaching behind him, Rugden pulled it ajar. "Yes?" he questioned in a clipped voice, still facing Christina.

"Lord Rugden," said the Marquess of Waldwick, "is Christina with you? I've come to say farewell."

Christina stepped forward eagerly as Austin Berringer entered the room. "Oh, Father," she cried with relief and ran into his arms.

" 'Fore heaven, what's this?" he queried, holding her close. "Why, Christy, you're crying." Deeply concerned, he tilted her chin upward. Her vision was suddenly blurred with tears. "Whatever's the matter?"

Christina's sobs broke through the thin veneer of poise she'd affected with the earl. "He's trying to keep me from going home with you. Let's leave quickly. At once, please!"

"Christy, you're not making sense," came her father's puzzled response. "You can't go with me this morning. You're a married woman now. You must wait and travel to London with your husband."

Looking into her father's determined eyes, Christina realized with crystal clarity that the ceremony in which she'd so grudgingly participated as a forced but necessary inconvenience was far more than that to the two men who stood quietly beside her. Both considered it legitimate, binding, and, worse, of glaring significance in her own life.

"Oh, no!" she said. "I've got to be in Cornwall in less than eight days. It's all been arranged. I'm meeting with my steward to go over the plans for Penthaven. The masons and carpenters have to be hired and the building supplies ordered as soon as possible. We want to get as much done as we can before the cold weather sets in."

The Marquess of Waldwick glanced over at his new son-in-law with a scowl and then looked at his youngest child once again. "Christy, the restoration in Cornwall is going to have to be set aside for a while. Your husband needs to use your inheritance to recoup some devastating losses in his family fortune. It seems the late Earl of Rugden made a large and very ill-advised investment."

Christina stared at her father in dismay. "You never told

me this! We agreed between us that I'd continue with my plans for Penthaven. You said you'd secure Rugden's agreement on it before the wedding."

"When I learned of the financial disaster Roderick had been left to face, I naturally assumed practical business matters would prevail over your philanthropic schemes."

"Then why didn't you tell me?" she demanded. "Had I known, I'd never have gone through with this travesty of a marriage."

"You were already upstairs dressing for that event, my dear." At his evasive explanation, Christina realized that the marquess, for his own reasons, had purposely kept the damaging information to himself.

A hysterical laugh bubbled up in her throat. "Yes, in a black wedding gown!" She turned on Rugden. "You sham! You imposter! Pretending to marry me for the protection of my reputation, while all along what you were really after was my fortune."

With a sinking heart, Roderick met her tortured gaze. He'd foolishly assumed that her father had explained all the terms of the settlements to her. She stared up at him as though he were some perfidious betrayer.

"Regardless of whom you married, Christina," Roderick answered grimly, "control of your inheritance would have moved from your father's guardianship to your husband's. Surely you realized that."

"Yes, but I'd always intended to pick out my own groom! I wanted someone who shared my interests, who had goals in common with my own. Not a false dissembler whose only desire is to cheat me out of my dreams." For a moment she covered her trembling lips with her fingers. When she spoke again, her voice cracked in despair. "That's why the preparations for the wedding were started long before my father even arrived, isn't it? You'd planned to take advantage of my vulnerability from the very start."

"Whatever your intentions yesterday, my child," Waldwick interrupted, "you entered into a true and irrevocable sacrament of matrimony. I admit, it was a union forced upon you for appearances' sake and borne out strictly for convenience. But surely you must see that if you set out for Cornwall without your bridegroom the very week you're wed, it'd be only too obvious to the scandal-mongers that what happened here was not what we wish it to seem." He took his daughter by her shoulders. "Believe me, dearest, I'd never have agreed to this alliance if I didn't have complete faith in Roderick."

"You lied to me, Father," she cried. "You promised that I could continue with my plans for Penthaven." She clutched his arm in desperation. "I want to go home."

"Christy," Waldwick replied with utter finality, "you are home."

Removing her fingers from the sleeve of his satin coat with gentle hands, he turned to face Rugden. "I'm sorry that her brothers and I must leave this morning, but our departure can't be put off. Francis is due back at the Horse Guards by tomorrow. And Carter and I must make our appearances at private gatherings as soon as possible to deflect any damaging suppositions. We'll meet you in London in one week to face all the idle prattle together. I don't want Christina to be alone when she reenters society. The entire family will present the bridal pair at the most lavish ball London's seen in years. By the time we're through, the entire town will believe the marriage was agreed upon years ago, and that it was her mother's recent death that required such a quiet ceremony. Considering the vast amount of wealth our two families symbolize, I don't think that you'll find yourselves pushed to the fringes of society. Among us all, we'll pull this off."

Waldwick kissed his daughter's forehead and started to leave the room. When Christina attempted to follow him, Rugden's muscular arm encircled her waist. She attempted to jerk away, but the earl only tightened his unrelenting grip.

"I want to say good-bye to my brothers," she said.

"We'll say it together."

Roderick took her firmly by the elbow and accompanied her outside. They stood on the wide stone porch, watching her brothers supervise the stowing of their gear. Then the Berringer men ascended the stairs to bid the newly married couple farewell.

Tense and somber, Carter stiffly shook Roderick's hand.

At the sight of his sister's tears, his narrowed eyes glinted a silent warning.

The marquess was nearly as grim. "Till we see you in London," he told Roderick. His worried look finished the unspoken words. *I expect you to live up to your promise.* Then he turned to embrace a sullen Christina.

Francis, however, wasn't nearly so solemn. His insouciant grin informed Roderick that, had he been asked to place a bet on which one would come out the winner in the newlyweds' struggle for domination, he'd put his blunt on his little sister any day. The debonair cavalryman shook his brother-in-law's hand soundly, then leaned a trifle closer. "In case you haven't figured it out by now," he said *sotto voce,* "in all fairness, there's something you probably should know. When she loses her temper, she throws things—sometimes with deadly accuracy. So if you see her chin go up and those big blue eyes start to crackle, get ready to duck."

Francis turned, chucked Christina under that stubborn little chin, and bent to kiss her cheek.

"You're all traitors, leaving me here with this scoundrel!" she called to their backs as the Berringers descended the steps.

Her father turned to look up at her and sadly shook his head. "Good-bye, daughter."

"Good-bye, Father," came her scarcely audible farewell.

As the coach-and-four pulled out of sight, Christina struggled to dash after them, and Roderick held his recalcitrant bride firmly to his side. She stared after the disappearing vehicle for long minutes in silent desperation. Then the sudden realization that she was still in his grasp brought her circling around to face him. Inches apart, their gazes locked.

"You fraud," she said through gritted teeth. "You lying charlatan. Do you think I could ever be a loving wife to a hypocrite like you? Someone treacherous enough to force himself on a woman just to acquire her fortune?"

Roderick looked into those gorgeous sapphire eyes, blazing now with wrath, and a sense of exhilaration swept over him. He slowly appraised the tousled honey-blond curls, the flushed cheeks, the heart-stopping loveliness that now belonged solely to him. Even more than her beauty, he admired her feistiness. He had no intention of destroying that incredible vivacity. Slowly but surely, he'd bend her passionate spirit to his own indomitable will without extinguishing the fire inside her.

With a chuckle of satisfaction, he pulled her to him, enjoying the marvelous feel of her slim, tense figure in his arms. "I haven't forced myself on you yet, Lady Rugden," he drawled. He could afford to be patient. Against his far superior strength, she didn't have a prayer of breaking free, and they both knew it. "Give me a chance, little bride," he coaxed. "You may decide you haven't made such a bad bargain after all."

He pressed his mouth against her unwilling lips and brought her even closer. The fragrance of roses enveloped him. Her firm, high breasts were crushed against his chest, and only the possibility of being seen by the servants kept him from cupping one soft mound in his hand. He hoped she'd respond with enthusiasm to the beguiling invitation of his kiss.

Instead she kicked him.

Despite the protection of his high boot, she managed to strike him sharply with the toe of her sturdy lavender kid shoe. He stepped back, more surprised than hurt by her unexpected assault. She was released so suddenly that she stumbled and staggered to regain her balance.

"Bargain?" she flung at him, her arms outstretched in her search for equilibrium. "I'll keep no bargain with a shameless fortune hunter. You'll rue the day you ever tried to trick me." She turned on her heels and disappeared into the manor house.

The earl bent down and rubbed his bruised shinbone through the soft leather. Damn it, that's what he got for marrying a child bride. What a hellcat! Throwing things wasn't the half of it. Francis should have warned him that she also kicked like a mule.

Roderick grinned in delight. Next time he'd be ready for her.

Self-incarceration in her bedchamber was Christina's hasty plan of defense for the rest of the day, and she was

relieved that no one attempted to disturb her. Late in the
afternoon a worried Mrs. Hawkins knocked to inform her
that dinner would be in an hour, and she'd be more than
happy to help her new mistress dress.

"Kindly inform his lordship that I'm unwell," Christina
demurred. "Then please bring a tray to my room."

The relaying of this simple message by the sympathetic
housekeeper brought an unfeeling response from Roderick.
"Inform Lady Rugden that meals will be served in the dining room." If she chose to sulk like a spoiled brat, she'd
be treated like one.

At eight o'clock sharp Roderick sat down in solitary
state before a sumptuous meal that had obviously been
prepared for two. He resolutely sipped the Rhône Beaujo-
lais he'd ordered up from the wine cellar early that morning especially for the occasion. But despite the curious
eyes of his devoted butler and batman, who hovered
around him with the oppressive silence of two professional
mourners at a funeral, the earl barely touched the food on
his plate.

One floor above him, Christina lay on her soft bed and
stared at the painted cherubs on the ceiling. Trying to ignore the hunger pains rumbling in her stomach, she imagined her husband devouring an enormous meal. He was
probably slavering over her share just like the beast he
was.

The hours slipped by. She remained in her bedroom all
that evening, trying to keep her fury kindled. Prowling
back and forth across the carpet, she memorized every biting word she'd say when he came to apologize. Sooner or
later he had to give in. Or did he? Perhaps it was his diabolical plan to let her starve until she was too weak to resist. If so, it was up to her to launch the first attack.

Roderick slipped quietly into his sleeping wife's bedroom in the middle of the night. His undetected entrance
was made through an adjoining chamber. He knew that
Christina had used the full-length mirror on the wall for
her toilette, never realizing that it was also the door to a
large dressing area. The ornate, gold-framed looking glass
had a handle cleverly shaped to resemble a flower, and to

the unsuspecting eye, the knob seemed a part of the floral design.

Shielding the flickering glow of the candle he held in his hand, he approached the bed. Her gold-colored tresses were spread across the pillow in a riot of curls; her long lashes lay across her smooth cheeks. One hand was flung across the counterpane like a small child's searching for a favorite stuffed toy.

He bent and checked her pallor in the shaded light. There were faint blue shadows under her eyes. He cautiously reached down and touched one silken forearm, worried that she might have become ill. She was cool to the touch and slept soundly. Still, he admitted ruefully to himself, he would relent and have a breakfast tray sent up to her in the morning.

Roderick stood by the bed and watched her sleep, a golden treasure so fortuitously tossed onto his beach with the last storm and now entrusted to his care. At last, at last his luck, which had run so badly in the past, was starting to change. For a scarred, hardened soldier like himself, she was a rare gift of sunshine from the gods, delivered into his hands after all the years of cynical, self-imposed alienation.

She was so young and innocent. And so astonishingly beautiful. Bending over her, he fought back the urge to pull off the thick coverlet that hid those delicate curves. He yearned to slip the demure nightgown she wore up over her head and free her fully to his view. Would she wake if he touched her again? Would she fight him? Racked with carnal desire, he longed to run his hot hands over her cool flesh, to penetrate the soft warmth of her mouth with his tongue and sip her sweetness like a honeybee on a trembling flower. God, he would show her such pleasures. He'd turn her cold fury into a blaze of desire, until she was writhing in ecstasy beneath him. Soon he'd teach her the erotic lessons of the marriage bed. In the meanwhile he'd force himself to be patient. After all, it was only a matter of a very short time.

She stirred in her sleep and muttered crossly, and his lips curved in a twisted smile of self-mockery. Before his disfiguring injuries, he'd been considered a handsome man. Women had fawned over him, or at least over the sight of his military uniform. The gods still retained their sense of comic irony. After all the adoring ladies he'd casually rejected, he'd married the one female in England whose only criteria in looking for a mate was whether he could play the violin. His mother had been right. He should have spent more time at those damn music lessons.

Chapter 6

Roderick sat staring with unseeing eyes at a stack of papers on his desk the next morning, when he was interrupted by a tap on the library door. "Come in," he called abstractedly and then rose from his chair.

Gowned in soft buttercup muslin with creamy lace framing her smooth shoulders, Christina entered the book-filled room. Her hair was tied up loosely with a lacy ribbon, the thick curls showing the lack of her usual hairdresser. In her yellow dress, with her yellow curls bound by the yellow ribbon, she seemed to be surrounded by a glow of sunshine.

He caught his breath at her radiant beauty.

"If you have a few minutes, my lord," she said shyly. She lowered her lids in that time-honored ploy of flirtation, then raised the thick lashes and smiled at him sweetly. "I'd very much like to speak with you."

He returned her smile with heartfelt relief. He had never dreamed her capitulation would come so easily.

Roderick came around the desk and leaned his hips against it. He nodded encouragingly to Christina. She stared up at him, her features grave, her enormous eyes wide and guileless, and an intense desire to be on better terms with his young bride flared up inside him.

"There's something you wish to say?" His tone was as gentle and mild-mannered as a man of his size and disposition could make it. Hell, he'd never been known for his docile nature. But now that she'd surrendered to his stronger will, he could afford to be unendingly patient.

His new countess stood in the center of the Persian carpet like a bright pool of sunlight. She clasped her hands tightly in front of her as though about to begin her morning prayers. "Yes, my lord," she said in a hurried, anxious voice. "I've had time to think things over, and I'd like an annulment."

He grinned at her ingenuous request. "As much as I appreciate your forthrightness, sunshine, the answer is no."

"But we have excellent grounds for a dissolution," she shot back. "There'd be no difficulty at all in obtaining one. In fact, I must insist upon it."

His smile faded. Apparently, she wasn't quite as ready to submit to his dominion as he'd thought. "If you're referring to the fact that our vows haven't as yet been consummated, Lady Rugden, I can remedy that right now." He jerked his head sideways. "Right here on the library floor."

She blushed at his plain-spoken words and looked down at the toes of her yellow silk shoes in discomfort. "I'd like to explain the reason that I can't be married to you." She spoke so softly he had to bend forward to catch her words. "I'd have made this information known before now, had I realized that my father planned on my remaining here at Rugden Court. When I discussed the settlements with him, Father agreed that I could go on to Cornwall immediately. So naturally I assumed it was to be a marriage in name only, followed a short time later by a quiet annulment." She looked up and met his gaze. "I can't be your wife," she said with finality. "I'm already pledged to another."

He glared at her in disbelief. "Your father never mentioned a previous betrothal."

"My father didn't know about it." She hung her head and once again spoke to the floor. "It was a secret from both our families, for we knew they'd never consent. Our plan was to wait and prove our mutual love. We agreed to say nothing about our feelings for each other until he was able to establish himself in his military career. Meanwhile, I'd endure two seasons in town to placate my father. When it became obvious that I'd refuse the suit of any other gentleman, our families would have to give in to our wishes and allow us to marry."

Roderick stirred from his relaxed position. Rising to his

full height, he strode across the room to tower intimidatingly over her. The news that she was in love with another man unsettled him—far more than he'd have ever expected. "Why in the bloody hell would the marquess be so adverse to your marrying the blighter in the first place? Isn't he respectable?"

Her brows snapped together at his cynical accusation. "He's the most honorable man I know! Why, we played together as children. 'Tis only that neither of our families would take us seriously. They claimed we were too young to be in love."

"Just how old is he?"

She tipped her chin up defensively. "Six months older than me."

"All of twenty. God." Roderick snorted in disgust. "Your families were correct in assuming it wouldn't stand the test of time. If he's as impulsive and irresponsible as you, the two of you are a pair of green cubs. Forget him."

"Never!" Christina avowed, her blue eyes flashing with mulish determination. "I won't give him up. It'd break my heart."

Her stubborn naiveté annoyed him. "Oh, I think you'll survive," he mocked. "There've been quite a few young girls before you who've undergone the same lovesick infatuation and lived to recover from it. If you think I'm about to release you for the sake of a childhood romance, you're even more foolish than I thought you were."

"He's no child," she countered. "He's a lieutenant in the Life Guards and presently stationed on the continent. He could be engaged in mortal combat on the battlefield at this very moment. He'll return a greater hero than you ever were."

Roderick's irritation rose at the childish gibe. "What *hero* would become secretly betrothed to a girl of nineteen? The fellow's an out-and-out scoundrel. Count yourself damn lucky he didn't try to seduce you as well."

Despite all her plans to the contrary, Christina's temper got the better of her. After all, Rugden was supposed to react with sympathy, if not profound compassion. Instead he was scoffing at the carefully fabricated story that had been designed to wring even the coldest heart. Hadn't he ever heard about Romeo and Juliet, for God's sake? What could be more touching than two young lovers kept apart by their own families?

"What if he did?" she taunted. "It'd be no worse than your behavior that first day when you kissed me." She propped her hands on her hooped skirt and sniffed dramatically. "How dare you stand in judgment over us."

"Are you trying to tell me that he was your lover?" Rugden's voice was deadly calm. Though his gray eyes were veiled, she could sense the shock her jeering words had evoked. The entire scenario, well-rehearsed in her own mind the previous evening, had suddenly taken a dreadful turn for the worse. And in a direction she hadn't dreamed of.

Go ahead and agree with him, she goaded herself. *Don't be afraid. If you're ever going to be free of this unwanted marriage, you've got to say it.*

She looked him directly between the eyes.

"Yes."

Rugden's granite chin jerked up. "Then why the hell did you consent to our marriage in the first place?" He turned, walked to the hearth, and braced both palms against the mantel's smooth Italian marble. The disappointment on his rugged features was distorted in the shattered mirror in front of him. He bent his head and massaged the back of his neck with one hand, then looked back at her over his shoulder. "Was it because you needed the protection of my name?"

For a minute she couldn't comprehend his meaning. When she understood at last, she forced herself to hide her astonishment at the preposterous suggestion. She lowered her lashes, bit her bottom lip, and shrugged her shoulders in an attitude of unbounded shame.

"Damn it to hell," Rugden cursed. "And I thought you were an innocent babe."

"It would seem that you've bought a mare with her blanket on, my lord." She stared at the rug and pursed her lips to keep from laughing out loud at his look of horrified revulsion. This was going to be easier than she'd thought. *"Now* will you allow the annulment?" She peeped up at him.

For an instant it seemed as though a deep, heartfelt pain was reflected in those silvery eyes, only to be quickly replaced by a look of icy dispassion. "How can there be a dissolution if you're with child?"

"Then divorce me," she answered with a flippant wave of her hand. "However you want to do it, just set me free."

"No, Christina. You'll serve my purpose, breeding or not." His voice was raw with a derisive acrimony, the venomous words clipped and tight. "You're my wife now, Lady Rugden. Forget your hero. He has no doubt long forgotten you. The world will assume the child is mine. You've caught not only me but yourself in an ancient trap, my lovely little deceiver. Make the best of it."

Furious at his insults, she snatched a splendid Oriental vase from a nearby table with deadly purpose. He wrenched it from her hands before she could send it flying.

"No one could make the best of a marriage to you," Christina cried, "unless she was a mindless nincompoop!" She lifted her skirts and ran toward the door.

She heard the deafening smash of glass behind her as the fragile blue and white porcelain crashed against the marble fireplace into what sounded like a million pieces. Heaven help her, she wasn't the only one with an undisciplined temper.

Up the stairs she raced, the thud of his footsteps directly behind her. She entered her bedroom and turned to slam the door, only to face her very large, very formidable husband as he stalked inside.

He kicked the door closed with a bang. In his fury, his gray eyes seemed almost black. The scar on his brow stood out against his bronzed complexion in a ghastly reminder of just how indomitable a foe he was. She knew instinctively that whoever had wounded him so horribly had never lived to tell about it. She backed away silently, cautiously; he followed her step for step.

"What's his name?"

Like a martyr being led before a tribunal of the Inquisition, she crossed her hands over her breast and looked up at the angels on the ceiling. "I'll never tell you."

Rugden grabbed her upper arms, lifted her off the floor, and flung her down on the feather mattress. Frantically, she scrambled to her hands and knees on the bed, kicking wildly at the yards of yellow muslin that tangled around her legs.

"You little vixen," he uttered with quiet scorn. "I should wring your pretty neck. But you'd hardly be worth the hanging." With a grimace of contempt, he turned and left the room.

Christina lay back on her bed and stared up at the painted cherubs dancing mistily above her. She'd tried a desperate ploy and bungled it with disastrous consequences. The words couldn't be taken back now. She didn't dare admit the entire tale was a bald-faced lie. His temper outmatched her own. Not that she didn't deserve every scathing word he'd said. Good God in heaven, what was truly amazing was that he'd actually believed her!

Entering the stables, Roderick brusquely waved away the approaching coachman and grabbed his own saddle and bridle. "Come on, Mohawk," he muttered as he led the large black stallion out of the stall. "We're getting away from here before I do something I'll regret."

Once clear of the courtyard, he urged the powerful animal into a gallop. Mohawk covered the ground in long strides, jumping hedgerows and fences with ease. When they reached a wide stretch of open meadow, Roderick gave the horse his head. The feel of the wind on his face began to cool the earl's burning anger, and he halted at the top of a rise. From his vantage point, the fifth Earl of Rugden looked down upon his home. Slipping from Mohawk's back, he walked the huge beast slowly along the ridge and gazed at the manor glowing softly in the late summer sun. Its old red bricks were mellow with age. The high mullioned windows sparkled in the light, reflecting glints of silver from each small, diamond-shaped pane. The magnificent country house represented the status, wealth, and power his forebears had gathered and held through the many years of civil war and political turmoil that had racked England. He stared down at it with a feeling of intense melancholy.

Roderick deeply regretted his hasty marriage. Had he known the full circumstances, he'd never have agreed to it. What an imbecile he'd been, falling all over himself at the first glimpse of those big blue eyes and golden curls. Damn it to blazes, the last thing he wanted was a wife who believed herself madly in love with another man.

There would have been plenty of opportunities to marry an heiress in London. He'd thought to find a docile bride. Certainly one more grateful for the title and position he'd bestow upon her in exchange for his deliverance from his present impecunious circumstances. A marriage to the daughter of a wealthy merchant would have been far more honest, for it would have been entered into with the complete knowledge of both parties' real intentions from the beginning.

Now he faced the prospect of being chained for life to an unwilling spouse in a loveless, antagonistic marriage. Not for a moment did he doubt that Christina was carrying her lover's child, for he knew all too well the fatal susceptibility of starry-eyed, impulsive young women. With her announcement of the pregnancy, the possibility of an annulment had flown out the window. And a divorce would only create the very scandal they'd all hoped to avoid, neatly and effectively precluding any chance he might have had for another advantageous alliance.

He'd caught himself in his own clever snare. He'd thought to gain a fortune and a loving bride in one skirmish. Hell, at least her inheritance was real. He'd recognize Christina's bastard child if it was a girl. If not, and he eventually fathered a son of his own, he'd set things in order when the time came. But, sweet Lord, to be twice trapped. He was as big a fool now as he'd been at twenty-two.

Roderick pushed aside the bitter thoughts and climbed into the saddle. Last night in her sleep, she'd looked so pure and innocent, like an angel adrift on a cloud. Oh, Lady Christina, Countess of Rugden, was a real angel, all right. With her fortune made in heaven and her morals forged in hell.

The countess entered the stables early the next morning dressed in a riding skirt and jacket of forest-green trimmed with gold braid. Inside the dim, cool building, she found both Rugden and Angus Duncan, his batman. She met her husband's hostile scowl with an unrepentant directness that appeared to rekindle his anger. Refusing to be intimidated by his frigid aloofness, she issued a curt request. "I wish to ride this morning. Please have someone ready a mount for me."

The little Scotsman looked questioningly at his lordship.

"Saddle up Sheba for the countess," Rugden said. As the batman hastened to prepare the mare, the earl turned to Christina. "I'll send Duncan to accompany you. Until you become familiar with our lands, you'll need an escort to prevent the possibility of getting lost. We wouldn't want to misplace you and have to waste several hours scouring the countryside to find you." His lips twitched in sarcastic amusement. "However, should such an event occur, I'm certain my neighbors would provide you with shelter until I could come and collect my wandering bride."

"I don't need an escort," Christina responded stiffly, tapping the toe of her boot with her riding crop.

"Nevertheless, Duncan shall accompany you. Try not to make it difficult for him to keep up. You'll only annoy him and tire your mount needlessly."

She felt herself being thrown up into the saddle and flushed at the touch of Rugden's hand and the contempt in his voice. As he started to adjust her leg around the side-saddle horn, she jerked on the reins. He barely had time to step back before she urged the mare to a gallop and sped out of the yard.

Angus Duncan brought his hackney out of the stable and mounted.

"Stay close to her," Roderick instructed.

Duncan nodded. "Aye, aye, Colonel. But this isna going tae be easy. The lassie rides almost as well as a Scotsman." He kicked his horse and raced after the countess.

During the ride with Duncan, however, Christina made no attempt to flee. They cantered over rolling hills and eventually came to the picturesque town of Rugford, where she was treated so kindly by its inhabitants that she was shaken to the core. All who spoke to her expressed with unquestionable enthusiasm how happy they were for their lordship on the occasion of his marriage.

At the end of the village, Christina stopped to admire an old Norman church. With Duncan in attendance, she wandered through an ancient graveyard, noting the frequency of her husband's family crest on various tombstones leaning at haphazard angles. One marker bore the name of the late earl whose memorial services she'd attended in London that past spring. Beside it was the grave of Rugden's mother, who'd written the beautiful sonata in her exquisite copperplate. The countess had died fifteen years earlier. As Christina turned to leave, she noticed a solitary white marble headstone set all by itself on a small, grassy knoll and walked over to it.

ELIZABETH MARGARET FIELDING AND BABY
DIED IN CHILDBED OCTOBER 1, 1751

Christina felt a chill go through her. This was the resting place of Rugden's first wife, buried with her stillborn infant in her arms. She'd heard the tragic story briefly from her father and later from Percy. She turned to the red-haired Scotsman who stood beside her, silently reading the same inscription. "What was she like, Duncan?"

The little batman shrugged his thin shoulders and spat on the gravel path. " 'Twas before ever I met his lordship, my lady. And the colonel hasna once mentioned her name in the ten years I've been with him."

"Then he must have loved her very much to have grieved so deeply for so long," Christina persisted as she accepted Duncan's help in remounting.

"Hmph," came his cryptic reply. He shook his head dolefully. "That I dinna ken."

Upon her return to Rugden Court, her spouse was waiting for her on the front steps. At his mocking look, Christina remarked with haughty condescension that she wouldn't risk racing a good horse over unknown terrain, regardless of the circumstances.

But the next morning, with Duncan in mad pursuit, she made a bolt for it. An excellent horsewoman, she'd carefully planned her escape route the previous day. Smiling in the surety that she could easily leave Duncan behind on his short-legged hack, she rode with elation, jumping one hedgerow after another, while the batman fell farther and farther behind. Christina intended to make for the village, give Sheba a breathing space, and then be off to the Proud Lion Inn, where she could hire a coach. Laughing out loud at her easy victory, she knew the glorious feeling of freedom for the first time in four days. She'd soon be in Cornwall.

The next moment she saw the dark outline of her husband silhouetted against the morning sun. He was astride a great black stallion, high on the rise ahead. Waiting for her.

Christina pulled on the reins, turning Sheba away from the village road and into the open fields. She knew from the moment she saw him that she'd never get away. Her spirited chestnut mare was already winded; his horse was fresh from the time spent leisurely awaiting her arrival. Rugden was the devil himself, to have been so sure of her route.

The stallion's hooves came pounding after her. Christina jumped a low brick wall with ease; the earl sailed right behind her. She brought her mare to a halt and carefully schooled her expression. Not for the world would she admit she'd been trying to escape.

"I'm so glad you decided to join me," she said as he brought his mount to an abrupt stop beside her. She flashed her most engaging smile and fought to control her erratic breathing. "It's such a beautiful day for a ride."

"Isn't it, though?" Rugden turned in his saddle and waved across the field to Angus Duncan, who'd brought his own lathered horse to a halt once he'd recognized his colonel. "I thought I'd give my batman a respite from his child-guarding duty and ride with you myself." He returned her smile with a brilliant one of his own and tipped his head politely. "That is, if you'll be so kind as to allow me?"

"Oh, pray do," she grated through her unwavering smile. "I couldn't think of anything more pleasant." Except, of course, to throttle the daylights out of him.

* * *

That evening the Countess of Rugden sat with outward serenity across from her husband at the dining table. They'd just finished the first course, and both were silent as Hawkins removed their dishes. Each had said only a minimum of words to the other during the meal, just enough to fill the obvious void in front of the servant.

The room was in semi-darkness with the heavy drapes drawn. Candlelight from the golden candelabras and wall sconces cast flickering shadows upon them. Christina peeped up at her husband from beneath her lowered lashes as he absently toyed with his wine goblet. Rugden's severe dark brown coat fit snugly across his broad shoulders. His sun-darkened complexion was set off by the pristine white of his stock and the simple ruffles of fine Holland linen on his shirt. She found it difficult to keep from staring at his extraordinarily handsome features.

It had been over forty-eight hours since their mad confrontation when she'd pretended to have a lover. Marital relations had not improved. Each party attempted to maintain an attitude of tight control as they sat across from each other at the center of the long, silver-laden table. Rugden graciously poured her a glass of wine; she quietly offered the salt cellar. Beneath the façade of detached politeness, however, each was inwardly seething at the other's treachery.

Hawkins stood in attendance at the sideboard and, when not serving the tempting dishes, sadly shook his head at their stilted, feeble attempts at conversation.

Roderick looked up from the glass of Burgundy in his hand and discovered his wife watching him covertly. Despite his feelings of disappointment and betrayal, he couldn't help but admit just how bloody beautiful she was in the soft, jade-striped satin gown. Her creamy shoulders were framed by the sheen of the rich green sleeves. The low decolletage of her dress, although edged with a wisp of lace, revealed an alluring glimpse of her firm breasts, pushed up by the boning of her corset.

Suddenly a booming voice called out joyously from the hallway. "By Jove, I knew I'd timed it just right! I can smell the roasted meat all the way out here! Roddy, ol' boy, where the devil are you?"

The two dinner companions turned simultaneously to behold a macaroni of the first order enter the room. He was garbed in the most exquisite suit of plum, with quilted brocade coat and breeches, multicolored silk waistcoat embroidered in gold thread, clocked white stockings, and a lace jabot that almost covered his chin. In one hand he carried a cane and a fan; in the other, a quizzing glass through which he surveyed the surprised table partners.

"Egad! Then 'tis true!" he fairly shouted in excitement. "I refused to believe the rumors! I had to ignore the papers. When has *The Gazette* ever gotten anything right? But I see it's all true. Why, you sly fox! To steal the toast of London right from under all our noses. I say, Roddy, it's too bad of you. And my own brother, at that. Snatching my heart's desire with not so much as a by-your-leave. 'Pon rep, I can't say I'll easily forgive you for this, old man."

By this time Rugden and Christina had risen from their seats and were moving toward their visitor.

"Percy!" she said. "How wonderful to see you."

"What's wonderful, by God, is that you've actually married this reprobate brother of mine! Come here and let me kiss your hand. No, 'fore heaven, I think I'll kiss the bride." While his older sibling watched in amusement, the tall dandy enfolded Christina in his lanky arms and gave her a resounding smack on the lips. Then he pumped Roderick's hand and offered his enthusiastic congratulations.

"Since you've timed your entrance so fortuitously, Percy, sit down and join us." With a grin of sincere pleasure, the earl gestured toward the chair next to his wife's, then motioned for Hawkins to lay another setting. "It appears that the two of you need no introduction. Christina mentioned that you were already acquainted."

"Acquainted? 'Fore gad! We're more than that! Oh, thank you, Hawkins. I say, that does look delicious," exclaimed Percy, eyeing the heaping plate set before him. "Why, thunder and turf, I've proposed to the lady! And a demn good job I did of it, too, though she wouldn't have me. Can't say I really wanted to get buckled," he continued, his mouth full of roast beef, "but if I had to do it with anyone, I'd as lief do it with you, Lady Christina." He rolled his eyes at her expressively.

Taken aback, Rugden looked from one to the other. "You proposed to my wife? This is the first time I've heard of it."

Christina flushed under her husband's accusing stare. She hadn't told Rugden that he'd succeeded where his younger brother had failed for the sake of Percy's tender feelings. Now here Percy was, blurting out the whole story as though it were a matter of little account. Apparently his emotions weren't as easily overset as she'd thought.

"If you didn't wish to get married," Rugden pursued, "why on earth did you propose?"

Percy looked at him in astonishment. "Why, because you told me to! When I asked how I could help us out of this bubble we're in, you wrote that the only thing I could possibly do of assistance was to marry an heiress. So I tried! But, as you can see, she'd none of me." He brandished his fork in the air for emphasis. "I vow, it wasn't for want of trying. I can't believe the posies and cards I sent. It was a push to get inside her front door, I can tell you, with all those moonstruck puppies hanging around. And it was a bang-up proposal—down on my knee and the whole bit. Right, Lady Christina?"

She smiled in amusement at Percy's artless efferves-cence. "It was a beautiful proposal, Mr. Fielding. The loveliest one I've ever received. And you know how flat-tered I was."

"Stap me, if you haven't given that same story to all your disappointed suitors. You can't imagine the hearts she's broken," he informed Rugden. "Why, Forthington swears he'll blow his brains out if the news of your mar-riage proves true."

"Who the devil's Forthington?" Rugden asked.

"Tsk, tsk," Percy clucked with a happy smile. "Now don't get jealous, ol' boy. There's far too many of 'em, even for you."

"Don't be absurd," Christina interrupted with a laugh. "Men don't commit suicide over unrequited love."

"Oh, I dare swear, Forthington'll be over it in a fort-night," her brother-in-law cheerfully concurred. "But your marriage has certainly turned London's gossip mill upside down."

"I must agree with Percival on that score, my dear," Rugden drawled. "Your desolate swains will be consoling themselves with less charming companions within a fortnight. I've yet to hear of a man actually doing away with himself over a blighted love affair."

In the flickering candlelight, Christina met her husband's taunting gaze. He tossed his napkin on the table and smiled unpleasantly. His hooded eyes were as cold as his mocking voice. "I do hope I won't have to face any of these grief-stricken beaux in a duel."

"Ha! Considering your reputation with a sword or pistol?" shouted Percy. "Not demn likely!"

"How fortunate for me then," her husband replied with a bored shrug.

But she was convinced that Rugden meant the exact opposite. He *wanted* to face the father of her unborn child on the field of honor. Thank heavens her phantom lover was a figment of her husband's own imagination.

Rugden stood, bent over his wife, and spoke softly in her ear. "Shall we retire to the drawing room?" He pulled out her chair and politely offered his arm. She wondered if he could feel her fingers tremble as she placed her hand on his sleeve.

Summer was quickly coming to a close, and the evening had grown cool, despite the day's bright sunshine. A fire in the small salon invited the trio to its warmth, where the bridal pair listened to the latest gossip from one who really knew all the scandalous tales of the kingdom's aristocracy. Percy regaled Christina with choice anecdotes from the parties and soirees she'd missed in the past week, adding many a scathing comment on anyone's unlucky choice of costume. He soon had his new sister-in-law giggling helplessly at his comic imitations of their mutual acquaintances, some of whom the earl had never met.

From his wingback chair, Roderick watched the two on the sofa from beneath seemingly bored, half-closed lids. He'd not as yet seen this bubbling, playful side of Christina's nature. Apparently it took an elegant town fop such as his brother to coax a giggle from his spoiled, wayward little wife. Despite his brooding thoughts, Roderick played the role of the long-suffering host. Had it not been his own beloved younger sibling, he'd have knocked the clever fellow down for entertaining his bride in such a droll fashion. If one could judge from the way Percy treated her like a princess—the way, no doubt, all of London's fashionable young bloods had been treating her—his brother couldn't possibly have guessed the hidden motives behind her sudden marriage.

Roderick all but ground his teeth in exasperation. He wanted to enlighten his naive brother to the ugly truth, and at the same time he wanted to protect Christina from the look of disgust she'd see on Percy's startled face once he learned of the bastard child she carried. Later he'd have to give his brother an edited version of the marriage contract, but he didn't want even Percy to know about his bride's shameful condition.

The evening grew late. At last Christina rose from the sofa in front of the cozy fire, and the two gentlemen came to their feet. "I'm so glad you're here, Percy," she said with a musical laugh. Her brilliant eyes were alight with humor. She took his long, thin hand in both of hers. "You continue to be absolutely outrageous, and I admit I've enjoyed it tremendously. I'll look forward to more of your shameless irreverence at breakfast."

"The evening's been my pleasure, little sister." Percy grinned and bowed over her small hand with a gallant flourish. "Till morning, then. Sleep well." He watched her thoughtfully as she left the room, then turned to his brother with a sober, questioning gaze.

Roderick put his arm around his brother's shoulder and led him back to the sofa in front of the fireplace. "Sit down, Percy. I'm afraid you may not like what you're about to hear."

For the next half hour, Percy listened to his elder brother's description of the coerced nuptials, including the reluctant bride's outrageous black wedding gown. Roderick made certain that his sibling understood the main reason behind the hasty union was her unchaperoned arrival at Rugden Court. But he allowed Percy to believe, as did her own family, that he was extremely taken with her beauty as well. In doing so, the earl hoped to prepare Percy for the pending announcement of her gestation. Although he hated to deceive Percy, he felt it was necessary to protect Christina from any ill feelings. She'd need all the family support she could muster in the months ahead.

Seeing the worry and doubt in Percy's eyes when he told him about her request for an annulment and his unflinching refusal, Roderick leaned forward and braced his elbows on his knees in morose contemplation.

"The best way out of this awkward beginning is to continue with the alliance," he said. He absently rubbed the throbbing scar on his forehead. "I'll use Christina's fortune to rebuild my own, then, if possible, allow her to go ahead with her own plans. Who knows, we may learn to rub along tolerably well together in the years ahead."

" 'Fore gad, is that all you can say?" Percy admonished. "She's had her sights set on that asylum in Cornwall since her grandfather died. It's supposed to be dedicated in the old gentleman's honor." His troubled gaze revealed his deep regret for the ill-starred marriage. And heartfelt compassion for his brother's unwilling bride.

Shortly after the unhappy interview between the two male members of the Fielding family, Roderick quietly entered his wife's bedroom. It was the first time he'd used the mirrored doorway while she was still awake. Their bedchambers were connected by a spacious dressing area, which the home's new mistress had as yet failed to discover.

Christina sat before her vanity table, not immediately aware of his presence. Her flowing satin robe, its long ribbons falling loosely to the floor, was draped open to reveal the embroidered white nightshift beneath. She'd removed the pins from her golden-blond hair, and the unbound curls cascaded freely down to her waist. She was just about to apply a cream to her face when she realized she was no longer alone. She pivoted on the dressing bench, her fingers poised gracefully above the pale green Wedgwood jar. At the sight of the gold-framed mirror standing wide open behind him, she gasped, stunned by the realization that she'd never been safely locked in her bedroom the entire time she'd been in his home.

Roderick crossed the room to stand beside the great four-poster bed. He leaned one shoulder on a carved post and folded his arms. Without saying a word to ease her alarm, he stared gravely down at her.

She was perched like a startled fawn, poised for flight on the edge of the seat, yet utterly defenseless. He could see, reflected in those magnificent sapphire eyes, the awareness of her own vulnerability. She bit her full bottom lip and pulled the front edges of her blue robe together in a gesture of constrained wariness. With her slight movement, the voluminous satin gown rustled seductively, and the fragrance of roses assailed his senses. He made no attempt to fight back the surge of rapacious desire that flooded through him. Rather he inhaled the bewitching perfume of her and released a long, labored breath. After months—nay, years—of enduring the primitive conditions of bivouac and battlefield, a man could die content in this silken, scented, rose-pillowed bower.

"What . . . do you want?" she gulped. Her fingers trembled as she hastily tied the robe's dainty white ribbons.

How many men had lain with her? Percy had said she'd had dozens of suitors. By her own admission, at least one had seduced her. Perhaps there'd been more. Why should he, her own husband, deny himself the delectable wares another man had already sampled?

"It would seem," he said brusquely, "that mine was not the only marriage proposal you've received. How many other half-wits like my foolish brother did you have down on their knees in front of you?"

Christina gaped at Rugden in astonishment, unable to comprehend why he was suddenly so angry. "What difference could it possibly make to you?"

He was still dressed in his severe dinner clothes, and the dark shadow of his heavy beard accented his overwhelming masculinity. Suddenly he straightened from his relaxed position beside the foot of the bed and moved toward her in swift, predatory fashion. He stopped only inches away. "How many?" he insisted.

Her words, stilted and unnaturally high-pitched, rang

out in the quiet room. "Father jested that it was an even dozen." At his ferocious scowl, she edged backward on the bench. I'm ... I'm not absolutely certain how many proposals there were, since most gentlemen consulted my father first for permission to court me. Naturally, he turned away anyone he considered unsuitable."

"Then he considered Percy suitable?"

Christina stared at her husband in surprise. " 'Tis obvious."

"But not your gallant cavalryman?"

So they were back to that again. Maybe a divorce wasn't as unobtainable as he'd first tried to make her believe. The idea of a husband willingly accepting his new wife's unborn by-blow seemed incomprehensible to her. Nearly as incomprehensible as the fact that Rugden actually believed she was pregnant in the first place. How could a man of his worldly experience be so gullible?

She rose from the padded seat and slipped past him. With exaggerated curiosity, she swung the looking glass door back and forth on its golden hinges while her mind raced through various possibilities. Then she shrugged with an air of jaded disinterest. "We were certain Father would come around if we just held out long enough. Instead, you've ruined all our chances for happiness."

"How many people knew about your liaison with this epitome of English manhood?"

"No one."

"Who is he?"

She sensed the scarcely veiled threat behind his question. But this time she was prepared with an answer. If he wanted a name, she'd give him one. She'd implicate someone so far away Rugden couldn't possibly harm him. Her husband could rant and rave and stomp on the floor in fits of wild anger. He could smash blue and white Chinese vases till he was wading knee-deep in broken porcelain. It wouldn't do him a darn bit of good. For the young man she'd identify as her lover would be completely beyond his reach.

"Why?" she taunted. She tossed her head in feigned unconcern. "So you can force a quarrel on him?" She peered with seeming fascination into the dressing room, then called back over her shoulder in a voice brittle with sarcasm, "Are you as deadly with weapons as your brother claims?"

He braced his hands on his hips, widened his stance, and smiled evilly. "Deadlier. However, forcing a quarrel on the snot-nosed little bastard would only succeed in bringing attention to the very item we wish to avoid. Namely, your pregnancy. I'm not going to call him out. But I insist on knowing his name. Who *was* your lover?"

Christina strolled back into the room and plopped down on the edge of her bed. She wound a narrow ribbon around her forefinger and then shrugged in surrender. "As you'll learn, anyway, I'll tell you. He's Edwin Whiteham, the second son of the Viscount of Beechym. His father's Wiltshire estates border my family's. It was only his age that my father saw as an impediment. Father refused to view us as anything but children. Ted has a fine, honorable reputation. We love each other desperately. He'll never give me up."

Rugden caught her by the wrist and dragged her off the bed. He slid his fingers around her throat and tightened imperceptibly. "Are you telling me the truth?"

"Leave me be," Christina whispered, immediately regretting her rash pose of worldly cynicism. Maybe this time she'd pushed him too far.

"Oh, aye, I'll leave you be," her husband responded. His deep voice was hoarse with contemptuous arrogance. He brought his face closer to hers and spoke through clenched teeth. "But not because you demand it, Lady Rugden. And not because your father insisted upon it. But because, when I do have a child of my own, I'll have no doubts who sired it."

He released her so abruptly, she sank back down on the bed's thick comforter. Then he strode out of the room, closing the gold mirrored door behind him with an insolent slam.

If they stayed together much longer, there wouldn't be an uncracked mirror or an unshattered vase on the premises.

Chapter 7

Justin Somesbury, the Duke of Carlisle, sat at his ornately carved Venetian desk and reread the crumpled note, penned in his cousin's hysterical French, for the third time.

> J.
>
> Whatever happened, you cannot blame me! Your coachman was an imbecile to take up a Painted Harlot in place of your Intended Guest. The rumors of the marriage are All True! Still, I overheard one of the family say that our little cabbage is Extremely Unhappy and Rebellious. An Annulment is not yet out of the question. They arrive in two days. I will await your instructions.
>
> M.

With a sneer of contempt for the ineptness and stupidity of underlings, he threw the wrinkled paper back down on the massive baroque desktop.

"More trouble, Carlisle?" his houseguest inquired with a bored yawn. Sprawled inelegantly on a nearby sofa, Oliver Davenport could barely keep his red-rimmed eyes open. They'd gambled into the late hours of the night, and the duke had enjoyed his usual run of phenomenal luck.

"Nothing I can't set right, my friend," Justin Somesbury said. He barely glanced at the portly gentleman half dozing nearby.

Davenport noted the implacable resolve in the arrogant voice and peered more closely through the lowered slits of his eyes. Carlisle's present calm demeanor belied a ferocity that his enemies had come to fear with good reason. The careless response failed to conceal the intensity of the lithe, muscular man whose body, despite his advancing middle age, reflected a life spent in vigorous sporting pursuits. The duke rode, hunted, raced, and dueled with a competitiveness that bordered on savagery.

Only the lines radiating from the corners of his eyes and the deep grooves carved into his lean cheeks indicated that he'd just passed his fiftieth birthday. That and the silver which winged out over his temples, cutting a swath through his ebony hair. The thin black brows were pulled together now in the straight line of an angry scowl.

"Ye gads, you're a cold fish!" chortled Davenport. He raised his bulk from the sofa and walked toward a nearby side table. "I'm surprised you didn't murder that buxom widow upstairs the night she arrived in your coach in place of the Berringer chit."

Carlisle glanced briefly at his guest as he recalled his inner rage upon discovering the voluptuous woman inside his carriage that stormy night just one week ago. It had been close for a while, but he'd managed to conceal his initial shock at seeing her mature, worldly face in place of Christina's angelic one. God, it was a wonder he hadn't beaten the jade to death in his disappointment. Her absolute astonishment had brought him quickly to his senses. It was obvious from her expression of startled dismay when he handed her out of the coach in the pouring rain that the handsome woman had nothing to do with the abominable mix-up.

Remembering his own smooth charm as he'd reassured Madeline Gannet that it was nothing but a silly mistake, his mouth curled up in a sneer. To have planned it all so carefully and ended up with Rugden's mistress!

"Yes, my dear Oliver, you're quite right. It's a wonder I didn't strangle the wench to death with my bare hands. But I'm convinced she wasn't knowingly involved in the aborted abduction. Certainly, she doesn't have a clue about the forced marriage that's just taken place. Mrs. Gannet's in for a rude shock. She's been under Rugden's protection since he returned to England this summer. Since her husband died, the wealthy widow has dropped every lover she's ever had the moment Colonel Fielding's come home on leave. No, I don't think she was any part of the whole fiasco. She is, perhaps, its only innocent victim—if one can possibly refer to Mrs. Gannet as innocent."

"Cognac?" Davenport asked from the console table. At the duke's nod, he splashed the amber liquid into two crystal snifters. "Well then, what next? he continued as he handed one to Carlisle. "Do you attempt a second kidnapping? Rugden could get rather nasty about someone stealing his newly acquired heiress. He's one of the finest swordsmen in England. I should know. I was almost removed from the face of this earth by his diabolical swordplay. Damn, it was like trying to duel with Lucifer himself! 'Twas Rugden's intention to kill me. Thank God, I was nigh mortally wounded. Had it been less, he wouldn't have had to leave the country. Zounds, I can imagine his chagrin when he learned later that I'd not died as expected. Not having seen him for the last eleven years, I can assure you that I'm most reluctant to renew his acquaintance."

Carlisle smiled, more to himself than in response to his cohort's timidity. "No, my good Davenport, I think a second abduction attempt would prove quite fruitless. Rugden's no fool. Since he obviously made short shrift of Christina's qualms and shackled her before she'd had a chance to leave his home, her inheritance will soon be put to use in rebuilding his lost fortune. What an ironic twist of circumstances that delivered her and her money into the hands of my worst enemy, while at the same time depriving me of her very delectable person. Damn!"

The stem of his brandy snifter snapped in his fingers, and Carlisle looked in bemusement at the broken shard embedded in the palm of his hand. Davenport hurried over to help, but was waved away with a contemptuous gesture. Calmly plucking out the glass, Carlisle bound up his wounded hand with a lace handkerchief, allowing Davenport to assist in tying the corners of the makeshift bandage tightly enough to stop the bleeding.

"If I believed in God, Davenport, I'd blame Him for this extraordinary mischance. Since I don't, I must curse blind fate and once again lay plans for Rugden's financial destruction. Oh, I'll have Lady Christina in the end. Never doubt it. As for Roderick Fielding, since he had the ill-chanced temerity to become the lady's husband, why, I'm afraid there's nothing left for me to do but kill him."

Carlisle turned his head to watch the Earl of Rugden's mistress quietly enter the salon. He rose from the desk chair and smiled ingratiatingly as he wondered just how much the lovely widow had overheard.

Madeline Gannet wore a flowing sack gown of bright orange and white stripes. Her lustrous, dark brown hair was drawn up off her brow and shaped into ringlets that curled about her head in artful disarray. Though petite in stature, she had a full-bosomed seductiveness that pulled both men's gaze to the embroidered bodice's low, square neckline.

Perceiving Davenport, she slowed. "Your Grace," she said in a husky contralto voice, "I didn't realize you entertained a guest." A tiny black patch accentuated the fullness of her lips, and the fragrance of musk enhanced the aura of ripe sensuality that surrounded her. It was easy to see why General Lucius Gannet, Rugden's former commanding officer, had been so easily entrapped by her beauty in the first blush of her youth.

"My dear Mrs. Gannet," Carlisle said with a flourish of his arm, "allow me to introduce Mr. Oliver Davenport."

Madeline graciously extended her hand. "Mr. Davenport and I are acquainted, Your Grace. We met in London at a soiree this past season."

"Your servant, madam," Davenport said as he bowed over her fingers.

With his younger brother in tow, the Earl of Rugden and his new countess departed for their town house in Berkeley Square on a brilliantly clear September afternoon. The journey from Buckinghamshire to London, which took place only three days after Percival's unheralded arrival, was singularly uneventful. After passing several tollgates with tedious regularity, Roderick settled back in the corner of his spacious, well-sprung berlin and watched his coxcomb of a brother make an idiot of himself entertaining his new sister.

The Fielding trio arrived at Rugden House only to be subjected to the shamelessly curious perusal of the entire staff. The servants had gathered in the entry hall to greet their new mistress. Each liveried footman, each white-aproned upstairs and downstairs maid, the beaming house-keeper, the plump cook, the dignified butler, indeed, every male and female on the premises vied for a chance to see the young lady who'd succeeded in snagging their re-nowned master. None knew the unhappy circumstances behind the wedding. Hence all assembled presumed that their distinguished employer had at last been smitten by a pair of fine eyes and rosy lips.

Composed and self-assured, the countess greeted each servant with her dazzling smile. Her sincerity was appar-ent to the lowest-ranking scullery maid and boot boy, and the staff withdrew singing her praises.

This unabashed capitulation of the entire household, however, did nothing to improve Roderick's already sour mood. While Christina was shown her chambers, an ele-gant suite of rooms on the second floor, and his brother napped on the sofa in the small salon, he proceeded to his study and began the arduous job of sifting through more of his father's papers. It was an onerous task he dared not put off. Any clue as to why Myles Fielding would invest his entire fortune in the ill-starred scheme euphemistically known as the Greater London Docks Company was of the utmost importance.

Upstairs, Christina was busily helping a ruddy-cheeked maid unpack her portmanteau. Annie, a strapping girl from the village of Rugford, had a ready smile that lit an other-wise plain face, making her hazel eyes crinkle at the cor-ners as she happily informed her new mistress that she was the cook's niece. The countess bathed and dressed for dinner with Annie's cheerful help and then went down-stairs to join her husband.

Upon entering the drawing room, she found Rugden and Percy awaiting her, accompanied by a man every bit as large as her husband. The two giants stood side by side in the center of the room, which seemed to shrink with their presence. Amazed, she came to an abrupt halt.

Roderick smiled at his wife's look of astonishment. He and Hugh Gillingham had been close friends since their school days at Harrow. Excelling in sports as well as academics, they were drawn to each other by their mutual talents and strong personalities. After Oxford, they both joined the Grenadier Guards. They'd fought side by side in the recent war and more than once had saved each other's life. Their last campaign together had been with General Wolfe at Quebec. Then Hugh had been transferred to Central Europe, while Rugden remained in the North American colonies. Despite the fact that they hadn't seen each other for three long years, they remained close confidantes.

"My dear, may I present my good friend and fellow soldier, Major General Hugh Gillingham?" Roderick said. "He surprised me this afternoon, for I thought him still stationed with our troops in Prussia. Hugh, meet my new countess."

The large officer, dressed in the scarlet tunic and blue breeches of the Foot Guards, moved forward and gently took her outstretched hand. He bent over it with consummate grace. "My pleasure, Lady Rugden," he said in a booming, gravelly voice.

Hugh's wide-set eyes were framed by thick, sandy brows. Even though Hugh was thirty-four years old, his ample pug nose was still decorated by a sprinkle of cinnamon freckles. His infectious smile displayed a slight gap between his two front teeth. "And my heartiest congratulations to this rawboned clod of a husband of yours," he added. "I didn't think Roderick had the good sense, let alone the personal address, to capture an angel like you."

At his sincere words of praise, the countess lowered her lashes. "You're far too flattering, sir. The honor is mine in meeting one of our country's gallant warriors." Another conquest was added to Christina's list by the time she raised those long, deadly eyelashes and turned her gaze on her brother-in-law. "La, Percy, but you do look grand indeed," she said in her musical voice. "Are we expecting more company on our first evening in London?"

That dandy, arrayed in his usual outrageous fashion, smiled triumphantly.

Roderick answered for him in an insolent drawl. "I'm afraid we're faced with a very dull evening, my dear, as only we three shall be dancing attendance on you tonight. But we'll endeavor to shower you with all the inane flatteries to which you doubtless have become accustomed since your successful entry into London's discerning society."

Percy and Hugh turned as one to stare in astonishment at his unmerited lack of courtesy. Both men took a step closer to the young woman and, without even stopping to think, each offered his elbow in a chivalrous gesture of protection.

With a proud toss of her golden head, the new Lady Rugden responded by turning her small, straight back on her husband and accepting the arms of her two gallant knights. "Gentlemen, your kindness precludes my making any choice. I shall simply have to allow you both to escort me to the dinner table."

They departed the room, leaving Roderick to gnash his teeth at the well-deserved set-down. Rather than join them immediately, which would have meant trailing after them like a chastened lap dog, he went to a gilded side table and poured another brandy. A shrill giggle errupted in the hall. He hastily tossed down the contents of his glass in one gulp and coughed, his eyes watering at the burning sensation. Laughter and hurrahs carried through the open doorway. The obnoxious threesome strolled back into the salon with a diminutive brunette between them, each exclaiming in delight over her sudden appearance.

"Heigh-ho, Roddy! Look who we have here! Our own little sister was standing on our doorstep, looking as forlorn as a gin-drinking waif from the poor house. I thought she was tucked up safely at some school for rich brats!" Percy hugged his sister joyously.

"That's exactly where she's supposed to be," Roderick answered in consternation. "Pansy, what the devil are you doing here? You must have received my letter refusing you permission to come to town. I wrote explicitly that you were to remain at school where you belong."

"Oh, bother, Roderick, I couldn't remain there any longer! I just couldn't." The young lady walked up to her eldest brother, a pout on her lovely heart-shaped face. "Not with all those Friday fish-faces staring at me."

She was so short she barely reached the middle of his chest. Her straight little nose crinkled in disapproval as she lifted her head and favored him with a look of complete disgust. "Every time I tried to have any fun, those old maids would cluck their tongues and prophesy doom and gloom for me. Who'd want to stay in such a dull place anyway? I begged Father not to send me there. And I won't go back! Not ever!"

"What is it you've done this time, scamp?" Percy teased. "Did you sneak food into your bedchamber again? Or a kitten you know perfectly well you can't keep?"

Pansy lowered her dark brown head, patently embarrassed. "'Tisn't what I sneaked into my rooms. 'Twas my stealing out of them. What a great to-do over such a little episode. I swear, they carried on as though I'd tried to elope."

Christina gave a startled gasp. Behind her, Percy groaned and Hugh chuckled softly.

"We'll speak no more of this now," Roderick interrupted. "But tomorrow, Lady Penelope, I'll have the whole story. The absolute truth, mind you. And you'll return to school the next day. You're too young to be let loose in London. And I don't have the time at present to provide you with the proper supervision."

The penitent girl looked around the group, her enormous brown eyes sparkling with tears. Her delicate little mouth quivered as she strove to keep back her sobs. The three adults stared at Roderick in silent condemnation, as if to say only a tyrant would so abuse a young girl by sending her back to that horrible institution.

Pansy knew how to play to an audience. She sniffed noisily several times, after which she cautiously peeped up at her new sister, whose identity she'd only just learned in the hallway, to survey the effects. To her delight, Lady Christina took up the cudgels in her defense.

The sight of the orphaned girl struck a sympathetic chord in Christina's heart, for she'd lost her own mother just that past year. She'd only been out of mourning clothes less than six months herself. As she looked at the unhappy girl, barely past her childhood, dressed in the severe black crepe of mourning that had, no doubt, been decreed by the fastidious females at the academy, Christina's heart went out to her.

She placed her arm around Pansy and glared defiantly at her autocratic husband. "There'll be no need for you to supervise your sister, my lord. I'll chaperone Pansy. After all, if she hates the school that much, it can't be a very good place for her. And since I'll be attending social events as a married woman now, there's no possible objection to my playing the duenna. If I can't attend a function, I'm quite sure my sister, Gwen, will be happy to accompany her. Why, Pansy can make her first appearance at the ball my family will be giving for us. 'Twill work out splendidly."

"Oh, dear, dear sister," Pansy cried in exultation. "It will be the most wonderful thing that's ever happened to me! We'll have the most glorious time imaginable!" She twirled about in a circle and clapped her hands for joy. "And you're so beautiful! You must have dozens of beaux sending you flowers and writing you poems. I'm sure you can teach me how to get some of my own!"

The entire group burst into laughter at her naive remark while Pansy bounced up and down in her excitement.

"Lady Penelope, I'll do no such thing!" Christina warned. But she laughed as she hugged her tiny sister-in-law. "If I'm to take responsibility for you, then you must promise to follow my admonitions to the letter. If not, it'll be off to the school of fish-faced old maids for you. I'll not be blamed for your high jinks. I've been in trouble enough for my own, and I refuse to suffer for anyone else's."

Pansy looked with hope at her oldest brother. "May I, Roderick? Oh, please! I promise I'll do exactly what Lady Christina says."

Roderick sighed in exasperation. "Very well, then. If my bride is willing to take responsibility for your appearance in polite society, you may stay. But I'll hold you to your word. And now, dear ones, shall we proceed to the dinner that awaits us?"

Taking his surprised wife's hand, Roderick placed it on his arm and led her out of the salon to the dining room, leaving the rest of the group to follow on their heels.

Chapter 8

Morning quickly became Roderick's favorite time of day. In an effort to make outward appearances seem completely unexceptional, his lovely wife joined him for a daily ride in Hyde Park. This routine had commenced their first morning in London, when he'd come downstairs to find her at the breakfast table dressed in a fetching green riding habit.

"You're up very early," he said. He eyed her outfit uncertainly. "Surely you don't plan to go riding?"

"Whyever not?" Christina's surprise seemed to match his own. She looked up from her soft-boiled egg and frowned at him. "I ride almost every morning. Why should I stop now?"

He was flabbergasted at her ignorance. Even a nineteen-year-old girl should be aware of the appalling dangers surrounding gestation and birth. He didn't want to frighten her needlessly. Still, there was no point in taking risks that could be easily avoided.

"Because you're with child, Christina," he explained patiently. "You wouldn't want to chance harming the baby or yourself." He poured a cup of coffee at the sideboard and went to sit down next to her. "I'm not so certain that you should continue riding at all."

The earl's statement had completely mystified Christina for a long, uncomfortable moment. She'd completely forgotten that she was supposed to be pregnant.

"Oh, oh, I see," she answered lamely. She became engrossed in buttering a piece of toast while she searched for an explanation for her seemingly witless reply. Inspiration struck as she smoothed on the orange marmalade. "But my sister hacked daily until her last few months. We're used to lots of vigorous activity in my family. I won't do anything foolish, I promise."

Roderick wasn't so easily mollified. He'd lost both his mother and his first wife in childbirth. An uneasy feeling had been growing inside him as the memories of both deaths, revived by the recent perusal of old letters and diaries, began to haunt him once again. When he'd first seen Christina ride at Rugden Court, he'd paid little attention. But the longer he'd thought about it, the more apprehensive he'd become. She was a bruising rider. Once the possibility of losing his young bride in premature childbed had reared its ugly head, he hadn't been able to set it aside.

"I think you should see our family physician, Christina. Let's be sure that it's perfectly safe. You can ride with me this morning, but I'm going to ask Dr. Bowles to have a look at you later this week and offer his advice."

"Nonsense!" she exploded. A blush crept slowly up her neck to suffuse her cheeks. "I won't have a man examine me! 'Tisn't decent." She nervously twisted the napkin in her lap. "Besides, my sister never had a doctor near her. A midwife handled everything. Gwen rode during both pregnancies, and I see no reason to act differently."

"Well, we'll see what Bowles says, nevertheless." He tried to keep his tone even and matter-of-fact. "Just how far along in your pregnancy are you?"

She lowered her head and stared at her lap. Her softly whispered words were filled with an excruciating shame. "Barely a month."

"Come on, then," Roderick told her. "Finish up your breakfast, and we can get an early start."

She lifted the piece of toast to her mouth and then laid it back down on her plate, as though unable to swallow a bite of it. Part of him felt sorry for her, having to admit such a dreadful thing to her new bridegroom. The other part wanted to turn her over his knees and whale the holy hell out of her. And after the child was safely born, he just might do that.

During that first week, their morning ride in Hyde Park

soon became a ritual. Both excellent riders, they found good horsemanship a common ground and, with unspoken agreement, set aside their differences to enjoy the pleasant canter on Mohawk and Sheba, who'd been brought to town in easy stages by Watt Keighly.

Since the evening hours usually found them far apart, Roderick treasured these morning rides, and they assuaged, if only a little, the frustration he felt at being held at arm's length by his maddeningly attractive wife. He set aside his objections to Christina's daily hack, at least during the early weeks of her pregnancy. He didn't want the rides to cease before it was absolutely necessary. And in deference to her strong feelings against being seen by a male doctor, he acceded to her wish to employ the services of the same midwife who'd attended her sister.

Meanwhile Rugden House reverberated with excitement. Christina and Pansy created a special glow that permeated the entire domicile, an establishment which, for fifteen somber years, had rarely heard the marvelous, lilting sound of high-pitched feminine laughter. Its quiet, meditative serenity had, as Percy astutely remarked, been blown to smithereens with the advent of two fragile powder puffs who, together, consciously planned their campaign for Lady Penelope Fielding to take London Town by storm.

In the midst of this lighthearted turmoil, Roderick attempted to maintain the solemn dignity of his late predecessor. It was an attempt sorely tried by the treacherous actions of his younger brother and his best friend. The three men would be involved in a learned conversation about the latest political imbroglio at court when, upon hearing the arrival of the beauties from an excursion, the two traitors would leap from their chairs, crowd around the women, snatch their packages, listen to their idle chatter, and gossip like a pair of old crones.

Gradually even Roderick began to admit that he'd become ensnared in Christina's silken web. He found himself listening for the peal of her musical laughter drifting down from her rooms as she discussed with her little sister-in-law the day's events or the plans for the evening.

His new countess appeared to enjoy Pansy's outrageous

remarks regarding society in general and men in particular. Not once had Christina indicated by a word, look, or gesture that she regretted committing herself to the Fielding household for the duration of the Little Season.

To the earl, Lady Penelope's appearance had been a godsend. The need to be a chaperone had kept Christina securely anchored at Rugden House. He suspected that she had considered jaunting off to Cornwall without his permission. She showed a regrettable lack of wifely submissiveness. Truth to tell, he doubted if it ever occurred to her that she was supposed to be submissive. That's what came of being a pampered pet of a large family. Still, at the end of each night's diversions, she was safely tucked up in bed, in the apartments next to his own. With that he was willing to be content until the birth of the child.

Probably the only person in the Fielding household less content with the present state of affairs than the master was Marie Boucher, Christina's personal maid. A veritable termagant, she'd arrived the day after Pansy in the Sanborn coach filled with trunks, bandboxes, valises, and various impedimenta. Stalking around her mistress's suite of rooms, she poked her sharp nose here, there, everywhere, rearranging all that Annie, the upstairs maid, had unpacked.

Thin to the point of being gaunt and as tall as most men, Marie appeared each day in a crisp black bombazine dress with a white starched mobcap perched precariously atop her severe chignon. She wore no apron, to signify her elevated status among the servants. The soubrette missed nothing that went on in the Fielding household.

"Peste," she snorted in disgust that first morning. "I have never seen such miserable care of a lady's garments." Turning to Annie, who was working alongside her in Christina's bedchamber, she snapped, "You can just lay those gowns down. I will be totally responsible for all miladi's things from now on. You needn't even come into this room."

Perturbed, Annie stared at the skinny abigail. She'd been an upstairs maid at Rugden House for five years; she wasn't about to be told what to do by some Frenchified upstart. "His lordship's housekeeper gives me orders,

Booshay, and thems what I follers. Ye'd best speak to Mrs. Owens, if ye be wishin' to change what's been going on here fer the last twenty years. And I'm thinkin' Mrs. Owens may just put a flea in yer ear, for all yer fancy airs."

Although her directions to Annie, who continued to come and go in all rooms of the home, were not upheld, Marie persisted in treating everyone as having less importance than a goatherd. She castigated fellow servants in colorful French expletives, all of which were as gibberish to the household staff. She attempted to construct an invisible wall around Christina's private quarters, but the Fieldings were oblivious to her baleful stares and came in and out of the countess's rooms with joyful abandon. For Rugden, Madame Boucher showed such obvious hostility that when the two of them came face to face, the atmosphere was charged as if with lightning.

Though the Frenchwoman dared say nothing in the least offensive to the master, it was clear to Roderick that she was aware of the unfortunate circumstances behind the sudden marriage. He attempted a truce after several days, certain that the sour-faced woman was intent on protecting her charge from further abuse at his, or any other man's, hands.

"I'm concerned about Lady Rugden, Boucher. Should she become overtired, I don't wish her awakened for our early morning rides. And if she wakes feeling poorly, I want to be told at once. I'll send for a doctor immediately."

His words came as a shock to Marie. No one in her care had ever been healthier than the countess. Whenever Rugden entered his wife's bedchamber, Marie hovered over Christina as though she were an invalid, but this had nothing to do with the state of the young woman's health.

"Eh, bien, Monsieur le Comte. If miladi seems ill, I will notify you immediately," Marie responded mechanically, pondering the meaning of his excessive solicitude.

The very next morning, as she entered the countess's bedroom to find her wide awake and waiting for assistance in lacing up her stays, Marie came to a startling, nearly unbelievable, conclusion. Rugden thought his new bride was with child. And being her lady's maid, she knew this was impossible.

"Here, my little cabbage, let me help you with those." Marie hurried to tighten the corset laces that bound Christina's slim waist.

"Monsieur le Comte was questioning the wisdom of your riding today, little one." The maid spoke casually, as though merely making conversation. "He seems to think you are perhaps *enceinte.*" She clucked her tongue in dismay. *"Mon Dieu,* how could he come by such a preposterous thought? I almost disenchanted him of that idea, but decided I should talk to you first before I said anything." She gazed shrewdly at Christina's horrified expression in the mirror before them.

The countess's worried blue eyes met the reflection of Marie's piercing brown ones in the glass. Though Christina stood perfectly still, saying nothing, she was unable to hide the stricken look on her white features. Marie moved around to face her, assuming an air of shock.

"You wish him to think so, miladi? But why? It is of no import that you do not carry a child. Few couples make so soon the *bébé.* The time is young yet for worrying about an heir. You should be truthful with your so strict husband, *n'est-ce pas?"*

"Oh, Marie," Christina rasped, her hoarse words echoing the panic in her eyes. "That's exactly what I haven't been! My husband thinks I'm pregnant because I told him I carried another man's child. I wanted to push him into obtaining an annulment. If you tell him differently now, his rage will be uncontrollable." The countess's golden head drooped in shame and misery. "Perhaps I should make a clean breast of it and tell him of my deception."

The maid put her arms around the dejected young woman. "But no, *petite.* None can expect you to remain in this miserable marriage with such a one as that man. I will keep your secret, this I assure you. Say nothing, at least for now, I beg you. I will pray that an annulment will eventually be forthcoming."

So while the rest of the household wondered why the countess employed such a waspish servant, the young bride continued to keep her maid nearby for support and encouragement. Though Marie was all sourness and gloom to the rest of the household, Christina never saw an unhappy look or gesture. Around the countess, the abigail was always indulgent and kind.

Roderick was hesitant to dismiss the hatchet-faced woman. He assumed that her irritating behavior was rooted in a very understandable concern over his wife's delicate condition, for which Marie evidently blamed him. It would be natural for Boucher to feel protective of her charge, especially since she should have been with her the night Christina came alone to his estate. Shrugging off the maid's annoying behavior, Roderick attempted to unravel his own problems, both financial and personal. He paid no attention to the notes, always written in French, that Marie frequently dispatched.

He sent a second letter of his own to Madeline, from whom he'd not heard a word since arriving in London. Watt Keighly had returned from the trip to St. James's Square with the information that Mrs. Gannet was not in town. The news of his hasty marriage must have been a severe shock to Madeline. She'd probably gone to stay with a friend while she nursed her bruised pride. Roderick regretted the pain that he'd caused his lovely mistress. Yet never by a word or a look had he given her reason to think he wouldn't someday marry a young woman of good family, who could present him with an heir. But he knew that the buxom widow sincerely cared for him. He'd not have purposely hurt Madeline, for he held a true fondness for her.

The thought of an heir brought him inevitably around to the dilemma of Christina's pregnancy. He wondered what he was going to do about the baby's father, Edwin Whiteham, when that soldier returned from the continent. If he harmed the young man, Christina might never forgive him, especially if she still believed herself in love with the fellow. Only one thing was certain. There'd be no divorce. No annulment. And, recalling the memory of his wife's sweet lips pressed against his own, Roderick reluctantly admitted that his decision had nothing whatsoever to do with Christina's money.

* * *

During their first week in London the Earl of Rugden and his new countess commenced their social activities even though they hadn't officially made their bow to society as a married couple. Their formal presentation was to take place in less than a week at the town home of the Marquess of Waldwick. The invitations were sent, the flowers ordered, the menu planned, and the dresses fitted. The excitement mounted to fever pitch.

As a respite from the week's hectic schedule, the couple was to enjoy an evening at the Theatre Royal Drury Lane, accompanied by Percy and Pansy. Lady Penelope had never attended a play before due to her father's strict sense of decorum. Watching the petite brunette enter the salon where they were patiently awaiting the ladies of the party, both older brothers looked on with easygoing resignation at her displays of maidenly giggles and lighthearted twirlings. She fairly danced into the room in her new satin slippers.

Dressed in a pale blue satin gown that fell over her hoops in the shape of a great bell, Pansy was caught up in the enjoyment of her own appearance. She pirouetted in front of a large mirror for the edification of her two siblings, her chestnut curls flying around her shoulders, her brown eyes glowing with pride. "Look at me! Look at me! Christina said I was gorgeous!" Pansy trilled in self-satisfaction.

"By gad, you are dazzling, baby sister," admired Percy. "Now, as soon as Christina comes down, we can be off. If we don't leave soon we'll miss the entire first act."

At that moment the countess entered the room in a rustle of taffeta petticoats. She laughed at his words of reproach. "Why, Percival, when have you ever been on time in your life?" She held her arms out gracefully and made a deep, elegant curtsy. "But, behold! I'm ready to leave. So you can't blame me if we arrive late."

Roderick's gaze roamed over his wife in open appreciation. Her honey-gold hair was piled high on her head with one long ringlet falling across her shoulder. Attired in a stunning burgundy velvet gown trimmed with beige lace and black ribbons, Christina appeared completely unaware of the effect she had on the two appreciative males who'd turned to watch her enter. She went over to her diminutive sister-in-law and put her arm around the girl's tiny waist.

"Pansy, you do look lovely. But you mustn't say so. *They* are supposed to say so, and *you* are expected to deny it," the countess pointed out as she kissed her sister's temple. "Didn't those fish-faces at that fine academy teach you anything about dissembling?" She shook her head in mock chagrin and lightly pinched Pansy's smooth cheek.

"But why should I say what I don't mean?" Pansy demanded. She tipped her head to one side and wrinkled her pert little nose in rebellion. "Especially to my own brothers."

"Because you need to practice on your brothers, that's why," Christina admonished. The corners of her full lips curved in a smile she was unable to suppress. "If you keep saying exactly what's on your mind, you just may have the social world howling with glee. And laughter is not what you're seeking, is it?"

"Oh, no!" Pansy cried in dismay. She clasped her hands in front of herself dramatically. "I'm seeking a rich husband! *Then* I can say exactly what's on my mind!"

Shouts of masculine laughter rang out in the parlor. Then the men gathered up their greatcoats and gold-headed canes and draped the two women in long, fur-trimmed capes.

Roderick carefully lifted the velvet hood of his wife's cloak over her elegant coiffure. "May I take the opportunity to say what's exactly on my mind?" he murmured. He stood directly in front of her, certain no one else could hear his softly spoken words. "You look incredibly lovely tonight."

Startled, Christina searched his gray eyes, astonished at the look of burning intensity he bestowed on her. "Why, sir, then I must protest that your flatteries are too kind and deny the possibility of what you say," she replied with a hesitant smile.

She lowered her lashes in confusion at his sudden change in tactics. It was a strategy that could prove far more perilous than his previous campaign of crushing aloofness. He was splendid tonight in his officer's uniform of scarlet and buff with the black hussar boots that reached just below the knee. The gold epaulets on the coat made his shoulders seem even broader, while the light dress sword belted around his red sash was a vivid reminder of his more lethal propensities. Christina drew in a quick breath. He had never looked more dangerous. Or more exciting.

They were to see *Florizel and Perdita,* David Garrick's celebrated adaptation of Shakespeare. Contrary to Percy's admonitions, however, the Fieldings were there well in time for the opening scene. The two ladies in the party chattered together gaily as they waited for the performance to begin. Lady Penelope was almost quivering with the excitement of watching her first stage production. Every once in a while, she'd erupt into a giggle of pure happiness. It was clear that, while she loved Percy, she positively idolized her eldest brother. Being allowed to accompany him and his new bride to a public function had raised her already high spirits to a plane close to perfect bliss.

Christina and Pansy waved to friends and acquaintances in nearby boxes while pretending to ignore the blatant ogling of the more aggressive bachelors on the floor. Those gaudy coxcombs boldly stared through quizzing glasses at all the attractive young females in the audience with open admiration and no show of reluctance to be seen themselves.

The countess was seated beside Pansy in the Rugden box located on the first of the three tiers that curved in a wide semicircle around the stage. Her husband and brother-in-law sat just behind them. As she listened to Drury Lane's talented company of actors weave their spell of enchantment, she slowly became aware of the earl's gaze fixed on her. From the advantage of his greater height, he looked down over her shoulder at the shadow of her cleavage. She shifted and turned slightly away from him, aware that his attention was directed totally upon her rather than the action taking place on the stage. Christina waved her painted fan back and forth and attempted to ignore the tantalizing nearness of her husband. It was an impossible task. She sighed softly with relief when the intermission brought the curtain down and the audience to life.

In the bright glow of the lanterns placed on the bare boards of the stage, Christina discovered that her husband no longed scrutinized her. She followed the direction of his gaze to a box straight across from them and recognized the Duke of Carlisle. With an uncomfortable start, she realized that the most persistent of her rejected suitors had also been watching her intently during the performance. Carlisle's steady perusal never wavered from her face as he nodded his head in a brief salute.

Seated beside the wealthy peer was a striking brunette attired in a scarlet satin gown that amply displayed her glorious bosom. Unlike her escort, however, she wasn't looking at Christina. The sultry, curvaceous woman had eyes solely for the Earl of Rugden. Responding to the look of near-adoration in her large brown eyes, Christina's husband gave the dark-haired beauty an almost imperceptible nod. The woman lowered her lashes to conceal her pleasure, but she couldn't quite hide the smile that flitted across her seductive mouth.

Rugden immediately turned to his wife. "I'll leave you alone for a few minutes, my dear, so that all the smitten beaux trying to squeeze into our box can find some room. If you'll excuse me?" He left before she could offer a word of protest. Unaccountably, Christina felt a sinking sensation at the bottom of her stomach.

"Thunder and turf," Percy expostulated softly under his breath. He scowled at his brother's retreating back, then glanced across the theater at the Duke of Carlisle's private compartment. Christina knew, without even looking, what Percy would find there.

The box was empty.

With Rugden's departure, several boisterous young gentlemen crowded into the loge, and Percy stopped frowning just long enough to introduce them to the ladies.

"Well, la," trilled Pansy, "I'd like to take a stroll myself." She peeped up roguishly at two gallants, who promptly offered their arms.

"Yes, Percy," the countess agreed, suddenly restless. "Let's not sit here, either. It'll feel good to stretch our legs."

A wide, artificial smile replaced Percy's scowl. "Egad,

Christina, the lobby will be a madhouse tonight. Might as well visit Bedlam. Why don't we stay here, safely out of the way of all that demn pushing and shoving?"

Before Christina could answer, Pansy disappeared with her two courtiers, and the decision had been made for them.

Arm in arm, Percival and Christina followed Lady Penelope and her admirers at a close distance. They were quickly surrounded by a throng of friends, many of whom stopped to give the new countess of Rugden their warm wishes upon her recent marriage. In spite of the swell of people, magnificent in twinkling jewels, floating ostrich feathers, fur-lined capes, and satin gowns, Christina was able to track her husband's progress through the crowd as she came down the stairs. He was a head taller than any man there, and garbed in the bright crimson uniform, his powerful shoulders and biceps were far wider and much more impressive. As he moved, people instinctively stepped back to give him room. She watched Rugden thread his way toward a tiny alcove in the densely packed lobby. He nodded briefly once or twice to someone attempting to capture his attention, all the while continuing to forge a relentless path through the crowd. With a feeling uncomfortably close to pain, Christina spotted the ravishing brunette in scarlet. The lady stood alone in the small embrasure, patiently waiting for someone to join her. She looked up and smiled as Rugden drew near. Christina had been right in her first assessment. It was an expression of absolute adoration. Then her husband's large form obscured the woman entirely as he braced his hands on either side of her head and bent forward to hear every delightful word she uttered.

Christina fanned herself with a languid, indolent sweep of her hand. Her heart might be beating a frenzied tattoo against her ribs, but she was determined that no one should guess at her inner turmoil. "Do you know, Percy, I believe you were right in the first place. The mob is almost overwhelming this evening. I think I'll seek the peace and quiet of our box."

Percy cast a worried glance at his fifteen-year-old sister, and Christina shook her head in answer to his unvoiced concern. She touched his satin sleeve to restrain him from fetching Pansy.

"No, no, I don't wish to tear Lady Penelope away from her new friends. You stay here with her, and I'll go back by myself. Don't worry, I'll be quite all right. I'll see you in a few minutes."

She closed the gold and black fan with a determined snap, turned, and made her way toward their private booth. In the dense throng, she was forced to move with exasperating slowness.

"It didn't take the great war hero long to be reunited with his lusty mistress," a shrill soprano voice sniggered from a group to her left. "The lines on his marriage contract aren't even dry yet."

Gritting her teeth in humiliation, Christina ignored the barbed but extremely accurate comment and wended her way around the tight circle of playgoers.

"Lud, he'll have to pry the dark-haired wench out of Carlisle's arms first," said a contralto.

"Out of the duke's bed, more likely," a tenor chortled.

"Shh," someone else hissed. "She'll hear you!"

At the belated warning, the clique of friends grew silent.

Christina lifted her chin, knowing they watched her covertly. She clamped her lips together in a tight, thin line and, with all the imperial hauteur of a royal princess, marched up the stairs that led to the first tier of private boxes. Opening the door to their loge, she pulled up short. Sprawled negligently in Rugden's velvet upholstered chair, the Duke of Carlisle sat waiting for her.

Justin Somesbury's powdered wig matched the fine white linen of his shirt and stock, providing a stark background for his ebony eyes, which burned now with an unconcealed fury. She was well aware of the cause of his anger. Twice that past spring she'd refused his proposal of marriage. Afterward, when he sought literally to buy her from her father with an offer of a bride's price approaching a small fortune, the Marquess of Waldwick had stood firmly behind his daughter's decision. But Carlisle was an extremely influential man with connections that reached as high as the king's personal advisers. For her father's sake and that of her family, Christina had no wish to make an enemy of the duke.

"Your Grace," Christina exclaimed. She struggled to maintain an air of gracious surprise. "What an honor to find you waiting for me. Or had you hoped to talk with my husband?" She tilted her head to one side in teasing, lighthearted inquiry.

A sardonic half smile twisted the duke's craggy face. He rose with the supple grace of a Bengal tiger and effortlessly pulled her into the box to stand beside him. "Why would any sane man wish to speak with that boor, my darling Christina, when he could talk with you instead? Especially a man who cares for you as deeply as I."

Unable to find a courteous reply to his deliberately provoking words, Christina stared up at him in disconcerted silence.

"You must pardon my atrocious lack of manners, *chérie*, if I fail to offer my felicitations on your recent nuptials." His low voice rasped with a finely honed resentment. "But I'm certain you wouldn't want to be paid in false coin. As you're only two well aware, it was the last piece of news I wanted to hear. Perhaps it's only my abominable pride, but I don't believe there are many women who'd spurn an offer of becoming a wealthy duchess only to turn around and marry an impoverished earl. Of course, with your own fortune, you could afford to follow the dictates of your heart, could you not?" Carlisle clasped her hand and lifted it to his lips. Insolently, he kissed the tips of her fingers. "I merely regret that you didn't allow me more time to establish myself in that same esteem before you acted in such a hasty manner."

Christina withdrew her hand and sank down into a chair. The golden butterflies on her ebony fan fluttered nervously. "You flatter me outrageously, Your Grace," she demurred.

His arrogant gaze swept over her. What Christina saw in those cunning eyes frightened her, as they'd always frightened her—with a hint of some unknown evil pulling her inevitably toward him while at the same time repelling her. What an insidious power this man held. She'd seen it at work in his careless use of other people, his self-centered manipulation of social situations, which inevitably ended in her being seated beside him at dinners or dancing with him at balls. Since she'd first met him, early that spring, he'd remained always close by, and many young men had been daunted by his proprietary actions. It had taken a blunt refusal by herself, reiterated by her father, before Carlisle had accepted her denial of any affection for him whatsoever.

He sank down in the chair beside her. Christina remained perched on the edge of her seat, desperately hoping for her new family's return and reliving in her mind the tightly controlled rage Carlisle had shown at her second refusal of his courtship. She'd not seen him since that day.

Recapturing one of her hands, Carlisle murmured caressingly, "Pray, tell me, little one, how do you like married life? Is it all that your girlish heart dreamed it would be? It's not often one hears about a true love match, especially for an heiress. A fortune like yours would tempt even the most honorable of men, would it not? You, of course, have no doubt of Rugden's intentions—such a great military hero as he."

The duke's acid tone of derision stung Christina's pride. She looked up at him, her icy hand in his strong one, his head bending close to hers. How much of what he'd implied was pure surmise? Good gad, the man was almost omniscient in his deductions.

Upon leaving his theater box, Roderick made his way at once to the alcove in which he knew he would find Madeline Gannet. They'd used that particular haven in the past to withdraw from the boisterous crowd. She was right where he'd expected her. Taking her by the shoulders, he eased her deeper into the small recess. He could see the hurt in her eyes as she looked up to meet his gaze.

"I'm sorry you had to learn of my marriage in the newspapers, Madeline. I'd hoped to tell you in person. As soon as I returned to London, I sent a note to St. James's Square asking if I could see you. Your housekeeper told my servant you weren't at home."

"I wasn't," she answered simply. "I was in Hertford-shire."

"What in hell were you doing there?"

"I wish I knew," she said. She lifted her dark eyebrows and shrugged fatalistically. "All I know is that I was taken to Carlisle Hall in what I believed was your carriage. When I realized I'd entered the wrong manor, I thought for a moment I'd been kidnapped for ransom. But it turned out to be just a foolish mistake. Like a simpleton, I'd hurried into a coach standing right outside my door. It proved to be the wrong one."

The implication of her words stunned him as he realized what Christina's destination had been. "The duke treated you well?"

"He was a perfect gentleman," she reassured him. "But there is something I overheard while I was there that I want to speak to you about."

He waited for her to continue. She reached up and touched his cheek in a caress filled with unspoken promises. "Not here, darling. Come to my home tomorrow evening."

"I'll be there in the morning."

Rugden took her hand, kissed it, and moved back into the crowd. He found his brother and sister in the middle of a large circle of friends and quickly went to stand next to Percy. "Where's my wife?" he demanded.

With a complacent smile, Percy waved his hand in a conciliatory manner meant to soothe the inexperienced husband. "She decided the press of the crowd was more than she could bear. Your bride returned to our booth some time ago."

"Alone?"

"She insisted I stay here with Pansy," his younger brother retorted defensively.

The thought of Christina feeling faint as a natural effect of her pregnancy set Roderick in motion. She could have fallen on the empty staircase with no one nearby to help her. He wheeled and sprinted swiftly up the narrow passageway to his private box. Without even slowing, he jerked the door open and entered to find his wife safe and sound and the picture of radiant health. She was also sitting hand in hand with Justin Somesbury.

Embarrassed at their seeming intimacy, Christina snatched her fingers from Carlisle's grasp, aware of the tension that suddenly swirled around her. Some tiny devilment inside her exulted at the look of ferocious displeasure on her husband's face. Fine, she told herself in satisfaction, let him get a taste of what it's like to be spurned in public.

Carlisle sprang to his feet with smooth grace. For long seconds no one spoke as Rugden's gray eyes locked with the duke's ebony ones. Each man's hand rested hopefully on the hilt of his dress sword.

"Sir, your very obedient servant," the duke said with the flourish of a mocking bow. "I was merely offering your charming bride my deep devotion to her future happiness. And you, I believe, are to be congratulated."

Shouldering Carlisle aside, Rugden moved farther into his theater box. He took Christina's cold hands and drew her up to stand beside him. Then he turned to face the duke with a contemptuous smile. "I accept your congratulations, Carlisle. As you see, I'm most fortunate in my marriage."

"Yes, Rugden, we have a great deal in common, you and I," Carlisle continued smoothly. "It seems that neither of us would hesitate to take an unwilling bride to our marriage bed. Nor draw back from a fight to keep her. Yet, for the moment, the lady remains in your hands. We'll see if your run of good fortune holds true. Somehow I think it will take more than mere luck for you to keep the prize as easily as you gained it." The duke turned to Christina and bowed. "Till later, my dear countess. I remain your most obedient servant."

Chapter 9

The small ormolu clock on the countess's dressing table struck twice in a musical chime. All was peaceful and still on the second floor. The Fieldings had attended a supper after the play, and each member of the party had appeared exhausted as they bade one another good night.

Christina's heavy lids were almost closed when the door that led to the adjoining sitting room swung wide, and Rugden stood on the threshold. He held a tall candlestick, its wavering light throwing shadows against the creamy silk curtains fastened to the tall bedposts. Startled, she lurched to a sitting position and pulled the coverlet up to her chin, ready to leap up and bolt to the other door.

He moved to the bed, set the candle down on a nearby table, and braced his hands on the canopy frame above her. "You enjoyed yourself tonight, I trust?"

The pleasant aroma of fine cognac wafted around him, reminding her that he'd been pouring a generous glass of the imported liquor when she'd left him in the small salon with Percy less than an hour ago. Rugden's ebony and gold dressing robe was loosely belted at the waist, displaying a glimpse of wiry black hair on his chest. A wild speculation that he was naked under the velvet garment brought a surge of panic.

"You've had too much to drink," she snapped. She scooted back against the pillow and glared up at him. "Whatever you wish to discuss can wait till morning when you're not inebriated."

The calculated insult failed to deter him. He sat down

beside her on the bed, one hand deliberately propped on the other side of her hip to keep her from sidling away.

"I'm not drunk yet," he murmured, "though God knows I may get there before the night's over. However, this particular talk can't wait." He lifted one of her curls in his long fingers and breathed deeply. "Did you know that the fragrance of your hair always reminds me of roses? It's most disconcerting when I'm trying to concentrate on serious matters."

"Such as?"

"Such as your relationship with the Duke of Carlisle. What did he mean about not hesitating to take an unwilling bride?"

"How should I know what he meant except a callous affront to you? The man knows more about our personal affairs than we'd wish him to, that's certain. And it seems he holds no warm feelings for you," Christina added with a sniff of sarcasm, "but that's no concern of mine. He was one of my suitors, as you may have surmised."

Rugden leaned forward until his face was only inches away. "It was rampantly apparent, sweetheart. Did he make you an offer—that is, an honorable one?"

"Certainly." Pulling the coverlet up closer to her chin, she favored him with a condescending smile. "More chivalrous than your gallant proposal to relieve me of my inheritance. As a matter of fact, Carlisle offered my father an enormous settlement for the privilege of gaining my hand in marriage."

"When?"

"About two months ago." She tossed her head in exasperation. "What does it matter? I refused him. Now go away. I'm sleepy."

Rugden's reply was a low, threatening growl. "Did he ever touch you, Christina?"

He wound her hair slowly around his hand, bringing her even closer. She could feel his warm breath on her lips as she inhaled the intoxicating fumes of expensive French brandy. She met his silvery gaze and realized he'd spoken the truth. He wasn't drunk. He was lethally, frighteningly, cold-bloodedly sober.

She pulled ineffectively at the lock of hair imprisoned in

his large fist. "Let go," she demanded, trying to sound braver than she felt. "I'll not ask about your personal relationships, nor will I answer to you about mine. I refuse to allow you to interfere with my friendships."

"Friendships! You'd be wiser to adopt a hooded cobra for a pet than befriend a snake like Carlisle. From now on I don't want you to have anything to do with the man." At her immediate scowl of rebellion, he tightened his hold on her hair and tugged just hard enough to assure her complete and undivided attention. "I'm ordering you, Lady Rugden, to cut the bloody bastard the next time you see him."

If Roderick had actually hoped for a display of wifely submission, he would have been grossly disappointed. He hadn't been so foolish. As it was, her beautiful sapphire eyes became the slits of sparkling indignation he'd expected.

"You command me?" she cried. "I refuse to follow any orders you might attempt to force on me. This sham marriage has addled your wits, if you believe I'll meekly follow your dictates. I'll see whom I please, when I please."

In her indignation she'd risen to her knees. Forgetting all about the barrier of safety provided by the creamy satin comforter, she shoved against his shoulders in a vain attempt to dislodge him from her bed. A suspicion rose in Roderick's mind that she'd seen him with Madeline Gannet, and it was jealousy over his former mistress rather than any fondness for Carlisle that spurred her wrath. That thought erased his own scowl completely.

Engulfed in the perfume of summer roses, he released her hair and slipped his hands down her silken arms to clasp her small waist. The abandoned bedcovers were bunched around her knees in soft, beckoning mounds of pale yellow satin. Through the voluminous folds of her pink nightdress, he could glimpse the lush contours of her full breasts. Against the diaphanous fabric, their budding crests were rosy circles of enticement. The pleasurable ache of sexual excitement surged through him, and he hardened. Under his velvet robe, his erection was thick and heavy, and he groaned deep in his throat. No other woman had ever brought about this headlong primal urge that threatened to sweep all rational thought before it. Beneath his rough fingertips, the transparent nightgown was no more than the sheerest gauze. He could rip it from neckline to hem in one quick, effortless movement.

She must have read his thoughts in the covetous gaze that raked over her. Her shaky voice belied her fierce words. "I'm not afraid of you, Rugden. If you lay a violent hand on me, I'll wait till you're asleep and shoot you. Or . . . or poison your food the next day."

At her audacious blustering, he threw back his head and gave a muffled shout of laughter. The idea of Christina boldly threatening his life delighted his sense of the ridiculous. Soft chuckles shook his frame. She tried to shove him away, furious at the swaggering amusement he made no attempt to hide. He cupped her little butt with his big hands and pulled her relentlessly against him. Seated on the bed, with Christina on her knees in front of him, he pressed his face against her firm breasts and breathed in the bewitching smell of woman. He wanted to slide down with her into the silken cocoon of her bed and drown himself in the satiny pleasure of her body. He could spend a lifetime making love to her. He smiled to himself. After the safe birth of the child, that was exactly what he intended to do.

"My little spitfire," he murmured. "I could have used your courage on the Plains of Abraham. You've more strength of will than most men, sunshine. But not, I think, more than your husband."

He slipped his arms around her, lowered her down to the feather mattress, and stretched out beside her. She tried to kick him, but with her frantic movements, the tangled bedclothes only wrapped her tighter in their folds. Luckily, there was nothing within her reach to throw. His beautiful little wife had the temper of a dockside tavern shrew. Prior knowledge of her preferred methods of battle was going to save him a whole lot of bumps and bruises in the years to come.

Part of her flowing nightgown was caught beneath his hip, and shiny waves of her golden hair were pinned under his arm. Catching both of her delicate, fine-boned wrists in one hand, he lifted them above her head. He wanted her to

feel the invincible power he had over her. A power she, as
yet, had refused even to acknowledge. Tonight he'd make
it impossible for her ever to deny it again.

With his free hand, he cupped her averted face and
turned it toward him. She looked up to meet his gaze, her
wide-set eyes blurred with tears of frustration. He softly
kissed her trembling eyelids.

"I'm not going to hurt you, sweetheart," he coaxed in a
voice ragged with desire. "Don't struggle against me. I
only want to pleasure you a little."

He bent his head and covered her parted lips with his
own. He swept her mouth with his tongue as he brought
her resisting body ever closer. From their hips downward,
they were separated by the tangled coverlet, and he started
to push the satiny material out of his way. He longed to
press his hard shaft against the folds of her feminine softness. He willed himself to slow down, aware of his brute
strength and the near-mindless intensity of his sexual ardor. Next to his solid bulk, she was so slender and dainty.
An inner voice warned him to beware of her fragile condition.

In response to the sensuous touch of his lips and tongue,
Christina felt her traitorous body mold against her husband
of its own accord. It was as impossible to move away from
his superbly muscled frame as it was to stop the sigh of
longing that came unbidden to her lips.

With her hands still imprisoned above her head, she
arched against him. Rugden trailed hot kisses down her
neck, caressing her with his tongue, grazing her skin with
his teeth.

"Ah, sunshine," he murmured, "you taste so damn
sweet."

He took her breast in his palm, his thumb flicking
across its erect tip. She could feel the heat of him through
the filmy lawn of her nightgown. Then he lowered his
head and covered the top of her breast with his open
mouth. She gasped at the unalloyed pleasure as he laved
the rigid bud.

He suckled her through the fine linen. A wave of intense desire, starting in the area of her groin, spread
through her. It was a compelling, intoxicating throb that

swept aside all sane thought except the hope that he wouldn't draw away until he'd tasted the other aching breast as well.

He didn't stop. Nor did he pull away. He moved to encircle the other nipple, drawing the firm globe of her breast into his warm, wet mouth. She whimpered in confusion at the awakening passion within her. He released her wrists and slowly moved down her suddenly languid body. He pushed the coverlet inexorably downward as his lips and tongue explored her ribs and stomach. The stubble of his beard caught in the gauzy fabric, making it swish back and forth against her overheated skin in a drugging, hypnotic sensation. Her hands fell to her sides, and she lay there, waiting for some unknown culmination to the dizzying responses that engulfed her.

Through the fragile tissue of her gown, he kissed the nest of springy curls at the juncture of her thighs. His warm breath caressed her in an intimacy she never dreamed existed between a man and a woman. With a sudden realization of the instinctive, pagan sensuality he'd aroused within her, she came to her senses.

"Rugden," she whispered in panic. She pushed frantically at his massive upper arms and shoulders. "Stop."

The sound of her frightened entreaty cut through Roderick's white-hot haze of sexual need. He pushed up on his hands and twisted off the bed, cursing himself for a fool to have let things go so far. The blood rushed wildly through his veins. Every fiber in his taut body throbbed with an unreleased tension. Bit by bit, the hammering of his heart slowly eased. Bewildered, Christina stared up at him from among the tousled covers, her cheeks flushed, her blue eyes dark with erotic excitement, her lips beestung with his kisses.

Damn! He had eight long months to wait before he could yield to the hot, searing need that had driven him tonight. In the meantime he'd do nothing, *nothing* to risk causing a miscarriage and the dangers it would involve. He dared not let such intimacy happen again until it was safe to take her completely. The next time he might not have the strength to stop.

When he spoke, his voice was hoarse and creaky with

the inner struggle he'd just waged and won. "I'll leave you to your rest, lady wife. You have a busy week ahead of you." Roderick quickly left the room, as though her life depended on it.

With Christina's returning sense of propriety came burning mortification. She rolled over on her stomach and buried her face in her satin-covered pillow. Why did she always respond to his nearness in this tempestuous, unpredictable manner? It had never been like that with any man until this rugged stranger intruded into her life with such devastating effect. If he hadn't kissed her in that shockingly intimate way tonight, she might have surrendered completely, and her hope for an annulment would have been destroyed forever. Good gad, she thought she knew all about what happened between a husband and wife. Apparently there was a whole lot more that her mother hadn't told her.

Roderick sat in his lonely bedchamber, staring at the hearth's small fire in deep reflection. Exhausted by the night's skyrocketing emotions, he slumped forward on a wing chair with his elbows resting on his knees. He felt as though he'd just returned from the battleground, scorched and singed by the powder and smoke of the muskets and cannons. How close he'd come to allowing his rampaging lust to endanger Christina. Not only that, he'd been willing to discard his pride and admit how much he wanted her despite the fact that she carried another man's child.

Once burned, twice shy. The old saying had proven true for eleven empty years. Not any longer.

The logs in the fireplace crackled and snapped, and in the shimmering flames, he saw once again a petite debutante smiling at him across a ballroom floor. Her flaxen hair curled in soft ringlets around her dainty head; her pale blue dress was the same shade as her luminous eyes. She smiled bashfully as he approached, a dashing blade in his scarlet regimentals.

Lillibeth. Sweet, enchanting Lillibeth. She'd floated around the dance floor, laughing with delighted abandon at his wry jests. In less than an hour she'd changed a serious, career-oriented young officer into a besotted swain. He adored her. She was everything a man could hope for, dream for, wait for. By the end of the evening she was in his arms, deep in the seclusion of an empty garden. By the end of the week he proposed, and to his surprise, she shyly accepted. Like a love-struck fool, he pushed for a quick wedding. They were married within a month—a month during which he was often kept from her side due to plans for the ceremony, the fittings for the trousseau, and visits with relations. Yet it had been speedily done. The vows were said in a lovely chapel in London. They spent their honeymoon in a charming country inn. That first night he'd waited downstairs while she disrobed, realizing her skittishness was normal for a girl of seventeen.

Roderick smiled ruefully to himself as he recalled his own nervousness. Barely twenty-two, he was scarcely a man of the world. Although he'd not been without experience, it was one thing to dally with a paid lady of the night and quite another to bed the girl of his dreams.

He remembered the shock, the overwhelming sense of outrage, when he learned his cherished bride was not a virgin. She carried another man's child. Had she only been honest before the wedding, he probably would have listened. But to have waited until he discovered her secret on their wedding night was to have succeeded in the ultimate betrayal. She cried and pleaded for his understanding. All for naught. Disillusioned and callow youth that he was, he couldn't forgive her. The only thing he asked of her was the man's name. And that she stubbornly refused to divulge.

The poignancy of his memories brought Roderick back to the present. He walked to the mantelpiece and pulled a Spanish cigar from an enameled box on the ledge. He lit the rolled tobacco leaf and sent clouds of smoke wreathing above his dark head, enjoying the unusual habit he'd acquired during his brief sojourn in the West Indies. Leaning against the marble, he pensively recalled the months of pitiable estrangement that had followed his honeymoon. While Lillibeth held fast in her refusal to name her lover, he turned a cold face and hardened heart to her tears. He returned to London, leaving her on his father's estate to brood over her transgressions. His nights were spent carousing, tempting fate at cards and dice, while bitterness grew like a canker within him and gradually eroded his cheerful nature.

Then after six months, an adolescent Percy appeared in London one still, frosty night to announce that Lillibeth was in labor—and that it was not going well. Roderick returned to Rugden Court to await the birth of his young bride's child, still not knowing the father's name. The labor had lasted for three tortured days. The delivery had been an agonizing one. The baby came breech and already dead. Lillibeth was torn, taking childbed fever. She screamed in her delirium and called for her proud husband. Holding his hand to her breast, she begged for pardon and confessed her lover's name.

Oliver Davenport.

A married man with four children, Davenport had, nonetheless, seduced her with practiced expertise. When he'd learned of the pregnancy, he'd callously deserted to France, leaving her to her own devices. Too frightened to confide in her parents, she'd entrapped Roderick, desperately hoping to provide a name for the child.

Roderick buried Lillibeth with the infant in her arms and became a man with a purpose. Yet despite his best efforts, he failed to kill Davenport, who'd foolishly returned to England after the young woman's death. The duel ended in a grievous but not lethal wound, and the scoundrel survived. The ensuing scandal saw the young officer quickly shipped out of the country by a well-meaning commander.

Roderick had longed for death, had openly courted it on the battlefield. But always during the next few years, the easy way out eluded him. He survived. And with his survival came the resolve never to be tricked by a woman again. Never again to believe in a pair of seemingly innocent eyes, or soft, sweet-talking lips.

Throwing the stub of the cigar into the fire, Roderick listened to the stillness of the sleeping household and remembered with self-derision those early years of bitter cynicism. In time he gradually began to see Lillibeth's youth and naiveté in a far wiser, more understanding light. He came to recognize his own immaturity and inexperience, and to regret deeply his harsh refusal to forgive his erring wife before she died. Seeing Pansy, so audacious, so filled with careless exuberance, he'd been reminded how easily an innocent girl could fall prey to a practiced seducer. The real blame fell not on his first wife, but on the adults in her life who had failed to guard and protect her. His harsh treatment of the seventeen-year-old Lillibeth was the one thing in his life of which he was truly ashamed.

In some ways the scars of the past were still with him. Lillibeth's excruciating death, coupled with the untimely loss of his mother at Pansy's birth only four years earlier, had left a cold, unreasoning fear in his heart when it came to women and pregnancies. It was a fear that had remained with him long after the memory of his first wife's features had faded and the sound of his own beloved mother's voice was as faint as the rustle of gossamer.

He recalled with a fond smile the single interlude of trust. Gentle as the Morning Mist was a doe-eyed Iroquois princess with more inner dignity and natural pride than most of the highbred ladies of the London aristocracy. That bitterly cold winter he'd spent snowbound in the uncharted wilderness of New France, she'd tended to his spiritual wounds with the dexterity of a surgeon removing a musket ball from a shattered limb. In her deft hands, his belief in the intimacy that can blossom and grow between a man and a woman had been renewed. A tiny seed of hope had been planted in his formerly barren heart that one day he would have the family he'd always secretly yearned for, with a wife and children who loved and respected him.

It was that closeness, that trust, that he wanted to have between Christina and himself. With each passing day he found himself more and more attracted to her. She fairly radiated energy and a marvelous strength of purpose. Like a ball of sunshine, she'd burst into his pessimistic world, warming his soul with her high spirits, her bubbling laughter, and her wonderful gift for music. Her touch set him on fire. He was no longer so green as to think he must be the first man to bed his wife, but he intended to make damn sure he'd be the last. In the meantime he'd do nothing that could possibly harm the unborn child or its mother.

* * *

Late the next morning, Madeline Gannet strove to present a picture of opulent sensuality. Arrayed in a magenta silk robe with quaint pagodas embroidered in silver thread, she leaned back languorously on her divan and gazed at the handsome visitor seated across from her. The Earl of Rugden was dressed in riding apparel. His forest-green jacket stretched tautly across his broad shoulders; his tanned features were a burnished gold above the white linen of his stock. Roderick was as handsome as the day she'd first met him six years before when her husband had been his commanding officer.

She peered at him over her dainty Chelsea teacup and smiled a slow, seductive smile. "I hoped you'd be able to come," she purred. "I was afraid your new marital state would hamper your movements."

The earl shrugged noncommittally. He absently tapped the sole of his shiny black boot with his riding crop. "Tell me about your visit to Carlisle Hall, Madeline. Exactly how did you happen to arrive there?"

"Lud, if I only knew!" she said. "I left my house in what I believed was your berlin and was delivered posthaste into the waiting arms of Justin Somesbury. He tried to hide his wretched disappointment as he handed me out of his traveling coach, but it was apparent that it wasn't me he'd been waiting up half the night to welcome."

A ghost of a smile flitted across Rugden's face. "I can imagine his chagrin when he discovered the wrong person had arrived in his coach."

For Madeline, his understated words brought back the staggering confusion of that strange night. "Whatever his real thoughts, Carlisle kept them well hidden." She looked up from beneath her lashes and smiled coyly. "He's been paying me court ever since. Naturally, after he shared the announcement of your marriage in *The Gazette* with me, I was uncertain whether you'd wish to continue our liaison."

Rugden watched her quietly, his honest gray eyes mirroring his compassion. He didn't want to hurt her, she knew that. But he'd tell her the unvarnished truth, regardless.

Certain what he was about to say, she quickly forestalled him. "But that isn't what I wanted to talk with you about, darling. While I was at his manor house, I overheard Carlisle mention your name to a guest."

"Not so surprising, if he'd been reading about me in the newspaper."

"He wasn't discussing your nuptials," she clarified. "I distinctly heard the duke declare his intention to kill you."

Roderick frowned. "Carlisle? I've no use for a man like him, nor he for me, I'd presume. But I don't suppose we've exchanged more than a few words since the day we met. There was some unpleasantness between him and my father. Whatever it was, it must have happened long ago while my mother was still alive. It would hardly seem likely that he'd bear me a grudge for something buried so deep in the past. You probably misunderstood."

"Perhaps," she said doubtfully. "What do you plan to do?"

Roderick met his former paramour's worried gaze. "Nothing, at least for the moment. I've far more important things to be concerned about than Carlisle's drawing room gossip."

Madeline rose and glided smoothly over to his chair. With a provocative wiggle, she settled her curvaceous backside in his lap. Tenderly, she reached up to trace the scar on his forehead with one manicured fingertip.

"Let me ease your cares, my darling," she entreated. Her husky voice was thick with unspoken promises.

Roderick gazed at her upturned face. Her cheeks were heavily rouged. A tiny black dot had been placed with practice skill beside her full lips. The morning light falling over his shoulder accentuated her jaded appearance. Against his will, the vision of a smooth brow, creamy skin, and deep blue eyes, fringed with the world's longest lashes, impinged upon his consciousness. Ruefully, he lifted Madeline off his lap and set her on her slippered feet, ignoring the look of disappointment in her eyes. He rose to stand beside her. He didn't want to damage her pride any further. Yet at the moment all he felt for his former mistress, beyond a genuine fondness based on years of friendship, was a nagging sense of responsibility for her present involvement with Carlisle.

"Need you go?" she queried softly.

"I must." His words were clipped. "We're meeting with my sister-in-law this afternoon to discuss the reception line at our ball. Since the affair is tomorrow night, I'm afraid I am most definitely committed." Roderick moved toward the door.

Madeline clung to his arm in one last attempt to entice him into staying the afternoon. But the disinterest on his rugged features made it clear that he had no intention of remaining any longer than necessary. She reached up to touch his cheek in a last farewell. "I'll contact you immediately if I hear anything worth reporting."

Upset at the plan she implied, he gripped her tightly by the shoulders. "Madeline, you're free to choose your companions as you please. But as one old friend to another, take my advice. Don't get involved with Justin Somesbury. He's killed at least five men in duels, one of whom was young enough to be his son. He's vicious and completely without mercy. You're liable to get hurt."

"He hasn't the power to hurt me," she replied in a choked voice. "Only someone I care about deeply could do that." She blinked back the tears and gave him a brilliant smile. "Besides, I find the duke rather intriguing in a dark, mysterious way."

Roderick put his arm around her in reassurance. "You know you can always depend on me. If you need help for any reason, don't hesitate to send word. I'll come immediately."

Madeline slipped her hands around his neck and pressed her face against his broad chest. She'd loved Roderick Fielding since the day, five years before, when he'd come to pay a condolence call after the death of her elderly husband. Rugden stirred restlessly in her embrace. She stood back to let him leave, proud of herself for not falling on her knees and begging him to stay. Heartsick, she watched him hurriedly descend the steps and mount the restless black stallion her footman was holding for him with such difficulty.

Chapter 10

Arriving at Rugden House after a busy shopping expedition that same afternoon, the ladies Gwendoline, Christina, and Penelope were informed that the anxiously awaited ball gowns had just arrived from the dressmaker. The trio flew up the wide staircase and into Christina's rooms. On the large canopied bed lay the gowns, wrapped carefully in delicate rice paper to protect them from wrinking.

"Oh, my," sighed Pansy. She lifted the peach taffeta dress with its delicate apricot ribbons and held it up before her. Twirling in front of a mirror, she admired the gown from all sides. "I'll be absolutely ravishing!" she cried ecstatically. "I'll have to dance with all my beaux at once because they'll refuse to wait their turns like proper gentlemen."

"You naughty minx!" Christina said with a laugh. "I forbid you to dance with more than one man at a time. Otherwise I'll tweak your nose till your eyes water. That'll teach a scamp like you some manners, despite all your care-for-nothing airs."

Dimples appeared in each plump cheek as Gwen smiled affectionately, clearly delighted with her new relative. "Faith, Pansy, you are going to be beautiful. I'm certain you won't miss a single dance. Now kindly stop prancing about, dear, and let's have a look at Christy's gown."

Three pairs of eyes were riveted on the creamy satin costume that Christina lifted from its nest of fragile paper. The sisters' audible gasps were simultaneous. They gazed in admiration at the billowing skirt which cascaded in folds from the tapered waist in yards and yards of off-white satin. The neckline was broad and low, slightly curving and trimmed with three rows of tiny Belgian lace; the stomacher was decorated with cream-colored ribbons tied in bows. Peeking out from the overskirt was the petticoat with layer upon layer of ruffles, graduated in width and growing ever wider as they reached the floor. The elbow-length sleeves ended in a froth of full, delicate ruffling. A satin moire bow of palest blue was perched at each elbow, and matching bows marched down the ruffles on the underdress. It was an exquisite creation fit for a bride.

Lady Gwendoline touched the gown in wonder. "Dearest, it's magnificent."

"It's a dress made for a fairy princess." Pansy smoothed the satin reverently with her fingertips. "You could have been married in it, Christy, if you'd been given the time for a real ceremony." Her low voice was tinged with sympathy.

The perceptive words caused Christina to turn in astonishment. How aware, then, was Pansy of her new sister's forced vows? Everyone thought the young girl had been kept in blissful ignorance.

Christina clasped Pansy's elbow. "Come on, Miss Outrageous, let's wait for the earl downstairs. I'll entertain you with some music to pass the time."

"I want to play the sonata composed by Pansy's mother," Christina said as she sat down in front of the harpsichord. "I brought it to town with me." She rifled through the stack of music and frowned. "It was here just this morning. I'll ask Marie. She probably put it in a special place."

_____ ____ ____ _ ___ minutes when the door to ___ _____ _____ _____ Gwen and Pansy, expecting to see the countess, stared in surprise at the tall figure of the Earl of Rugden.

He was unable to contain a smile at their startled expressions. "You weren't expecting me? I thought our get-together had been all arranged." He moved into the room to stand beside them. "How nice to see you again, Lady Gwendoline. It's been many years since I've had the pleasure." He took her hand and kissed it politely, his eyes glowing with warmth. "I understand you've been busy this week with two sick children."

Responding with a curtsy, she smiled up at him. "Yes, and I was dying to discover if you'd really changed into the redoubtable war hero that everyone's described. You don't look any more frightening then you did at twenty-two, though you are the size of a small mountain."

Roderick gave a crack of laughter and released her hand. They were interrupted by the entrance of his wife.

Delighted over the discovery of the missing sonata, Christina came flying into the room. "I've found it!" She waved a sheet of music in the air. "That is, Marie found it." At the sight of her husband, she came to an abrupt halt and added lamely, "Oh, Rugden, you're back."

His smile faded at her lackluster greeting. "Our agreement was to meet this afternoon and go over some plans for tomorrow night, I believe."

"We were so involved with our music, we quite forgot the time," Gwen explained with a warm smile. "Christina was just going to play a piece composed by your mother."

"Oh, please, do," interjected Pansy. "I've never heard it. I didn't even know it existed, though I'd been told she was an accomplished musician. I'd love to hear something she wrote."

The countess sat down at the harpsichord and beckoned for Pansy to sit beside her on the bench. "This lovely melody, my dear little sister, was written in your mother's own hand. You watch the notes she penned before you were born, perhaps waiting with happy anticipation for your birth, while I play them for you." The room's other occupants were as still as figures in a tableau while Christina played the piece with all the skill and feeling she could render.

Awestruck, Pansy listened for the first time to her mother's beautiful composition. When she looked across the room with tear-blurred eyes to meet her brother's gaze, she saw a matching sparkle in his gray ones. Just as she longed to be closer in some way to the lovely woman she had never known, she realized he must be remembering again the deep loss of his beloved mother. No one moved when Christina finished. No one spoke. A hush filled the salon, until it was shattered by the grinding of carriage wheels and the clatter of horses' hooves on the pavement outside, and, at last, the spell was broken.

"We'd better get busy with our final arrangements for tomorrow night," Christina said with determined cheerfulness. She stood and arranged the sheets in a neat stack against the harpsichord's music board.

"By the way, Lady Gwen, did you find the letter from Lady Muggleton about the antique lute?" Roderick asked from his perch on the arm of the sofa. "I'm curious to see it."

Gwen shook her head. "We searched every inch of Sanborn House the minute I got your note requesting that I save it for you. We couldn't find it anywhere. It must have been tossed away by a careless servant. When I questioned my staff, no one remembered seeing it after my butler gave it to Christina." She turned thoughtfully to her younger sister. "Perhaps you took it with you that night and later mislaid it."

"No," the countess answered emphatically. "I left it on the dressing table in my room. If only it hadn't been thrown away, I could prove it was Lady Muggleton's writing. You'd only have to look at it to know."

"But, lud, Christy," Pansy said as she looked in confusion from one serious adult face to another. "Why should you need to prove anything? Everyone here trusts your word."

"Of course they do," said Gwen lightly. She put her arm around Pansy and pulled her down beside her on the sofa. "Now let's discuss the receiving line at the ball tomorrow night. That's far more important." She smiled up at Roderick. "Don't you agree, my lord?"

The afternoon passed quickly with each member of the group enthusiastically offering ideas for the coming celebration. Rugden was just outlining his final thoughts when the butler brought Christina a calling card with a note on the back requesting a private audience. After instructing the servant to show Jacob Rothenstein into the study, she said a brief farewell to Gwen and withdrew, leaving her husband to see her sister to a waiting carriage.

Opening the study door, Christina found her elderly friend before a wall of books with his back to her, his snowy head tilted up to peruse their titles through his reading spectacles. When he heard the door close, he turned to face her and slipped the glasses into his pocket. His deep brown eyes beamed with affection.

"Jacob, what a lovely surprise!" She quickly crossed the room to take his hand. "I didn't expect to see you until tomorrow evening. What's so exciting that you wanted to talk to me before then? You've discovered another antique?"

The merchant smiled at her fondly. Holding his cane in one gnarled hand, he leaned on her arm and allowed her to guide him to a leather chair near the fireplace. "First of all, please accept my good wishes on your marriage," he said as he sank down gratefully on the comfortable cushion. He peered up at her with his astute, intelligent gaze. "Since you'd failed to mention it the last time we met, I must assume it was all rather sudden."

She made no attempt to deceive her old friend. "Sudden and unwanted," she admitted. She plopped down on the ottoman in front of him. Her elbows resting on her knees, she propped her chin in her hands and wrinkled her nose in unhappy resignation. "But apparently necessary for my father's sake and that of my family." She smiled in curiosity. "Now tell me why you're here."

Jacob pulled a folded paper from his coat pocket. "Child, I'm afraid there's been a bit of confusion involving your newly acquired marital status. The draft you just recently sent for the purchase of the three instruments requires your husband's signature. Since you obviously didn't realize that, I came here to let you know. I wanted to warn you personally, Christy, before you were embarrassed in front of a tradesman or worse. In the future your spouse must sign every note of hand against your account. The Bank of Rothenstein can no longer honor your name on any certificate, dear heart."

"Due to my marriage settlement?" Christina took the paper. Her hand shook as she unfolded it and read the brief explanation written across the top. She'd realized from the start that Rugden could spend her fortune as freely as he chose. What she hadn't considered was that he could effectively block her from using it for her own purposes as well.

Jacob shook his head in sympathy. Pursing his lips, he absently stroked his long white beard. "Then you didn't realize the full stipulations of the contract? I thought as much, for I'd never have believed you'd sign away so completely the inheritance your grandfather left you. All that was required, however, was your father's signature as guardian of your trust. Your moneys, my child, are securely in the hands of your new husband. I'm deeply sorry to tell you this, for I know the plans you'd made for Penthaven. But you'll no longer be able to spend your fortune without the written approval of your spouse."

Christina rose and jerked the bell pull. When a lackey entered, she directed him to ask His Lordship to come to the study immediately.

"Nothing needs to be done about this draft at the moment," Jacob said kindly. "The last thing I want to do is cause problems between you and your new groom." He started to rise from the chair. "Perhaps it would be best if I leave now."

"No!" she cried. She struggled to speak calmly. "No, Jacob. I want you to wait. Please."

She paced back and forth in front of the hearth, unable to make polite conversation. The moment she heard Rugden enter the room, she whirled to face him. Her voice trembled when she spoke. "Kindly sign the draft I wrote to pay Mr. Rothenstein for some items I purchased. The note now requires your signature." She handed Rugden the letter of credit, fighting to keep back her tears of outrage.

Roderick glanced down at the bill. He expected to find the exorbitant price of the two fashionable ball gowns the ladies in his family had recently purchased. They'd been chattering about their arrival earlier that afternoon. In fact, he'd already prepared a stern lecture for both young women on the importance of thriftiness. When he read the sum, he nearly swore out loud in astonishment.

The note was for the staggering figure of nine thousand pounds.

A hundred dresses wouldn't cost as much. Not even

adding in shoes, fans, ribbons, and undergarments for three more ladies. Incredulous, he looked up to meet the merchant's calm gaze. The only possible reason for such a fantastic debt was a loan to cover excessive gambling losses. The wily old fellow was a damn cents-per-center from the City. Roderick glared at him and spoke with barely concealed contempt. "What exactly did my lady wife purchase?"

"Three antique instruments of the highest quality," Rothenstein replied with an unworried smile. "They were heirlooms and had been stored by their original owner with great care for many, many years."

Roderick looked over at Christina, who stood in front of the fireplace with her chin tilted high, her arms folded across her chest pugnaciously.

"Instruments? What kind of instruments?"

"Musical." They both answered at the same time.

Roderick strode over to his desk and placed the draft carefully on its top. He turned to face the two, who waited in silence for his answer. The financier seemed completely undisturbed by the mix-up. Apparently, he believed that the Earl of Rugden's funds were unlimited and the purchase of near-priceless antiques a mere bagatelle. Christina bristled with unveiled contempt that her new spouse couldn't provide the funds she wanted to spend on a collection of old, useless objects. Damn, it was an unnecessary and exorbitant luxury at a time when funds were so straitened and his own finances in such a state of crisis.

"Please accept my apologies for the inconvenience, Mr. Rothenstein," Roderick said with cold formality. "I appreciate your kindness in coming here to speak to my wife. Henceforth, however, I will supervise her monetary dealings. I will sign all bills personally. The antiques in question will be returned to your possession immediately. Thank you again for coming." His sharp words were an undisguised dismissal.

"If circumstances at the moment make it impossible for you to purchase the instruments, my lord," Rothenstein answered with unruffled serenity, "consider them a present to the new bride." Leaning on his cane, he rose from the chair.

Stung by the fact that he was in such financial straits that he hadn't been able to give Christina a decent bride gift, Roderick stared at the wealthy merchant in haughty disapproval. "My wife will accept no gifts from any man but her husband."

Rothenstein bowed graciously and moved toward the door. "I understand your possessive feelings, my lord, and respect them. Still, the instruments will remain in Lady Christina's collection at Penthaven." He paused and smiled mischievously. "Unless you wish to pay an eighty-year-old man the ultimate compliment of calling him out over your nineteen-year-old wife."

Speechless, Roderick watched the elderly gentleman calmly blow Christina a kiss and leave the room.

His wife, however, was not at a loss for words. The moment the door closed, she spun to face him, her skirts swirling around her like a whirlpool. "You great, braying ass! Jacob dangled me on his knee when I was a baby. He was my grandfather's business partner and dearest friend."

"I didn't realize you had such close connections to the City," he bit out.

"Yes, I have friends in the City. My grandfather was a businessman just like Jacob." Two bright spots of anger glowed on her high cheekbones. She strode over to him and held her hands in front of his face, her fingers splayed apart. "I have the smell of the City all over me. But at least Grandfather Hilliard's money was made honestly, with hard work and the sweat of his brow. He didn't stoop to marrying a young woman solely for the use of her fortune, while turning her into a penniless pauper."

"You're not a pauper, Christina," he snapped.

"I'm so happy to hear you say that, my lord. For I've absolutely no intention of giving up my plan to establish a home for musicians at my estate in Cornwall."

"At the moment, there'll be no large expenditures without my approval. I absolutely forbid it. However, I do intend to provide you with a small allowance for trivial purchases."

"An allowance?" With whitened fingers, Christina gripped the straight-backed chair beside his desk as though holding on to an anchor in a hurricane. She spoke through

tightly gritted teeth. "You take my inheritance from me and then dare to offer me a small stipend?"

Rugden's gray eyes grew icy. His jaw clenched, and a muscle twitched in his right cheek. He appeared to be struggling hard to maintain his frayed composure as he moved to stand behind his desk and jerk open a drawer. Pulling out a bank draft, he answered with glacial calm. "Here, my extravagant wife, is a voucher for your new ball gown. I wouldn't want you to appear in rags at our postnuptial ball." He handed it to her across the desktop.

Christina snatched the note of credit and tore it into shreds. "I'll not live like a child given small tokens when I behave in a proper manner," she cried. She threw the pieces of paper at him and raced to the door.

"I didn't say you were behaving in a proper manner, damn it!" Rugden shouted as the tiny bits of vellum floated lazily to the ground around him. "In the future, madame wife . . ."

The door slammed with a bang on his uncompleted ultimatum.

An overwhelming need for privacy drove Christina out of the house. She flew through the now empty salon and into a side garden, slowing to a walk on the brick pathway that led to a small stable housing the few mounts kept in town. Mohawk's shrill whinny pierced the quiet, and she followed the sound to the stall of Rugden's magnificent stallion. Stepping up on the lowest board, she peered over the top railing. The sight of the powerful animal always filled her with a grudging admiration that her husband was able to control him with such ease.

"Mohawk, you beautiful beast, what a sniveling coward your master is to cheat a defenseless girl of her fortune. Why don't you throw him off some fine day so he can break his bloody, avaricious neck?"

A voice sounded from the next stall. "Tut, tut. I've heard the colonel called many a name, now, lass, but I havena ever heard him labeled a coward. How do ye think he earned all those fancy ribbons he wears on his dress uniform?"

Christina turned to find Angus Duncan peering at her

over the high boards that divided the stalls. "I think he must have stolen them!"

The little batman laid down a rag he'd been using to polish Rugden's saddle and came around to the other side. Pushing his cap back on his head, he scratched his chin in bemusement, looking for all the world like a red-haired elf gazing up at a foolish mortal.

"Nay, lassie, he earned every one of them. I ken verra weel, since I was with him through the thick of it. He tricked the Frenchies at the battle of Quebec. 'Twas on his account we were able tae land at Foulon Cove."

She clambered up and perched on the top rail. Still scowling, she reached out to pat Mohawk's velvety nose. "Tell me about it, Duncan," she requested sullenly.

The Scotsman sat down on a bale of hay nearby and took a piece of straw he'd been chewing out of his mouth. Pointing it at her for emphasis, he began his tale. "Weel, lass, we had almost given up hope of ever taking the city of Quebec. There wasna a place for a single piece of artillery, and it wasna possible for the infantry tae approach the walls. Then the young officers met with General Wolfe himself and devised a plan tae sneak up the river and enter the city by the Heights of Abraham. The colonel and his men set out on board ship with the hope of making it safely through the French blockade. Twice he and a fellow officer replied tae a sentry's challenge in some fancy French words. He fooled them right smartly. And then he and his volunteers climbed up that steep cliff face and overpowered the Frogs guarding the summit. Before dawn, the whole blasted British army was moving on Quebec. And the man ye think cowardly nearly lost his life in the battle."

Impressed by the description of Rugden's bravery, Christina sniffed defensively. "But he's still behaved dastardly toward me."

"I dinna ken anything aboot that, my lady. Nay, and I dinna believe it, either," came Duncan's gruff reply. "The colonel isna capable of anything dishonorable. If he has a fault, lass, it's that he imposes the same strict code on others that he does on himself. He willna tolerate deceit of any kind." The batman stood, tipped his cap, and walked out of the stables whistling.

Mohawk gently nudged Christina's elbow. Absently patting the quivering muzzle, she thought about the enigmatic man she'd married. He seemed to have the admiration of everyone who knew him—with the sole exception of the Duke of Carlisle. Even her father seemed to be in awe of Rugden, else he'd never have signed that dratted marriage agreement. Could so many honorable men be hoodwinked by an unscrupulous charlatan? And why did she find herself so attracted to him, in spite of the fact that he stood resolutely between her and her plans for Penthaven?

She turned her thoughts to the terrible lie she'd told about Edwin Whiteham. Her childhood friend would be appalled to learn he'd been named as the father of her unborn child—a child that existed only in her husband's imagination. From what Duncan had said, she'd been right in keeping her lie a secret from Rugden. Only after she was safely divorced would she tell him the truth. And not until there was sufficient distance between them. Two or three counties might just do, if she was lucky.

Chapter 11

By the time the evening of the ball arrived, Christina could barely contain her apprehension. Since she'd thrown the offer of an allowance back in Rugden's face, she'd treated him with cold disdain, barely acknowledging his presence when he came into the room. She'd considered and rejected every conceivable plan for avoiding the whole affair, from pleading illness at the last possible moment, when it was too late to reschedule, to simply disappearing for a week, preferably to Cornwall. But all her dread couldn't hold back the appointed hour. Like it or not, she was going to be formally presented to society as Lady Fielding, the new Countess of Rugden.

In Grosvenor Square, her family's magnificent Waldwick Mansion was thrown open to the balmy fall weather. Flambeaux lit every window. The golden candlelight blazed out onto the street to illuminate the way for the guests as they departed their coaches and sedan chairs and mingled on the wide stone steps. The chattering crowd entered through the high doors of the elegant town house and were solemnly announced by a green-liveried major-domo.

At the head of the reception line, Lady Helen Berringer, the Dowager Marchioness of Waldwick, splendidly costumed in royal purple, greeted the callers. Standing at his mother's side, the Marquess of Waldwick, though not as tall as his parent or as regal, was no less finely arrayed in gold brocaded satin, a wide purple ribbon across his chest, and a white bagwig tied with golden threads on his head.

On the other side of her father stood Christina in the cream satin gown that had cost her husband so dearly. It had taken Marie nearly an hour to pile her mistress's thick hair on top of her head in a riot of careless curls. Fragrant yellow roses were strategically placed above one long ringlet that fell across her shoulder.

Next to her loomed the Earl of Rugden. Resplendent in the dress uniform of the Forty-third Regiment, Grenadiers, he towered a full head above every other man present with the single exception of Hugh Gillingham. Completely at ease, he greeted new arrivals with the natural skill of a diplomat, responding to their sometimes ribald attempts at congratulations with a smooth charm and answering each question with a personal comment. He impressed his new bride with his easy grace and open manner. It was with a surprising sense of pride that Christina introduced her husband to her friends and acquaintances for the first time.

The steady stream of guests slowed to a trickle and then, at long last, came to a halt. The reception line began to disburse, each family member to his appointed position. Lady Gwen and Lord Henry Sanborn joined the throng in the crowded ballroom to mingle and converse, while Carter and Francis departed to oversee the card tables. With a sense of relief that the worst was probably over, Christina bent her head to sniff the bouquet of yellow roses she held just as her father's major-domo announced the evening's last arrival.

"Lieutenant Edwin Whiteham."

Dear God above!

From the corner of her eye, she could see Edwin bow formally and kiss her grandmother's gloved fingers. Then he was shaking hands with her father. "Very sorry for the uninvited intrusion on your gala, Lord Waldwick. I'd only meant to make a brief call on Lady Christina this evening. I'm to return to my regiment in Prussia as quickly as possible and only just arrived in town this morning."

Shocked, Christina straightened slowly, her thoughts whirling crazily with the horrendous possibilities that had just walked in the door with her childhood friend. She'd been wrong in her earlier assumption. The evening could get much, much worse before it was over.

Whiteham wore the stunning uniform of the Horse Guards, and the deep azure jacket complemented the light blue of his eyes. He turned from her father to Christina with a carefree smile on his handsome face. She stiffened and instinctively lifted her hand to silence him before he unknowingly gave away her preposterous secret. Despite her heroic attempt at self-control, her knees buckled dangerously beneath her. She sank slowly toward the floor and reached out unthinkingly to Edwin for support. Through a haze she felt her husband's strong hand clasp her elbow as the steel of his arm held her in an upright position. His quick action and instantly taut frame indicated that he'd already surmised the identity of their latest guest.

Edwin, of course, remained oblivious to the desperate scene being played out before him. He carried his steel helmet nonchalantly under one arm, its long horsehair plume cascading to the floor and swishing against his long knee boots as he turned to the bridal couple. His frank gaze sought Christina's, then moved on to the silvery agates of the tall grenadier colonel standing so possessively beside her. With a quizzical smile, the cavalryman reached for her outstretched hand.

"Edwin." Her trembling fingers touched, then grasped his, her hoarse voice barely above a whisper. "I didn't know you were in London. No one told me you'd arrived."

Her shaky grasp and raspy speech brought a frown of concern to the young man's fair features. His honest face, with his sandy hair smoothed back over a wide, clear forehead, evoked the epitome of the brave and true English soldier. Barely inches taller than his childhood playmate, he leaned closer and spoke in a tone of unalloyed cheerfulness.

"How could you have known, Christy? I was given an unexpected leave to bring dispatches from our headquarters at Liegnitz. It was a total surprise for me as well. I've been involved in military debriefing all day and was unable to call on you before now." He glanced questioningly at the Marquess of Waldwick, who stood beside them. "But I intrude, I believe, on some special occasion, my lord?" he added politely, as though only just remembering his manners.

Rugden moved even closer to Christina, till the hem of her full skirt half covered his nearer boot. He addressed the junior officer in a daunting tone. "A special occasion indeed, Lieutenant. I have the honor tonight of introducing my new countess to society. Since my wife seems to have lost her tongue, I'll introduce myself." The earl extended his hand. "Colonel Roderick Fielding."

Edwin glanced briefly at Waldwick, as though in hope that the marquess would refute the unexpected disclosure, then clasped Rugden's hand and shook it. "Colonel Fielding, it's an honor, sir. We've toasted your bravery many times at the Horse Guards. Congratulations on your marriage." He turned to Christina in stunned amazement. "I didn't realize you were betrothed. You never mentioned it in your letters."

"You never mentioned your leave," she answered in a daze. "I never dreamed you'd be back so soon."

Sensing that something was strangely amiss, Lord Waldwick put his arm around Edwin's shoulders. The marquess had a contagious good humor that sparkled now in his blue eyes. He chuckled as though it were all a marvelous jest. "Why, these young gels will forever be surprising us, will they not? My little girl is a married lady now, and I hope it won't be long before I've a passel of grandchildren." He retained his hold on Edwin and guided him past Rugden's inquisitive brother and sister into the ballroom.

The Honorable Percival Fielding and Lady Penelope stood next to their eldest sibling, their mouths nearly agape with curiosity. Percy was the quintessence of a London macaroni that evening in pink brocade with silver waistcoat and clocked pink stockings. He peered at the retreating backs of the marquess and the young lieutenant through his gold quizzing glass, then swerved to eye the bridal pair who stood frozen to the spot.

"Odd's fish!" he scolded them. "Everyone's waiting for the married couple to lead out the first dance. The orchestra won't begin till you're on the floor."

With the oppressive silence of a cloistered monk, Rugden took Christina's arm and led her down the steps and onto the parquet dance floor. Not by the flicker of an eyelid did he betray what thoughts he hid behind his mask of icy indifference. Guiding her into place at the center of the circle of waiting guests, he held her hand aloft while the beginning strains of the sprightly minuet rose above the gabble of voices.

It was the first time they'd danced together. Shaking with delayed fright, Christina turned to face her taciturn husband and sank into an awkward curtsy. His returning bow was exceedingly graceful despite his great size. Garbed in a scarlet tunic with gold satin facings, his chest covered with medals, he was clearly an object of envy to his fellow officers. And a source of unmitigated delight to all the scatterbrained females who could barely keep their eyes off his corded thighs encased in the skin-tight buff breeches. Rugden's scar, rather than detracting from his appearance, only served to enhance the aura of male virility he evoked.

Following his lead, Christina regained her poise and executed the courtly moves of the minuet, all the while steadfastly meeting his cold gray eyes. Neither spoke. The sound of the harpsichord, viols, and oboes soared around them while the hushed audience watched with unabashed curiosity. They met and separated, gliding gracefully past each other, approaching and retreating, searching and evading in the ancient dance play of courtship. The swirl of her cream-colored skirt on the oak floorboards became a dizzying blur, and Christina feared she might faint. After the last curtsy, she unfurled her fan and waved it back and forth in a vain attempt to hide the feeling of panic that threatened to overpower her. She had to find Edwin and explain the horrible lie she'd told about him. And even more important, she had to talk him into keeping her secret!

The assembly applauded, and the dreamlike quality was replaced by a sharp sense of impending doom. Lord Waldwick appeared at his daughter's side, and they danced together while Rugden gently guided Grandmother Berringer, the indomitable dowager marchioness, in the steps of a merry gavotte.

At its conclusion, Christina left the dance floor on her father's arm and was met by her younger brother. Like Edwin, Francis wore the blue dress tunic, white bucksin pantaloons, and long knee boots of the Horse Guards. Unlike his friend, Francis's tow-colored locks were hidden beneath a fashionable powdered wig. She smiled at him briefly before her distraught gaze swept the room for a glimpse of another blue uniform.

"Egad, Christy." Major Francis Lord Berringer chuckled complacently, totally unaware of her plight. "You look like a Botticelli angel tonight, all pink and gold and white." His blue eyes beamed with pride. "Come say hello to an old friend of ours. He's waiting for you in the small salon."

With that, Francis drew his sister out of the ballroom and down the central hallway till they reached a simply furnished drawing room decorated in the lush, verdant colors of an English forest. Standing near the fireplace, in deep discussion with Rugden's closest friend, was Edwin Whiteham.

She hurried over to them, Francis at her side. "Major General Gillingham, Lieutenant Whiteham, I hope you're both enjoying the ball."

"How kind of you and Major Berringer to join us for a moment, Lady Rugden." Splendidly arrayed in his scarlet regimentals, Hugh smiled down at her. His broad face glowed with admiration, the boyish gap in his front teeth deceptively hiding the shrewd military cunning Rugden had told her he possessed. "Roderick is a very lucky man indeed. You're a vision of loveliness to this poor soldier's eyes, my dear. You'll be pursued for the next dance even in this out-of-the-way corner."

Hugh glanced at Edwin and continued. "We were just asking Lieutenant Whiteham how it fares on the continent. He's only recently arrived with communications from Silesia. We're anxious to hear the latest news."

Francis clapped his friend's shoulder. "It's great to see you again."

"It's wonderful to be in London again, I can tell you that." Edwin favored Christina with a smile that didn't quite reach his rueful eyes. "And here you are a married lady, and I knew nothing at all about it."

She gulped and prayed that Hugh had no inkling of the supposed relationship between her and the young dragoon. Though she strove to keep her voice coolly unemotional, she failed miserably. "It was a very brief engagement, Lieutenant. The earl and I have known each other only a short time." She glanced up to find Gillingham studying her thoughtfully.

"Then here's to impetuous love." Edwin lifted his wineglass in a salute. His fair complexion was flushed, and bright red spots blotched his neck near the jacket collar. "General Gillingham was correct. You'll be pursued for a dance even here. May I have the honor, Lady Rugden?"

She gladly accepted Edwin's proposal and quickly made her excuses to Hugh and Francis. But instead of allowing the lieutenant to lead her into the crowded ballroom, she pulled him to a stop in front of a pair of French doors that opened onto the mansion's small side garden.

"Let's not dance," she urged. "It's been so long since we've seen each other, I'd rather step outside in the fresh air and visit for a while. There's something important I want to tell you."

He shook his head in misunderstanding. "I'm much better at dancing than I used to be, Christy. Honestly. This time I promise not to step all over your fancy new ball shoes."

She pursed her lips in a tight line and met his troubled gaze. "I really need to talk with you, Ted. In private."

At the seriousness of her tone, he nodded a quick agreement. Opening one of the double doors, he led her out into the coolness of the night. They followed a brick path to an arbor covered in honeysuckle and bathed in the candlelight beaming from the second-story windows. When they reached the stone bench in front of the trellis, he turned to face her.

"What's so mysterious?" he asked.

"Oh, Ted," she blurted, "I'm so terribly unhappy."

He took both her hands, searching her face with sincere regard. "What's wrong? Is it your marriage?"

Miserable at the awful mess she'd gotten herself and Edwin into, she stared bleakly up at him. "Yes." She removed her hands from his grasp, turned, and faced the arbor, afraid she might give way to the tears that threatened to spill. She reached out and touched a cluster of pale yellow flowers with her gloved fingers, disturbing the night-flying insects busily collecting their pollen. The woodbine's sweet fragrance lifted on the warm evening air and swirled about them.

"Rugden and I are totally unsuitable," she said in a suffocated voice. "He doesn't have any interest in the things that are important to me. He's forbidden me to refurbish Penthaven as I'd always planned. He even tried to force me to return three precious antiques I'd purchased before we were married. We shall never, never suit. I'm convinced of it."

"If you felt that way about him, why did you marry the fellow in the first place?"

She swung around to face the baffled cavalryman's shocked gaze. "I can't explain it now, Ted. Not tonight, when we could be interrupted at any minute. But I have to be free of this dreadful marriage or face a lifetime of unhappiness."

Edwin clasped her elbows and anxiously drew her to him. His smooth forehead was furrowed in misgiving. "The man's a bloody hero, Christy. He's known throughout England for his courage. Surely you're mistaken."

"He's a brute and a miser!" she exclaimed. "And . . . and a philanderer."

Astounded at her vehement words, Edwin drew her even closer. His voice was low and harsh with anger. "Has he hurt you? You have to tell your brothers about this. Neither Carter nor Francis would stand for the man abusing you."

She shook her head. "It's much more complicated than that. I need to see you alone as soon as possible. Will you meet me at my sister's home tomorrow?"

Edwin frowned thoughtfully. "I can't. I'm supposed to be at the Horse Guards all day. But I'll come to see you the day after tomorrow."

"Not to my house," she insisted. "Send me a note, and I'll meet you at Gwen's." She clutched the scarlet cuff of his blue jacket. "Oh, Ted, it's so important that I see you. Please, please come as soon as possible."

The click of the double doors interrupted them as another guest sought the privacy of the garden. Edwin released her and instinctively stepped away to protect her from idle gossip. Christina spun around, one hand still on his sleeve, and the warm autumn breeze stirred the satin ruffles on her evening gown. A large figure stood silhouetted in the light streaming from the mansion.

"Here you are, my dear," Rugden said in a tone of jaded boredom. "How uncivilized of me to interrupt your little rendezvous, but the bride and groom are wanted for the next part of the festivities."

Beside her, Edwin tensed at the cruelly indifferent words. In the stillness of the darkened garden, the two men stared at each other in silent appraisal. From behind Rugden came the happy noises of the celebration as two chattering couples hurried down the hallway.

The young guardsman swung around to face her. He took her hand and squeezed it reassuringly. "I'll speak with you later, Lady Christina." With a curt nod to the earl, Edwin brushed past him and reentered the home.

"Problems with your young lover, sweetheart?" queried Rugden. He moved to stand in front of her and block her escape. "The young puppy certainly left fast enough. Did you tell him he was about to become a father? Or were you merely setting up another assignation?"

When she looked away, ignoring his insolent remarks, he reached out and caught her face in his hand. Christina tried to jerk her head free, but he held her chin in his strong fingers with maddening ease. She met his gaze, vainly trying to pierce his mask of cynicism.

His deep voice was as silken and soft as the fragrance of honeysuckle that floated around them. "I had no control over what happened in your past, Lady Rugden, but believe me, I do now. And I'm not going to stand idly by while I'm cuckolded by that pimply-faced little bastard. If you value the young lieutenant's life, you'll not meet with him privately again. Do you understand?"

With her jaw trapped in his relentless grip, she glared mutely up at him.

"Not at your sister's home," he continued with ominous calm, "not at your father's home, and not at our home."

If Rugden thought he'd intimidated her, she was quick to disillusion him. The moment he slackened his hold, she answered his implied threat. "I told you before that I'll choose my own friends. If you think . . ."

He slipped his fingers down to encircle her neck and squeezed just hard enough to bring her angry words to a halt. "Be extremely careful, my dear, or you'll be attending one of your *friend's* funerals."

"You're the bastard," she whispered the moment his hand left her throat. Tears stung her eyes and she blinked them away, determined that he wouldn't reduce her to sniveling like a two-year-old.

With a sardonic grin, he took her hand firmly in his. "Then you must feel very comfortable being married to me. Now we must return to our company. After all, the ball's in our honor. We should attempt to look as joyous as possible. Smile, sunshine, and pretend you love me. And I shall pretend that I love you."

At his mocking words, she tossed her head and tried to pull free. When that proved impossible, she squared her shoulders, pointed her nose in the air, and ungraciously condescended to allow him to escort her into the house.

The party was so successful it was being pronounced a great squeeze. Various alcoves framed groups of lovely young ladies sipping punch and flirting gaily behind their fans with any bachelor brave enough to come near. Older gentlemen moved in and out of the card rooms, dice boxes in hand, searching for a convivial group to join. Stout matrons, enthroned on equally stout chairs, sat in clumps around the sides of the dance floor like a herd of resting rhinoceroses dozing and grumbling to themselves on the edge of a swirling river.

Rather than join the stream of dancers, Christina stood at the door of the salon where her father, Carter, and Percy were overseeing games of whist, hazard, and faro. At their hearty greeting, she waved in a valiant attempt at gaiety. She was leaning on the doorjamb, pensively contemplating her brief, interrupted meeting with Edwin, when someone touched the ruffles at her elbow. She recognized his foreboding presence even before she turned to face him. Once again, the Duke of Carlisle brought with him an eerie sensation of looming entrapment.

"La, Your Grace! How you startled me!"

Justin Somesbury bowed over her hand. "With your

kind permission, my dear countess, may I have this dance?"

He was dressed entirely in black, the stark white folds of linen at his neck the only contrast in his dolorous costume. A tiny black patch in the shape of a crescent moon accented one corner of his thin mouth. He smiled at her coldly.

"My heart's delight, your beauty never fails to dazzle me," he said with smooth charm as he led her onto the dance floor. "But you surpass even yourself this evening. Could it be that you're responding to the pleasures of marriage with enthusiasm?" Christina stared at him in shock. Uncertain of his deeper meaning, she concentrated on the steps of the lively quadrille.

Carlisle led her down a row of couples, passing a giggling Pansy and her equally boisterous young partner. Giving Christina no time to recoup, the duke leaned closer to her. "Your new sister-in-law is also looking very lovely tonight. Quite a riddle, is she not?"

"A riddle? How so, Your Grace?"

The duke raised his shoulders in an affected shrug. "Then you never remarked how very different she is from her brothers? Strange, I thought it would have fairly leaped to your attention. So tiny she is beside them. And so unlike them in coloring. When you think about it, she hardly seems to resemble anyone in her family."

Not having met Pansy's mother, Christina lifted her eyebrows in puzzlement. She glanced again at Lady Penelope, who was just gliding by with her adoring partner. "Such things are not so uncommon, are they?"

"As you say," came his cryptic reply.

At the completion of the dance, Carlisle led her to Lady Gwendoline, who was standing at the side of the room with the dowager marchioness. He lifted Christina's gloved hand to his lips and kissed her fingers in a lingering, provocative manner. With an air of thinly veiled arrogance, he addressed her sister and grandmother. "Though I relinquish her to your loving hands for now, I have every intention of claiming Lady Christina at a later time."

Gwen stared in surprise at the presumptuous words that sounded unbelievably like a threat. "Perhaps my sister's dances are all promised, Your Grace. You may find it difficult to reclaim her tonight."

Carlisle's haughty smile widened. "Rest assured, Lady Gwen, I will reclaim her. If not tonight, soon, and for a more satisfying length of time." He bowed slightly to the dowager marchioness and withdrew.

"Why, his manners exceed all bounds," Gwen said indignantly. "The man's truly brazen!"

"He's a blackguard, granddaughter," Lady Helen replied. "And how he procured an invitation to this ball is a mystery to me. I've known the Duke of Carlisle for many years. He may be powerful with his friends at court, but he's beneath us in everything that counts—lineage, status, and honor. Christy, I warn you to beware of him. Your refusal to his offer doesn't sit well with the arrogant duke. Justin Somesbury won't forget, or easily forgive, your rejection."

Christina placed her arm on her grandmother's shoulders and pressed a kiss on the wrinkled cheek. "Pooh, what poppycock! Refusing a marriage offer hardly constitutes scorning a man. His wasn't the only proposal I turned down. I can't live in fear of every suitor I rejected."

Before Christina could persist in arguing further, they were joined by her husband. "I was hoping to meet your friend Lady Muggleton this evening," he said to the dowager marchioness.

Roderick glanced pointedly at the group of elderly ladies sitting nearby. He wanted to question the woman whose invitation had succeeded in setting Christina off on the aborted journey to St. Albans.

"She's not here," Lady Helen replied. She seemed nearly as disappointed as he. "Muggs is suffering an attack of the gout and has been confined to her London town house. She sent her apologies to your wife just this afternoon."

Christina's soft lips curved in a smile. Her beautiful eyes twinkled with amusement. "I think Lady Muggleton's suffering from more than just the gout. Her memory is starting to fail her as well. I wrote to thank her for inviting me to see the antique lute. I apologized for any inconvenience I might have caused her friend before he left for

Scotland. She said in the note that she'd never heard of Mr. Zachary Noyes and didn't have the slightest interest in lutes, English or Italian."

"At seventy, a lapse in memory isn't all that unusual," Gwen offered compassionately.

"I'm seventy-three, and I'll match my mental abilities with anyone here," retorted Lady Helen. Her patrician features and proud bearing made it obvious from whom Christina had inherited her fine bone structure and regal posture. The dowager marchioness met Roderick's gaze, the challenge clear in her alert blue eyes. She knew why he wanted to interview her elderly friend. He suspected his wife's grandmother knew more about the unusual mix-up of coaches than he did.

"Then if you ladies will excuse us," Roderick said with a polite smile, "I'd like to dance with my wife." Before Christina could say a word to the contrary, he took her hand and led her onto the floor. As she sank into a deep curtsy, she lifted her sapphire gaze to Roderick and smiled up at him as though he were the only man in the room.

"So you've decided to take my advice," he goaded, returning her curtsy with a smooth bow. Intrigued by her sudden change of behavior, he took her hand and led her forward in the first steps of the minuet.

She'd barely spoken to him since he'd offered her the voucher for the ball gown, which she'd spitefully torn into little pieces. He hadn't brought the subject up again, nor had he pushed her to reconsider. He'd recognized his error in judgment immediately and did what every good commander does when he finds himself outflanked through a tactical blunder. After sending a profuse apology to Jacob Rothenstein, along with a draft for nine thousand pounds, he had retreated to fight again another day.

They turned to face each other. She fluttered her long lashes and peeped up at him disarmingly. Three short strands of milk-white pearls encircled her delicate collarbone, and matching pearl drops dangled enticingly from her tiny earlobes. She'd slipped the ribbon of her fan over the wrist of one long white glove, and it swayed rhythmically as they danced. They dropped hands and took two steps to the right.

"You've offered me so much instruction in the past few days, my lord, I'm sure I don't know which piece of advice you're referring to."

They moved two steps to the left.

"The part about pretending to be in love with me."

"I'm a consummate actress," she boasted as they passed each other and turned, "but even my incredible skills aren't up to that hypocrisy." A smile skipped about the corners of her mouth, belying the sharpness of her words. "It's just that I suddenly remembered that I haven't as yet introduced you to three very dear old friends of mine. As soon as this dance is over, I'll do so."

"Just how old are these dear friends?" he questioned sardonically. They took two more steps to the right. "About the same age as Lieutenant Whiteham?" And two to the left. "You've known that idiot since childhood."

Her musical laughter floated around them as they glided past each other and turned. "They're a little older than Ted." She grew serious and gravely searched his eyes. "My grandfather was their patron for many years. When he died, I continued to support them with the inheritance he left me." She looked over at the orchestra, and he followed her gaze. Three very elderly musicians smiled at her over their violins.

"They need our help, Rugden," she continued as they executed the counterfigure and returned to their original position. A worried frown creased her forehead. "If you cut off the stipend I've been giving them, they'll be destitute."

"What kind of cold-blooded monster do you think I am, Christina, that I'd turn my back on three old men who are dependent upon my help to survive?" He bowed stiffly, his voice harsh with anger.

Relief flooded her lovely face as she rose from her curtsy. "Then you'll continue to support them?"

"Yes," he bit out. He took her hand and led her forward once again. "And you don't even have to bat your eyes and pretend that you like me."

"Good," she hissed furiously. "It was starting to become very tiresome."

They finished the dance without another word.

Roderick was irate at Christina's insistence on portraying him as a despicable fortune hunter. He didn't covet her money. It was merely a means to an end. Besides, everyone knew that females were incapable of understanding the harsh world of finance. When he married her, he'd taken it for granted that he was to be the guardian of her inheritance, accepting the responsibility from her father. That was a husband's role. Any other woman would have been grateful to rely on her spouse's guidance. Belatedly, he'd come to realize that Christina wasn't like any other woman. She wanted to make her own decisions.

Roderick was astounded by her radical thinking. He placed no importance whatsoever on an impulsive female's preposterous notions of changing the world. He was a practical man, not a dreamer. Money was to be used to protect and enhance what one already had, not thrown away in pie-eyed schemes. After all, music was a rather unimportant part of life, a hobby to keep an otherwise bored female busy. He believed, like every other logical, down-to-earth male, that a woman's first interest should be in studying how to please her husband.

Chapter 12

It was not Lieutenant Whiteham's intention to force a quarrel on anyone when he left his apartments the evening following the Berringer ball. All through the afternoon, as he'd been briefed at Whitehall for his imminent return to the continent, he'd considered penning a cartel in the most polite language possible and sending it round to Rugden House with a fellow guardsman, whom he knew could be easily persuaded to act as his second.

Whiteham had learned from Francis the reason behind the hasty marriage and was certain Rugden had planned his own bride's entrapment. But Edwin had no prior claim on Christina. He hadn't even spoken to her of his intentions. When it came to romancing the lady of his dreams, he was still as tongue-tied as he'd been at seventeen. And in the eyes of the world, it was the responsibility of her two brothers to protect the young woman from an abusive husband. So it was the unexpressed hope that he'd be able to imbibe enough liquor that blustery night to drown his inner pain that sent him into the dark streets.

The September evening had grown cool with the advent of an approaching rainstorm. Following numbly in Major Francis Berringer's wake, Edwin passed through every available gaming house in London, drinking all the while. He paid no attention to the gambling hell they entered under the unlikely name of Madame Clarissa's Fortune Parlor. Although he'd never been inside this particular establishment, it resembled every other one they'd visited that evening. Even-Odd tables were set out in the nearer salon. Smaller rooms were crowded with dandies and town swells trying their luck at deep basset, hazard, or piquet. In the back of the house was the inevitable faro bank, presided over by the corpulant proprietor, Madame Clarissa herself.

Repairing to a small table in one corner, Francis and Edwin joined a group of acquaintances in His Majesty's Horse Guards. Edwin groaned with fatigue and disillusionment as he sank down beside a beet-faced captain of the Blues. Whiteham lifted a glass of port to his lips, gazed distractedly about the noisy room, and scowled in sudden consternation. At the large faro table, placing bets with an air of refined, punctilious boredom, sat the Earl of Rugden. He was sprawled casually on a massive baroque chair, attended by two voluptuous demireps perched on each of the seat's carved and gilded side arms. A statuesque redhead massaged his neck and shoulders as he leaned forward to toss the rouleaus on the green felt. Her dazzling blond counterpart ran long, graceful fingers seductively up and down the sleeves of his red coat as though she were petting a dozing lion.

The sight of Christina's brutish husband, married less than two weeks and already being fondled by a pair of harlots, sent Edwin's morose self-pity scuttling like a lobster across a tiled floor. The melancholy desire to drink himself into unconsciousness was quickly replaced by the near uncontrollable urge to throttle the knave where he sat. That any man could be married to an angel and spend his time and favors in such a lewd fashion outraged the lieutenant's sense of decency. From what Francis Berringer had confided, the arrogant earl would be penniless except for Christina's fortune.

Edwin turned to his companions and snorted loudly and contemptuously. "Egads, I wasn't aware of the scum that patronized this establishment, else I'd never have agreed to come in here."

His colleagues gaped in astonishment.

Francis, noticing his brother-in-law for the first time, apparently realized just which one of the scum this scathing comment was directed at. "I say, Ted, we won't stay here at all, if you don't like it. Plenty of places to drop one's blunt. No need even to finish our drink." He set his glass down and tugged nervously on the sleeve of his friend's blue tunic.

"Should we go, Berringer?" Edwin countered with undisguised revulsion. "Or should we chase the swine out?"

The room buzzed with conjecture. Fellow gamblers leaned across the faro table and whispered to each other, debating the identity of the sandy-haired, foul-tempered dragoon. The entire company tingled with delighted anticipation, while every man under sixty mentally examined the weapon—pistol or small sword—carried on his person for just such an occasion.

From her place on the arm of Rugden's chair, the redhead met Edwin's stare. "Come over here, darling," he called to her, "and I'll show you what a real man is like."

She gave the earl a sly glance from the corner of her eye. Engrossed in the card play, the colonel didn't even bother to look up. With the languid air of a practiced courtesan, she slipped from the chair and crossed the short distance that separated them, her lime satin petticoats swaying enchantingly with her deliberate movements. The strumpet touched Edwin's hair in a light caress and then slipped across his knees.

Pulling her down on his lap, Edwin called for another round of drinks for his fellow guardsmen. He looked insolently at the dark-haired man she'd just abandoned at the faro table. "You'd make no attempt to keep the woman?" he taunted. "Then send the other little doxy over here as well. Unless you're not too chicken-hearted to try to keep her!"

The room fell silent.

Gaming stopped.

No one spoke.

Not even the snap of a card being turned interrupted the crowd's attempt to hear the large gentleman's answer. Only the faint sound of dice on the E.O. boards in the front salon clicked steadily on.

With unruffled indifference, Rugden pulled a stack of coins across the green cloth and then leaned back in his chair. "Miss Gardiner is welcome to join you if she wishes," he drawled with bored complacency. "I wouldn't hold her against her will."

"That's certainly out of character for you, isn't it?" Whiteham snarled.

Major Francis Berringer, appalled at the sudden turn of events, leaned across their small table. "I say, Ted—this won't do! You're being insolent without provocation. I think you've been dipping a trifle too heavily."

Impatiently, Whiteham shook his head. "I'm not that drunk, Fran. By God, I'm sober enough to recognize a cowardly poltroon when I see one."

The silence was broken by someone's audible gasp. The curvaceous wench at Rugden's elbow gave a nervous titter, then quickly covered her mouth.

With enormous difficulty, Roderick kept a tight rein on his growing rage. He'd recognized Lieutenant Edwin Whiteham the moment he'd entered the room. For the past ten minutes the earl had repeatedly warned himself that it would be morally wrong and socially unacceptable to give in to his baser instincts and send the young idiot into well-deserved oblivion. The rash fool was more than ten years his junior and had obviously been drinking heavily.

"I never fight over women in gaming establishments, my good fellow," Roderick explained with exaggerated patience. He gave the cavalryman a derisive smile. "Perhaps you should listen to your companion and go home before you get yourself into serious trouble."

Whiteham leaped to his feet, discarding the redhead in all her pulchritude with total disregard. She hit the floor with a plop, her indignant yelp ignored by every observer. All eyes were fastened upon the two potential combatants.

"Are you telling me to leave? Plague on't, I think a cur like you needs to be taught some manners." Wineglass in hand, Whiteham stalked toward Roderick, who'd remained seated throughout the entire exchange.

Recognizing the irrational fury in the cavalryman's liquor-blurred eyes, Roderick knew their altercation wasn't over some insignificant faro's daughter. He rose slowly from his chair and made one last attempt to deflect the probably unavoidable duel. "I'm willing to accept your apologies, Lieutenant."

"Apologies be damned!" Whiteham roared. "Let's see if this will make you act like a man!"

He tossed the full goblet of red wine into Roderick's face. The port splashed against his eyebrows and lids, then ran in cool rivulets down his cheeks to drip from his chin.

With lightning reflex, Roderick reached out, picked up the junior officer by the front of his blue jacket, and shook him like a terrier with a rat. "You sniffling little schoolboy. It's you who needs the lesson, and by God, you'll find me a most demanding instructor. Damn, I should thrash the bloody hell out of you right now."

Major General Gillingham, who'd come into the room from the front salon to investigate the shouting, hurried over. A scowl marred his usually good-humored features. "Easy, Rugden. As much as he needs a good whipping, this is neither the time nor the place."

Roderick released Whiteham's coat and shoved him away. "You may consider your challenge accepted, Lieutenant. Name your seconds."

With a grin of satisfaction, Whiteham turned to his companion. "Francis?"

Major Berringer nodded reluctantly. "Oh, aye! If it has to be!"

Spying a fellow from his own regiment in the corner group, Edwin called, "Lieutenant Dearing, will you assist?"

The astounded guardsman leaped to his feet and gleefully nodded his acceptance.

Roderick wiped the wine from his face with a linen cloth someone handed him. He smiled in genuine pleasure. "If you'd be kind enough to second for me, Hugh? I'm certain my brother will be happy to oblige as well. I'm going to teach this fresh-faced recruit the manly art of the duello."

Resignedly, Gillingham swore under his breath. "The choice of weapons is yours, Rugden. And the date."

"I'll instruct the little whelp in the use of the short sword. Any day this week will be fine."

Whiteham brashly interrupted. "Tomorrow, if you please. I'm due to leave for the continent the next day."

"I'll be happy to oblige," Roderick told the father of his bride's unborn child. "Tomorrow in Oaks Crossing at dawn. We shall arrange for the physician." He turned to

Hugh and put his arm around the general's shoulder. "And now, my friend, let's get out of this rat's nest. There must be some establishment more fastidious about its guest list. This place stinks of the hoi polloi."

"Christy! Wake up! You must wake, up dearest!"

Sound asleep, Christina heard her sister's persistent voice calling her. She rolled over and stubbornly tried her best to ignore it.

"Wake up, Christy," Gwen said again, this time directly into her ear. She leaned across the enormous canopied bed and shook her little sister insistently.

Christina forced her heavy lids open and slowly focused on the blue-green eyes of her eldest sibling. Only inches from her own, they were wide with alarm. Except for a single candle, the bedroom was still enshrouded in darkness, and a bolt of fear went through her. Wide awake, she sat up and reached frantically for Gwen's dimpled hand.

"What is it? Is it Father? Oh, Gwen, no!"

"It's not Father, Christy. It's Edwin Whiteham. You must get up at once. Only you can prevent the disaster that's about to overtake us."

Christina released her sister's cold fingers, threw off the coverlet, and slipped out of bed. She yanked her satin brocade robe on over her thin nightgown. "What's happened to Ted? Tell me, Gwen!"

Lady Gwendoline placed her hands on Christina's shoulders and held her fast. "First calm down. Nothing's happened yet. But I overhead Francis talking to Henry last night. It was well past midnight, and they didn't know I was still awake. I couldn't sleep and had slipped downstairs for my embroidery."

Lifting back the velvet hood of her ermine-trimmed cloak, Gwen untied the twisted silk cords at the base of her neck. Her hands were shaking so much she could barely manage to undo the knot.

"'Tis a duel, Christy! Rugden is meeting Edwin this morning at dawn." Gwen's soft voice was filled with worry. "This so-called affair of honor is somehow related to Edwin's fondness for you. For some unknown reason, he believes you're being mistreated by the earl. I couldn't sleep all night for fear of what might happen. Surely, you can talk your husband out of this madness."

Christina fought the panic and guilt that threatened to immobilize her. She pressed her fingertips to her temples and forced herself to remain composed and clear-headed. No matter what the cost, she had to tell her husband that she'd lied about the pregnancy. She had to convince him of Edwin's innocence before it was too late.

"I'll talk to Rugden," she cried. She spun away, then paused in mid-stride to look back. "Please don't go, Gwen. Wait for me here."

With a strangled sob, Christina dashed through the door and raced across the sitting room that separated her bedchamber from her husband's. Without stopping to knock, without even considering what she was going to say, she shoved the door open and rushed inside.

Despite the early hour, Roderick was awake and dressing by the light of a candle placed on the mantelpiece. Angus Duncan had just put away the shaving utensils and was turning to empty the basin when Christina entered her husband's sleeping quarters for the first time in their married life. Both men stared in surprise at her unannounced entrance.

"Rugden, I must speak to you alone! Please!"

His wife stood framed in the open doorway, the room's faint candle glow painting her in soft, lambent hues. Her lemon-colored robe was partially opened, revealing a glimpse of the pale batiste nightdress hidden beneath. Golden curls tumbled across her slim shoulders and down her back in glorious disarray. When she saw the little Scotsman, she hurriedly closed the braided gold frogs that marched down the front of her dressing gown.

The shock and dread in her marvelous blue eyes made it all too clear why, at long last, she'd entered Roderick's private sanctum. It had taken an unreasoning fear for her lover's safety to bring Lady Rugden into her own husband's bedchamber. God, he wanted to turn her over his knee and smack some sense into her with his open palm. Then throw her on the bed and pound his own flesh into her, over and over, till no trace of Edwin Whiteham's memory was left in that conniving little brain. If it weren't for the unborn child ...

"That will be all, Duncan," Roderick ordered. He inclined his head in dismissal. "I'll finish dressing by myself. You may leave us. And tell General Gillingham that I'll be with him momentarily."

The batman nodded silently. He set aside the folded linen towel draped across his arm and left.

Bare-chested, Rugden hooked his thumbs in his belt, widened his stance, and stared insolently down at Christina. The warm candlelight suffused his sun-bronzed face. In the flickering glow, the jagged scar that crossed one black eyebrow stood out in stark relief on his high forehead. His chiseled features showed absolutely no emotion.

"You have exactly two minutes," he said tersely. "What is it you wish to say?"

Christina advanced upon her husband. Unspilled tears blurred her sight. "You can't do this, Rugden," she begged. She clasped her hands in front of her in an open plea for mercy. "I swear to you, Edwin's innocent. You can't kill a blameless young man."

"Young?" he bit out savagely. He reached for his boots, and the quick, jerky motion betrayed the strain of the forced interview. "Yes, I grant you, he's that all right. But not too young to father a child. And innocent? Perhaps that, too, my darling wife. Having met the boy, I'd readily believe him the seduced, not you."

Clad only in buff breeches and woolen stockings, he sat down on a bench at the foot of his enormous bed and tugged on one knee-high top boot. His deep voice, when he spoke again, was choked with suppressed rage. "No, not you, Christina, with your lying lips so ready to beguile and betray."

The muscles on his upper body bunched and rippled in the room's mellow light as he viciously yanked on the second boot. From shoulder to waist, a ghastly battle scar stretched through the thick mat of hair on his chest. Yet even that failed to mar the perfection of his magnificent physique.

"Whiteham didn't have a chance, did he, Christina?" the earl continued before she could gather her rattled thoughts and begin her confession. "You lured him into your silken trap, only to discover that you were caught as well. How frightened you must have been when you discovered you were with child and the baby's father had just left for his tour of duty on the continent. Was that when you devised your plot to ensnare the first unsuspecting male you found?"

Rugden stood and reached for the white shirt that hung on a chair nearby. He pulled it on, stuffed the tails into his breeches, and hastily fastened the lace cuffs at his wrists.

Christina moved to stand in front of him. She placed a shaking hand on his forearm. Her voice broke when she tried to speak, and she had to start anew. "Yes . . . yes, I lied. I admit it, I lied. But it's not what you think. Spare his life, Rugden. Please, give me time to explain!"

Cursing softly, he shook her off and strode to a massive armoire, where he snatched up his scarlet coat. He grabbed his scabbard, sash, and belt, and moved abruptly to the door. With his hand on the knob, he paused and looked back at his wife, who'd followed him.

"Spare me the ridiculous theatrics, Christina," he said. "At the moment I wouldn't believe you if you told me the sky was blue, or the grass was green. If it's any consolation, however, it's not you we're fighting over this morning, but some damn trollop from a gaming hell. That should relieve any slight twinge of responsibility you might feel over his death."

She reeled back in shock at his heartless words. "You bastard," she gasped. "I don't believe you! You're acting in needless, despicable vengeance."

"Suit yourself, madame wife," he replied and slammed the door in her face.

Christina could hear the stamp of his booted feet as he hurried down the central staircase. She threw the bedroom door open.

"Come back here, Rugden! I have to talk to you!"

At the bottom of the stairs, Major General Gillingham had been waiting patiently for his closest friend. The look of barely controlled rage on Roderick's face when he appeared forestalled any comment over the commotion Hugh had just overheard from his spot in the entry hall. Without a word of explanation, the earl buckled his sword belt over his red sash and stomped out of the house.

The muffled sounds of a scuffle going on abovestairs drew Gillingham's attention. He turned and looked up to see Lady Rugden on the wide second floor landing. She was held fast by her petite sister and her tall, skinny maid, who stood on each side of the struggling countess and together prevented her from charging madly down the steps after her husband.

"Rugden!" she screamed hysterically. She tried unsuccessfully to pull free of her self-appointed guards. "Dear God, Rugden! *Don't kill him!*"

Hugh stared in silent horror, appalled at the sight of the exquisite countess actually begging her husband for the life of her young friend. Shaken, the general turned and crossed the threshold, leaving the home's high, carved door standing ajar in the cool morning mist.

The two grenadiers rode side by side in the faint light of dawn. They turned off Oxford Street to Edgware Road in silence, each one fearing to utter what was uppermost in his mind. They reached the inns at Oaks Crossing well ahead of the other participants in the *passage d'arms* and rode to a nearby spinney surrounded by the tall trees that gave the place its name. After dismounting, they tied their spirited steeds to a low branch and walked slowly across the soaked clearing, searching carefully in the grass for any holes or ridges that would trip the unwary swordsman. The morning's first rays of sunlight broke through the leaves overhead and cast a dappled shadow on the two soldiers, who propped themselves against a huge fallen oak and waited for the others' arrival.

Gillingham broke the self-imposed silence first. "Whiteham's a rash young lad, but he's always seemed an honorable one. I've come to know him fairly well in the past few years. There's no reason to doubt his integrity. He's a good man to have beside you on the battlefield, I can tell you that."

Roderick was disinclined to discuss his child bride's quixotic lover. "Yes, well, I did try to avert this whole asinine encounter, Hugh. But you certainly have my permission to try once more for an apology. Lord knows, I'd be willing to accept one and avoid the bloody affair. You say you knew him on the continent?"

Major General Gillingham's wide brow was creased with worry. "I'll be sworn, we were stationed together every step of the blasted way, from Liegnitz to Torgau. I was delighted to see the poor fellow had finally pulled some leave. Two consecutive years away from home is a long time, as you and I both know."

Stunned, Roderick pushed himself away from the tree trunk and stood up straight. He turned aside and fidgeted with his scabbard and belt in an attempt to hide the shock of Hugh's offhand remark. "He's had no leave for the last two years?" he asked. "Are you certain?"

"'Fore gad," Hugh protested, "we've been attached to Brunswick's campaigns the entire war. No, the lad's not been home until now, nor have I. Does that change your mind about continuing with this travesty?"

Roderick didn't answer immediately as he considered the possibility of refusing to fight. When he spoke, there was a tinge of irony in his voice. "The duel is, and always has been, Lieutenant Whiteham's intention, not mine. If he's willing to back away from this confrontation, so am I. I've no wish to spill that young madman's blood if it can be avoided."

With an air of resignation, Gillingham rested his hand on the hilt of his cuirass and gazed up into the branches overhead. The golden leaves rustled ominously in the breeze. "I'll do my best. But the fellow was none too reasonable the last time we saw him."

They turned at the sound of a cabriolet pulling into the grove and strolled toward it. The Honorable Percival Fielding rode beside the two-wheeled conveyance on a large, snorting bay.

"Percy's brought the surgeon," Roderick said. "Now all we need is my brother-in-law and his hotheaded friend."

In a matter of minutes Lieutenant Whiteham bowled up in a borrowed carriage, accompanied by his seconds, Major Berringer and Lieutenant Dearing. The two principals nodded briefly to each other. Then they quickly stripped off their coats and rolled up the lace cuffs of their white linen shirts. The other men walked over the ground, which, though nearly flat, with no hidden holes to trip an unwary combatant, was still dangerously wet from the night's storm. Next the seconds investigated each antagonist's sword to be certain the double-edged blades were the accepted length and weight. Following the amenities, Hugh approached Whiteham with one last request for an apology.

"I'll see him in hell first," Edwin said.

The words were sheer bravado, for the young officer was engaging in his first duel. Like many other wartime soldiers, he'd faced death on the battlefield amid the thunder of cannon and the screams of dying men and horses, where there was little time for preparation and none for sober reflection. He'd spent hours during drill practicing the art of fencing with a buttoned foil, but never before had he faced a man over naked blades in single combat. On the way to Oaks Crossing that morning, Francis had told him confidentially that Colonel Roderick Fielding had fought several duels, almost killing one opponent, who'd survived only by a miracle.

But the lieutenant couldn't draw back now that it had become a matter of honor and his own personal courage. He grasped his sword and tested the steel's flexibility with a deft turn of the wrist. The cool feel of the hilt in his hand had a calming effect. He turned to face the Earl of Rugden, now armed with a similar weapon.

"On guard!" called Major General Gillingham.

The two small swords *par excellence* flashed to the salute.

Rashly, Whiteham opened with an attempted flèche, depending on the initial surprise of the running attack for its success. Rugden evaded him, sidestepping with ease. Edwin's failure submitted him to the possibility of a hit from the back as, arm extended and fighting to maintain his balance, he passed the earl on his quarte side, nearly slipping on the spongy grass.

Rugden didn't attempt a strike, however, but calmly turned to face his opponent. Both adversaries resumed the guard position. Though Edwin knew his face was flushed with excitement, not a flicker of emotion crossed the colonel's impassive features. If anything, he looked bored.

Rugden's height gave him the advantage, but he didn't attack, seeming content to parry Edwin's wild thrusts in sixte and quarte. Vainly, the lieutenant sought to control the measure. He knew Rugden's superior reach could be a shorter man's downfall. The anger that had prompted the first mad attack had cooled enough for Whiteham to follow the techniques he'd been taught by his fencing masters. But Rugden easily parried each lunge, and Edwin, though he maintained the offensive, failed to find an opening in his opponent's guard.

Suddenly the earl took the offensive. Whiteham, like a rank beginner, failed twice to riposte and merely held his parry. With a strongly executed graze, Rugden thrust diagonally downward and deflected Whiteham's blade. The lieutenant's weapon flew out of his hand and landed in the soft dirt beneath a holly bush.

Roderick stepped back and waited for Hugh to approach. "Ask Lieutenant Whiteham if his sense of honor's been satisfied," he instructed, his breath coming slow and even. The dampness of the ground had hampered the speed of his footwork, but he'd managed to maintain his balance despite the slippery turf.

Panting audibly, Edwin Whiteham quickly retrieved his sword. His pale eyes were deep hollows in his white face.

"I won't be satisfied till your blood's been drawn," he said.

Roderick accepted the refusal with stiff formality. "Very well, then, Lieutenant. On guard!"

After that Whiteham never regained the attack. From an engagement in sixte, Rugden made a feint disengage into quarte, drawing Whiteham's lateral parry and deceiving it by rounding his guard into the open sixte line. The hit was delivered to Edwin's sword arm, and his blade fell to the ground with a soft thud. The last skirmish was over in seconds.

Francis ran up to Whiteham, supporting him with one arm around his shoulders. Lieutenant Dearing and Dr. Bowles assisted in laying the wounded man on the thick grass. They propped his head against a tree and pillowed it with his own tunic. After ripping off Whiteham's shirtsleeve with a small knife, the surgeon examined the cut.

Roderick stood apart with Hugh and Percy, waiting to hear the extent of the wound. Some minutes later Berringer approached the somber trio. "He'd like to talk to you, Rugden. Alone."

The earl nodded assent and left his companions. Kneeling on one knee beside his defeated adversary, he sent a questioning glance toward Bowles.

"It's a clean cut, my lord. Though he'll not have the use of that arm for a while, it should heal without complications. He's young and strong and foolish. But weren't we all, at his age?" With that brief, acerbic lecture, the portly doctor gathered up his instruments and bandages, replaced them in his bag, and returned to his carriage.

Roderick looked down at the pale face. The lids were closed, the lips bluish. "You wish to speak with me?" he asked quietly.

The prone lieutenant opened his eyes. He raised his shaky hand to the earl's forearm. "Give her up, Rugden."

"She's with child, you bloody fool," he said in a whisper.

"Give her to me," came Whiteham's insistent reply, despite the dismay in his glazed eyes.

"You'd take her now? Carrying another man's seed?"

Whiteham sought to rise up on one elbow. White with shock, he gasped at the pain in his arm and shoulder. "Yes, I'd take her. She's miserably unhappy, and I've always adored her. I'd accept your child as though it were my own. None of this misfortune can possibly be her fault."

Roderick stood again, towering over the injured man. "If you believe that, Whiteham, you're a bigger fool than I thought. Perhaps I should have released you permanently from your miserable delusions about women." Turning abruptly, he walked over to where Hugh waited beside their horses.

Gwen looked over the blue and orange yarn of her colorful needlework at her youngest sibling. "Christina, you'll wear out your fancy carpet if you don't sit down and stay still. I'm certain either Percy or Francis will come as soon as possible."

"That's right, Christy! If Roderick doesn't return straight home from the duel, I'm certain that Percy will come and tell us all about it. Just think how exciting! To have two men actually fight over you. How very splendid!" Pansy clasped her hands and crumpled on the sofa in a mock swoon.

Christina reeled to face her sister-in-law and raised her arms wide in disbelief. "Lady Penelope Fielding, I'm shocked at your scandalous attitude. Edwin Whiteham could be lying dead at this very moment."

"What about my brother? He might be mortally wounded also." But it was obvious neither Pansy nor any one else considered that suggestion even a remote possibility.

"Both of you are conjuring up a great tragedy," said Gwen, "when we have every reason to hope that the affair was averted completely. Francis promised to make very effort to reach a peaceful solution. I'm certain Percival and Major General Gillingham were of the same mind. Now let's try to remain calm. Christina, you sit down here," she commanded. She pointed to the velvet armchair. "Pansy, you take this seat on the sofa beside me, and I'll pour the tea."

Reluctantly, the young ladies did as directed. Christina sat on the edge of her seat and pulled distractedly on the Brussels lace at her elbow while the fifteen-year-old helped Gwen with the china cups and saucers.

The crunch of carriage wheels pulling up to the front of Rugden House brought all three women to their feet. Both Christina and Pansy flew toward the door, bumping into each other on the way.

As he came into the salon, Percy called to them in a booming, cheery voice. "Zounds, Christy! Pansy! It's all right! Everyone's safe."

Christina met him with outstretched hands. "Thank God! Oh, Percy, come in and tell us what happened."

The Honorable Percival Fielding gathered his two sisters in his arms with a laugh. "Sink me, if they're not both alive and well. Whiteham was pinked—nothing serious.

My brother, of course, is unscratched. Francis watched over Edwin after the surgeon left, so he's being taken care of quite nicely. And Roderick called for breakfast for all of us at the Oaks Crossing Inn. That's what took me so long, ladies," he apologized. "I couldn't resist the sight of sirloin and eggs, accompanied by a nice bit of kidneys. I must say, for an out-of-the-way place, their fare was quite good. Nothing fancy, you understand, but still totally acceptable. And the claret was as fine as you could wish for in any hostelry outside London."

Christina pushed him down on the settee and stood over him. "You're telling me that all of you sat down to a meal together? While we waited here on pins and needles, terrified of the outcome, all of you were swilling like pigs at a trough? I've never heard of such a disgraceful affair."

"Odd's fish, Christina, it happens all the time. Once it's settled, it's settled. Why bear a grudge? It was a fair fight. And everyone knew Roderick would never kill that young man."

"Everyone knew that? *We* didn't know that! We sat here like three hen-witted simpletons preparing for a funeral. Good God, I *begged* Rugden to spare Edwin's life. I practically got down on my knees." The countess flounced away from her astounded brother-in-law and sank into a chair. She covered her face in mortification.

"Thunder and turf! Don't be such a ninnyhammer, Christina. Two men aren't going to fight to the death over some doxy they just met the night before in a ramshackle gambling establishment." Sensing her discomfiture and wanting no part of her further recriminations, no matter how justified, Percy rose to go.

His premature departure, before a detailed narration of the duel had been given, was not to be allowed, however. Pansy leaped to her feet and grabbed his hand. "Was *that* what they were fighting over?" she asked. "But I thought . . ."

"Never mind what you thought, little miss," interrupted Lady Gwen. She sat down and deliberately started pouring tea into four Wedgwood cups. "Both gentlemen are safe, and that's what's important. The rest is irrelevant and not to be discussed by genteel young ladies. Now, we promised Grandmother Berringer that we'd call on her today. We'll go as planned and not say a word about this. Promise?"

Christina placed a icy hand to her forehead. "You and Pansy go, Gwen. I can't face Grandmother right now. She'd know immediately that something was wrong. Tell her I've a headache and I'll see her tomorrow."

"Very well. And Percival, since you took your own leisurely time in getting here with the news, you can accompany us this afternoon on our call and help dispel any suspicions our intuitive grandparent may have. It'll serve you right." Lady Gwendoline took hold of the dandy's satin-clad arm and pulled him down on the sofa beside her.

"Odd's fish, I say, you Berringer females are bloody termagants," came Percy's indignant retort.

The determination to forswear all contact with the male members of the human species had taken firm root in Christina's mind during the brief, solitary minutes following the departure of her family. This silent avowal was reinforced by the sound of carriage wheels stopping again in front of Rugden House. Inwardly bracing herself for the impending encounter with her husband, she was surprised to learn from the butler that Lieutenant Edwin Whiteham had arrived and was asking to see her.

At the sight of his injured arm encased in the spotless white sling, she was filled with guilt. "Ted, I'm so sorry."

Whiteham walked slowly toward her and bowed. He shook his head and gave her a wry half smile, his sandy hair glinting silver in the window's light. "Don't be," he said. "It wasn't your fault. I forced the issue for reasons of my own. And I didn't acquit myself all that badly for my first encounter, in spite of this." He nodded toward the bandaged limb, and his smile faded. "I came to say goodbye. I depart for Portsmouth in the morning. From there I sail to Brussels."

"I was going to leave London as soon as possible myself," she said eagerly. "I could travel as far as Portsmouth with you and then go on to Penthaven from there. My sister will chaperone Pansy while I'm gone."

Taking her hand, Whiteham smiled wanly. "'My dear

girl, that would never do. Not after this mangled affair. In any case, you'd have to travel on alone from Portsmouth, which wouldn't be wise in your delicate condition."

"I'm not expecting a child!" said Christina.

Baffled, the lieutenant looked at her with a puzzled frown. "But Rugden told me this morning. I hardly think he'd lie about it."

"Oh, he thinks I'm with child, Ted. I told him that so he'd agree to an annulment. But he still refused, even when I told him the baby was yours."

"My God, Christy, you didn't tell him that I forced myself on you?"

"No, no. Only that you seduced me. I made it very believable."

Edwin dropped her hand and asked in a scandalized voice, "Christy, how could you say such a thing? You could have gotten me killed."

Christina caught hold of the satin facings on his blue jacket. Her eyes glistened with tears. "It was wrong of me, and I'm truly sorry. But please, Ted, take me with you."

Without warning, the deep, familiar voice of her husband spoke quietly from the doorway. "I'm afraid I must interrupt this heartrending drama. You were about to give my wife your answer, I believe, Lieutenant. May I suggest you do so now, and then say your farewell?"

The startled pair drew apart. Christina, rigid with guilt and fear, turned to look at Rugden, who stood with arms crossed on his chest, feet braced apart, and sword hanging threateningly at his side.

Whiteham grew pale, but proudly stood his ground. "I only came to tell Lady Christina that I leave for the continent tomorrow. May I assure you, sir, that there'll be no repetition of this morning's challenge. Nor will I make any attempt to remove the countess from your protection. Since there's to be no annulment, she must remain with you or suffer the absence of genteel society. I'd never place her in that position."

"It's most gratifying to know that we agree on my wife's future, Lieutenant Whiteham," the earl replied in a tone just short of insolent. "When you return from your tour of duty, you must pay us another call."

The guardsman bowed stiffly to his host, and then, turning again to Christina, kissed her hand one last time. "Good-bye," he said quietly.

The moment he'd gone, Rugden caught her arm and roughly pulled her to him. "I learned only this morning that Whiteham has been in Europe for two uninterrupted years. Who *is* the child's father, Christina?" His narrowed eyes were nearly black with anger as he searched her face. "Or is there a child at all?"

She stared up at him, debating the wisdom of telling another lie. But good gad, there was no point in blabbing the truth at this late date. Edwin was safe. And she wanted the annulment more desperately now than ever. She started to speak, and he slid his forefinger across her lips, silencing her.

"Don't," he warned. "Don't say a thing. I wouldn't believe it anyway." He released her. "We'll set the matter aside for the moment. I've more important considerations at the present time. I've just come from Whitehall. Hugh and I are to report to the British ambassador in Paris for the peace negotiations, and you're to accompany me."

"I can't," she said. "I need to travel to Cornwall as soon as possible."

"Your scheme for Penthaven will have to wait, my dear, until our finances are on a more stable footing. It may take a while, but I've a hunch that eventually much of my father's unfortunate investments may be recovered. Then, and only then, I'll take you to Cornwall myself. In the meantime I can't afford to indulge your impractical notions of saving the world. You'll have to leave that to the politicians and the clergy. That's their responsibility. My duty lies with my country and my family. Period. Your duty, Lady Rugden, is to accompany me to Paris, where you'll be an obedient wife and play the role of your husband's charming hostess."

"But no Englishman's been to Paris in over three years!"

He smiled triumphantly. "We're going to be the first. We'll be escorted through our fleet's blockade, where a French guard of honor will be waiting for us at Le Havre. Since we're due in the capital in two weeks, we'll need to leave immediately. You'd best begin your packing now. And take your fanciest wardrobe. We'll no doubt be put on display."

"I'll never be packed in time!"

"Then you'll have to leave without your clothes, won't you?" her husband replied in a bored tone and left the room.

Chapter 13

They sailed from Portsmouth the next Tuesday aboard the H.M.S. *Mediator.* As they drove up High Street into the town that was the country's largest naval base, Rugden pointed out the cruiser with its three tall masts, waiting in the harbor to take them to France. Christina felt a thrill go through her at the sight. The ship bobbed patiently by the quayside in readiness for her coming voyage, her sails tightly furled, her decks alive with sailors, her cargo being hoisted aboard to the calls of "Steady, there! Ease her on, lads."

In the harbor, Christina could see the vast fleet that had come in for refurbishing and supplies. The *Mediator* was only a small cruiser in comparison to the first-rate ships of the line, which stood four stories high above the water. But she was proud to sail on any member of the renowned Channel Squadron, which had played such a formidable part in the sea blockade of France and the winning of the war.

They were piped aboard. Accompanied by Major General Gillingham, Colonel Fielding and his countess were welcomed by Captain Duckworth and the *Mediator*'s junior officer, First Lieutenant Charles Thompson. Behind them stood almost two hundred sailors at rigid attention. The preciseness of their perfect rows gave mute testimony to the hours of drill inflicted upon them by their gruff captain. Duckworth beamed at Christina. Despite the piercing blue gaze that pinned her, she liked him instantly.

"I intend to see that your stay on board the *Mediator* is as comfortable as possible, Lady Rugden. I've put you and

Colonel Fielding in a nice little cabin." His weathered face crinkled at the corners of his eyes when he smiled. Beneath his tricornered hat and slightly skewed bagwig, deep furrows ran down his sun-browned cheeks, attesting to a lifetime spent battling the sea.

He turned and addressed the serious-looking officer at his side. "Lieutenant Thompson, show the countess her quarters and see that she has everything she needs before we sail."

Thompson, striking in the blue and gold uniform of the Royal Navy, smiled at Christina. He had dark hair and warm brown eyes. His skin, swarthy from hours in the sun, was slightly roughened, the vestige of a mild case of smallpox. "If you'll please follow me, Lady Rugden, I'll be happy to take you to your quarters."

Back on top a short time later, the countess stood on the *Mediator*'s quarterdeck, watching and listening to the ordered hubbub as the trim ship left the harbor. Able seamen scurried aloft to unfurl the top gallants, while others of the crew winched the capstan and hauled on the shrouds. The fair wind and rising tide pushed the sloop along the formidable ramparts guarded by the batteries and past the fleet anchored at Spithead. Soon they glided by the Isle of Wight.

A smile was hovering about her lips when she was joined on the deck by her husband. He'd removed his coat, and with his full shirtsleeves billowing in the wind and his straight black hair tousled, he appeared more relaxed and approachable than she'd ever seen him.

"You seem to be enjoying the sea, Christina. Many people are quite ill when they sail. I was afraid you might be sick during the channel crossing."

"Oh, no, not me! As a child I sailed frequently with my brothers on our family ketch." But Christina didn't as yet have her sea legs. The deck beneath her lurched without warning, and she teetered backward. Rugden's arms were around her instantly. "Whoa," she said. She laughed as she tried in vain to catch her balance. She placed one hand on his chest and grasped his forearm with the other. "I'm not as good a sailor as I thought."

Roderick pulled her slim body next to his and inhaled the delicious scent of her. He could feel the curve of her tiny waist beneath his palm. One firm breast was crushed against his rib cage. The light, tantalizing pressure of her fingertips seemed to burn through the linen of his shirt.

"Lean against me," he said. "I won't let you fall."

To prove his point, he drew her even tighter, bringing her shapely legs, hidden beneath the layers of petticoats, against his steady thighs. Despite all his resolutions to the contrary, he couldn't keep his hands off his beautiful wife.

She looked up at him with startled eyes, and he wondered if she could feel the accelerated beat of his heart beneath her fingers or read the longing in his gaze. Desire rushed through him, hard and fast. Damn. It happened now every time he so much as brushed against her. In the close confines of the ship, he was about to learn the true meaning of the words *tortured* and *tormented*.

He wanted to learn if she was really pregnant. There was no doubt that she was a liar. She'd had the incredible nerve to name an innocent man as the father of her unborn child. Hell, if she could lie about that, she could lie about anything. She was a heartless, scheming witch. But in the web of deceit she'd spun, where did the truth end and the falsehoods begin? Perhaps she was with child and wasn't certain whose bastard it was. Or perhaps she was so much of a child herself that she hadn't fully comprehended the wickedness of such a dangerous fabrication.

Aware that they were surrounded by scores of curious men, he forced himself to release her and step back. "You're fortunate to be so well acquainted with the sea. It'll make the crossing that much easier for you."

"Yes, I'm very lucky," she murmured as she moved to take hold of the ship's rail.

That evening Christina stood on the quarterdeck of the *Mediator,* snugly encased in a primrose wool cloak, the fur-trimmed hood surrounding her face with its soft warmth. She watched a seaman check the tautness of the halyards below her on the forecastle. Canvas slapped and shrouds creaked as the sloop crested the waves like a dolphin in sportive delight. Overhead the full moon wandered in and out of thin wisps of clouds, revealing the scrubbed planking of the deck, now shining in the phosphorescent light, now cast in shadow.

Since that dreadful morning of the duel, Christina had felt totally estranged from her husband. Except for the incident on the deck when he'd rescued her from falling, this evening at supper had been the first time Rugden had so much as smiled in her presence. Relieved that his anger had finally dissipated, she recalled the cold, banked wrath that had seemed barely under control for over a week. He'd spoken to her only when necessity demanded it. Not that she was afraid of his displeasure, she told herself, leaning over the railing to enjoy the full force of the wind. Yet still, now that the rift between them was not quite so wide, she admitted she was much more at ease.

Bemused, she recalled the discussion they'd all enjoyed at the captain's table. From the comments made by the others, it was evident that her husband was a respected war historian and a brilliant military strategist. His knowledge of the world's great conquerors and the logistics of famous battles was detailed enough to fill a war encyclopedia. In addition, Hugh had mentioned that if Rugden should stay in the army, an important promotion would be immediately forthcoming.

Her husband had spent the greater part of his life, since he was twenty-two, outside England, and most of that in the field or on bivouac. The only music he seemed to be familiar with were bawdy camp songs and military marches. They had so little in common. Yet in the past two weeks she'd become more and more attracted to the stern, straight-backed, no-nonsense colonel. She'd begun to question her own judgment. Why should she yearn to be held in his arms? He was nothing but a rough, uncouth soldier, for God's sake.

In a splash of moonlight, Christina saw the scarlet coat of Major General Gillingham coming toward her. He walked with a strong stride against the roll and buck of the ship.

"You're still awake, Lady Rugden," he said as he came to stand at her side. His merry grin was infectious, the gap between his front teeth enhancing his small-boy charm.

"You'd make a good sailor with your sea legs already under you the first night out."

Christina turned to face Gillingham. The wind was blowing briskly, and she held her hood snugly under her chin. "I've been enjoying the beauty of the ocean, General Gillingham. I hope my absence from my cabin hasn't worried anyone." She pivoted to face the sea again and gazed out on the whitecaps glinting silver in the moonlight.

"Your husband knows your whereabouts. He mentioned you were here when I inquired after you. I hope you don't resent my intrusion. Sometimes a person prefers to be alone."

She glanced at the large man beside her and smiled. "Not at all, Hugh. I just couldn't bear to stay cooped up below deck when the night's so splendid. It's very romantic on the sea."

Gillingham propped his hip against the railing and crossed his arms. He gazed at her thoughtfully. "Females sometimes mistake a smooth tongue and a glib manner for romance. Often the most infatuated men say the least—possibly because they feel so deeply."

Christina wondered if he were hinting at his own past disappointments. "Such as yourself, General?" she questioned softly.

"Such as your husband," answered Hugh. "It's always been a source of wonder to me how a man who's so adept at conversation with all sorts of people, great and small, can become near tongue-tied in the presence of one particular little lady."

"I understand that my husband is quite a hero," Christina cautiously remarked. "Duncan told me of his exploits in Quebec." She realized Hugh was concerned about her unhappy marriage. It seemed the wise general had no idea of the feigned pregnancy and its disastrous effect upon her relationship with Rugden.

"That was just one of his many courageous feats, Lady Christina. Roderick wouldn't have been chosen for the position he'll soon hold at the negotiating table if he didn't have a record of uncannily shrewd martial tactics behind him. And he's going to need all his talent and wits about him, for he'll be pitted against some of the best minds our enemies can muster. In Paris we'll set aside our weapons to fight with words, and, damn, I can't say I like it. But when it comes to bellicosity, Rugden is even more agile with his tongue than with his sword, if that's possible."

Having been a victim of his tongue-lashings, Christina found it very easy to believe. "Were you stationed in the North American colonies with my husband, General?"

"Aye, for several years. We spent some time together with our allies, the Iroquois. We wintered with them in '59, having been caught after the defeat of Quebec with our supply lines cut by the frozen rivers. Nothing you've seen in England can equal the freezing temperatures and blowing drifts that sweep through the region. Without the help of the Indians, we would have died."

"You lived with the savages?" asked Christina with curiosity. "How appalling!"

"What was appalling?" Rugden said. Her husband had joined them unexpectedly. The sounds of the ship running before the wind had muffled his footsteps.

"I've read about the aborigines of the New World," Christina answered. "They have the most abominable practices. I shudder to think what it must have been like to spend a whole winter with them."

"Despite what you may have read, Christina," Roderick replied, "we found them not without hospitality and even possessing a nobility of their own." His lips twitched with amusement as he looked down at his astonished wife, who stared up at him as though he were half savage himself. "They taught us how to survive in the terrible snowstorms. The Iroquois have a rigid code of honor, which they live up to at all costs."

The two male friends exchanged glances. Neither mentioned, of course, the serenely beautiful Iroquois princess who'd fallen deeply in love with Roderick and had spent the snowy winter with him in the warmth of her lodge.

"Aye, 'tis true, my lady," Hugh added. "But on the battlefield, the very sound of their war whoops would freeze the French's blood in their veins. The Iroquois show no mercy in combat, and they expect none."

The fascinated countess was full of questions about their exploits in the colonies, but she'd promised Marie, who'd taken ill the minute they'd set sail, that she would check on her before retiring. Christina asked them to tell her more about their adventures in the morning, and having received their pledge, bade them good night and went below.

Watching her disappear down the stairwell, Major General Gillingham gave his friend a resounding clap on the shoulder. "Your wife is very inquisitive," he said with a laugh.

The earl raised a scarred eyebrow in reply. "Yes, and so is my friend," he said crushingly.

Unimpressed with the colonel's daunting manner, Hugh grinned. "Well then, I might as well be hung for a whole loaf as a half. I'll just continue to be meddlesome. How goes the investigation?"

Roderick gazed across the poop deck into the star-filled night. "Not well. The men I've hired to delve into the finances of the Greater London Docks Company have found no records whatsoever. There were no plans drawn up, no rights of way secured, no customs officials bribed, no attempts to buy out existing waterfront properties or assume ownership of one of the legal quays. No one in either Lords or Commons, other than my sire, seems to have invested a single pound in the corporation. The two men whose names are listed as its directors haven't as yet been located. There's no sense in applying to the courts. I've seen the notes paid by the bank. They're written in my father's hand."

"Why, by all that's holy, would Myles Fielding sink his entire fortune into a venture that no one else ever heard of?"

Roderick's eyes narrowed in thought. "My father was a most conservative and cautious man. Why he'd invest such an enormous amount in any scheme, let alone such a foolish one, is impossible to fathom. I can't believe he would."

"Then the entire affair could be a goddamn swindle perpetrated on the late earl just before he died."

"It's possible."

"Did your father have any enemies?"

"I remember some turmoil involving the Duke of Carlisle just before Pansy was born. I know my father hated the man—there may even have been a duel, but I was never told. Whether the secrets surrounding the Greater London Docks Company involve Carlisle or not, I have to find the major shareholders and prove them criminally liable. Or I'll have lost forever nearly my entire fortune."

Despite the risk of offending his closest friend, Hugh continued his interrogation. "The acquisition of Lady Christina's inheritance was quite timely then?"

Rugden bent forward, propped his elbows on the quarterdeck rail, and watched the whitecaps splash beneath him. "You're correct on that point, Hugh," he said in a terse, frustrated voice. "I had to swallow my pride and come to my new bride with the resources of a damn pauper. I'm forced to use her funds. As you may surmise, the investigation is outrageously expensive. And it must be continued at all costs."

"Oh, Lord, aye! But don't let your inordinate pride stand between you and your exquisite wife, man. You've more than a fortune to lose, and you'll never find another Christina."

Staring into the wind-whipped ocean, Rugden straightened and clenched the rail with his strong hands. "I won't lose my wife, Hugh. Whatever else may happen, that much I can promise you."

Hours later, when he was certain his wife was sound asleep, Roderick entered the cabin. With Marie's help, she'd managed to remove her corset, and it lay, along with her gown and petticoat, on a trunk in the corner. Christina was sleeping peacefully on the top bunk, one arm draped over its edge, the other curled beneath her pillow. She wore a high-necked cotton nightdress, and the pure white ruffles framed her chin, making her look even younger than her nineteen years.

He walked over and stared at her, making use of the seldom acquired opportunity to study her close up and unimpeded: the fluid line of the high, arched brows; the feathering of her thick brown lashes against her cheeks; the finely molded lips slightly parted in sleep, their corners curved up as though she were dreaming of her coming excursions in Paris. He took the graceful hand that dangled free of the bunk in his own large one. Her pale fingers were fine-boned and delicate, the pink, oval-shaped nails exquisitely feminine against his callused palm.

Sexual desire, which had smoldered all evening, carefully banked, now roared through his veins like molten fire. He throbbed with a primal male drive that surged through every pore, till he could taste the hunger in his suddenly dry mouth. Jesus, he wanted her. He wanted to lift her down onto his own bunk, to push the prudish nightgown above her silken breasts and cover her soft body with his hard one, to thrust his thickened, pulsating staff into her sleep-drugged woman's flesh and have her slowly wake to find him inside her. In his mind, he could see her beautiful blue eyes, heavy-lidded and drowsy, gradually become aware of his taut flanks pressed between her ivory thighs, of his turgid manhood buried deep in her slick folds as she drifted into consciousness. But by then he'd have brought her slumbering, passive body to full arousal, and they'd sail together into that fevered sea of erotic ecstasy.

His heart booming against his ribs like an artillery barrage, Roderick kissed the tip of each dainty finger. She stirred, and he gently placed her hand on the woolen blanket that covered her. Then he glanced around the small quarters, found his tin of cigars, and retreated up the companionway to the quarterdeck. It was going to be a long, long night.

Chapter 14

When they came down the gangplank at the Port of Le Havre the next morning, the English visitors were met by a detachment of Louis XV's own Life Guards. Capitaine Antoine Duvergier, Comte de Chastellux, snapped a salute to Gillingham and Rugden, and proudly introduced himself. Then he turned to kiss the hand of the British colonel's lady. Though Duvergier's green eyes rested only briefly on Christina's face, his fierce blond mustachios seemed to quiver in anticipation as he bent over her gloved fingers.

"I've been sent by the Duc de Choiseul to ensure your comfort and safety during your stay in our country, Monsieur le General," Duvergier said. "If you'll be kind enough to allow us, we'll accompany you to Paris."

Christina and Marie rode in an enormous, old-fashioned coach with a large part of the luggage. The overflow was transferred to a farm wagon that brought up the rear of the entourage. At the sight of the two great, lumbering vehicles, the Englishmen quickly accepted the captain's generous offer of mounts.

The travelers were overtaken by an accident near Mantes on the morning of the sixth day. The coach's right wheel came off and the vehicle had to be abandoned. A spirited filly was procured for the countess, who continued the journey in a riding habit hastily pulled from a trunk, while Marie sat atop the luggage on the rickety farm wagon.

Christina entered the city of Paris on horseback through the Porte des Ternes, riding beside Rugden, Gillingham,

and Duncan, and accompanied by a detachment of His
French Majesty's Life Guards. They moved slowly along
the crowded Rue du Faubourg-St.-Honoré, inching their
way through the diverse populace of peddlers and shop-
keepers, craftsmen and beggars, clergy and noblemen.
Turning south, they passed the classical buildings of the
Chateau of the Tuileries, which once housed the kings of
France, and crossed the Pont-Neuf, whose high stone
arches spanned the Seine. At last they rode into the charming St.-Germain suburb, where a hôtel on a wide, tree-
lined boulevard leading from the river had been rented for
them by the British ambassador.

They called at the British embassy their first morning in
Paris. Lord Hertford, the ambassador, and John Russell,
Duke of Bedford, the English king's special envoy, met
with their countrymen for over an hour. The two diplomats
explained to the new arrivals some of the personages they
would face across both the bargaining and the dining tables.

Hertford leaned back in his heavy chair and folded his
plump, beringed hands across his velvet-covered paunch.
"At this point the negotiations remain strictly unofficial.
We don't want our Prussian allies even to suspect that
peace proposals are being discussed. Hence, later along,
we'll be meeting secretly at His Majesty's summer palace
at Fontainebleau."

The ambassador was seated at an enormous desk, over
which he peered at his fellow negotiators. "The French
king feels that he is above the bargaining—says he won't
act like a common merchant. The real power behind the
throne, as you well know, is the Marquise de Pompadour
and her group of confidantes—Choiseul, Bernis, and the
Maréchal de Belle-Isle, to name a few. Don't underestimate her. She's intelligent, well-educated, and shrewd in
political affairs. It's rumored that she's ill and anxious to
end this war. But only if France can retain some shred of
dignity throughout the peace process."

The Duke of Bedford, from his place beside a high window, shook the delicate lace of his sleeve, snapped open
his snuffbox, and added, "The other person to watch

closely is the Duc de Richelieu. He's clever as a fox and has the king's ear. Though not a friend of the marquise, he's too powerful for her to dispense with entirely. Especially after his victories over our troops, unbelievably lucky as they may have been."

Hertford smiled pleasantly at Christina. "But Louis does want to meet you and extend a formal welcome. Till then, you're free to relax and enjoy the city. The other members of our team will be arriving in the next few days. You'll be meeting them as soon as they reach Paris."

He rose to his feet and continued pleasantly, "You'll find the court at Versailles congenial to foreigners, but very snobbish. If they value anything in this world—and sometimes I doubt they do—it's wit and clever conversation. Many of them have considered this entire war a great joke. Some of the nobility have laughed openly at the defeats of their own generals. But don't underestimate them, either. They can cut you to ribbons with their tongues."

"I appreciate what you're saying, Lord Hertford," Rugden said. "I spent some time here just before the war and also during my studies as a youth. I'm familiar with their penchant for gossip and sly puns. But I think we can hold our own in their salons as well as at the negotiating table."

"Egad, I'm glad you have so much faith in me!" Gillingham burst out. "I'm the one who stammers when a pretty face appears, remember?"

"Nonsense," said Christina. She smiled up at the large man beside her. "I've a feeling the French ladies will treat you very gently." She frowned thoughtfully and added, half to herself, "I only hope my wardrobe will pass their critical inspection. Thank God for Madame Boucher's unfailing sense of fashion."

Four days later they were presented at Versailles. Christina pondered long and hard over her choice of costume for this auspicious occasion. With Marie's unerring advice, she'd finally decided on a gold moire-silk gown trimmed with dull gold lace and black satin bows. At Rugden's suggestion, she bravely left her curls unpowdered and placed only one tiny black patch beside her nervous lips.

Standing next to her husband, who towered above her in his scarlet dress uniform, she gazed about the long state rooms filled with milling courtiers. Major General Gillingham and Ambassador Lord Hertford waited beside them, attired in equal splendor. They'd been instructed in the old-fashioned etiquette of the court by their stately usher, Dufort de Cheverny. He'd left them momentarily to prepare their entrance in the Council Room, but returned now to guide the way through a throng so preoccupied with precedence that a quarrel could easily arise over who would walk through a doorway first.

"Pray, follow me," Monsieur de Cheverny said. "His Majesty is ready to receive you." He led his charges through the crowd in the Oeil-de-Boeuf with the smooth, detached professionalism of a pickpocket working his way through a Martinmas fair.

In the Council Room, more courtiers, peers, and ministers elbowed one another. They gathered in front of Louis XV, who stood alone behind a balustrade, which the English visitors had been warned not to cross without the king's express permission. Christina resisted the temptation to grab hold of her husband's hand.

Louis was a tall man with a long face and a large nose over quite nice brown eyes. His wig was curled and powdered in a rather conservative style, with a large black bow in the back. The king was bored. There was no doubt in Christina's mind that he barely looked at them.

"We welcome you to our country and hope you have a pleasant stay," he muttered, just loud enough to be heard. He dismissed them with a nod.

Astonished, Christina managed the three required curtsies, gracefully kicked aside the heavy train of her court dress, and walked backward to the door.

Outside the Council Room, Lord Hertford smiled and rubbed his chubby hands together. "Well, that came off splendidly, splendidly. Considering the king's innate shyness and the purpose of your stay, we couldn't have hoped for more! After that presentation, you'll be permitted to visit Versailles whenever you receive an invitation to a supper or ball. And seeing the rampant curiosity on the faces of the onlookers, you may expect quite a few."

"But the king barely noticed us," Christina said in a low voice. She tried to keep her disappointment from being too apparent.

There was a suspicious glimmer of laughter in the earl's gray eyes. "Oh, he noticed us, Christina," her husband said. "Or at least he noticed *you.*"

For the rest of the week Rugden devoted his time to exploring Paris with his bride. "Take a pair of stout shoes, if you possess such an item, and a wide bonnet," he told her the morning after their presentation at Versailles. "We'll be walking all day—or until you cry enough."

It was the first of October. The fine weather of early autumn only served to enhance the beauty of the two-storied city, with its cobbled quais at the water's edge and its stone balustrades that held back the press of buildings, while providing a gallery from which to view the river. The stone walls were hung with ivy, atop which were perched fishermen who lowered their long poles over the Seine. On the quais below were benches and shrubs, creating little gardens.

The river itself was a long, lovely park meandering through the heart of the city. There was a thicket of bridges, under which Christina and Rugden floated in a small rented boat, viewing the lovers and vagabonds who sheltered beneath them. On water turned bronze in the sunlight, they glided past barges gleaming with fresh paint, past the boats of laundresses and fish sellers, past splashing bathers on the edges of the islands. They stopped for lunch at a café and feasted on *choucroute garnie.*

"Who'd believe sausages and cabbage could taste so wonderful!" Christina exclaimed. "What shall we do next?"

"You're insatiable, sunshine," Rugden scolded. But his smiling eyes belied the criticism, and they were off again, like children, to see the Cathedral of Notre-Dame on the Ile de la Cité.

Together they gawked at the Palais Royal and then finally sought shelter from the sun in its cool garden.

Perched beside a bubbling fountain, Christina looked into her husband's eyes, and suddenly, without cause, without warning, felt painfully shy. It might have been the unprecedented tenderness with which he treated her that day. Or maybe it was the city itself, so magical in the fall sunshine. Whatever the cause, this unexplained bashfulness was accompanied by the tremendous physical response she always felt in his presence. Could it be possible that she was falling in love with him? Or was it simply the normal reaction to his tolerant indulgence of her every whim during their happy excursions?

All day Rugden's behavior had remained unfailingly polite. He'd uttered no word to indicate that his feelings toward her had altered, one way or the other. Fearing to show the change in her own heart, she chattered endlessly about the things they'd seen. She was determined that he'd never guess the wild ideas that raced through her mind. It was useless to wonder about his thoughts. She had no option but to continue the deception she was living. If he did begin to have tender feelings for her, he'd soon change his mind, once he learned that she'd lied to him so wickedly.

Whether or not France's Bien-Aimé had noticed the countess of Rugden, the couple returned to Versailles four days later to attend a ball given in honor of the Maréchal de Belle-Isle. Once again Rugden had refused to don a wig, or even to powder his raven locks. Neither would he carry a cane, fan, or quizzing glass. He was, however, impeccably dressed in dark brown satin. His thick hair was pulled back ruthlessly from his scarred forehead and secured at the back of the neck with a ribbon. There was nothing of the delicate courtier about him. Except for his flawless French, he was the complete opposite of the court hangers-on whom Christina had seen in the Oeil-de-Boeuf the day of their presentation.

She paused in admiration at the drawing room door when she came down to join him for their departure that evening. He was truly magnificent in his stark severity. "I've never seen you look more handsome, Rugden," she blurted out with frank honesty.

"Nor have I seen you more devastating, Lady Rugden,"

he answered with a crooked smile. His silvery gaze glinted with amusement as he helped her with her cloak. "Hugh's driving out with Lord Hertford and the Duke of Bedford. We'd best be on our way, or we'll find ourselves at the end of a very long procession."

His words proved correct. For this court function, neither they nor anyone else needed a special invitation. All that was required by the liveried servant at the door was one's name and the proper dress. As they drove up the Avenue de Paris amid a solid stream of coaches, two abreast and each lit with its own bright lanterns, Christina peered at the river of light stretching from the city of Paris to the palace in the countryside.

To Christina, stepping down from their coach at the foot of the marble staircase, it seemed as though the entire populace of Paris must have decided to attend that night. The English couple were swept through the queen's state rooms into the Galerie des Glaces and on to the reception rooms, where both a buffet and an ensemble had been provided in the hope that the crush in the gallery would be relieved.

The Galerie des Glaces was ablaze. The candlelight reflected in the tall gilded mirrors dazzled the eye and made the crowd seem even larger. The high ceiling was lavishly decorated with bronzed figures of mythical beings that surrounded the countless chandeliers suspended from the center on long ornate chains. Christina looked down in distress at her new satin slippers, studded with diamonds on the heels, certain they were doomed to be stepped on. It was hard to find a place to put her own feet, harder still to find room to flutter her gold-edged fan.

Rugden guided her to an alcove by a high, arched window in the hope she might have some air. "Wait here, sunshine, and watch for Hugh. I'll see if I can make it to the buffet and back with something for you to drink."

Christina surveyed the panorama of the French court stretched out before her and made a determined effort to hide her excitement. It seemed that everyone knew everyone else. Many curious glances were sent her way, with casual asides made behind spread fans or lifted quizzing glasses. Grateful that she'd chosen to powder her hair, she glanced down at her beautiful cream-colored gown with its rows of tiny blue ribbons. Then she held her head high, proud that she was an Englishwoman, but also happy she was fluent in their language. Spotting Capitaine Duvergier, who'd escorted them from Le Havre, she waved politely.

Duvergier immediately left the circle of courtiers and made his way to her side. "Madame la Comtesse, what a pleasant surprise to find you in this mob. One has to be mad to come to Versailles at a time like this. But I, for one, had no choice. I was specifically requested to be here for the maréchal's honors."

"You know Belle-Isle, then?"

"Yes, *chérie.* The maréchal's son and I were close friends. The Comte de Gisors was killed in the war. Everyone thought the loss of his son would destroy Belle-Isle, but he is determined to stay on in the Ministry of War, as the king has begged him to do. That was de Gisors's young widow you saw me with just now."

"War brings great losses to us all, Capitaine. My family was incredibly lucky to have my brother Francis survive. He was present at some of the terrible defeats in which we suffered such heavy casualties at the hands of the Duc de Richelieu."

Someone approached, and Christina looked up with a smile, expecting to see her husband. Startled, she stared into the arrogant face of Justin Somesbury, Duke of Carlisle. "Your Grace," she said, recovering her wits, "you're here in France! I hadn't heard that you were a part of the English colony in Paris. May I present you to the Comte de Chastellux?"

"I'm not, *ma belle,* a member of the negotiating team, if that's what you're referring to. I came to Paris on a more personal errand." Carlisle, dressed as always in unrelieved black, negligently tipped his head to the guardsman. "Monsieur le Capitaine and I are acquainted. The comte is married to my cousin's sister-in-law. How are the Comtesse de Chastellux and your two so charming offspring, Duvergier?"

A wicked smile gleamed on the hussar captain's face. His thick mustache curled in a golden frame about his perfect white teeth. *"Touché,* my dear relative. My family was well the last I had news of them. Due to her poor health, my wife rarely leaves our chateau on the Loire."

The Duke of Carlisle took Christina's hand and brought it to his lips. "If you'll permit me, *ma petite,* I have some friends who've begged for an introduction. When they discovered that I was acquainted with the fair English angel everyone's talking about, they wouldn't cease their clamoring until I agreed to bring you over and present them."

"I'd be happy to comply, Your Grace, but I'm waiting for my husband to return with some refreshments. If I leave this alcove, he might never find me in this crowd."

"I dare swear," drawled Carlisle, as he took her hand and placed it on his sleeve, "our good friend Duvergier will be honored to wait here and inform the earl of your whereabouts." Without bothering to hear the captain's reaction, Carlisle led her across the gallery to a large group of people and presented her with a courtly bow.

A ravishing beauty about Christina's own age, with lustrous brown curls, stepped up to her. Her dark eyes flashed with friendliness. "I'm Septimanie, Comtesse d'Egmont, madame. You must pardon all the boorish stares of my compatriots. It's not often that such a handsome pair as your husband and yourself are seen. Usually in France, a beautiful young woman is married to some decrepit old roué like my father."

At the burst of laughter that accompanied her words, Carlisle leaned closer to Christina and spoke softly in her ear. "Her father is the Duc de Richelieu. At the moment he's angling for an alliance with a lady far younger than himself. The old mummy is indefatigable in his amours."

Christina returned Septimanie's warm smile. "You're very gracious to have noticed us, Comtesse."

"Vraiment, I must be honest. It is your husband who has attracted the notice of all the ladies." Septimanie twirled her fan with a dramatic flair. "Such a physique! Such magnificent legs! We are consumed with envy."

The Duc de Choiseul intervened at this point. "Since the fair angel's legs must, alas, be left to our imagination, may I simply state for all the leering young men surrounding us, that Madame la Comtesse de Rugden is as fine an example of English porcelain as we've seen."

Choiseul was in roistering good spirits. His brick-red hair showed in patches through the inadequately applied powder. Bright blue eyes above a turned-up nose gave him the look of a pugnacious bulldog. Beside him stood his quiet wife.

Madame de Choiseul's grave brown eyes surveyed Christina. She spoke calmly and graciously. "Please ignore these incivilities, Madame de Rugden. You'll find that no one is safe from our ironic sense of humor. We welcome you to our country."

Roderick joined the group, along with Gillingham and Bedford. He was pleased to see that Christina had made the acquaintance of some ladies near her own age. He met the hostile gaze of the Duke of Carlisle for one brief moment and then turned to Septimanie. "What's this about incivilities?" he asked with a smile.

"Ah, my handsome colonel, we were just discussing your magnificent legs," Septimanie told him with an infectious giggle. "And wondering if your charming wife would share you with us." At the high-pitched titters behind her, she hastily added, "Your company, that is, monsieur."

"Before you frighten them away entirely, Comtesse d'Egmont, I'd like to present our visitors to Madame de Pompadour," said the Duc de Choiseul. "The marquise has expressed a desire to meet them."

He led them out of the gallery and into the Petits Appartements, where they were ushered into a salon decorated entirely in white and gold. At their appearance, Madame de Pompadour rose from a divan in the corner of the room. She moved across the floor with the innate grace of a born dancer. De Choiseul presented them with a flourish.

"So these are the English visitors I've heard so much about," said Jeanne-Antoinette in a breathy voice. She was gowned in blue satin, and pink and blue flowers ornamented her lightly powdered hair. She looked worn and frail. It was obvious that she was in failing health, although she was not much older than Rugden and still retained much of her beauty.

One by one, Bedford, Gillingham, and Rugden bent and kissed her hand. Christina dropped a graceful curtsy, and the marquise smiled at her.

"Ah, *chérie,* I can see why they call you Madame de Rayon de Soleil. You outshine the sun. Your praises have been sung up and down the state apartments. For our jaded court that is high honor indeed!"

Christina looked into the tired, lovely eyes and flushed with embarrassment. "Madame la Marquise is too kind."

"No, no, I speak the truth. I no longer dissemble, *ma fille.* I've seen too much hypocrisy in my life to add to the falsehoods which permeate these walls. But thank you for your gracious reply."

Her friendly gaze took in Rugden, who stood straight and severe in his uncompromising costume of dark brown. "And you, Monsieur le Comte. I'll not repeat the name our courtiers have given you, but you've also been aptly described.

"Monsieur le General," she said to Gillingham, "I hope an equitable peace will soon be reached. May your visit to our country be most pleasant."

She smiled at the Duke of Bedford and extended her hand. "When you return to England, you must give my fondest regards to my dear friend, the Duc de Nivernais, who stays in London in your stead. He writes that the English are a hard lot to bargain with. Perhaps we can better reach an agreement in Paris than in London."

The gentlemen bowed and prepared to leave. As an afterthought, Madame de Pompadour turned again to Bedford. "It is my wish to present the duchesse with a gift before you leave, Your Grace. May I ask what would please her most?"

The duke thought for a moment. "She greatly admires the beautiful dishes we've been using in the Hôtel de Nivernais."

The marquise smiled. "Then I shall send her a set of Sèvres china to take home with her. And a service for you, Madame de Rugden. I understand you are newly married. It will be a wedding gift."

As they returned to the Hôtel de Fontaine late that evening, Hugh, Christina, and Rugden reviewed the ball and its participants.

Gillingham was sprawled on the seat across from the

couple in their borrowed carriage. "Whatever the reputation of the French court, Lady Rugden," Hugh said, "you seem to have taken the citadel by storm."

Flustered at the reminder of the name the courtiers had given her, Christina studied her fingernails.

Merciful heavens! Lady Sunshine.

With growing inquisitiveness she recalled that Rugden had been dubbed with a sobriquet also. "I wonder what title they've given my husband," she mused aloud.

An unrestrained chortle escaped the general. "Tell your wife what they call you, Rugden. 'Fore gad, man, don't be so shy!"

The earl folded his arms across his broad chest. He glowered at his fellow grenadier. "You tell her, Hugh, if it amuses you so much."

Gillingham leaned forward, his hand near his mouth in a pseudo attempt at secrecy. *"Fier Barbare,"* he whispered theatrically.

Christina translated with slow precision. "Proud Barbarian." She glanced at her husband, who sat aloof and detached beside her.

"Oh, I see," she said. She unfurled her fan in one smooth motion and quickly concealed her grin of delight.

Chapter 15

The affluent denizens of the city dedicated to St. Genevieve deluged the English visitors with invitations following their formal presentation at the court of Versailles. During the cool October mornings, while the earl spent his time at the conference table, his countess received visitors in their luxurious Petit Hôtel de Fontaine.

Capitaine Duvergier soon became a frequent visitor, despite the forbidding looks of the lady's husband whenever he stumbled over the cavalryman in his drawing room. Taking advantage of the crisp, clear autumn weather, the hussar invited Christina to go promenading down the Champs-Elysées. Through his introductions, she made still more acquaintances. The cliquish French aristocracy was amused by her forthright enjoyment of their ancient city and indulged her extravagantly.

One person, however, made no attempt to gain admittance to the Hôtel de Fontaine. Justin Somesbury was neither so bold nor so foolish as to attempt to breach the Rugden fortress. But whenever the Duke of Carlisle discovered Christina at a supper or ball, he attached himself to her with ruthless determination. The frequency with which Carlisle succeeded in attending the countess at the various functions did not go unnoticed by the worldly Parisians. The possibility that the large colonel was being cuckolded by his countryman was avidly discussed.

Roderick was not unaware of the idle talk and attempted to warn his unsuspecting wife. He met Christina as she came down the staircase of their home early one morning.

When she explained that she planned to ride with a group that included Carlisle, he tried to warn her off.

"Sorry to be the one to pull in the string on your high-flying kite, Madame Flirtation, but it would be better if you were more cautious about whom you're seen with. The French are fond enough of tale-bearing. They take real delight in marital scandal. We're all on stage here, and your partiality for Carlisle's company has become a source of great interest to the gossipmongers. I suggest you keep the duke at his distance in the near future, before your names are irretrievably linked together."

Poised on the bottom step, Christina finished tugging on a pair of gray kid gloves. She interlocked her fingers to complete the fitting of the snug leather and frowned up at him in annoyance. "Like Lancelot and Guinevere," she questioned flippantly, "or David and Bathsheba?"

"No, I was thinking more in terms of Don Quixote and Dulcinea."

Her blue eyes widened in suspicion at his sardonic tone. "Are you becoming a jealous husband, perchance?"

Roderick propped his elbow on the gilded rococo balustrade beside her. While privately admiring his wife's trim figure, smartly decked out in a gray and black riding habit, he schooled his features to give no hint of his captivation. He had no intention of joining her long list of moonstruck admirers.

"Hardly," he said. "I'm more concerned with the political ramifications than the romantic, my dear. Since I face the French across the bargaining table daily, I prefer to maintain a certain degree of respectability. That's hard to do while my wife is making a spectacle of herself. Though you may not care what the courtiers of Versailles are whispering about us, I do. Perhaps I need to change the word *suggest* to *command* to make my intent clear. I'm ordering you to keep Carlisle at arm's length while we are in Paris."

The insinuation that she was becoming a public laughingstock bruised Christina's pride. His unfortunate choice of words heightened her aggravation. If she gave in to his autocratic demands on this or any other important issue, he'd soon succeed in wresting away her right to make her own decisions. She met his overconfident gaze and gave him back measure for measure. "Why, truly, I'm quite fond of His Grace. He's the most entertaining companion I know. I don't intend to give up his company on a casual whim of yours. Best keep your *commands* for your junior officers, my dear husband."

Christina flounced away, and Roderick was left to ponder the exact meaning of the word *fond*.

Later that morning, as she rode alongside the subject of their dispute, Christina resolved to discover if an open flirtation with the Duke of Carlisle could stir more than mere concern over appearances on the part of her exasperating spouse. Don Quixote and Dulcinea indeed! She'd make him eat those words.

Upon further consideration, she decided that it might be amusing to see just how much provocation Rugden could withstand before he admitted to jealousy. The chilling thought that he might never reach that point intruded on her inner ramblings. She strove to fix her attention firmly on Carlisle, who was addressing her for the third time with a smile of labored patience.

The next Thursday evening Colonel Fielding and his wife, along with Major General Gillingham, attended a soiree hosted by the Comte and Comtesse d'Egmont. They discovered upon their arrival that a musicale had been planned by their hostess. Septimanie begged Christina to accompany the renowned Italian virtuoso, Signore Calzabigi, who was the evening's center of attention.

While her concentration was devoted entirely to her playing, Roderick had the opportunity to watch his entrancing wife with frank enjoyment. The fact that her own attention, as well as that of the rest of the audience, was riveted on the performance allowed him to relax for once and study Christina with the lingering and appreciative eye of a connoisseur.

As he listened to and watched Christina, the rest of the ensemble faded into the background. But the irritating occurrences of the past week spent at the conference table kept intruding. The peace negotiations were not going well. Roderick reviewed in his mind the machinations of Louis XV's skilled diplomats. They had an extraordinary knack for anticipating every move the British made. Whenever the Duke of Bedford's negotiating team privately agreed to yield to one of their adversaries' demands, the French seemed to know beforehand. They accepted what should have been a hard-won capitulation with haughty assurance and remained unimpressed with British flexibility. Yet each time the Englishmen secretly concurred not to back down on a specific item, the damn Frenchmen agreed to the item without a quibble, pointing out their own willingness to compromise. The French were shrewd when it came to politics, no doubt about it.

At the conclusion of the recitative, the audience responded wholeheartedly. Praising both the brilliant singer and the gifted musicians, the guests drifted into the dining room.

Roderick was joined at the buffet table by the English ambassador, and Hertford voiced the earl's unspoken thoughts. "Well, Colonel, I must say, we don't seem to be doing too well with the French. They have an uncanny way of predicting our every move. It would have been disastrous had they been so perspicacious during the war."

"They've anticipated us at every step of the way, Lord Hertford. I could have sworn, from my parlor conversations with the French nobility, that we would have no trouble suggesting the inclusion of Canada in our reparations demands. I can't believe the New World territories mean so much to them. It's almost as though they're toying with us—as though they know just which items we'll hold firm on and which we'll negotiate.

"It's unfortunate that Major Gillingham and I are the only members of our team who have ever been to the American colonies," Roderick continued. "Believe me, Lord Hertford, you can't overestimate the value of the territories we could gain. There's untold wealth there, not just in the trackless wilderness that the French trappers have only begun to explore, but in the fertile land and immense virgin forests which stretch as far as the eye can see. We must not deviate from our original intention to acquire as much domain in North America as possible."

The British ambassador heaped delicacies on the plate that rested precariously on his round paunch. Studying the tarts, eclairs, and cream puffs piled in mounds on their crystal pedestals, he wagged his head at Roderick absent-mindedly. "Ecod, my good fellow, I'm not so sure that un-civilized land, filled with wild animals and naked savages, is as important to the British empire as you think. Maybe the French are correct—it's just a country inhabited by bears, beavers, and barbarians." He speared a chocolate pastry with his fork and added it to his pile. "Well, here's your colleague to support your views. I'll leave you to commiserate with General Gillingham on our lack of prog-ress while I further my acquaintance with our lovely host-ess. By the by, your lady wife plays exceeding well. You must be quite proud of her."

"Lady Rugden is very talented. I'll convey your compli-ment to her, Lord Hertford," Roderick said, attempting to keep the frustration out of his voice. Once again he had failed to convince the narrow-minded diplomat to push more strongly for the acquisition of Canada.

Hertford wandered away to seek the beautiful Madame d'Egmont, and Roderick greeted his friend, who'd been moving through several rooms, trying the various dishes set out on long buffet tables. "Have you seen my wife, Hugh? I won't be staying late tonight. We've early hours in the morning. I'd best collect Christina and say our fare-wells."

Hugh flashed his gap-toothed grin. "I'm not ready to leave just yet, old man. This place is filled with gorgeous women. The last I saw of Lady Rugden she was being se-duced into the opera by that sawed-off runt of a *castrato*. He was promising her a career unequaled in the annals of music."

Tired and irritable, Roderick gave a low groan. Cal-zabigi was only a minor problem, but still one more nui-sance to deal with. Roderick left the general and strode into the larger salon. He stood near the doorway and searched for his lovely bride, half expecting to find her be-ing pawed by the effusive tenor.

But Christina was not with the short signore.

Roderick's wife stood with her back to the wall. The Duke of Carlisle was directly in front of her, only inches away, and hovering over her as though she were some delectable trifle served up for dessert. The countess, gorgeous in a lime-colored confection of frothy lace and chiffon, smiled up at Somesbury, her expressive eyes locked on his goddamn arrogant face. Roderick was reminded forcibly of a huge, black beetle crawling over a trembling magnolia leaf. He crossed the room and brushed against the bastard's elbow. "If you'll excuse me, Carlisle, I've come to collect Lady Rugden."

Christina didn't even bother to look at her husband. "Oh, Rugden, no!" She pouted. "It's far too early to go home. His Grace was just telling me one of his amusing stories. I can't leave now."

It was a struggle, but Roderick kept his voice low and even. "I must keep early hours in the morning, my dear. The peace treaty can't wait upon our socializing."

A practiced exploiter of the opposite sex, Carlisle knew instinctively that he was being used to bait a jealous husband. Without compunction, he seized the golden opportunity to cause Rugden further misery. He glanced over at the earl and smiled mirthlessly. "There's no need to ruin the evening because of your onerous duties, Colonel Fielding. If the countess wishes to stay, I'll be delighted to see her home."

Roderick clutched the hilt of his dress sword. He surveyed the duke, purposefully taking his measure and praying that Somesbury would offer him the smallest excuse for a fight. "That won't be necessary. I'm certain General Gillingham will be happy to bring my wife back to our hôtel when he returns."

Christina barely glanced at the enraged male beside her. "Splendid, Rugden! Lady Septimanie would be so disappointed if I left her soiree early. And now, Your Grace, why don't you finish that naughty tale you were telling me? You can complete it while we find something to drink. It suddenly seems very warm and oppressive in here." Christina reached for Carlisle's arm, turned her back on Roderick, and sauntered across the drawing room floor in a brazen display of flirtation.

Livid, Roderick watched his audacious wife walk away with his enemy. Short of creating an ugly scene in a room filled with nosy French aristocrats, there was nothing he could do but acquiesce politely and leave Christina at the party. But once he had her home, he'd make damn sure it never happened again. After speaking briefly with Hugh, Roderick left.

Christina felt a chill go through her at her husband's abrupt departure. The fury blazing in his eyes as he'd said good night to Madame d'Egmont was something she'd never seen before—not even after the duel with Edwin. She could almost feel the intensity of his gaze across the room when he curtly nodded farewell to her. Frightened and suddenly filled with an aching loneliness, she had wanted to call out for him to wait for her. But the knowledge that he was so terribly angry only because of his concern for the political consequences of the gossip strengthened her resolve. She'd never let him know he'd hurt her pride. Let him feel a little jealousy over Carlisle. It would do him good.

On the ride home, Roderick gazed out the window at the night sky with unseeing eyes and brooded over the happenings of the past week. First had come the letter from London, telling him that the investigation into the Greater London Docks Company had ground to a complete standstill. So far the only thing Roderick had learned was just how expensive solicitors and private investigators could be. Next had been the frustrating negotiations with the French. His dream of bringing the Canadian territory under the British crown had never seemed so remote. Finally there was the matter of his wife's incomprehensible intransigence. He'd asked her to keep Carlisle at arm's length—not such a dear favor, surely, considering the duke's ugly reputation. Bad enough that she continued to encourage that swaggering hussar Captain Duvergier. One besotted admirer was apparently not enough for the greedy little countess. What was the saying? Lucky in war, unlucky in love? He sure as hell wasn't about to accept blind chance when it came to his wife's fidelity.

The silence of the Hôtel de Fontaine infuriated him even further. He nodded curtly to the footman who opened the door for him, and stormed into the house. He strode inside the darkened library, feeling the loneliness of the room seep through him to cause a restlessness he seldom knew.

He tossed his sword belt and coat over the back of a chair and rolled up his shirtsleeves. He went to a cabinet and poured himself a snifter of brandy. Then he sat down on an overstuffed chair and pulled off his boots. One by one, he dropped them with an annoyed thud on the rug. There was no other sound in the drowsing hôtel. Roderick finished the brandy and poured another, taking it with him up the wide stairs leading to the second floor.

His wife's bedroom door stood open and he paused, leaning against the jamb, to stare into that holy of holies which he had never entered. By God, he thought savagely, he'd enter it tonight. He stalked into the forbidden boudoir and looked about.

Against one wall stood a delicately carved dressing table, carelessly strewn with ornaments of jewelry and jars of cream. He lifted a cut-glass bottle of scent. Removing the stopper, he inhaled the sweet fragrance of roses, then set it down and wandered farther into the room.

His eyes became accustomed to the soft light provided by the single candle on the vanity table and reflected in the high mirror. He spotted the gossamer ivory negligee laid out carefully on the bed. It rested like a nest of swan's feathers on the green silk comforter. Roderick stared down at the nightdress and then slowly brought the smooth, cool satin to his lips. The wonderful smell of roses emanated from the gown, from the comforter, even from the curtains pulled back and tied with tassels on the four oak posts of the bed. The fragrance of his beautiful, elusive wife seemed to taunt him. Why did Christina prefer every other man to him?

An ache of desire wrenched through his body, and he hurled the gown from him with a curse. She might prefer other men, but, by God, she'd not have them. He wouldn't be cuckolded by every panting roué that came her way.

After picking up his goblet from a side table, Roderick sat on his wife's sumptuous bed. His stocking feet rested on the green coverlet; his shoulders relaxed on the tall headboard. He'd wait for Christina's return. Then he'd turn this charade of a marriage into a real one.

* * *

Less than an hour after the earl's departure, Hugh Gillingham suggested to Lady Rugden that he was ready to leave, as the morning in conference would be a long and demanding one. Relieved to be going, Christina hastily said good-bye to the Comtesse d'Egmont.

The ride home with the general was unusually quiet. Neither seemed inclined to discuss the musicale. When they arrived at the Hôtel de Fontaine, they bid each other a subdued good night, so as not to disturb the slumbering household. Each took a candle and climbed the stairs. Nodding again to Hugh, who was padding down the hallway to his own room, Christina entered her bedchamber and softly shut the door.

The room was dimly lit by one candle flickering on the dressing table. She set the candle she held next to it. Abstractedly, Christina removed her earrings and bracelet and laid them beside her brush and comb. She loosened the strings of her lime overskirt and let it fall to the floor with a soft swish. Her underskirt followed. Then she released the straps of the whalebone panniers, which landed on the silk petticoat at her feet. She stepped out of the garments and tossed them on the chaise longue nearby. Her stomacher was laced in front, and, watching her own nimble fingers in the mirror, she plucked at the strings that held it tightly secured over her chest. With a soft murmur of pleasure at her release from its confining restraints, she slipped off the bodice and draped it on the chair in front of the vanity. The marvelous feeling of freedom brought another sigh of contentment. She reached high over her head in one long, relaxing stretch, clad only in her sheer, knee-length chemise, silk stockings, and garters. She breathed deeply, and her breasts strained against the gauzy undergarment.

There was a soft rustle of bedcovers. She looked into the mirror directly in front of her and met the silvery gaze of her husband. She whispered in shock to the reflected image, "You! Here!" then whirled to face him.

"I've been patiently waiting for you to get into bed," he drawled. "Come over here, sweetheart, and I'll help you finish disrobing."

Rugden sat on top of the covers dressed in breeches and

stocking feet. His fine lawn shirt was unbuttoned, the sleeves rolled up to his elbows. The thick mat of hair on his chest, with its battle scar crossing slantwise to his waist, showed up starkly against the white of his shirt. A strand of his straight black hair had broken free of its queue and fell across his scarred temple.

She saw the empty brandy snifter on the bedside table and curled her lips in distaste. "Go to bed, Rugden."

"My intention exactly, sunshine. But first I'm going to administer a lesson in wifely obedience. Since asking you to avoid the Duke of Carlisle didn't work, I shall now instruct you on how a young bride should strive to please her husband. I'm afraid I must insist upon it. Your clever little parlor game of taunting the emasculated spouse went a tad too far tonight. I have absolutely no intention of standing by and watching another man make love to my wife."

"Don't be ridiculous!" She tossed her head impatiently, anxious to be rid of him before she betrayed the intense physical longing his presence in her bed had aroused within her. "Neither Carlisle nor any man has made love to me."

"No man?"

Christina spun to face the dressing table. She straightened the brush and comb and restoppered the bottle of scent with compulsive, jerky movements. Her voice shook with fright when she answered the sharply uttered question. "Except, of course, for the father of my child."

The earl left the bed with the silent grace of an Indian hunter, his footsteps muted on the carpeted floor. Coming up behind her, he slid his hands around her neck, then slowly massaged her bare shoulders with his long fingers. The blood pounded through Christina's veins as he slid his hands down her arms and entwined her fingers with his. Their gazes locked in the mirror.

"Come to bed with me, Christina." His voice was thick with passion. "I'll make you forget him, whoever he is. I'll show you pleasure no other man can match. I can bring you to heights you've never dreamed of and keep you there. Let me show you, darling."

An ache of desire seared Christina, leaving her breath-

less and flushed. Her breasts rose and fell under the fragile
lace of the chemise, despite her attempt to remain calm.
Her husband stood full against her. She could feel his sin-
ewy thighs press her buttocks. His silken words enticed
her, leading her to imagine what it would be like to lie
with him. Since the time he'd come to her bedroom and
kissed her so intimately, she'd been tortured by dreams of
stretching out beside him. Letting him kiss her. Kissing
him freely in return.

"You promised my father you'd not touch me without
my permission," she whispered hoarsely.

He released her fingers and turned her to face him. His
large hands framed her face, his thumbs stroked her jaw.
"When I made that pledge, Christina, I believed you were
a shy young virgin. Do you honestly think I'll stand idly
by while other men seduce you?"

He bent and kissed her. His tongue traced the line of her
lips, then boldly entered her mouth. She gave one quick
sob of need before regaining control of her shattered emotions. But it was too late. He'd heard it.

His arms enfolded her as the kiss became more passionate, more demanding. She could feel his satisfaction at her
uncontrollable response. If he weren't so busy kissing her,
he'd be smiling. She was certain of it. Somehow, she also
knew that he wanted her to explore his mouth in return.
He willed it, and she complied. She swept the moist cav-
ern with her tongue, and he met her in a duet of primal excitement. Her heart banged like a jungle drum, its rhythm
wild and erratic.

She thought she'd been trying to push him away and realized, half frantically, that she was clinging to him instead. With a will of their own, her hands had slipped
beneath his shirt. She traced the outline of his rib cage and
the ridges of his corded muscles with her splayed fingers,
then buried her fingertips in the thick black hair that covered his chest. He was thrillingly, uncompromisingly male.
She tried to stifle the moan of hunger that came from deep
in her soul.

He lifted her up against him. She could feel the hardened bulge of his manhood through her thin undergarment.
His hand slid beneath the chemise to cup her bare but-

tocks, and he groaned low in his throat. Then his fingers touched the very core of her femininity. She whimpered over and over, half sobbing in confusion as he stroked her into mindless submission. God, she'd never felt anything so wonderful.

She had to stop and think before it went any further.

But he intended to give her no time. He slid one muscular arm beneath her thighs, lifted her up, and carried her toward the bed. In those few seconds it took to cross the room, Christina regained her senses. She looked up to meet his stormy gaze, and the memory of his terrible rage earlier that evening shook her. Was this what he meant by a lesson in wifely obedience? He'd promised to instruct her in how to please him. This, then, was no more than a blatant attempt to dominate and control. She panicked at the thought that he'd nearly succeeded. The earlier feelings of passion dissipated in a surge of anger, directed as much at herself as at him.

"Put me down, Rugden."

He dumped her on the bed, placed one knee beside her thigh, and leaned over her. She immediately rolled on her stomach and began to crawl across the feather mattress toward the other side. Rugden caught her ankle and pulled her back to him with maddening ease, and the thin gauze of her chemise slid upward to bunch around her waist.

Christina tried to push up on her hands and knees and heard the sound of lace ripping asunder. She held the torn strap of her undergarment with one hand as she twisted around in her frenzied attempt to break free. Her breath came in short, ragged gasps. Her hair tumbled down around her shoulders in the fruitless struggle, and the long curls caught beneath her elbow as she tried to scoot away. She found herself pinned to the silken coverlet in front of him.

"The French are right," she told him scornfully. "You *are* a barbarian! You lived with the savages too long."

She tried to kick him, and he swung one heavy thigh across her bare legs in a casual move of unworried self-defense. He looked bemused, as though he was almost as amazed as she at the swirl of primitive emotions that charged the air between them. She was angry enough to scratch his eyes out, and he knew it. But he didn't mind her unbridled ferocity. Not one bit.

A wicked gleam lit his smoldering gray eyes. He grinned in slow, delighted self-mockery. "Then let me show you, my feisty little wildcat, how the savages treat their women."

Chapter 16

Before his wife had time to scratch and bite like the infuriated kitten she resembled, Roderick locked her fingers in his. He pushed her back down on the soft mattress and pinned her small hands on either side of her delicately boned face. She looked up at him, her blue eyes enormous with excitement and fear.

"I'm not going to hurt you, baby," he coaxed, purposely gentling his voice. He didn't want her frightened, only aroused and in desperate need of the bedding he intended to give her. He buried his face in the silken warmth of her partially covered breasts, then pulled the remaining strap of lace over her shoulder with his teeth, freeing the firm ivory globes completely from the torn remnants of the tattered chemise. His heart kicked in his chest at the sight. She was perfection.

He traced his tongue across the smooth silk of her skin and breathed in the female scent of her. As he suckled the rosy crests, he heard her reflexive sigh of pleasure. Her fingers slowly relaxed as the soft buds of her nipples grew hard and erect. He could feel the lethargy move through her, languid and erotic, as her entire body responded to his kisses. He nudged her legs apart with his knee. She lay with her eyes closed, sprawled motionlessly on the bed as though powerless even to move without his help. He released her hands and slid his battle-scarred palms over her sweet, sweet body, memorizing each smooth valley and plane. His starved lips tasted every delicious inch his hands explored. His fingers sought and parted the golden-brown curls at the apex of her thighs and caressed the soft pink petals of her womanhood. With a whimper of need, she lifted her hips up against his touch, marvelously responsive and uninhibited. He lowered his head and laved the rigid nub with his tongue.

"Rugden," she gasped. She pulled on his hair, her voice filled with shock and confusion. "What are you doing?"

He smiled to himself. So she'd never experienced this kind of mating before. His heart soared with the knowledge that, by introducing her to this voluptuous love play, he would establish a bond that would tie her to him both physically and emotionally. At last he would begin to exert the male power over her that he should have had from the very beginning.

She tried to squirm away. He wouldn't allow it. He captured her hips in his hands and held her firmly in place. Then he stroked her again and again with his tongue and his lips, till she was writhing and sobbing beneath him, her hands limp at her sides, her fingers curled loosely. He knew the second she reached fulfillment. There couldn't be any doubt. Her body convulsed against him, racked with spasm after spasm of pleasure, as she cried out in a long, low, ongoing sob of total female surrender. He'd been with too many women not to know she'd responded with a deep, unreserved eroticism. All the sensitivity and passion she brought to her music had been channeled tonight into a prelude of unqualified sensuality. She was made for love. His love.

He shed his clothing as she lay supine and passive, barely aware of her surroundings in the pulsating afterglow of her release. Her eyes were closed, and she didn't see the thick shaft that sprang, heavy and swollen, from the black mat of hair at his groin. He throbbed with desire. Gently, he raised her knees and positioned himself between her pale thighs. Bracing up on his hands, he leaned over her, ready, poised to enter.

"Christina," he called tenderly, and her lids drifted open. She looked up at him with thick-lashed, languorous eyes. "I'll go very slowly, very gently, darling, so as not to harm the baby."

Even now, racked with desire, he was totally aware of the urgent need to be careful. Her slim form showed no visible signs of gestation, but, by a few discreet questions to married friends, he'd learned that at nine weeks that wasn't at all unusual. He'd also learned that in the first few months any pregnancy was precarious at best. He met her worried gaze, letting her know his intentions, yet silently reassuring her that it would be all right, that he was still in control of his rampaging lust.

She reached up and brushed the stubble of beard on his cheek with trembling fingers, a look of dazed wonder on her delicate features. "Roderick," she whispered. "I have to—"

Her soft, hesitant words were interrupted by a wild pounding on the bedroom door. Roderick reacted with the instinctive purpose of a trained soldier startled in the middle of the night. He rolled off the bed and crouched, naked and wary, prepared to ward off any intruder with his bare hands.

"Who is it?" he shouted.

The unlocked door swung open, and Marie Boucher rushed into the room, clutching a brown woolen wrapper to her thin form. One long braid fell over her shoulder, the silver streak from her widow's peak crisscrossing back and forth through its coal-black strands.

"Miladi, is everything all right?" she cried. Her obsidian eyes darted from Roderick to Christina, who'd quickly covered herself as best she could with the torn chemise. "I came to check on you and heard voices."

Her abrupt, unexpected, and completely inappropriate entrance was as sobering as the fording of an icy river on horseback. Roderick straightened but made no attempt to cover himself. "Get out," he said ominously.

"Madame?" the maid questioned, foolishly ignoring him. She pressed her hands to her flat chest and moved three tiny, involuntary steps backward to the opened door.

"Now!" Roderick roared. He took a menacing stride toward her.

Behind the frightened maid, Duncan appeared in the doorway, a confused scowl on his sleep-wrinkled face. His bright red hair was nearly hidden by a long pointed cap; his bare toes stuck out from beneath a garishly striped nightshirt. As he took in the scene before him—his master's bare ass, his mistresss's wisp of an undergarment—the little batman grinned with undisguised glee. "I'll get the old witch out of here, Colonel," he offered. He rubbed his hands together in anticipation.

Holding the torn lace of her chemise over her breasts, Christina watched from the other side of the large four-poster. Her hands shook uncontrollably. Her legs felt as though they might give way beneath her as she walked around the bed, hastily scooped her night robe off the floor, and slipped it on. "Pray, leave us, Marie," she said breathlessly. "Everything's quite all right. Go, and I won't need you again till morning."

The maid stalked out of the room without another word. Duncan, pursing his lips and giving a silent whistle, closed the door behind them with a soft click.

Christina moved to the dressing table and sat down. She picked up the golden brush and faced her own dazed reflection in the mirror. Her lips were swollen and tender from his kisses. Two bright splashes of red highlighted her cheekbones. Nervously, she brushed at her tangled curls with quick, jerky movements in an attempt to calm herself and regain some small measure of self-control.

"She goes," Rugden said. He stood in the center of the rug, his hands propped on his hips, completely at ease with his nudity. "I want her dismissed immediately."

Christina refused to turn and face him. She'd already gotten a good, long look at the massive torso, the lean flanks, the corded thighs, the well-endowed maleness of him, as he'd addressed her rattled servant. Good gad, the sight was enough to overwhelm any woman. If she'd thought he exuded raw power in his scarlet regimentals, she now found his naked virility absolutely devastating. Only minutes before, she'd almost blurted out her deception. She had to have time to regain her equilibrium. Otherwise he'd press his advantage in this campaign for total domination, and she'd crumple like an insecure little child.

Her voice cracked as she spoke, but she was determined to provoke an argument. "Why? Because she interrupted your lesson in wifely obedience? I can't be left without an abigail here in Paris."

"There are plenty of French maids to be had."

"Not one who can speak fluent English like Marie. I need her in the midst of all the affairs we're attending."

Roderick pulled on his breeches and walked deliberately to the door. He turned to face her, his hand on the knob. Completely sober now, he looked his beautiful wife over from head to toe in a long, searching gaze.

"Are you all right, Christina?" he asked in a low voice.

She gripped the brush handle with whitened knuckles. "Perfectly. You haven't frightened me, if that was your intention."

A wry smile curved his lips as he opened the door. "That wasn't exactly what I had in mind, sunshine. Boucher can stay until our return to England. Directly there, she's to be discharged. You may give her a reference and a parting salary, but she's to go. That's my last word on it."

"Your *word?*" Christina said. She turned in the chair and looked pointedly at the rumpled bed.

"Yes, my lady wife, you have my word on it." Roderick left the room before he decided to finish what he'd started.

For the third time that morning Christina rearranged a bouquet of bright yellow chrysanthemums in their tall crystal vase. She carried the flowers across the blue and gold salon to set them on a spindly plant stand beside the tall windows. Sinking down on a sofa, she leaned her head back on its soft cushion and listened to the gentle patter of the autumn rain on the paving in front of the Hôtel de Fontaine.

How could she have been so foolish as to think she was falling in love with her husband? The magnetic attraction Rugden evoked was merely a symptom of some mindless infatuation—nothing compared to the higher plane of mutual communion she'd always dreamed she'd share one day with a man who fit her ideal. All she needed to do was regain control of her shattered emotions.

Her plan to arouse Rugden's jealousy had worked far better than she'd dared hope and with far worse results than she'd ever imagined. Previous experience had in no way prepared her for his fierce reaction to her ill-advised game of flirtation. She picked distractedly at the yellow fringe on the sofa pillow she clutched in her lap. Her scheming had almost ended in complete disaster. Dear Lord, she'd nearly babbled out the truth.

Christina's reverie was interrupted by the butler, who announced the visit of the Comtesse d'Egmont. Septimanie came rushing into the room behind him, her lustrous brown curls flying.

"Madame de Rugden, I wanted to thank you again for saving my musicale last night. It was a complete success! Everyone was praising your talent, especially Signore Calzabigi. You'll be receiving tickets to the opera this afternoon for tonight's performance. I'll also be attending with my husband. Say you'll go with us. It's always so dreadfully boring when I go alone with Monsieur d'Egmont."

Christina pulled the volatile girl down beside her on the settee and smiled wanly. "I'm not sure Rugden will feel like another evening of musical entertainment tonight. He was up and gone this morning before I came down to breakfast. Do you always find an evening with Comte d'Egmont boring, Lady Septimanie? Or just tonight?"

The lovely young woman shook her head. "You've met my husband, Comtesse. Surely you could tell how little we have in common. He was my father's choice, and no matter how I pleaded against the marriage, my father was implacable. I was madly in love with a young man, and he loved me. We begged my father to allow us to marry. The proud Duc de Richelieu would have none of it. He ridiculed us, saying we were foolish children to think we might wed for love, for there would be no political gain in my alliance with the son of a French nobleman. Oh, no! I was to be used as a pawn in the politics of France and Spain, regardless of my love for the Comte de Gisors." Teardrops glistened on the tips of her dark lashes.

"I'm so sorry." Christina reached out and took Septimanie's hand in her own. "The Comte de Gisors was killed in the war, wasn't he? Capitaine Duvergier told me about the death of his best friend."

"Yes, *chérie*. How I despised my father for separating us. When we told him that we would never get over our love, he scoffed at us and said there was no need to—that we could continue to see each other after our weddings. But, ah, *mon Dieu,* we could not bear even to look at one another, knowing that each was tied in marriage, forever beyond reach. I thought there were no more tears to cry, until I learned of his death. Oh, Christina, how lucky you are to be married to the man you love, and who loves you."

"What makes you say that?" Christina asked. She dropped Septimanie's gloved hand and scooted back on the sofa. Perhaps Rugden had been correct in his warning that all of Paris was discussing their affairs.

Her deep brown eyes glowing through her tears, Septimanie reached over and pinched Christina's cheek. "Silly cabbage, anyone can see that he's wild for you. His eyes follow your every move from across a room. *Vraiment,* the way he looks at you reminds me of my mama, when she was still alive, looking over a box of candy, trying to decide which to eat next. He looks at your hair, your eyes, your nose, your mouth, your lovely figure, as though he doesn't know which he'd like to sample first."

Christina's startled laugh pealed out. "My husband reminds you of your mama perusing bonbons? I can't believe it!"

"Oh, it is true, *je vous assure,"* Septimanie said with a giggle. They leaned back on the sofa and laughed uproariously.

At that moment Rugden stepped into the drawing room. "You ladies are full of good spirits this morning," he said. He moved to the sofa and bent to kiss Septimanie's gloved hand. Drops of rain glistened on his scarlet uniform and trickled off the gold braid of his epaulets.

"We were talking about you, Monsieur le Comte. But don't ask us what we were saying, for we'll never tell." Septimanie's chestnut curls swung back and forth as she shook her head.

Christina decided to brazen out the smothering embarrassment that afflicted her at the sight of him. After all, Rugden could have no idea that what had happened between them the previous night was something she'd never experienced before. Good God, never even dreamed of.

"We were wondering if you liked bonbons," she told him sunnily.

Rugden's eyes twinkled. "I suppose I like them as much as most men. Is this your inimitable way of telling me I'm gluttonous, or did you have some other defect of my character in mind?"

"Mercy, if we were to list all your faults, we'd be here most of the morning," she countered with a smile. "Besides, we're much too busy making plans for this evening. Are the negotiations going so well that you can return home this early?"

"Unhappily, no," Roderick told his wife. He reached down and twined a golden curl around his forefinger. "I forgot some documents. I thought I'd left them in my case, but I found them just now in my armoire. They shouldn't have been left lying about," he added with a frown. "I'll have to speak to Duncan later." He didn't add that he'd chosen to come back for the papers himself in order to check on her well-being.

Septimanie rose from the settee and turned the full force of her marvelous smile on her host. "Speaking of later, Monsieur le Comte, I've just invited you and Madame de Rugden to the opera with my husband and me. Please say you'll join us. Signore Calzabigi will be sending tickets this afternoon so we can sit in his private box."

"If my wife wishes to attend, Madame d'Egmont, I'll be happy to escort her." He extended his hand to Christina and drew her up from the sofa. "Are you planning on studying the *opéra comique,* my dear? Or merely Calzabigi's personal style?"

Christina's blue eyes sparkled, though she adopted a serious tone. "Oh, lud, aye! The opportunities for fame and fortune awaiting me in the opera would be limitless, I daresay. If I wish for some additional excitement, I could even go on tour through the capitals of Europe. An English countess on the Viennese stage would be quite a sensation, don't you think?"

Septimanie burst into laughter. "Oh-la-la, it would be scandalous! But if you go, I'll go with you. I can play the lute. We'd be the musical prodigies of the civilized world."

"I'm truly tempted," Christina replied. Her soft lips curved engagingly as she peeped up at him. "But it may be wiser for us to attend the performance tonight and just hum along softly."

Retaining his bride's hand, Roderick turned to Septimanie. "Perhaps you and your husband can dine with us after the performance. Now, ladies, I must return to my duties." He brought his wife's hand to his lips and kissed her tapered fingertips. "Till this evening," he said. He strode to the door, then stopped and looked back over his shoulder. "By the way, sunshine, if you leave that list of defects on my bureau, I promise to set aside time next week to study them. Then we can work on my reformation together."

At the earl's departure, Septimanie sank back on the yellow cushions and yanked off her dark orange gloves. "So you don't believe he adores you? Perhaps that's why you've chosen such dangerous playmates—to make your husband jealous. I'm surprised he allows you even to speak to the likes of the Comte de Chastellux and the Duc de Carlisle. Surely he's warned you away from them both?"

Christina tipped her chin up defensively. Joining her visitor on the sofa, she addressed her with obvious skepticism. "What's so dangerous about Capitaine Duvergier? He's always behaved with exceptional politeness."

"The capitaine is a notorious duelist, *chérie.* I'm amazed that no one has told you of his exploits." In her eagerness to convince Christina of the truth, Septimanie grabbed both her hands.

Stubbornly, Christina refused to be impressed. "What notoriety can there be in dueling?" she protested. "Lots of men have affairs of honor. My husband just fought one."

"*Naturellement.* But not every man has killed seven opponents, all of whom had the misfortune of having a very foolish wife who took an inordinate fancy to the capitaine's blond mustachios. Beware, Christina. Duvergier is fearless, and the fact that you are married to the fierce colonel means absolutely nothing to him. If the capitaine is moving slowly and cautiously, it is an indication of the depth of his desire for you. And he is a strong-willed man, used to having his own way where women are concerned."

Christina leaned back on the sofa with a worried frown. "And the Duke of Carlisle? Is he notorious here in France as well?"

Septimanie thoughtfully wrinkled her nose. "What is His Grace but enigmatic? Remember that Justin Somesbury is French on his mother's side. That hot Gallic blood runs in his veins. We're not so phlegmatic as you English, Christina. There's nothing a Frenchman likes better than a dalliance with a beautiful married woman. And if the husband should object, well, that's so much the worse for him!"

The visiting Italian opera troupe was extremely popular with the Parisians. In attendance that Friday evening to see the delightful opera written by Goldoni and set to music by Piccini, was almost every person Christina had met in her two short weeks in France. Members of the audience strolled about before the performance, visiting with friends, insulting enemies, and making romantic assignations. Surrounding the main floor were three tiers of private boxes, and the buzz of conversation reached high above the stage, where the Comte and Comtesse de Rugden sat, accompanied by the d'Egmonts, in Signore Calzabigi's private loge.

"Comtesse de Rugden, someone is trying to get your attention." Glorious in scarlet velvet, Septimanie spoke in a whisper as she touched Christina's arm.

Looking down at the brilliant panorama of the French aristocracy, Christina spotted Capitaine Duvergier studying her through a raised quizzing glass. When he realized she was looking at him, he lifted the glass in salute and gestured emphatically that he wished to talk with her. But the words of caution given only that morning by the lovely young friend seated beside her were fresh in Christina's mind. She shook her head at the aggressive hussar.

Clearly disappointed, Duvergier scowled and glanced at Rugden, who stood behind her, then accepted the momentary defeat with good grace. He shrugged his shoulders fatalistically, as if to say that if the lady didn't wish her husband aware of the capitaine's attentions, it would be as she desired. At least for now.

The Duke of Carlisle wasn't so easily warned off. He approached Christina during a long intermezzo after Rugden had wandered out of the loge for some fresh air. The silvery streaks etched on Somesbury's temples and the snowy white of his shirt were the only relief to his somber black costume. When the kiss he placed on her hand lingered too long, she tried to pull away. He ignored her and kept her fingers clasped firmly in his own.

Despite the nearness of the d'Egmonts, he leaned even closer. "Last night at the musicale, *ma mie,* I thought I'd breached the citadel at last. Now once again I find the princess has withdrawn behind the castle walls. What has happened since we were together?"

"Tonight the princess is safe within the keep, and the crocodiles have been loosed in the moat. Mind, Your Grace, that you don't get your hand bitten off," Christina replied, tugging unsuccessfully on her own. "After all, the lady *is* married. Some very malicious rumors have been spread about her. She feels it wise to avoid the Black Knight's company for a while. Considering the nature of her husband's position in this country, you can appreciate the need for circumspection."

Justin Somesbury raised his eyebrows in surprise. He hadn't expected Christina to be so frank about the rumors, which, he admitted to himself, he'd done his best to encourage. He retained her hand in his own and spoke in a raspy whisper. "Why, *mignonne,* I'd run a sword through any knave vile enough to disparage your reputation. Point him out, and I'll put a quick and sudden stop to his lying tongue."

Her fan fluttered nervously. "What folly! I've no names to give you, sir. And should I need protection, I have a husband who can enter the lists for me."

"If these innuendos have reached your lovely ears, *ma fille,* he'd better see to his lance and poniard."

With a strong, determined jerk, she freed her hand at last. She tipped her chin up in an obvious gesture of dismissal. "If Your Grace will be so kind as to excuse me . . ."

Roderick wandered through the crowded lobby. He nodded briefly to several acquaintances as he left the building, then stood at the top of the wide steps that led to the street. Gazing thoughtfully at the starry night sky, he reached into his waistcoat pocket for a cigar. A candle burning in a sconce beside the entrance provided a torch. He hadn't missed the interplay between Christina and Antoine Duvergier. He toyed with the idea of warning the hussar away and then discarded it. Such an overt step would most likely lead to a formal challenge, and a duel between one of the English negotiators and a popular military hero wouldn't endear the French populace to the peace treaty soon to be ratified by their king. That his gorgeous bride had absolutely no intention of keeping the Comte de Chastellux at arm's length seemed likely. Moreover, her acceptance of Carlisle's attention the previous evening had indicated her refusal to accept her husband's guidance in that matter as well.

He leaned against the iron railing that led down to the cobblestones and exhaled the fragrant tobacco smoke. Ignoring the several footmen, who were watching the puffs drift upward in amazement, he mentally calculated the effects of his own behavior the night before.

As irritated as he'd been at the time with the entrance of that damn interfering maid, he had, paradoxically, been relieved the next morning. The last thing he wanted was to chance harming either Christina or her unborn child. He realized he was being overcautious, but the deaths of both his mother and his first wife in childbirth were losses that had left their painful marks. All his hardheaded logic couldn't change his deep-seated fears. He knew the safest course was to wait until after the birth.

In the meantime he was being flayed alive by his primal need and his growing jealousy. Christina believed herself deeply in love with the baby's father. Yet last night she'd surrendered to her husband, if only for a moment. He intended to use all the skill and expertise he possessed to make her forget the nameless bastard. In the meantime he wasn't going to wait around like a half-wit while other men seduced his wife.

He pitched the cigar butt into the street and reentered the opera house. Walking onto the crowded main floor, he glanced up to Calzabigi's private box just in time to see

Justin Somesbury kissing Christina's hand. How long would it be, Roderick wondered, before he faced the Duke of Carlisle behind drawn swords? Or turned his naughty little wife over his knee and administered the spanking she so richly deserved? He honestly didn't know which he'd enjoy more.

During the performance of *La buona figliuola,* Christina was once again impressed by the pure talent of Signore Calzabigi. She prayed silently that the proud tenor would never realize that he was being continually upstaged by two curvaceous, auburn-haired dancers who looked enough alike to be twins. That the bachelors at floor level noticed nothing but the beautiful Ramillies sisters became obvious to most of the audience. The whistles and cheers at the end of the performance made Christina laugh at the misdirected uproar.

She turned her head and met Rugden's amused gaze. "I only hope Signore Calzabigi never looks around to find those two redheads stealing all his applause with their antics," she said. "I doubt his fragile ego could withstand such a shock."

Rugden stood behind Christina, holding her cape up for her. "Calzabigi must be the only person in the theater unaware of their unique charms. No doubt he's only heard them singing from behind him and never watched the ladies parade their talents before the appreciative crowd. I've bespoken a meal at La Palette. We can continue our discussion of his performance over a bottle of fine champagne." He placed his wife's gold cloak on her bare shoulders, and his strong fingers lingered to caress her neck and sensitive earlobe.

The Duchess of Bedford was a blathering idiot. Arms folded across his chest, Roderick leaned against the doorjamb of the ballroom in the ancient Hôtel de Nivernais, two nights after the opera, and watched with disgust as that rotund lady simpered and flirted with a handsome French cavalryman. The soldier was half her age and half her weight, if truth were told—not that she'd be willing to hear it.

Roderick frowned at the comic scene. No doubt the middle-aged lady was flattered by the attention of the young Adonis. He hoped that in her lighthearted coquetry, she wouldn't let slip any political information to which she might be privy. As the wife of the special envoy in charge of the British negotiating team, she'd have had ample opportunity to acquire knowledge not meant for the ears of any Frenchman, let alone a hussar lieutenant. How many other English ladies in that spacious ballroom had knowledge that the French would pay dearly to gain?

The parquet dance floor was filled with their representatives. Choiseul, Belle-Isle, and Duvergier were all leading English ladies in a spirited gavotte. Was it possible that this was the answer to their adversaries' uncanny ability to predict every move the English team made?

His unhappy speculations were interrupted as the Duc de Richelieu entered the room side by side with Justin Somesbury, and he realized for the first time that the two men were cronies. Just behind them came First Lieutenant Charles Thompson, whom Roderick hadn't seen since the day he'd departed the H.M.S. *Mediator* in the port of Le Havre. He immediately made his way through the crowded room to the naval officer.

"Lieutenant, I wasn't aware that you'd arrived in Paris. I've been waiting for the dispatches I assume you're carrying."

Thompson saluted. "Yes, sir. I arrived in the city less than an hour ago. After changing into my dress uniform, I came directly here. I have the documents on me, Colonel Fielding. I was instructed to hand them over to you in person."

Returning his salute, Roderick took the papers held out to him and slid them inside his coat. "Well done, Lieutenant. I'll read them later in private."

Excitement glittered in Thompson's brown eyes. "There's one thing more, Colonel. I was told, just as I left Whitehall, that the first four pages are to be disregarded completely. Upon receipt of your suggestion that our intelligence may be landing in the Frogs' hands, sir, the first few sheets were added as bogus information. If the data they contain show up at the bargaining table later this week, we'll know for sure there's a spy among us."

Roderick smiled at the junior officer's fervor. He'd written to his superior in London of his suspicions, and this, then, was the answer.

"Good. Now we'll find out if there's a rat to be ferreted out, or just a careless old lady babbling to her young lover. Meantime, Lieutenant, I suggest you enjoy some of the refreshments set out by our hostess. But first, let Major General Gillingham know you've arrived with the dispatches. You'll find him enjoying supper, no doubt. After that you can help us partner all the elderly French wives on the dance floor while their husbands wonder what's in these papers we've just exchanged."

Twenty minutes later, her gloved fingers trembling, Christina peeked down at the note which the Duke of Carlisle had placed there only moments before. Since the evening at the opera, she'd steadfastly refused to be seen in his company. She had avoided a gathering only the day before which she suspected he might attend. Christina was determined to squelch any idle gossip about them, and she'd ignored his arrival that evening without compunction.

The cold glitter in his jet eyes and the uncompromising set of his jaw when he placed the folded paper in her hand had unaccountably frightened her. Slipping out into the hallway, she read his brief message.

Fair Angel,
　　Pray cease this cruel torment. How can you continue to deny your Exquisite Presence to me when you know how devotedly I worship you?
　　Meet me at eleven in the solarium and allow me to allay your fears. I demand you grant me this chance to reinstate myself in your good graces. You must not refuse me.

　　　　　　　　　　　　　　　　　　　　　　　　C.

Horrified at the bold insistence of his words, Christina drew a deep, inward breath. On no account would she

meet Justin Somesbury in an empty room. If they were to
be discovered, all her efforts to debunk the rumors would
be destroyed. She hurried to the nearby library, mercifully
deserted, where she discovered writing paper lying atop a
large desk. She would slip Carlisle a note, refusing unequivocally to meet with him. Scratching out the hasty
words, she folded the paper into a narrow slip and enclosed it in her fan. When a chance was provided, she'd
drop it into Carlisle's hand.

The stately minuet came to an end, and the dancers in
their glorious evening clothes slowly cleared the floor.
Roderick delivered the Comtesse de Choiseul to her
husband's side. Glancing around the crowded room, he
searched for his own wife. "Have you seen Lady Rugden?"
he asked.

The comte's round blue eyes twinkled with humor. He
scratched his snub nose with one pudgy finger and answered with a wide smile. "As a matter of fact, Madame
de Rugden was just going into the library a few moments
ago, Monsieur le Colonel, when I came down the hallway."

Leaving them with a polite nod, Roderick circumvented
the noisy throng in the ballroom and entered the almost
deserted hall. At the end of the corridor, beside the open
library door, stood Christina, exquisitely arrayed in a rose
silk gown. Next to her hovered the ebony figure of the
Duke of Carlisle. She was handing him a tiny piece of paper.

Roderick interrupted the cozy tête-á-tête without a
qualm. "Here you are, my dear. I've come to claim your
hand for the cotillion."

At the sound of his voice, Christina jumped visibly. A
guilty flush spread across her cheeks as she turned to face
him. Her beautiful eyes were enormous with surprise. Obviously stupefied at his sudden appearance, she gazed at
him like a tongue-tied simpleton.

Roderick kept his words low and deliberate as he approached the culpable pair. "I fear I've startled you,
Christina."

With the silent grace of a slithering cobra, the duke

placed the folded note inside his black coat pocket. He stared contemptuously at Roderick through narrowed eyes.

Christina's tremulous laugh put the lie to her innocent words. "Oh, not at all, though you have the softest tread of anyone I know. I was just directing His Grace to the library."

The pulse on Roderick's scarred temple throbbed, and a muscle in his cheek twitched spasmodically. "And what in the library could be of such fascination?" he said, his words clipped and staccato. "You were just there yourself, I understand."

Without hesitation, Carlisle interrupted Christina's stuttering attempt to reply. "The Hôtel de Nivernais houses a fine collection of rare manuscripts. Would you care to inspect them with us?" Flourishing his hand in an infinitely polite gesture and bestowing a mocking smile, he seemed to dare the earl to contradict him.

Roderick glared at the enemy standing so insolently close to his wife. "I think not, Your Grace. I'll postpone that pleasure until after I dance with Lady Rugden." He took Christina's elbow and led her into the ballroom.

During the lively cotillion, Christina's agitation became quickly apparent. She missed steps, lost her partner, and bumped into a fellow dancer within the first measure of the round.

"You're not quite yourself, my dear," Rugden stated as they re-formed their square. "Perhaps we should sit down and just converse."

The thought of a lengthy conversation with her husband frightened Christina even more than her awkward missteps in the dance. "No, no. I'm fine. I was just not concentrating, I'm afraid."

Had he seen the note? She pivoted to face the gentleman across from her, and they linked arms to start the grand chaine. If her husband thought she had a rendezvous with Carlisle, he was certainly taking it calmly.

Could it be possible, Roderick asked himself as he wound in and out of the line of swaying women, that Christina was responsible for the leak in communications? Could she be giving information to the Duke of Carlisle? The son of a bitch was half-French, and never, at the best of times, had he indicated any feeling of patriotism for England. Hell, he'd just entered the ballroom arm in arm with Richelieu himself. Damn! It would all fit together, if it were true.

That first night, when Christina had appeared on the doorstep of Rugden Court, she'd claimed that she had mistakenly taken the wrong coach. If they'd been having an affair, it would have been Carlisle's coach she'd expected, and no mistake about it. Was Justin Somesbury the father of her unborn child? That in itself would be motive enough for Christina to cooperate with the bastard. Roderick had inwardly accused Lady Bedford, when it could be his own darling little wife who was passing secrets to the enemy.

Early the next morning, having dressed with Duncan's assistance, Roderick remained deep in thought. Long after his batman had left with a pile of shirts over his arm for the laundress, the earl sat on the edge of his bed and stared in silence at the sheaf of papers in his hands. The evidence they'd soon produce would either free his bride from suspicion in his own mind or condemn her absolutely. He wondered if he really had the courage to entrap her. The idea of setting a snare for his beautiful countess to prove her a traitor to her own country, as well as unfaithful to her husband, was perhaps calling for more patriotism than he had. Yet if he didn't know, if he never proved her innocence to himself, it would haunt their chances of happiness for the rest of their lives. Summoning up an iron resolution, Roderick stood and placed several pages of the dispatch inside his coat, secure in the knowledge that no human being would read those papers without his permission. The first four pages he left in a neat stack on the tall walnut bureau and resolutely left his room.

Chapter 17

"I won't go!" Christina said. Her knife dropped with a clank against a fragile china saucer. "You can't send me home like a naughty child. I won't let you." She clasped her hands together in her lap and stared, wide-eyed and guileless, at her husband seated across from her at the breakfast table. "Besides, I've already planned an excursion with Septimanie this week. She's arranged a visit with Jean-Philippe Rameau. It's a great privilege, for he's been very reclusive in his old age. In case you don't recognize the name," she added, "Monsieur Rameau is a brilliant composer whose works are well-known to everyone in the civilized world."

Roderick threw his linen napkin down beside his plate. His wife's insistence on portraying him as a uncouth, half-savage soldier was a minor irritation. It was her pose of artless innocence that disgusted him. He rose and stood glaring across the table at the heartless little baggage.

When he'd returned the evening after the Bedfords' ball to find the papers apparently undisturbed, he'd been filled with hope. The trap remained unsprung, proving that his terrible suspicions were unfounded. And then the very next day, the information surfaced. The French had smiled politely, cocksure and smug, while Roderick sat across the conference table as stunned as if a piece of flying shrapnel had just struck him in the chest. Right in the region of his heart. If Christina was giving Carlisle her country's secrets, then most certainly she was also giving the duke her own exquisite body. And yet Roderick still couldn't bring himself to turn her over to the British authorities.

He leaned across his coffee cup and placed both hands on the highly polished mahogany tabletop. His deep voice was low and even. "You are going back to England, Christina, because I desire it. There need be no other reason. You've been here long enough to sightsee and shop. Now stop making a nuisance of yourself and go upstairs. I've already notified Boucher. She probably has the packing nearly completed by now. You leave tomorrow morning, madame wife, if I have to put you bodily into the carriage."

"Making a *nuisance* of myself?" Christina rose from her high-backed chair and leaned across her own place setting. "I deserve some explanation for this sudden curtailment of my visit. You can't fob me off without a reason. If it's because you're jealous of the Duke of Carlisle, you're a fool."

Rugden's silvery eyes glittered with rage. "Whatever my reasons, Christina, foolish or otherwise, you will obey me on this. You have the rest of the day to say your farewells, but they'd better be brief. I won't be home until late this evening. When I see you tomorrow morning, I'll expect the packing to have been completed." He left the room without a backward glance, closing the door with a bang.

Christina snatched up a china plate from among the breakfast dishes and hurled it at the closed portal. It shattered with a satisfying crash. She waited in vain, however, for the door to reopen.

Outside the Petit Hôtel de Fontaine, the Earl of Rugden entered an antiquated coach on loan from Versailles, his stormy visage warning the lackey who held the door to refrain from offering his usual cheery greeting. The strain of the preceding interview was still on Rugden's face, and, leaning back on the seat, he momentarily covered his eyes with his hand. Seated across from him in the large conveyance, Hugh Gillingham maintained a compassionate silence, wisely imitating the footman and keeping his own counsel. His unvoiced sympathy betrayed his concern for his closest friend, who was suffering the agonies of hell over his bewitching wife.

Avoiding Hugh's questioning gaze, Rugden dropped his hand and stared out the window at the Palais du Louvre with unseeing eyes. He admitted to himself one more time that Christina was right. He was a fool and a coward. He could no more turn her over to the authorities than he could murder a member of his family. And with her reprieve came Carlisle's, for in protecting his wife, he shielded his foe. Had any man been caught in such an ironic triangle? The only solution was to send her home immediately and put a quick end to her dealing in political secrets. There'd be no suspicion placed on his wife, of that he was reasonably certain, even though the contents of those four insidious pages had turned up at the conference table only two days after they'd been placed in his hands. Surely no one on the English negotiating team would suspect that a young lady of quality was a spy for France. He'd send her away and look for consolation elsewhere. Perhaps he'd develop a penchant for red-haired opera dancers.

Marie Boucher leaned over the green coverlet on the sumptuous four-poster and grumbled under her breath as she folded the sleeves of her mistress's cream satin ball gown around the fragile rice paper. *"C'est incroyable!* We come. We go. Unpack. Then pack. *Bonjour. Au revoir. Voilà!* Your husband has lost his wits, miladi."

Her own head bent low, Christina worked quickly beside the maid, laying sheets of tissue between each dress the servant placed in the large trunk. She didn't want Marie to see how upset she was. To be forced to leave Paris after only three weeks! She'd made such great plans with her new friends. She'd even discussed a trip with Septimanie to visit her chateau in the Loire Valley.

Earlier that morning the Comte de Chastellux had called. He'd taken the news of Christina's departure poorly. Seeing her unshed tears, Duvergier had offered to remove Rugden's foul presence from her life permanently, and she sensed that the bold hussar had spoken only partially in jest. He hadn't been joking when he'd asked her to run away with him.

* * *

The next day dawned bright and clear, a glorious morning for a broken heart. The autumn sky was a brilliant blue, with puffs of clouds drifting lazily above the city. Some of the leaves had begun to turn, giving a tantalizing intimation of the coming riot of fall colors that would soon paint the French countryside before the cold weather set in. But the Countess of Rugden wouldn't see Paris in the wintertime. She turned from the pastoral beauty framed by the front salon window to face bravely, once again, the crowded room. Word of her unexpected departure had spread like wildfire. The bell on the front portico of the Hôtel de Fontaine hadn't stopped ringing since breakfast.

She moved across the drawing room to greet a gray-haired lady who had just arrived. "Madame de Belle-Isle," she said brightly as she took the woman's gloved hand. "How very kind of you to call. It's such a pleasure that so many of my new friends have stopped to say good-bye."

"Dear Comtesse," came the soft-spoken reply, "we shall all miss you dreadfully. But I understand your family is in need of you at home."

Christina hid her disgruntled surprise. So that was the tale that Rugden had given out to explain her sudden departure. Faith, she could embellish on that lame excuse!

"As you know, Madame la Duchesse, none of us can avoid our family duties. But that's only part of the reason. I fear my husband is worried that I'll purchase so many fashionable frocks in Paris, he'll have to hire a flotilla to transport them across the channel." She lowered her voice to a dramatic whisper, one certain to carry to any curious listeners near by. "You know how miserly British husbands can be."

The Comte and Comtesse d'Egmont entered the salon, and Septimanie ran to embrace Christina. *"Mais non,* my little friend! I don't wish to say good-bye. You've only just come to us. I shall miss you so."

The Comte d'Egmont bowed and kissed Christina's hand. "I too, señora, shall miss your lively presence. My wife shall be downcast for weeks to come, for she has so enjoyed your friendship. *Vaya con Dios, mija."*

The arrogant Spanish grandee didn't seem nearly as aloof or as cold as when she'd first met him. "Thank you for your kindness. I shall never forget you," she said and kissed them both on the cheek.

She crossed the room to join Capitaine Duvergier, who stood beside the Duc and Duchesse de Choiseul.

The hussar's eyes glistened with sadness as he looked at her for the last time. "When you think of me, *chérie*, don't be too harsh in your judgment. I was married at seventeen to a young woman I'd never met. A woman who's as dour and gloomy as you are full of sunshine." He took her hand and lifted it slowly to his lips. *"Au revoir,* Madame de Rayon de Soleil. I shall never forget you."

Suddenly Rugden was beside her. "The escort is waiting, Christina. I'll assist you into the carriage."

It seemed the only person in the room not sorry to see her leave was her own husband. He appeared untouched by all the sad farewells, as proud and remote as the savage she'd accused him of being. No mercy, no kindness could be found in his cold eyes, though she searched them with a brazen, unrepentant look of her own. Feeling his firm grasp on her elbow, she smiled intrepidly at the people who'd gathered to bid her farewell. Implacably, Rugden escorted her out the door of their hôtel.

Hugh Gillingham stood on the top step, and, at Christina's appearance, he lifted her down from the porch and enclosed her in a fierce bear hug. "Courage, little one," he said softly. "All will come a'right in good time."

Over his shoulder, Christina saw her well-wishers, who'd come out of the mansion and stood watching her on the stone portico. She gave them all a carefree smile and a flamboyant curtsy, then waved a plucky salute.

"Adieu, my friends!"

Rugden opened the coach door and guided her up the carriage steps. The door closed with a click of finality. "Good-bye, Christina," he said quietly through the open window. Despite his look of impenetrable detachment, he clutched the sill with whitened knuckles.

Christina leaned out the window and stared into her husband's icy gray eyes. Their faces were only inches apart. "I shall never forgive you for this humiliation, Rugden," she whispered. "I shall hate you for as long as I live." Then she sat back in the carriage seat beside Marie.

Mounted on a spirited bay, First Lieutenant Charles Thompson, who had been ordered to escort the Countess of Rugden to the port of Calais and see her safely aboard the *Mediator*, moved closer to the impassive colonel. Thompson waited for orders, not making any attempt to hide the compassion he felt for the beautiful young countess.

Rugden glanced up at the naval officer. "I entrust my wife's safety to your care, Lieutenant. Carry on."

With a smart salute, Thompson turned his horse around and led the way down the wide, tree-lined boulevard, accompanied by a detachment of Life Guards provided most generously by His Royal Majesty, Louis XV.

Inside the coach, a dry-eyed Christina vowed never to forget who was to blame for the premature and disgraceful end of her visit to the ancient city of the Capetian and Carolingian kings.

The sailing from Calais to Dover was marred by an ominous sighting. The unseasonably fine weather had continued during their journey to the coast, and the friendly seas allowed even Marie to remain on deck during the crossing. Early in the voyage they spotted a sleek yacht, dark as ebony and trimmed in scarlet. She was sailing fast with the wind on the quarter, abaft the beam, and passed them easily, her foresails and topgallants stretched taut.

Christina stood on the poop of the *Mediator* with her servant and watched the weatherly sloop go by. "Oh, my," the countess exclaimed appreciatively, "she is bonny!"

Spotting Lieutenant Thompson striding toward them from the quarterdeck, she pointed to the magnificent ship. "Look, Lieutenant. Whom does she belong to?"

A smile lit his warm brown eyes. The officer came to stand beside the mistress and her maid, the tails of his blue coat flapping in the breeze. He shielded his eyes with his hand and gazed out across the green sea, then nodded his agreement of her praise. "She's a beauty all right. That's the *Crimson Queen* out of Ramsgate. She's owned by the Duke of Carlisle."

In that instant Christina recognized the figure in black standing on the sloop's deck. He was staring across the waves at her. He lifted his dark hat with its white plume and bowed with a gallant flourish. Watching the corsair pull away from them and move out of sight, Christina felt the grip of fear engulf her. No wonder Justin Somesbury hadn't bothered to say good-bye in Paris. She had the desperate feeling of a hare being run to earth by a hound.

Thompson must have noted her stricken reaction, for he moved closer. "Are you well, Lady Rugden? You look a little white."

The cool breeze tugged at Christina's curls, pulling them out of the snug blue hood with its fur trim. "You may think me quite deranged, Lieutenant Thompson, but I just had the most fanciful thought. What if it were the old days, when pirates captured good English vessels and took innocent passengers prisoner?"

The naval officer smiled kindly. "I can assure you, Countess, not even a pirate as fearless as the Duke of Carlisle could capture the H.M.S. *Mediator.*"

His words were proven correct. Late that afternoon they reached Dover safely, and, after saying farewell to a solicitous Captain Duckworth, Christina, under the conscientious supervision of Charles Thompson, spent a peaceful night at the Land's End in a room overlooking the waterfront.

In the morning she was met in the inn's courtyard by the lieutenant, who'd been supervising the packing of her trunks and boxes into the capacious boot of a large hired berlin. Near the vehicle, ready to escort her to London, waited a small detachment of Light Dragoons beside their mounts. The familiar sight of their colorful red and blue jackets brought a feeling of reassurance to Christina.

Thompson's expression was somber. "I'll send the rest of your luggage on a cart, Lady Rugden. It won't be far behind you. I'm afraid we say our good-byes here. I must return to the *Mediator,* for we sail to France on the evening tide. I've just received more dispatches, which must be placed in your husband's hands as soon as possible. It's a matter of greatest urgency."

"Is there some trouble, Lieutenant?"

"Nothing that need concern you, Countess. We've been

attempting to ferret out a spy among the English delegation. Apparently someone in Whitehall has cast upon a likely suspect."

Christina smiled and held out her hand. "Then I wish you godspeed, Lieutenant Thompson. I hope this traitor will be apprehended and quickly brought to justice."

"Thank you, my lady." Thompson took her hand and spoke hesitantly. "Er, I would like to say—that is, Lady Rugden, I couldn't help but note your sorrow upon leaving France or your cheerful and courageous behavior during our journey. If you ever need a friend, if you ever need help of any kind, I pray you'll not hesitate to call upon me. Please believe that I am your most devoted servant." Despite his worried scowl, Thompson's brown eyes expressed the tender feelings that, as an officer and a gentleman, he would never allow himself to speak.

Christina's wounded heart ached at his kindness. "I'll remember, Lieutenant. Thank you for all you've done for me. I shall not forget your goodness."

The naval officer assisted her up into the waiting carriage and signaled the curious sergeant to be on his way. Leaning out of the departing vehicle, Christina waved her lacy kerchief in a sad farewell, and First Lieutenant Charles Thompson stood in the middle of the roadway and watched the coach until it disappeared from sight.

It was evening, and the streets of London were empty and morose. The hired coach's huge iron wheels clattered and creaked as it crossed Westminster Bridge. Christina watched the rain falling steadily on the River Thames. Only the water boats tied along the banks seemed peaceful, the soft glow of their lanterns seeping through the tiny windows, their inhabitants secure inside. What would it be like, Christina wondered, to live on the river? To go up and down its banks, through all the unending seasons, perhaps selling one's daily catch or offering rides to visitors going down to Pimlico Gardens or Vauxhall? Would it be as carefree, she thought, as it had always seemed to her, or did those boat people, too, suffer the heartaches of rejection and estrangement? Of one thing she was certain. She had no wish to return to a cold and lonely Rugden House. Not now. Not in the dark and the rain.

Impulsively, Christina pounded on the carriage roof and steadied herself while the vehicle lurched to a stop.

"My lady?" the sergeant questioned as he opened the door.

"Take me to Sanborn House in St. James's Square," Christina ordered.

"As you wish, my lady."

The rain was coming down in sheets by the time the coach pulled up in front of Gwen's home. A liveried houseman responded to the clang of the knocker. When he saw who sat waiting in the berlin, he hurried down the steps with an umbrella, and Christina was soon inside the warm foyer.

The servant smiled as he placed Christina's wet cloak over his arm. "Lady Gwendoline is in the front salon, Countess. There's no need to announce you." He escorted her to the drawing room, and without a word ushered her inside, then left to arrange a room for Marie in the attic.

Gwen sat beside a fire, swathed in a comfortable wrapper and engrossed in a novel. She was alone for the evening. Lord Henry was at his favorite club; her houseguest, Lady Penelope Fielding, was visiting with Grandmother Berringer; and the children were sound asleep in their beds. When she heard the door open, she looked up in surprise.

"Christy! Of all things! I wasn't expecting to see you for another month, dearest." She laid the book quickly aside and rose to meet her little sister.

The Countess of Rugden hurried into the room and closed the door. "My visit was cut short, Gwen." Her voice shook with unhappiness.

Gwen looked more closely at her unexpected visitor. "Something's wrong, isn't it? What is it, darling?" She opened her arms wide, and Christina flew into them.

"Oh, Gwen, everything's wrong. My husband hates me. He sent me home by myself. I've never been so humiliated."

The dam of pride that Christina had so carefully erected dissolved. She clung to her older sister, no longer attempting to hide the misery she felt. Then, smiling through her tears, she looked down at Gwen. "This is ridiculous! Here I am, all grown up and four inches taller than you, and crying like a baby."

"Well, you are my baby sister, so go ahead and bawl your heart out. But first come over here and sit down with me." Gwen led her to the sofa. Taking the handkerchief clutched in Christina's hand, she patted her sister's wet cheeks. Then she put her arm around her shoulders. "Now what could be so bad that your husband had to send you home in disgrace? What did you do—flirt outrageously with all the French courtiers?"

Gwen's soft blue-green eyes and teasing smile helped ease the dull ache Christina had felt inside her for the last two weeks.

"Well, to tell the truth," Christina admitted, "I did flirt. And now Rugden despises me."

"I can't believe that!"

"Oh, but it's true. When I asked him what I'd done wrong, he refused to tell me. Oh, Gwen, he looked at me with such contempt."

"Surely this problem can be rectified?" questioned Gwen. She looked at her sister in dismay. "Is there no affection between you at all?"

Christina met her sister's troubled gaze. "Sometimes I've thought perhaps Rugden had begun to care for me. He can be so tender and thoughtful. But lately he's been so cross and mean I don't know what I think or feel when I'm with him."

Lady Gwendoline hugged her sister and laughed. "Why, Christy, I think you've fallen in love with your husband."

Christina pulled back. "Gwen, what's it like being married? Do you feel, well, sensations that are different deep inside you?"

Gwen's eyes sparkled with humor. "Christy, when a woman loves a man, she has these sensations you're talking about. It's a part of married love, dear. If you trust your husband, you'll find that you can show these feelings without fear or embarrassment. And because he loves you, your husband wants you to enjoy them. There has to be a deep, emotional bond between a woman and a man before

she can let him see her as she really is—and not as the refined lady that society tells her she ought to be. Don't be
afraid of your feelings when you're with your husband.
And don't be ashamed to let him see them."

"I can't let Rugden know how I feel inside," Christina
said. "He doesn't love me. To him, our marriage is only a
financial arrangement."

Gwen frowned. "Did he tell you this?"

"Not in so many words." Christina jumped up and
walked restlessly to the window. Mortified by the disclosure she was about to make, she kept her back to her sister. "He's not aware that I know he has a mistress. But he
makes no attempt to hide his dislike of me."

"Perhaps, like you, he's hiding his real feelings."

Christina covered her face with her hands. "All he feels
is lust."

Gwen stood. "Oh, Christy, married love can be the
physical bond that ties two people together and sustains
them through the tragedies of life. Intimacy with your husband can be truly beautiful. Sometimes it can feel like
you're soaring without wings."

Christina was incredulous. "You mean like a bird?"

Dimples showing, her sister chuckled at her astonished
reaction. "Exactly."

Christina's peal of laughter filled the room. "Oh, Gwen,
you're fantastic!"

Chapter 18

Paris was titillated. The gossip flowed down the rococo halls of Versailles, hopped by coach over to the Palace of the Tuileries, jumped from mouth to mouth in the luxurious hôtels of the St.-Germain suburb, floated down the Seine with the canaille on dilapidated barges, streaked through the Latin Quarter on clever scholars' tongues, to return, where it had begun, in the Opera Quarter, till every blasé Parisian was bent over with laughter, enjoying the scandal with loud, bawdy, rollicking appreciation.

London was more circumspect. Beginning quietly at Whitehall, the word spread slowly up and down the Thames, pushed its way with self-righteous vigor into St. James's Palace, crossed with increasing speed through worldly-wise Piccadilly, and oozed with sly repetition into the wealthy town homes of the West End. A long, low, smothered laugh was on the lips of the insular Londoners, breaking out, every once in a while, in a high-pitched shriek or a boisterous guffaw, only to be covered over by the clap of a parochial hand.

The Countess of Rugden, moving serenely in the eye of the hurricane, remained blissfully unaware of the commotion around her, for not one person, male or female, dared share the hilarious tidings with the deceived wife herself.

By the beginning of November the weather watchers were predicting an early and severe winter. In the City, sudden gusts blew piles of garbage down Cheapside and Ludgate Hill. Two days after her return from Paris, neither the fall storms nor the perils of the narrow streets in the

Barbican discouraged Christina from calling upon her banker.

Inside the Bank of Jacob Rothenstein & Son, row upon row of clerks sat on high stools. They bent over thick account books, methodically dipping plumed quills in and out of their inkhorns. The older clerks wore scarves around their necks, shawls over their dark jackets, and fingerless gloves on their hands to ward off the chill.

Several customers in bright satin coats glanced her way, seemingly surprised at the appearance of a young woman in such a masculine enclave. At the announcement of her name, a low rumble of conversation spread through the large room. On one side, several young clerks seated around a high table looked up at her with rampant curiosity. Christina stiffened in exasperation. Good gad, if they'd never seen a woman in a bank before, it was high time!

She was escorted into the private office of the bank's junior partner. Anselm Rothenstein hurried from behind a wide desk piled high with stacks of papers. His dark brown eyes twinkled a welcome. "Lady Christina," he said, "how good to see you again." He took the hand she offered and grasped it warmly. "You look lovely, child."

Christina glanced down at her fitted lavender traveling coat trimmed with deep blue piping. "I did a little shopping while I was in Paris. But it's still me, beneath all the finery."

"Sit down, my dear," he said. He pointed to an upholstered chair in front of his desk.

"How is Jacob?" questioned Christina.

"My father's hale and hearty for a man of eighty. He comes into the bank only about twice a month now. He's more interested in his art collection than in buying stocks or collecting dividends." Anselm sat down and folded his hands together on the desktop. "I have all your records ready for you, Lady Christina." He tapped the open pages of a large ledger with his forefinger.

Suddenly nervous, Christina peeled off her gloves and clutched them tightly in her lap. She tried to smile, but the effort was more than she could manage. "Thank you, Anselm, but it isn't necessary for me to look at the books. I have complete faith in you and Jacob. Please, just tell me how my finances have progressed since my marriage. Have there been any exorbitant withdrawals on my funds?"

The financier stared thoughtfully down at the columns of figures on the pages in front of him. Then he stood, dragged his wooden chair around the desk, and placed it next to hers. The childless widower peered at her for several long moments before he began. "Well, my dear, there have been some rather significant debits, I'm afraid. Your husband has diverted large sums to ease the shortages on his own estates."

Christina returned the banker's honest gaze. Determined to face the truth, no matter how painful, she cleared her throat and lifted her chin. "How . . . how large, Anselm?"

He knew her too well to soften the truth. "About a quarter of your entire fortune, Christina."

She stared at him in disbelief. "My God," she said, "I'd not have thought it possible in so short a time."

"Don't take this news too badly, my dear," Anselm advised. "I've personally seen to the disposition of the funds. Each and every draft has gone either to cover the expenses of the earl's many estates or to pay for the extensive investigation into his late father's investments. Using a large part of your fortune to secure his own is logically and financially a wise move. Your husband, in his written directives to me, has shown himself to be a conservative and prudent manager who takes great interest in the running of not only his properties, but yours as well. In fact, we've discussed by letter the possibility of selling Penthaven to recoup some of these immediate losses."

"Sell Penthaven!" she cried. Aghast, she leaned forward in her chair. "On no account will I allow it! I spent my summers in Cornwall as a child. All my memories of my grandfather's home are precious. I shan't lose them or it."

Rothenstein stood and walked around his desk. He looked down at the large account book, turning several pages and reading the entries before he answered her. "That particular estate has been a drain on your assets for several years, Lady Christina. The total cost of renovation would be staggering. Part of the roof is threatening to collapse, and at the moment the building is uninhabitable. It's only natural that your husband has considered selling it."

"Well, I won't!" she said. "I'll speak to Rugden about it when he returns from France. In the meantime, please do nothing to further its sale." She rose from the chair and pulled on her lavender gloves.

"One thing more, child, if an old friend may offer a bit of advice to a new bride. Compared to other men who've married young heiresses, your husband, in spite of the sizable withdrawals, appears to be most judicious. Nothing has been for his personal use, which is amazing, considering that all of his own funds have been wiped out. Were you aware that his country home was to have been locked up, with no one on the grounds except the gatekeeper? Financially, in my opinion, your father has made a wise choice for you. If the Earl of Rugden proves that the Greater London Docks Company was a fraud perpetrated on his deceased father, he stands to regain his lost fortune, once the swindlers are identified and apprehended. With his shrewd understanding of business affairs, the two of you could someday be one of the wealthiest couples in Britain."

But Christina knew she wasn't the fortunate bride the banker believed her to be. Considering the heartless way Rugden had packed her off to London, her husband's openhanded use of her small fortune appalled her. For once she held her ready tongue. She offered her hand to Anselm, and he led her out of the office.

"When my father was in last week," Rothenstein told her, "we discussed the investigation. Jacob's very intrigued. He'd never heard of the Greater London Docks project. He knows the factors of every merchant house in the City, as well as the brokers and underwriters up and down Exchange Alley. It seems unbelievable that he wouldn't have heard of this vast scheme to build wharves along the Thames." He smiled and patted her hand. "If anyone can find out about a venture to raise such a huge amount of capital in London, my father can."

"I hope to pay a visit to Jacob as soon as I'm settled at home," Christina said. "Maybe by then he'll have learned something."

As she entered the main lobby, the group of junior clerks in the corner looked up at her and started to snigger. They rolled their eyes expressively at one another and seemed to hold back their laughter with great effort. One even held up his ledger to hide his grin, till he saw Anselm's thunderous scowl and gave a sickly grimace instead.

Marie, who'd spent the duration of the visit knitting in a chair by the room's huge fireplace, placed her needles and yarn carefully in her satchel and rejoined her mistress. Her dark eyes crackled as she glared at the smirking young men. Then like a huge crow trailing after a lavender-blue parakeet, she followed Christina out of the treasury, her black umbrella tucked tightly under her arm.

Christina turned to her maid. "Pray, tell me, Marie," she said, "is there something wrong with my appearance?"

"Not that I can see, miladi."

"Perchance my hat is on backward?"

"No, miladi."

"Is my coat inside out?"

The soubrette didn't appear surprised by the ridiculous question. "No, miladi," came her serious reply.

"Then why do I have the feeling that everyone's talking about me?"

"Indeed, why would such a thing be?" Marie responded. She seemed as bewildered as her mistress.

Exasperated, Christina signaled her footman. "Something's going on, Marie, and I intend to discover what it is."

The Countess of Rugden's unexpected arrival at Sanborn House coincided with teatime. In the elegant drawing room, Lady Sanborn was just about to lift her favorite teapot, hand-painted with delicate lilies of the valley, when her sister hurried in, petticoats flying, and unannounced as usual.

As she entered, Christina spotted her husband's sister, whom she hadn't seen since her arrival in London. Lady Penelope sat beside Gwen on the rose damask settee, just about to stuff her mouth with a warm, buttered scone. "Pansy," she cried. "How good to see you, darling. Did you enjoy your trip to Tunbridge Wells with Grandmother Berringer?"

"Christy!" Pansy choked, coughing on a crumb in her excitement. She sprang up from her chair, crossed the room with one great bound, and hugged Christina fiercely. "Oh, lud, I missed you! You have to tell me all about Paris! Did you get many new gowns? Did you bring one home for me? Tell me all about those romantic Frenchmen. Did you have an *affaire de coeur?*" In galloping spirits, she twirled her brother's wife round and round, the bright green and white stripes of her satin overskirt ballooning out in a dizzying blur.

Christina laughed at the outrageous scamp. She returned the girl's tight squeeze, then turned to hug Gwen as well, keeping one arm around Pansy's tiny waist all the while. " 'Fore heaven, I've much to tell you. We were presented to Louis himself. And I met the Pompadour also. She promised me a set of china for a wedding gift. But nothing so unusual happened in France as has been happening to me here in the City today."

A furrow creased Gwen's brow. She moved to the tea cart and adjusted a porcelain cup on its saucer. "What's happened that's so unusual, Christy?" Her blue-green eyes, usually so open and forthright, were hidden beneath her lowered lashes.

Christina looked from one sister to the other. "All day long, wherever I went, it seemed as though people were laughing at me."

A smothered cry escaped before Pansy could clap her hand over her mouth. The young girl's deep brown eyes, enormous in her small, heart-shaped face, peered over her fingers.

Like a prosecutor in a courtroom, the countess whirled on her tiny sister-in-law and shook her finger accusingly. "If you know anything about this, Lady Penelope, I demand that you tell me at once!"

"Gwen made me promise I wouldn't tell you," she said. She twisted her hands together nervously as she backed across the room to the safety of a wing chair beside the fireplace.

Lady Sanborn moved swiftly to Christina. She took her

younger sister's arm and gently pulled her to the sofa. "Sit down, Christy," she said, settling on the cushion beside her and retaining hold of her hand. After a moment's hesitation she raised her eyes, took a quick little breath, and continued, almost painfully. "There's been some rather unusual news from Paris, dearest. A *passage d'arms* of some notoriety is being bruited about."

"A duel!" cried Christina. She jumped up from the sofa and paced across the floor. She struck her forehead with her palm in exasperation. "I vow, I was afraid this might happen. I begged the Comte de Chastellux not to do it. He's called Rugden out, hasn't he?" She turned to find Gwen's eyes filled with sorrow. "Dear God, my husband wasn't seriously wounded?" Genuine alarm brought her voice to a high pitch. "Rugden isn't . . . ?"

Gwen rose and walked over, compassionately taking hold of Christina's shoulders. "No, no, he's perfectly sound and well. Christy, your husband didn't engage in combat with anyone. Nor did Capitaine Duvergier. But the affair of honor did concern Rugden. Now come and sit down, dearest. There's more to tell."

Bewildered, Christina allowed her sister to guide her back to the sofa. Gwen sat down beside her. Her smooth brow knitted in her effort to find the right words. "Christy, the duel was *over* your husband."

"Over Rugden? That's not possible."

Pansy leaped up, unable to keep the secret any longer. "Yes, it is! Two women quarreled over him, Christy. Only think! Isn't it romantic? How I wish I'd been one of them. I'd love to fight a duel."

Dramatically pacing off to her own count of ten, Pansy turned and assumed the dueler's sideways stance. "Ready! Aim! Fire!" she called. She leveled an imaginary pistol. "Bang! Bang!" she shouted, shooting the mantelpiece over the fireplace dead center. "Imagine, two ladies actually fought a duel over my brother," she added proudly. She turned to face the two shocked women, who watched her in fascination.

"They were hardly ladies, Pansy," Gwen interposed dryly as she quickly regained her composure. "Now hush and let me talk to Christy." With an authoritative gesture, she indicated the chair by the fire.

Christina's brain refused to comprehend what her sister-in-law had just told her. "This is incredible! Women don't fight duels. Whoever heard of one female challenging another?"

Teatime completely forgotten, Gwen reluctantly nodded her head and leaned back on the settee in unhappy resignation. "It did happen, Christy. Last week in Paris. Two redheaded opera dancers tried to shoot each other. The earl, being the cause, managed to talk them out of it before a shot was fired. According to the gossip, he really was quite brave, walking in between the loaded guns."

The full meaning of the news began to sink in. Slowly but surely, she comprehended the enormity of the scandal. "The Ramillies twins!" she said to herself, barely able to frame the words on her stiff lips. She rose awkwardly from the sofa and stood in the center of the room. "Those overblown, red-haired hussies." She gasped. "He could hardly wait for me to leave. Scarce wonder, when he was after not one but two stage doxies. That was why he sent me home. And I thought I'd done something wrong!"

Frightened by her passion, Pansy looked up at her brother's wife. "Christy, you're white as a ghost."

Gwen spoke firmly. "Pansy, you promised to take the children to Hyde Park this afternoon after their nap. I just heard Joanna's voice upstairs. Why don't you see if Nanny has her and Alexander ready for their walk, while I talk to Christina."

Tears sprang up in Lady Penelope's velvety eyes, and her bottom lip trembled. She flew to the countess. "Don't hate me, Christy. I'm sorry for what I said! I only wished I had fought in a duel, that's all. I didn't mean to hurt your feelings."

Stricken, Christina looked down at her, barely able to speak. "I don't hate you, Pansy. I merely despise your brother. Now please, let me be alone with Gwen for a while." After Pansy had left the drawing room, the two sisters looked at each other.

"What are you going to do, dearest?" Gwen questioned

softly from her place on the sofa. "Why don't you stay here with me tonight?"

Christina remained standing, calm now that the decision had been made for her. "I'm leaving him, Gwen. Annulment or legal separation, it makes no difference. May Pansy stay here with you until Rugden returns from Paris? It wouldn't be seemly if I took her with me. Besides, it'd be far too hard on her emotions. And mine."

Lady Gwendoline rose and tenderly enfolded her little sister in her arms. "Oh, my poor, darling girl. How I prayed that you'd never have to be told. I truly underestimated the notoriety of this scandal when I thought I could keep it from you."

Dry-eyed, Christina gave a brittle laugh. "How could you possibly have protected me from it, Gwen, when all of London is talking about me behind my back? Me! The Berringer heiress who was sought after by the most eligible bachelors in England."

The Countess of Rugden returned from her sister's home late that afternoon, seething with anger. Flying up the central stairs with Marie at her heels, she raced into her bedroom suite and started pulling out gowns, stockings, shoes, and bonnets from the high, carved wardrobes. She piled everything in one huge stack on the canopied bed as she called to her abigail, who'd spent the visit at Sanborn House in its cozy kitchen getting her ear filled with the tale of the outrageous duel.

"Marie, ring for Mrs. Owens. I need all my trunks, valises, and bandboxes brought up here. Pack all my things. And everything you own. Every last item. I'm leaving this house for good."

The soubrette's black eyes danced with excitement. "We are leaving, *ma petite?* But of course, I will begin packing at once." With a jaunty step, she moved across the chamber and happily yanked the rope to send the bells clanging in the servants' quarters.

Shortly after Mrs. Owens entered the bedchamber, wiping her hands on her white apron. When she saw the confusion that reigned in the room, she looked at her mistress in surprise. "Yes, my lady?"

Seeing the gray-haired housekeeper staring openmouthed at the upheaval, Christina stopped flinging her clothing around and spoke abruptly. "Have all my trunks brought up here, Mrs. Owens. And then send Annie up to help Marie pack."

"Surely you're not leaving this evening, my lady?" Mrs. Owens asked. Her worried glance took in the shoes tossed haphazardly upon the yellow silk coverlet and the boxes of powder and rouge piled high on the lacy white pillows. She walked over to the bed and conscientiously lifted a pair of gray kid boots down onto the rug.

Taken aback, Christina stopped in her tracks. It was early evening, and it might take her most of the next day to complete all her packing. "No, not tonight. But I'll be leaving for Waldwick Mansion tomorrow afternoon. You may as well know from my own lips, for you'll learn of it soon enough. I'm moving to my family's town house. I'm leaving Rugden."

Dismay filled the elderly woman's kind eyes. "Are you sure, my lady? Pray, think what this will mean to the earl, to your family, and to yourself. It will create a scandal you'll never live down."

"Ha!" exclaimed Christina. She hurled a whalebone hoop across the carnage that littered the room. "Rugden already has me beaten on that score. I'm presently the laughingstock of London. I think I prefer good, honest vilification to that."

Mrs. Owens turned to the Frenchwoman, who was busily folding corsets and chemises, and, despite her dislike of the woman, pleaded in a desperate attempt for help. "Madame Boucher, can't you reason with her? Surely you must see how disastrous this would be for your mistress?"

The maid didn't even look up from her work. "Nothing could be more tragic than this marriage in which miladi has been trapped. It would never have taken place except for a terrible mischance. I blame myself for being ill that night and not being there to protect my little cabbage from your diabolical master. You know the slander that's befallen this innocent girl because of that ruthless man's shameful affairs. How can you suggest that she stay with him, after this final humiliation?"

From the look of chagrin on the housekeeper's face, Christina realized that Mrs. Owens had already heard the gossip that was apparently flying through all levels of London society. Good gad, was there anyone, except for herself, who hadn't heard it before today? "My mind is quite made up, Mrs. Owens," she said. "Please send up my trunks."

A fierce storm rocked the house that night. The windows rattled and the rain beat in torrents against the glass panes. In her large bed, the Countess of Rugden tossed about, prey to vivid dreams of squadrons of red-haired women dressed in fusilier uniforms, loading, aiming, and firing artillery at her.

Christina awoke exhausted. She felt as though she'd spent the night on a battlefield, dodging cannonballs. She peeked out of the yellow silk curtains that hung from the four-poster. All around her in her lovely bedroom were her belongings, stacked in neat piles in still-open trunks. No one could have accused Marie of being recalcitrant in the packing, and although it wasn't completely finished, many of the boxes were ready to be hauled down the wide central staircase immediately after breakfast.

Halfheartedly, the countess crawled out of bed to face the chilly room with a shiver. During the night the fire had died, and the floor, even with its thick Persian carpet, felt icy to her bare feet. With the recollection of the previous day's events, the cold seemed to seep inside her, freezing her very spirit.

With a light tap, Marie entered, her bombazine skirts rustling. She beamed a rare smile, like a shark just before it devours its prey. "After I help you dress, miladi, I will have Watt Keighly move the baggage that's ready down to the front hall. Then I will get right to work on the rest of this. I myself am all prepared to go."

Christina nodded in agreement. With her handmaid's expert help, she was soon dressed and downstairs in the dining room. Though she did her best to appear serene and unruffled by her butler's disapproving look as he pulled out her chair, she felt cross and tired. "I only want some coffee, Rawlings," she said. "I have a great deal to do this morning."

"As you wish, Lady Rugden," he replied with a dignified bow. He set a cup and saucer in front of her and poured the rich brown liquid. Its delicious aroma filled the room. "I understand that your maid has directed Keighly to carry down your luggage, my lady. I was hoping you would, under further consideration, countermand that directive. I'm certain the earl would do so, were he here."

"Well, he's not here, Rawlings," she snapped. "He's off somewhere busily seducing sets of twins."

The astonishment on her butler's face only increased her feelings of ill-use. "You needn't look so shocked," she said. "You know very well what I speak of, as does the whole of London. I want my things in the entryway and ready to go by noon today. And I don't want anyone offering me any more advice," she added in warning.

The servant's reply was forestalled by a loud, boisterous halloo from the hallway. Only one person would enter the mansion so precipitously: the Honorable Percy Fielding. Next to Rugden, he was the last person she wanted to see.

But there was no escaping him. He entered the dining room, dressed in a magnificent costume of peach and silver, and rushed to kiss her on the cheek. "My sweet sister, how delightful to have you back again." Lifting a quizzing glass, he looked thoughtfully down at her. The optical instrument's magnifying lens distorted the eye peering through it, and Christina felt as though she were an insect pinned to a mat for inspection. She squirmed uncomfortably against the chair.

Not waiting for her reply, he continued in a rush. "When I arrived yesterday afternoon from Bath, I was greeted with the astonishing news that you were back from Paris." He smiled and then waved one hand in a lofty gesture, the glass's ribbon flying above her head. "Never mind what ungodly reason took me to Bath at this time of the year. To tell the truth, and be done with it, it was horses, or one horse, to be exact. And an empty errand at that, for, odd's fish, I never saw such a bowlegged, swaybacked hack in all my life." He stopped only long enough to catch his breath. "But you're eating breakfast. Zounds,

I think I'll join you. Those kidneys smell delicious. And how are you, Rawlings?" he said, turning to the butler who stood quietly waiting.

The usually cheerful servant failed to vouchsafe even the glimmer of a smile. "I shall be glad when the earl returns to Rugden House, sir." He turned to the sideboard to dish up Percy's breakfast.

Percy dropped his gangly frame down on the chair beside Christina and rubbed his hands together. "Brrr, rather chilly in here this morning, hey? They say it was the tail end of a hurricane we had last night. Thought I'd never get any sleep. You look a trifle out of sorts yourself, Christina." He rolled his eyes sideways and looked at her searchingly.

The Countess of Rugden passed him the butter for his toast and replied in a monosyllable under her breath.

Not about to be put off, Percy resumed his artless conversation. "Say, I couldn't help but see you still have your trunks piled up in the front hall. Thought you'd be all unpacked by now. Don't look as if you'd even begun. Not going on another trip, are you? My, those eggs do look beautiful, Rawlings," he added as he eyed the plate set in front of him.

Christina handed her husband's brother the salt and pepper with a scowl. "No, I've had all the trips I want for a good long while, thank you. To tell the truth, I'm going home."

"Home?" squeaked Percy. "But, little sister, you are home."

"You can't possibly think I'd stay in this house after the gossip that's been bandied about."

"Gossip? Thunder and turf, I've heard no gossip!" he lied, wholly without expertise. His face turned red, and he tugged with one finger at the lace of his stock. "Why, I've been in Bath all week. How could I have heard any rumors? Mustn't pay any attention to scurrilous talk, Christina," he added. He wagged his finger at her. "Nine out of ten times, it's all a cloud of smoke. No substance, a'tall."

She rounded on him in fury. "Every human being in Britain seems to be giving it credence, Percy. You deny that two shameless, red-haired hussies fought a duel over my husband? You can tell me, for certain, that it's all a hum? Can you give me your oath on that?"

"Two women dueling? Well, now there you have it," he replied, feigning relief. " 'Tis so absurd, it can't possibly be true. Why, whoever heard of two females, hussies or otherwise, actually trying to kill each other with pistols? I had a great aunt who used to fence. A veritable Amazon, she was! But she never took the button off her foil. And, to my knowledge, never tried to kill anyone, either. Sink me, if it's not all a lot of folderol!"

"I never mentioned pistols," Christina said.

Percy's gray eyes opened wide. He popped up out of his chair like a cork out of a bottle of fine French champagne. "So you hadn't. Well, I say, I think it's time I'd best be going. Nice to visit with you, little sister. I presume Pansy's staying with Grandmother Berringer?"

"No, she's at Gwen's house. She'll be perfectly fine there until Rugden comes back—if he ever dares to show his face in London again." Christina pushed back her own chair and stood. She glared at Percy, daring him to attempt a defense of his wretched brother.

Like a stork daintily exiting a pond at the approach of a crocodile, Percy wisely headed for the door.

"If you ever talk to your poltroon of a brother again, give him my contempt!" she cried.

She picked up the table's crystal centerpiece and smashed it against the opposite wall. But Percy had already closed the door behind him.

Chapter 19

Percy didn't wait until the next time he saw Roderick to relay the message entrusted to him by his feisty new relative. By the following week the earl received his younger brother's letter.

Roddy,

The fat's in the fire now, big brother. I've just come from Rugden House and there are valises, trunks, bandboxes, and portmanteaus littering the hallway and halfway up the stairs. Seems your Dutiful Wife ain't so dutiful. She was crackling and snorting like a fire-breathing dragon and appears about to fly the love nest. If you don't come home soon, old boy, you may not need to come home at all.

Odd's fish, maybe it would've been better had I married the chit. I don't seem to get her hackles up the way you do! Stap me, if this time she don't have Good Cause. Your name's on every tongue and linked tight as a drum with two redheads. Wish I could have been there! What a prodigious duel that must have been! (Naturally, I denied everything to your lady wife.)

Bought old Noodle's mare yesterday. You'll agree when you see her that I couldn't let the chance pass by. Admired her for two years, and when Noodle said he'd let her go—well, there you have it! She's a beaut. Turned down Evans flat, however. What a nag he tried to bamboozle me with!

Take care with those treacherous Frogs about!
Your very obedient, etc.,
Percy
P.S. Lady R. sends her contempt.
P.P.S. She threw the table centerpiece at me, but she
missed!

Roderick wadded the sheet of paper into a ball and
threw it in the fire burning on the grate. He strode to the
open library door and shouted.

"Duncan!"

Angus came running at the earl's angry bellow, wondering what could have happened to put his master in such a
pucker. "Colonel?"

The earl had been almost unbearable to live with since
that black day he'd bundled Lady Rugden into a borrowed
coach and sent her off with the serious young naval lieutenant. Then, adding more fuel to the already raging fire of
his temper, those two buxom harpies had to fight over the
colonel before a large crowd of Parisians, like two cack-
ling hens squabbling over the same rooster. Duncan
sighed. Though he lived to be a hundred, he'd never forget
that legendary day.

The Earl of Rugden had received word through a junior
officer that the Mademoiselles Danielle and Antoinette
Ramillies had issued each other a cartel, prompted by their
mutual jealously regarding a certain handsome English officer. They were to meet that very day in front of the opera
house where they were both employed. By the time
Rugden and his batman arrived on horseback, carefully
wending their way through the throng of curious onlookers, the sisters stood back to back, each holding a huge
dueling pistol up in front of her heaving breasts. What a
sight! They counted off the paces, the buoyant silk of their
skirts swishing around their trim ankles, their matching
curls of flame wisping around their faces in the breeze, the
low decolletage of their bodices exposing their overripe
endowments to the friendly autumn sun.

Just as they turned to aim, the colonel jumped from the
saddle to land softly on his feet between them. He held up
his hands in farcical surrender, and the high-spirited crowd

applauded zealously. Rugden took off his hat and bowed low, as though he were a performer in a Shakespearean comedy. This impromptu mummery brought the cheers and hoots of the men and women surrounding the little drama echoing in the plaza. The twin coquettes had no recourse, short of wounding the hero himself, but to lower their weapons and curtsy to one and all. Laughing, they each ran to Rugden and put their arms about him possessively. Then all three bowed once again, to the delight of the crowd. That was the last time Duncan had seen his master smile.

It had been two weeks ago, and the Scotsman was tired of creeping about like a man tiptoeing though the cage of a sleeping lion. It was with great reluctance that he approached the earl, whose gaze was even stormier, if possible, than on that wretched day.

"Sir?" Duncan questioned again. He cautiously watched his master pace back and forth across the library rug.

The lion had awakened.

"Pack our bags, Duncan. We're going home. We leave in three hours."

"Yes, sir," Angus responded happily. Nothing could have pleased him more. Perhaps now the colonel could put matters right between him and his bonny lass. "We'll be ready to go in two," he added over his shoulder as he hurried away to pack.

The subject of all this commotion was herself in a turmoil. After debating for several days on the wisdom of moving out of her own home, Christina finally decided to put her rash words into action.

Her reception at Waldwick Mansion was not auspicious. The dowager marchioness, tall and regal in a stylish mauve gown, met Christina, surrounded by her luggage, in the entry hall.

"You can just send those bags right back where they came from, young lady. You're not spending one night here." Lady Helen waved her gold-headed cane like a marshal's baton at her surprised granddaughter. "Turn yourself around and march back to your own house where you belong."

Christina blinked in astonishment as she slipped off her cape. "No, I won't, Grandmother. You can't possibly know why I'm here to begin with. And you haven't the right to bar me from my father's home."

Rapping her cane against the nearest trunk, the white-haired woman replied with the conviction of authority, "We'll see about that, Christina. I'm still in charge of what goes on at Waldwick Mansion, though you may think I'm old and useless. I do have ears, you know, even though they don't always work so well. It would have taken a deaf person not to hear the skimble-scamble tales entertaining all London for the last two weeks. Now come into the salon with me and stop filling the servants' ears with more unnecessary gossip. Though I know you're all listening," she added, raising her voice to the closed doors lining the hallway.

Leaving Madame Boucher to stand by the trunks, Lady Helen led her granddaughter into the drawing room. "Now, young lady, just what is it that would justify such an unheard-of scandal as a marital separation?"

Christina could feel her cheeks flush with indignation. "Well, I am justified, I can tell you that, Grandmother. The entire city of London is laughing at me. I won't have it. I refuse to live with that . . . that barbarian."

Grandmother Berringer walked over to her own soft chair by the glowing fire. She leaned heavily on her cane and sat down with a stifled groan. "If you're referring to his affair with the opera dancers, you're wide of the mark. A husband can only be expected to look elsewhere for sexual favors when he's barred from his own marriage bed. I believe that was the bargain struck between your father and your husband on the day of your wedding, was it not?" She snorted in disdain. "I knew it'd never work. Did you really expect that rugged grenadier colonel to wait in the wings like some sniveling lackey until you were ready to beckon him into your boudoir? Ha! He don't look like the celibate type to me."

Christina sank down on a nearby settee. "This husband was not of my choosing," she said mutinously. "I was forced into the marriage."

"Nevertheless, the vows were spoken. Marriage isn't

just the joining of two young people. It's the combining of two families, a merger from which will spring the future hope of both lines. We were thrilled at the union. Think what sons and daughters you and Rugden will give us." The dowager marchioness stood and pointed her finger at her rebellious granddaughter. "Your puffed-up conceit shan't deny us this promise, Christina. Go back to your home and your husband."

The possible truth of her grandmother's words stung the countess. She rose to stand beside the marchioness. "I refuse to be a sacrifice on the altar of my family's ambitions. Already Rugden has squandered a quarter of my fortune. Do you expect me to wait until I'm a pauper? I'm going to Father. He'll let me stay at Waldwick Abbey."

Lady Helen sniffed. "Hmph! Your father agrees with me, young lady. You can travel to Wiltshire if you wish, but you won't find any sympathy there. The entire family is behind this union, including your sister. Now go home and see if you can put that well-recognized Berringer charm of yours to good use when your husband returns. And you'd better pray that he does."

Christina stormed out of the mansion. When she visited Sanborn House that same day, she discovered that it was just as she'd been warned. Gwen sadly delivered the family's directive. Christina could not set up residence with her older sister.

Back at Rugden House, the countess raged impotently. She wouldn't admit defeat, and she ordered her belongings piled high in the entryway and front hall until she decided where to go. Two days later, she welcomed Pansy back amid the confusion. Her little sister-in-law's luggage was carried through the parcels and valises standing in the entry and on up the wide center staircase.

Christina refused to be seen in public. She ignored Pansy's pleas to attend at least some small private gatherings. Like a nun immured in a convent, she remained inside the confines of her elegant town house, unwilling to face the cruel smirks and jeering looks of London society. By the end of the week, she'd sent off a letter to Waldwick Abbey, begging her father to allow her to come to Wiltshire. She waited morosely for his answer, uncertain if it would be a loving summons to her childhood home or a cold refusal to allow even a short visit.

The coachman called out to his team of six, and a well-sprung traveling berlin, its braking wheels screeching on the cobblestones, pulled up with a rush in front of the elegant mansion in Berkeley Square. With a clatter, the brass knocker on one of the great double doors was banged against its shiny pediment by a sergeant of the Grenadiers. One door was flung open wide, and then its matching partner. Footmen scurried down the steps to unload the trunks piled high in the boot of the carriage. The butler came to lend a hand and carried more items inside, which he added to the hodgepodge in the already crowded entryway. All was a flurry of excitement. The master of Rugden House had come home.

Pansy heard the noise and rushed out of the drawing room, where she'd been avidly studying the fashion plates brought back from Paris. When she saw her eldest brother standing in the center of the hall's confusion, she impetuously flung her arms around him. "Roderick! You're back!" she cried as she kissed his cheek. "I didn't even know you were coming home."

Roderick hugged his little sister and kissed her fondly on the forehead. "It's good to be home, Pansy." His smile quickly disappeared as he took in the chaos. His front hall resembled the waiting room of a busy inn. "What's all this?" he asked.

"Oh, it's Christina's things," Pansy replied airily. "She's going to move, but she doesn't know where. In the meantime, she's insisted that everything remain stacked right here. But you needn't worry, for she's refused all callers. So no one's seen the mess except us."

"Where is she now?" he asked tersely.

"She's in her room, but, lud, don't go up there. She'll never speak to you as long as you live. She hates you." Pansy pulled on his elbow in a futile attempt to keep him from going up to the mansion's second story. "It's about the duel, you know," she explained as she hung on to his sleeve.

Gently but firmly, Roderick freed himself from his sister's clutch. "You wait here," he told her. He took the stairs two at a time.

"What was it like having two women fight over you?" Pansy called to his back. "I always miss the excitement!"

Christina rested back in her porcelain hip bath and relaxed in a profusion of bubbles. On the far side of the chamber's canopied bed, Marie was laying out her ladyship's gown for supper. Both maid and mistress turned their heads toward the door at the sound of booted feet pounding up the staircase.

Christina knew immediately whose boots they were. Beside herself at the thought of Rugden brazenly returning to face her after his heinous behavior, she stood up, poised in the bath, the water swirling around her calves. The door opened with a bang, and Rugden charged in.

With surprising accuracy, his wife hurled her sopping wet cloth. Not even breaking his stride, Roderick dodged the flying object with the instincts of an Indian brave. The cloth barely missed his head and smacked against the doorjamb, where it slid down the woodwork and plopped softly on the floor.

"You vile, loathsome wretch!" she screamed. "You perverted devil's progeny! How dare you come in here! Get out of this room at once!" Lost in her indignation, she didn't even stop to think about the circumstances in which he'd found her.

Roderick came to an abrupt halt. He gazed at his gorgeous bride, standing in the bath like Venus rising from the sea. Her honey-golden hair, which had been piled high atop her head, fell in damp tendrils around her neck. His hungry gaze feasted on the sight of her. Captivated, he followed the soap bubbles as they slid lazily over her pink-tipped breasts, across her flat stomach, and down her smooth, ivory thighs.

Seeing her target remain so tauntingly still in front of her, Christina reached down into the water. Her nimble fingers quickly found the bar of soap, and she hurled it at him. But that missile's flight was also untrue, for its sudsy slickness had deflected her aim. She looked behind her at the low table beside the tub, which held a bottle of perfume and a box of combs for her hair, frantically searching for another rocket to launch at him.

Like a squawking black magpie, Marie joined the fracas. "Miladi, miladi, cover yourself," she scolded. The old crone had comprehended immediately the erotic vision that had halted Roderick's forward assault. Valiantly, the maid attempted to throw a large cloth to her mistress from across the wide bed.

Roderick reached up and caught it with ease as it flew by. He draped the linen casually over one scarlet shoulder. Still gazing at his wife, he addressed the servant in a quiet voice. "If you value your life, Boucher, get out." The icy calmness of his demeanor frightened the woman. She backed out the door without uttering another sound and closed it quietly behind her.

Christina froze. Realization of her nudity had dawned with her maid's first screech. She could feel a rosy flush spread over her bare skin. She clenched her hands and ground her teeth at her own impulsiveness.

"Odious beast!" she said. "Contemptible lecher! One mistress isn't enough for you. Oh, no! You must seduce two women at once. And make me the laughingstock of two countries while you're at it! There are no words vile enough to describe a man who cheats his wife out of her inheritance and then sells the manor her grandfather left her. Is it your intention to leave me destitute and homeless?"

Like any husband caught making a foolish blunder, Roderick resorted to a major offensive barrage. "Just when is the baby due, Christina? By my estimation, you must be well over three months along. Yet you're as slender as the day we met."

He moved to the edge of the tub. Spanning her small waist with his fingers, he lifted her out of the bath as though she were a child and set her down on the fluffy rug in front of the blazing hearth. "Allow me, my lady," he said, his voice suddenly husky. "I'll be happy to attend you at your bath." He took the towel from his shoulder and started to dry her off.

In spite of the warmth of the fire, Christina shivered convulsively. Her teeth chattered when she spoke. "The

. . . the baby is months away yet. Many women don't show until the very end."

He slid the linen slowly and methodically across her slick, wet body. With lingering thoroughness, he wiped the cloth over each satin breast, brushing the pink nipples with his thumb as he did so. He knelt on one knee in front of her and caressed her abdomen and thighs, then brought the towel between her legs and around her little butt.

She tried to slap his hands away. When that didn't work, she attempted to step out of his reach. "But I won't be here at the end of my pregnancy," she continued, her words breathless and harsh with anger. "I'm leaving you."

He rose, and with the linen cloth looped behind her, pulled her hips against his thighs, where he held her effortlessly. Desire raged through his taut body. But he'd seen the hurt in her eyes when he'd first entered the room. After the humiliation she'd endured, for which she held him solely responsible, she'd fight him tooth and nail before she'd let him make love to her.

"You're not going anywhere, sweetheart." He wrapped the toweling around her and tucked one end of the damp linen in the cleavage of her full breasts. His fingers lingered in that silken valley until Christina jerked defiantly away.

Roderick continued in a lazy, conversational manner. "My intuition tells me that if you had someplace to go, you'd have been gone by now. So, madame wife, get dressed. I'll be sending the servants up with your trunks in thirty minutes. What gala were you planning on attending tonight?"

"I haven't stuck my nose outdoors for two weeks, thanks to you," she said indignantly.

"What? Hiding like a timid little mouse, Christina?" he mocked. "That isn't like you." He caressed her bare shoulders. "Tonight we'll go to whatever ball you've been invited to. And tomorrow being Sunday, we'll attend services at Westminster. Until this whole thing has blown over, we're going to act like a pair of lovebirds. And it will blow over, never fear."

"Yes," Christina agreed, "in about ten years."

Rugden threw his head back, and his laughter filled the

room. "I'd forgotten your sweet, docile nature, darling. I've been gone much too long."

Marie waited on the landing and stared with horror-struck eyes at the closed door of Christina's bedchamber. She leaned against the carved balustrade and wondered what was happening inside. To her immense relief, in less than fifteen minutes, the earl opened the door and stepped out. The smile hovering on his lips disappeared when he saw her.

"Your mistress's trunks will be moved upstairs shortly," he said with thoughtful deliberation. "See that they're un-packed and her clothes put away. See also that my wife is dressed for the evening in proper style. Then, Madame Boucher, you had best gather together your references, for you have exactly two weeks from today to procure a new employer, or you will find yourself on the streets. I trust I make myself clear?"

Marie nodded. She dared not show him the hatred she felt. Bobbing a stilted curtsy, she waited for him to run lightly down the wide stairs. Then she hurried into the countess's bedchamber.

Christina was sitting at her dressing table, wrapped in the enormous linen cloth. She rested her chin on her folded hands and stared into the looking glass with haunted eyes. "He knows, Marie," she said. "I can tell by his eyes that he knows I'm not pregnant."

The maid came swiftly across the room to stand beside Christina. She folded her arms across her chest and tapped her foot thoughtfully. "He may suspect, miladi, but he cannot know for certain. No man could."

"I'm going to have to tell him the truth," Christina whispered in despair to her frightened image in the mirror.

Marie's dark eyes narrowed. "You know what he'll want from you then, miladi. If you admit the truth to him now, you'll be chained to a philanderer for the rest of your life. Is that what you want, little cabbage?" She lifted a lacy chemise from the bed and carried it to her mistress, who'd risen and doffed the toweling.

Christina slipped into the delicate undergarment. "I can't stay wed to him." She nearly sobbed in her frustration. "Not after this scandal over those two harlots. My father will never insist upon letting the marriage stand once he knows the truth. I'll get an annulment then."

"Till then, miladi, you must keep the earl at arm's length." The maid handed the countess her silk stockings and garters.

Christina sat down on the bench to pull them on. "But he'll know the truth eventually, Marie. I can't keep up this pretense much longer."

"No, but you can bring it to a conclusion that will prevent him from ever knowing for certain whether you were with child or not."

Christina stepped into the wide cage of her whalebone panniers and looked up into the maid's shrewd black eyes. "How?"

"Quite easily, madame. A miscarriage. You will soon be in the time of your monthly flux. A small but disastrous fall, and you could lose the child. Naturally, you would be heartbroken and unable to talk about it. But I would bear witness that you had, indeed, lost the baby."

Christina slipped the taffeta overskirt with its printed floral design over the stiff framework and stood still while Marie fastened the ties at her waist. "It would work, wouldn't it?" she said breathlessly, overjoyed at the idea of freeing herself from her own web of deceit.

A rare smile spread across the servant's thin face. "Nothing could be easier than deceiving a man when it comes to pregnancy, miladi. Women have been doing it since the beginning of time."

"But it'll be several days. What shall I say in the meantime, if he questions me again?" Christina turned for Marie to lace up the brocade stomacher.

"Tell him that you are worried about your lack of girth yourself. That you had thought to have felt movement by now, but none has come, and you are fearful something is wrong. That will put him off for the time being, and make the miscarriage even more plausible when it happens."

Christina took both of Marie's hands in her own. "What would I do without you?"

"Miladi is too kind," the handmaid replied.

* * *

Marie was correct on one account. Roderick wasn't positive that his wife was not with child. But he was nearly certain of it. All his mental calculations brought him to one conclusion. Though most women would be obviously pregnant by now, not all would be. But only a few weeks more would end the doubts, one way or another. It was possible that when Christina had been delivered by mistake to Rugden Court that rainy summer evening, she had truly thought she was carrying Carlisle's child and then discovered later that she'd been mistaken. A common enough error, especially for a frightened young girl. Knowing his wife, he found it easy to believe she'd have kept up the deception in an attempt to force a dissolution of the marriage. Whatever the case, all he had to do was wait. The answer would soon be forthcoming.

The Earl of Rugden and his beautiful countess appeared in public the very evening of his return to London. They arrived arm in arm at the mansion of the Duke and Duchess of Olwood, to the delight of their hostess. Their unheralded attendance at her soiree meant that it would be talked of by the *ton* for weeks to come.

A startled silence descended upon the chattering guests the moment Roderick and his wife entered the drawing room. He was furious at the notoriety his activities in France had drawn down upon her. He realized that for Christina, who'd not appeared in society for almost two weeks, it was as though she must run the gantlet down that elegant salon.

"Courage, sunshine," he murmured through clenched teeth. "Unless I enlighten them, not one person in this room knows exactly what happened in Paris. After I tell my own version of the duel, no one will lend an iota of credence to the stories that have been setting this town on its ear. Now shall we begin our counteroffensive?"

The evening passed slowly as Roderick moved from group to group, his quiet wife on his arm, enthralling his audience with the tale of how he'd saved two complete strangers—and fishwives, at that—from stabbing each other with their scaling knives on the bank of the Seine. Soon the gentlemen were howling with laughter at his colorful description of the "duel" while the ladies smiled politely behind their fans. Whether anyone believed his story, no one vouchsafed to say. But neither did anyone deny it. Not a person there hadn't suffered, at one time or another, from a false rumor started by an enemy or envious acquaintance.

Unexpected support arrived toward the end of the evening with the appearance of the Duke of Carlisle and his companion, Mrs. Gannet. The Duchess of Olwood led them into the drawing room and announced to the company at large, "Here, at last, is someone to corroborate Rugden's tale. Carlisle has himself only recently come from Paris. I'm sure he'd be happy to satisfy our curiosity about the exceptional combat between two females."

"Tell us, Carlisle," a large matron tittered, "were you present at the notorious passage of arms? Were the ladies fighting over Rugden or a catch of trout?"

With his arm around Madeline's waist, Justin Somesbury looked about the room and found Christina standing beside her husband. An unspoken plea shone in her lovely, frightened eyes.

"Unfortunately, I can shed no new light on the subject," he told his hostess. "I left Paris before the affair of honor took place. However, I have no doubt that it was fish the ladies squabbled over."

"How can you be so sure?" the duchess demanded.

"The answer is obvious," replied Carlisle. Leaving Madeline, he walked across the room and took Christina's gloved hand. He bent and kissed it, then held her trembling fingers in his own as he addressed the fascinated audience. "What man, married to the exquisite Countess of Rugden—and in his right mind—would so much as glance at another woman?"

As they returned to Berkeley Square from the Olwood ball, Christina sat straight and tense on the carriage seat beside her husband. She tried to blink back the tears of abject relief that brimmed in her eyes, gave up, and wiped them away as surreptitiously as possible. It had been an interminable, nerve-racking evening as she waited in dread for someone to challenge Rugden's version of the duel.

The presence of Madeline Gannet had all but pushed her over the edge of hysteria. Had Rugden gone to his sultry mistress, or danced with her even once, Christina would have fled the ballroom in utter mortification.

Now in the darkness of the coach, Rugden must have sensed the misery she was trying so hard to hide. Without a word, he swooped her up and settled her on his lap. He rubbed his chin back and forth across the curls on the top of her head in silent reassurance. Surrendering to the comfort of his strong arms, Christina laid her wet cheek against his shoulder and released a long, ragged sigh of unhappiness.

"The worst is over," he soothed as he gathered her even closer.

The rhythmic sway of the coach, punctuated by the steady clop of the horses' hooves on the cobblestones, worked its comforting magic, and Christina gradually relaxed. Wriggling contentedly, she locked her arms tighter about his secure bulk and cuddled closer. Even through the layers of her ball gown and cloak, she could feel the bulge of his manhood grow and harden. Cautiously tipping her head back, she tried to discern his features in the darkness. She could feel his warm breath on her tearstained cheeks. Then as the coach turned a corner, the glow of a street lantern streamed in through the window, revealing his rugged face. His silvery gaze glittered with sexual desire, while a teasing smile played about his lips, only inches above her own.

He chuckled softly. "In this position, it's pretty hard to hide my intentions, sweetheart."

She tried to scoot off his lap, but he held her in place effortlessly. "Stay right where you are, beautiful," he murmured. "I've waited far too long for this moment." He kissed her, his open mouth covering hers, his tongue probing insistently. Before she had a chance to protest, his hand slipped inside her velvet cloak to fondle her breast.

Christina felt the flame of passion ignite inside her, as she returned his kiss, their tongues meeting in wild excitement. She gasped as his long fingers slipped inside the low bodice of her satin gown. He teased the tightening bud of her nipple with the pad of his thumb till she squirmed on his lap, desperate for his touch. Then he bent his head and suckled her.

Roderick could feel his wife respond to his caresses, and his heart leaped inside him. Somehow, someway, he'd make her forget the humiliation she'd suffered because of his idiotic behavior. He slid his hand under her petticoat and followed the slim, smooth curve of calf and thigh to the matted curls hidden beneath the flimsy chemise. She took a deep breath and tried to pull away, but he held her locked securely in his embrace.

"It's all right," he whispered hoarsely. "Don't worry, darling. I won't take any chances. Just lie back in my arms and let me touch you." Slowly, carefully, he eased his finger inside her as he rubbed the nub of her womanhood with his thumb. "You're so moist and warm. Your body's aching for release. And after tonight's travesty, you deserve it."

The steady, unceasing rhythm of his strokes created a fever of mindless, urgent need. Christina closed her eyes and felt the throbbing pulsations spiral higher and higher. She clutched the wool of his scarlet coat, frantic for him to continue, praying for him never to stop touching her as the outside world slipped away. There were only the two of them, their breaths commingling, while her heart raced and her body arched back against his muscled strength. Her release came with a smothered sob as she covered her mouth with her hand to suppress the plaintive sound of her fulfillment. She opened her slumbrous eyes to find him watching her.

Roderick met her bemused gaze, his own heart thundering in exultation at his victory. In the dim light, her eyes were enormous, velvety soft, and filled with confusion. As the coach drew to a stop in front of Rugden House, he fought back the raging desire to carry her up to his bed and continue the lovemaking. But she was exhausted from the emotional havoc he'd put her through for the past two weeks. Whether it had been necessary or not, he'd already waited this long, thinking he was protecting her from a possible miscarriage. He could wait a little longer. First he would earn her trust. And her forgiveness.

* * *

The Fieldings attended ten o'clock Mass at Westminster Abbey the next morning. To Christina's relief they met Lady Gwen and Lord Henry, with the two children, on the lawn before services began and invited them to sit in the Rugden pew.

Supported by their presence, Christina sat with her sister on one side and Rugden on the other. Try as she might, she couldn't concentrate on the liturgy. Her eyes roamed about the cathedral, where she'd worshipped so many times in the past. Her wandering gaze came to rest eventually on the wall past her husband, who sat at the end of the pew. On the stones above his head was an inscription marking the tomb of a knight who'd fallen in battle. The Fielding name leaped out at her. Their pew was located beside the burial place of one of her husband's ancestors. The Rugden coat of arms, crennelated in marble, proclaimed his military family's ancient maxim: *Honor and Duty Above All.*

Just before the Scripture readings, Joanna Sanborn, in the restless manner of all four-year-olds, joined her aunt. Clambering down from her seat beside Lady Gwendoline, the little girl slid past Christina and stood, staring thoughtfully up at her new uncle. With her large blue eyes and golden curls, she resembled a cherub. Rugden gently lifted the little angel up and wedged her between his wife and himself.

Christina's attention was caught by the preacher, whose first exhortation was taken from the Book of Ruth. "Whither thou goest, I will go," he boomed from the pulpit, "and where thou lodgest, I will lodge."

The countess glanced uncomfortably at the proud man seated beside her. Did he remember that was the very passage chosen by the Reverend Hotchkiss on their wedding day?

Rugden turned his head to meet her gaze, and she was certain that not only her family, but the Almighty Himself, was conspiring against her. Somehow she managed to focus her attention on the religious rite unfolding in front of her. Gradually the two Sanborn children became quieter during the long service. Christina lifted a sleepy Alexander onto her lap to give his mother's tired arms a rest, and the two-year-old curled up and promptly fell asleep. Turning to check on Joanna, Christina saw that the little girl had dozed off as well. She sagged against her tall uncle, her tiny arm and hand resting trustfully upon Rugden's corded thigh. The poignancy of the child's delicate limb, as fragile as a bird's, lying atop the massive bulk of muscle struck Christina like a thunderbolt. She stared at Rugden, no longer seeing him only as her husband, but as the potential father of her children.

Suddenly she comprehended all that he stood for. As his family crest above his head proclaimed, he would indeed lay down his life to protect his family. And what a loving and nurturing father he would be! He'd returned from Paris before the preliminaries of peace had been completed in order to shield her from the vicious gossip. Seated beside her courageous husband, she knew no one would dare continue to utter salacious talk about them. She saw at last, with crystal clarity, the qualities her father and grandmother had recognized in him.

In Paris, she'd been astounded at the deep respect and admiration the world held for the man she wanted to believe was unrefined and uncultured. Little by little, she'd been forced to acknowledge that his gifts for brilliant diplomacy, keen understanding of national issues, and shrewd pragmatism were as admirable and important as any talent in the field of music. As she'd observed him in his role as one of the chief negotiators of the Treaty of Paris, her reluctant admiration had grown. She'd fought the ever-deepening physical attraction to this primal male, who was the antithesis of the scholarly gentlemen she'd hoped to marry. The traits she'd taunted him with—soldierly discipline, practicality and common sense, commitment to family and honor—were the very traits she'd come to love in him the most. Aye, she loved him. But it was too late.

Why did it have to happen now, when he'd surely realized that the story she'd told about a fabricated lover and a feigned pregnancy was a despicable lie? Now, after she'd disgusted him with her flirtations with Carlisle and Duvergier? After he'd sought solace in the arms of other women? In heaven's name, why did it have to come too late?

Chapter 20

It was the fragile beauty of the costly Sèvres china that depressed Christina the most. She unpacked the dishes one by one from the crates in which they were nestled, and her spirits sank lower with each bowl, plate, tureen, and platter she admired. Guided by the discriminating counsel of the earl, the Marquise de Pompadour had chosen a pattern of roses in shades of cameo-pink to deep ruby. It was an exquisite design. All Christina's youthful dreams of running her own household as a loving wife and mother seemed to be embodied in that magnificent collection of porcelain. Its very perfection silently taunted her for the charade of a marriage in which she remained a virgin.

Earlier that morning Marie had entered her bedchamber, carrying a breakfast tray. "Wake up, *petite,*" the maid called with a toothy smile. Her stiff skirt rustled portentously as she moved to the bedside. "I thought you would enjoy a little extra pampering today." The hidden intent of her words glittered in her black eyes.

Christina had stared down at the cup of coffee placed solicitously in front of her and frowned. Disgruntled that Marie would remind her so brazenly of their hastily conceived plan, she ignored the woman's conspiratorial tone. "I'm feeling perfectly fine," she said, setting the tray aside. "There's no need for this coddling. In fact, I think I'll get dressed right now and have breakfast downstairs."

Marie held out her hand to stay her mistress. "But, miladi! By my calculations, you will begin your flow today. The accident must take place this morning."

Irritated by the maid's persistence, Christina lifted the

bedcovers and slipped off the feather mattress. "I'm not so sure that a staged fall is a good idea. Who knows, I might actually get hurt." Refusing to meet the narrowed eyes of her abigail, she walked over to the large armoire and opened it. She stared indecisively at the array of gowns within, then pulled out a stunning lavender creation brought back from Paris.

Marie hurried to stand beside her irascible mistress. *"Mais non,* there would be no danger, I assure you. You need only roll yourself down a few bottom steps and cry out for help as you do so. It would be quickly and safely done."

Christina shrugged her shoulders noncommittally, and Marie had no choice but to attend to the task of dressing her lady for the morning. Neither spoke another word about the scheme during the uneasy toilette.

By midmorning Christina had bitterly reviewed in her mind, while unpacking the thirty settings of china, all the lessons her mother and father had taught her as a child on the value of a clear conscience. She understood, at last and with devastating clarity, to what degree she had uncannily trapped herself. She toyed with the idea of making a clean breast of the sham pregnancy and pictured herself approaching her stern husband and blurting out the truth. He'd be furious to learn she'd played him for a fool. No doubt about that. But surely he could forgive her, if she was willing to forgive his widely publicized infidelities.

She laid down the last saucer with a shaky hand and drew a deep, steadying breath. Her head throbbed with a blinding headache. Marie was partly correct. A day spent in bed might, if nothing else, improve her despondent frame of mind. Christina left the dining room and climbed slowly to the top of the curving stairway. As she reached the landing, Marie appeared from the sitting room.

Holding on to the balustrade with one hand to steady herself, Christina put the other to her clammy forehead. Beads of moisture stood on her top lip. "I'm going to lie down for a while, Marie."

The maid sprang forward. "Only think, little cabbage, what an opportunity you are throwing away." Marie's voice creaked with excitement. "It is your only chance to be rid of this subterfuge without admitting the truth to your husband. Mark my words, he will never forgive you if he learns of your duplicity."

The two women stood eye to eye at the top of the staircase. Below them in the study, Rugden and Percy, who'd arrived earlier to take Pansy on a ride through Hyde Park, could be heard in a friendly discussion.

Painfully, Christina shook her pounding head. "Nay, Marie. Rugden will eventually understand and come to forgive me. Even if he doesn't, anything is better than the deceitful role I've been living. I'm going to go back down and tell my husband the truth." Christina brushed the servant aside and turned to descend.

Panic gripped Marie. The foolish chit was about to sabotage all her ingenious plans, and she reacted without hesitation. She struck the young woman in the small of her back with one hand as she trod on the hem of the lavender frock.

There was a ripping sound, and Christina tottered in mid-air. Arms flailing helplessly, she hurtled through space. She cried out once in terror as she rolled over and over, crashing almost headfirst down the long flight of stairs. Her shoulders and arms took the brunt of the fall. Her head struck the newel post with a sickening thud, and she came to a stop, unconscious, on the marble entry floor.

High above her, Marie gave a piercing scream. "The *bébé*! the *bébé*! Help!" she called with heartrending sobs. "Someone help! Miladi has fallen, and she will lose the *bébé!*"

Roderick came tearing into the hallway with his brother fast at his heels. Christina lay sprawled in an ungainly heap at the foot of the stairs. An icy chill clutched Roderick's heart. Crouching on one knee beside her still form, he felt her pulse, then bent his head to check her shallow breathing. A gash on the side of her forehead was bleeding copiously.

"Christina," he called. He cautiously moved her head to inspect the cut. "Darling, can you hear me?" He glanced up at Percy, who stood bending over them. "Quick, fetch Dr. Bowles! Hurry, man! Go as fast as you can! Her life may depend on it."

On the landing above, Pansy appeared. "What's happened," she cried in alarm as she came to stand beside Marie. "Is Christy hurt?"

"There is no need for a physician, my lord," Marie interrupted, suddenly galvanized into action and coming down the stairs to stand beside the two gentlemen. "The mistress has merely hit her head. She will wake up shortly." Leaning across Roderick's shoulder, she attempted to pat Christina's cheek.

"Get back," he snarled. He turned once again to his brother. "Go, Percy! Now! Bring Bowles as fast as possible. Don't come back without him."

White-faced, Percy looked aghast at the fallen countess. "My God, Roddy, is she pregnant?" he asked in bewilderment, suddenly realizing the meaning of the abigail's cry for help and the potential complications of the mishap. With his brother's answering nod, he sprang into action. He whirled for the door, shouting for Duncan and Rawlings.

With infinite tenderness, Roderick lifted his wife in his arms and carried her to her bedroom, where he placed her on the soft yellow coverlet. Pansy and Marie followed close behind, crowding around the inert countess.

Christina was ashen. Blood streamed down the side of her face. A purple blotch was quickly appearing around the cut on her temple. Carefully, the earl examined her head and neck for further injuries. "Please be all right, little one," he prayed softly.

At that moment Rawlings and Mrs. Owens came running into the room. The housekeeper glanced with disgust at Marie, who stood watching at the bedside, then spoke to the butler. "Get some hot water, quickly. And some cloth for bandages from the linen pantry." Rawlings darted out of the room.

Roderick, having made certain there was only one cut on Christina's head, began to staunch the blood with a clean pillowslip handed to him by Mrs. Owens. They were joined by Duncan, who had years of experience in repairing battle wounds.

"We'd better undress her and check for broken bones," Roderick said quietly to his batman.

Together, with the aid of the competent housekeeper, the two army veterans slipped off the brocaded stomacher. They eased the pale purple overskirt and petticoat down around Christina's legs. Roderick untied the straps of the whalebone cage that surrounded her hips and gently pulled it off. He flung it across the room, leaving the countess clad only in her lacy knee-length chemise, shoes, and silk stockings. Duncan checked each limb, searching painstakingly for a break or a lesion.

Mrs. Owens caught her breath in horror as she saw the spreading red stain on Christina's pure white undergarment. "She's bleeding."

"Damn!" Roderick swore.

Angus glanced up momentarily. "The lass carries a wee bairn?"

"Yes," came the clipped reply.

The batman finished his meticulous inspection. "No broken bones, Colonel. But her shoulder is dislocated. Shall we wait for the doctor?"

"No, do it now, while she's unconscious."

A low moan escaped Christina's lips as the Scotsman worked on her with skilled hands. He quickly and expertly slipped the bone back into the socket. Roderick's eyes flew to her face, hoping desperately she wouldn't regain consciousness till the worst was over.

Rawlings entered with pieces of bleached linen over his arm and carrying a basin of hot water, which he handed to Mrs. Owens. Then he placed himself just inside the doorway and waited for further orders.

Deftly, the housekeeper tore cloths to be used for a sling and a dressing for the gash on Christina's temple, while Roderick and Angus turned their attention to the head wound. Between them, they washed, closed, and tightly bandaged the lesion. Lifting Christina carefully, they immobilized the injured shoulder by wrapping her bent arm securely against her side with wide linen strips. Finally they slipped a folded sheet under her hips and laid a blanket lightly over her.

The batman shook his head and muttered in frustration, "I can fix the shoulder and the cut, but I canna do a thing aboot the bairn."

There was nothing left, except to wait for the arrival of the doctor.

Less than an hour later, Dr. Bowles, accompanied by Percy, was met on the front steps by the distraught earl, who grabbed his hand and shook it briefly. "Thank God, you're here at last! It's my wife, Bowles. She's taken a bad fall. She's hemorrhaging."

"What happened?" the elderly man questioned as the three raced up the stairs.

"Apparently, she tripped on the hem of her gown," Roderick answered. He tried to keep his voice calm, but his heart was pumping madly. He opened the door to the bedchamber and ushered the doctor and Percy inside. "She fell all the way from the second floor landing and struck her head on the bottom post. She's been unconscious since it happened."

The surgeon shook his head grimly at the news, but made no comment.

The moment they entered the bedchamber, Marie darted wildly across the room to stand in the physician's way. "She won't be examined by a man," the maid wailed in a shrill voice. "Miladi would never agree to this, I tell you." She flung her thin arms out in an insane attempt to prevent the doctor from reaching Christina.

"Get the old bag out of here," Bowles growled impatiently. He removed his satin coat and rolled up the lace on his immaculate white sleeves. "Mrs. Owens can assist me with my examination. I want everyone else to leave."

"*Bête!*" Marie screeched in warning. "Fool! You cannot do this, I say. Miladi would never allow it."

Disgusted, Roderick flashed an unspoken command to Duncan.

The sergeant grinned fiendishly. Spitting on his palms, he rubbed them together with relish. "Aye, howl like a witch if ye wish," he said, "but ye'll be coming with me." He placed his hands behind her back and shoved her ruthlessly out the door in front of him.

Dr. Bowles bent over the prone woman and lifted a closed eyelid. "She's probably suffered a concussion, Lord Rugden. Her breathing seems normal, but I'll need to examine her. You go on downstairs and take the rest of this menagerie with you. If she's as shy as her maid says, she'll not appreciate learning that she had an audience when she regains consciousness. She'll be all right. Now go on, everyone." With an impatient gesture, the portly gentleman motioned them out of the room.

Roderick, in shirtsleeves and with his stock dangling loose, paced up and down the front drawing room. Though Percy and Pansy, seated woodenly beside each other on the sofa, waited with him, neither said a word, their thoughts riveted on the injured woman on the floor above.

All the fears of the past rose up like a specter to haunt the Earl of Rugden. He'd lost his mother and his first wife in childbirth complications. The memories of their tragic deaths came back now, crystal clear and exquisitely painful. Like a man stretched on the rack, he faced the very real possibility of losing the beautiful young woman he'd grown to love so completely. God, he'd never been so scared. If he lost Christina now, before he'd even told her that he loved her, he'd never be able to endure the agony.

The tall pendulum clock in the corner slowly ticked off the minutes as the three Fieldings waited in tortured silence for the doctor to join them. At last Bowles appeared in the drawing room doorway, wiping his hands on a linen towel. "Your countess will be fine, my lord. She sustained a nasty bump on the head, but she's young and healthy. She'll be as fit as a fiddle in no time."

Roderick bowed his head in relief. "Thank God." Then he grabbed the surgeon's hand and pumped it up and down in delirious joy while he grinned like a madman. "And thank you, sir!"

"Hooray!" shouted Pansy. She leaped up from the settee and executed an impromptu dance step.

"Sink me, if I don't feel a little woozy myself," Percy added with a wan smile.

Peering compassionately from under his bushy white brows, the physician returned Percy's smile, then addressed both the earl's siblings. "I wonder," he asked politely, "if I might have a few words with your older brother alone?"

"Of course, Dr. Bowles," Percy answered. He rose from his seat. "May we go up and see Christina?"

"I think not. She's still unconscious. Mrs. Owens is sitting with her. At the present time Lady Rugden needs quiet and rest."

After the younger pair had left, the surgeon looked quickly around the salon. He spied a cut-glass decanter and matching goblets. Laying the linen cloth he held in his hand on the side table, he poured out a glass of claret and handed it to Roderick, then poured another for himself. "I think you could use this, my lord. Come on, drink up. Doctor's orders."

The two men lifted the glasses in salute. Bowles took a sip of wine and then sank down on the sofa. He absently twirled the dark red liquid in the crystal glass. "My good friend," he said at last, "there's no need to be embarrassed about all this. You'll be surprised, but I've seen it happen before. An older, experienced man weds a lovely and innocent young girl, who's never been told what to expect as far as the consummation of the marriage. Discovering her totally ignorant and extremely frightened, the overconscientious groom can't bring himself to deflower her." The physician looked up to meet the earl's questioning gaze. "Your wife is flesh and blood, Lord Rugden, just like any other woman. She won't break."

Stunned by the doctor's words, Roderick listened mutely, not trusting himself to venture a comment on this staggering revelation. Mechanically, he sat down on a chair facing the sofa and gulped the wine. He felt like he'd just been kicked in the gut.

"Today's hemorrhaging is no more than a woman's monthly flow," Bowles continued thoughtfully. "You and I both know for a fact, of course, that Lady Rugden couldn't possibly be carrying a child, as she remains a virgin. But she apparently doesn't know that. It happens all too often, I'm afraid, despite all our modern knowledge. She's only one of many young girls kept in ignorance—this time understandably so. Her mother was ill for some time before she died a year ago. Mrs. Owens tells me that the countess has an older, married sister. She should be the one to tell her the facts of marital intercourse. Then take your lovely bride on a holiday. All women yearn for romance. She may return expecting the baby she so obviously desires. And you'll have a wife in more than name only."

After a few moments of shocked silence, Roderick was able to find his voice. "I believe I shall take your advice, Dr. Bowles. What my wife and I need is the honeymoon we never had. I appreciate your forthrightness in the matter. And I know I can trust in your sense of confidentiality. Will you need to check on her again before you go?"

The kindhearted gentleman shook his bewigged head, sympathy showing clearly in his eyes. "No, but I will stop by to see her tomorrow. She should have regained consciousness by then. In the meantime someone must remain with her until she rouses, for in cases like this a lapse of memory isn't uncommon. And as long as I've gone out on a limb already, I'll offer still another bit of unsolicited advice. No more duels or affairs, eh? With a wife like the countess, you don't need opera dancers."

"I'll stay with her myself," Roderick replied. "Thank you for coming so quickly." He stood and assisted Bowles from his chair, then encompassed the doctor's pudgy hand in his large one in heartfelt gratitude. He helped the physician on with his coat, which had been brought by a footman, and walked him to the door. Roderick then returned to the front salon and poured another glass of wine. He felt as if he'd been caught in the midst of a cavalry charge and trampled by several hundred galloping horses. Of all the things he'd suspected, he'd never once guessed the truth. But who would have dreamed an innocent girl would fabricate such a scandalous story? He mentally reviewed every conversation he'd ever held with his exasperating bride.

Just when *had* she told him she was carrying her lover's child? Hell, not until he'd first accused her of it. He realized with a jolt that he'd created the entire tale for her with his own ridiculous accusations. All she'd done was lower her lashes and go along with him. He'd been a stupid, stupid ass. Only a man blind with jealousy wouldn't have recognized the truth after the duel with Whiteham. Once he'd learned the young soldier couldn't have fathered her child, he should have caught on to her deception. Instead he'd continued to accuse her. And when she'd started to speak, he'd silenced her: *Don't say a thing. I wouldn't believe it anyway.*

He drained the wine and set the glass down. Engrossed in his reverie, he walked to the window and stared with unseeing eyes at the wintry street below. What an idiot she'd made of him! She'd succeeded in treating him like some castrated eunuch, playing on his inordinate male pride and his irrational fear of harming the unborn child like the consummate artist she was. He braced his hand on the window jamb and silently laughed at his own folly.

My clever, scheming, wicked, darling, wonderful, virgin wife. What a treat I have in store for me when you're well again.

Percy found his older brother standing in front of the window, his head bent, his shoulders shaking convulsively. He went up to Roderick and placed his hand on his arm in a comforting gesture. "I say, Roddy ol' boy, don't take it so hard. She's going to be as good as new. I just spoke with Mrs. Owens. She said the doctor insisted there was no reason why Christy couldn't have a half-dozen children in the future. Thunder and turf, man, you'll have lots of little Fieldings to carry on our name. I'm sure of it."

The earl turned to face his younger sibling. Placing his hand on Percy's shoulder, he gave his brother a courageous smile. His gray eyes glistened with moisture. "You're absolutely right, Percy. Christina and I will have children. You can count on it."

Had the Honorable Mr. Fielding not known better, he'd have sworn that the tears in his brother's eyes were tears of joy.

A solitary beeswax candle lit the pale yellow chamber, casting its soft, flickering glow on the still figure lying under the coverlet in the enormous four-poster. The silk bed curtains were drawn slightly ajar to allow a view of the bed's occupant. Outside, the chill winter rain froze on the leaded windowpane, leaving crystal proof that the first snowstorm of the season was about to reach London.

A small blaze flickered in the nearby fireplace. The Earl of Rugden bent over the grate and tossed a log atop the andirons. He resumed his post in a chair strategically placed beside the bed. Dressed in a warm jacket and buckskin breeches to ward off the chill, he thrust his booted feet under the bedstead. The clock on the mantel ticked monotonously in the quiet sickroom, measuring the hours since Christina had fallen. It was three o'clock in the morning, and she'd still not regained consciousness.

Roderick watched her in worried silence. His thoughts were filled with memories of his brief marriage with the girl-woman who rested so quiescently before him. How cleverly she'd pulled the wool over his eyes. He'd thought her a practiced flirt, carrying on her love affairs beneath his very nose, when in actuality she was still part child, completely inexperienced in the ways of love.

The bedclothes stirred with a soft rustle of satin. Christina thrust her free arm up above her head and brushed against the bandage. Her hand came down with a jerk, and she scowled in pain. Gradually she lifted her lids. Feeling his presence beside her, she turned and stared at him, her expressive blue eyes filled with confusion.

Roderick leaned forward, his elbows propped on his knees. He sat so close to the bed that his legs touched the coverlet. "Christina?" he called softly, fearing she'd slip back into unconsciousness.

After several moments she spoke in a voice so faint he could barely hear the words. "What happened?"

He lifted her hand as his heart soared with relief. "You fell, sweetheart. You're all right now." Then he added, in the hope of surprising her into a confession, "But you lost the baby."

Christina frowned in concentration. "I misplaced an infant? I'm not usually so careless. Whose child was it?"

"No one seems to know," he answered in a whisper. He lifted her fingers to his lips and then gently released them. "Do you recall anything about the fall?"

Her hand went to her forehead to touch gingerly the edges of the dressing. She tentatively explored her immovable shoulder and arm. "No, I can't seem to remember falling."

"Do you know who I am, Christina?" he murmured.

"Aye. We're ... we're married, aren't we," she said haltingly, as if it was painful to think.

He bent over her and lightly placed a kiss on the bridge of her nose. "Yes, darling, I'm your husband. Now close your beautiful eyes and sleep. I'll be right here beside you."

It was ten o'clock in the morning when Christina awoke to find Mrs. Owens hovering nearby. At her shaky "Good morning," the housekeeper turned and beamed at her.

"Ah, my lady, it is a good morning indeed, seeing you awake and clear-eyed. How do you feel, dear?" She bent over and tenderly pushed aside the tangled curls that fell across Christina's brow. Looking intently into her eyes and apparently satisfied with what she saw, the housekeeper stood up straight. "How about a little breakfast? Do you think you could drink some tea?"

"Yes, and I would like some muffins, too, please," Christina said. She smiled more bravely than she felt. "I'm starving."

The cheerful woman pushed back the yellow curtains all round the bed and came to stand beside her mistress. "And well you should be, my lady. You haven't eaten since yesterday morning. How does your head feel?"

Christina's hand flew up to the bandage. "Oooh! Sore! What happened?"

"You fell down the stairs, my lady. You've been unconscious since midmorning yesterday."

Christina closed her eyes and tried to recall the events leading up to the accident. Like a distorted scene from a feverish child's nightmare, she vaguely remembered arguing with Marie about faking a tumble down the stairs in order to feign a miscarriage. Mortified at the hoax she'd apparently perpetrated, the countess closed her eyes, unable to meet the honest gaze of her servant. About the fall itself, Christina remembered nothing. A light tap at the door brought her eyes open once more.

Lady Gwendoline peeked inside. "Is she awake?"

"That she is, my lady. And calling for breakfast."

Gwen hurried into the room and approached the bed. She was dressed in a warm merino ensemble, and her round cheeks glowed like winter apples. "Oh, you poor little thing," she said. She clucked her tongue in sympathy. "Look at that bandage! How are you feeling, sweetie?"

"Like I walked into a wall." Christina chuckled. "And the wall didn't move."

"I just spoke with Percy," Gwen continued as she patted her younger sister's hand. "He said you lost the baby." Her blue-green eyes were filled with the certainty that Christina had never been with child. The two women were far too close not to share such a marvelous secret, had it been the truth and not a mere fabrication.

Christina flushed and lowered her lids. She squeezed her sister's hand gratefully. "Where's Marie? I need to get up and dress." She leaned on her good elbow and scooted awkwardly back against the headboard.

Mrs. Owens hurried to prop the pillows behind her. "Easy, easy, my lady. His lordship is very upset with your fancy French maid. He's refused her permission to wait upon you until he talks with her. But Annie and I will be happy to take care of you."

Gwen interrupted cheerily. "I'll help you this morning, Christy. But are you sure you feel up to getting out of bed?"

Christina leaned her head back on the pillows and blinked her eyes to clear away the blurred images swimming before her. "Perhaps I'll just lie here awhile, till the dizziness clears."

The housekeeper carried a dressing gown over from the wardrobe. "Here, my lady. Slip this on. You have a sitting room full of company out there waiting to see you."

Together they helped Christina put on the blue robe, easing it cautiously over the injured right arm and then replacing the sling they'd removed. That nursing task over, Mrs. Owens opened the door. "The Countess is awake and ready to receive visitors," she announced. The door was flung wide, and Percy and Lord Henry Sanborn entered.

"Zounds, Christy, what a start you gave us," Percy said. "Why, if something happened to you, we'd never forgive ourselves."

Lord Sanborn went to stand beside his wife. His infectious good humor split his face in an ear-to-ear grin. "Indeed, this world wouldn't be the same without you, little lady. So no more bouncing down the stairs on your head, if you please."

Christina grinned back. She knew she must be a sight.

With the heavy bandage encircling her head and one arm encased in a sling, she probably resembled a refugee from a war zone. "That's one promise I can make and keep, Henry," she said. "Soaring down the staircase headfirst isn't nearly as much fun as jumping horses over the forbidden fence at Waldwick Abbey." She looked at Lady Gwen. "Where are Joanna and Alexander?"

Gwen put her arm around her husband's ample waist and smiled contentedly. "Pansy is entertaining them downstairs. You don't need two wild savages rampaging through your bedchamber until you're back on your feet and able to defend yourself."

"Speaking of savages," Percy interrupted, "I think I hear my brother's voice."

The sound of a deep baritone came from the adjoining room of the suite. "This rampant flattery has got to stop, Percival." Rugden peered around the edge of the doorjamb and smiled at Christina. "I'll be in shortly. There's a messenger just arrived that I must attend to first."

Christina sat up straight, twisting the bedclothes with nervous fingers. Her breath caught high in her throat, and her heart pounded erratically. She didn't remember speaking to her husband since before the accident. What would he say about the miscarriage?

Her agitation increased when a portly stranger entered the room. The corners of his kind eyes crinkled with friendliness as he smiled at her. "And how's my little patient today?" he inquired. "I see you're fully awake this morning."

Christina sent Gwen a look of mute desperation, and her sister came swiftly to the rescue. "Dr. Bowles was here yesterday, Christy. Percy fetched him. The doctor examined you to determine the extent of your injuries."

Incredulous, the countess looked from Gwen to the physician, trying to read from their expressions just what his examination had revealed. She willed herself to keep breathing. She was determined that she wouldn't faint, and she wouldn't start bawling, either. "Ah . . . what is your prognosis, Dr. Bowles? Will I survive?"

"Absolutely," he replied with a jovial smile. He came over to stand by her bedside. "I predict a complete recov-

ery. Now, let's have a look at that cut on your head, Lady
Rugden." He bent over his patient and removed the long,
bloodstained strip of linen.

Rugden came in the room and immediately moved to
stand beside the physician. The earl was dressed in a riding jacket of light brown suede. His white shirt enhanced
the color of his neck and face, making him resemble a burnished god of war straight out of Greek mythology. He
took hold of Christina's hand while the doctor changed the
dressing. His somber gray eyes watched the procedure intently as the last of the gauze was lifted from the wound.
"How is she, Bowles?" he inquired, and the quiet gravity
of his words betrayed his apprehension.

"Right as rain. All that's needed is time to heal."

"Can she travel, if she takes it easy?"

A jolt of pure anguish lanced through Christina. He
knew. He knew her pregnancy had been all a charade, and
he was going to send her away without even giving her a
chance to explain. Heartsick, she swallowed back the tears
that clogged her throat.

The surgeon readjusted the linen sling that supported
her injured arm and shoulder. "Certainly, Lord Rugden.
Just be sure there are no rambunctious high jinks till we're
certain the wound is staying closed and healing well and
the dislocation no longer pains her."

"Travel?" yelped Pansy, who had followed her brother
into the room. "Christina is going away again?"

Rugden squeezed Christina's hand as he smiled at the
diminutive brunette. "Yes, but don't look so disappointed,
Lady Penelope. This time you get to go along, too. In fact,
we're all going." He looked at his wife again. "A messenger just arrived with a letter from your father," he explained. "He wants you to visit him at Waldwick Abbey."

"Did . . . did he say anything else?" Christina asked,
wondering if he'd read the marquess's reply to her pleas
for an annulment.

The earl quirked his scarred eyebrow and smiled at her,
a warm light glowing in his silvery eyes. "Yes. He invited
all of us to join him there for his birthday celebration. It
seems he'll be turning sixty next Saturday."

"Oh, Christy," Pansy trilled happily, "how wonderful

that you're going to be all right." She hurried over to clasp Christina's hand and continued with genuine sympathy, "I'm so sorry that you lost the baby. I didn't even know—"

Lady Gwendoline interrupted, mid-sentence. "How kind of you, Pansy. And I'm sure you express all of our thoughts. But the important thing is that Christina is going to be fine."

Mortified that all the caring people around her had been duped by her vile chicanery, Christina looked down at her hand resting in her sister-in-law's tiny one. "Thank you, Pansy," she answered in a trembling voice. She looked up at the family that had hurried to her support so lovingly, and her eyes filled with tears. "Thank you, everyone, for being so good to me. I don't deserve it."

"Pshaw!" Percy exploded. "That's plain fustian! We don't know anyone more deserving!"

"I'm sorry to break this up," said Dr. Bowles, "but if Lady Rugden is to travel to Wiltshire, I want her to spend the remainder of the day resting quietly."

"An excellent idea, Doctor," Rugden affirmed. He opened the door to usher the entire group out, then returned to her bedside. "I respect Bowles's opinion highly, Christina. He's tended my family's illnesses and accidents for many years now. He said you'd suffer no further complications from your tumble."

Christina lowered her lids to conceal the panic that threatened to suffocate her. She was afraid to speak, certain her guilty tone would give her away. But she had to know if he knew. "What else did the doctor tell you?"

"That there's no reason why you can't have children in the future."

Her startled eyes flew up to meet his grave ones. Breathless, she waited for him to continue.

"Now, sweetheart, I suggest you lie down and get some rest. There'll be no going to Waldwick Abbey unless I'm convinced that you're able to travel. By the way, do you remember anything about the fall?"

Relieved, Christina slid down, and he readjusted the pillows beneath her head. She tried to meet his gaze, but the effort was too painful. She was a lying, deceitful brat, and his tenderness was more than she could bear. "No, I remember nothing from the time I was unpacking the china until I awoke this morning," she replied. She stared down at the coverlet bunched in her hand.

He wrapped one of her curls around his forefinger and absently rubbed it against his thumb. "Well, maybe the intervening events will come back to you in time. Meanwhile, don't tax yourself. You've a big family gathering ahead of you. Mrs. Owens will be bringing up some breakfast shortly. After that try to sleep." He cupped her chin and brought her face up so he could look into her eyes.

"Christina ..." he said in a voice tinged with tender amusement. His lips curved in the hint of a smile. But whatever it was that he had been going to say, he changed his mind. Instead he bent and kissed her gently, lingeringly on the mouth.

That afternoon the earl interviewed Madame Boucher. It wasn't a comfortable discussion for the abigail, who stood in the center of his study and faced him across his large desk. The master of Rugden House informed her in cutting words and with a tone cold enough to freeze Hades, that he'd prefer to dismiss her summarily and would do so were it not for the kind regard his wife held for her.

"Your actions of yesterday," he curtly informed her, "were such that I am counting the days until your two weeks are up. In the meantime you may wait on your mistress as long as I'm not in the room. But keep out of my sight. I trust I make myself clear?"

"Quite clear," she answered, careful to keep all trace of emotion out of her voice. She dared not risk the chance of being flung bodily out of the home. And he was just mad enough to do it.

She left the room and raced down the central hall, startling a footman, who jumped visibly when he saw her.

"Out of my way, *imbécile!*" she hissed.

Watt Keighly watched her hurry away, her black eyes glittering with hatred and her dark skirts swirling around her bony ankles. "Creepers," he muttered to himself, "if she doesn't look like a witch flying over a graveyard on All Hallow's Eve, I don't know who does."

Chapter 21

The glories of autumn had faded, and the chill November wind steeped the bleak Wiltshire landscape in mist. Christina gazed out the window of the Rugden coach at the dreary countryside and listened to the dismal creak of iron wheels on the frosty ground. Blissfully content, Pansy rode on the seat across from her, happy that she was finally being allowed to go somewhere, anywhere, with her family.

Lord and Lady Sanborn, along with the two children, were following immediately behind in their smart carriage. The third vehicle, a huge, antiquated coach, carried Gwen's abigail, the children's nanny, Christina's maid, and Percy's valet. Angus Duncan had taken one glance inside the crowded coach, snorted contemptuously, and mounted his own fine mare.

Earlier that morning, after an overnight stay at the Five Willows in the small village of Chippenham, Christina had been bundled into their finely appointed berlin by her husband. Rugden had placed her tenderly amid a mountain of pillows piled high on the velvet seat and covered her with a thick bearskin rug, a memento of his winter spent in the Canadian wilderness. Now the two Fielding brothers, mounted on Mohawk and Sheba, cantered alongside the coach, matching the brisk pace set by the team of bays.

When she heard Rugden whistling cheerfully, Christina wondered once again about his inscrutable reaction to the supposed miscarriage. He hadn't indicated by so much as a word that Dr. Bowles had said anything to cast suspicion on the staged fall or the pregnancy that never was. Since her accident, Rugden had treated her like a semi-invalid. Even Marie, who also remained strangely reticent about the mishap, didn't fuss over her as much as he did. He'd never have insisted that his wife be coddled and cosseted until she squirmed with embarrassment, if he knew of her odious deception. Whenever she looked at her husband, there was a flicker of humor lighting his silvery gaze. A hint of a smile played around his handsome mouth, despite his obviously sincere concern over her injuries. Only once had that sanguine expression disappeared. When she'd asked that he postpone Madame Boucher's dismissal, he'd clenched his angular jaw and coldly shaken his head. He'd offered no explanation, except to say that Marie was to be replaced the day they returned to London.

Suddenly noticing the familiar landmarks, Christina leaned forward with excitement. "Look, Pansy, just around the bend. Waldwick Abbey!"

The young woman pressed her nose to the cold pane as she tried to get her first look at the Berringer family's beloved country estate.

Across the frozen River Avon, on a slight knoll, stood a weathered stone abbey rising four stories high against the leaden sky. Its dozen chimney stacks, fluted and coiled in gothic style, pierced the gray horizon like spiraling steeples on a French cathedral. Row upon row of arched, mullioned windows looked down on the lawn, now a blanket of frost that stretched all the way to the riverbank. It was old. It was faded. It was surpassingly beautiful.

"Oh, Christy, how you must love it," Pansy said.

Christina's heart leaped with joy as the coach-and-four took the curving graveled driveway at a spanking pace. On the broad front steps waited Austin Berringer, the Marquess of Waldwick. Next to him were her brothers, Lords Carter and Francis. And there on the top of the stairs stood Grandmother Berringer. She was home at last!

The Earl of Rugden was given a guest room beside Carter's, well down the long hall from his countess. He accepted his father-in-law's unspoken rebuke with a shrug and a rueful smile. No doubt the news of the notorious Parisian duel had traveled into Wiltshire. Roderick considered himself fortunate not to have been assigned one of the bare cells on the ground floor, once inhabited by long-dead Augustinian monks and now only by their ghosts. The first floor rooms had been left almost completely untouched since the building's days as a monastery. He glanced indifferently about his bachelor accommodations and then left Duncan unfolding shirts and cravats. At the moment the earl had worries of far greater concern than Waldwick's displeasure in his son-in-law. Lost in thought, he hurried down the hallway to the central staircase.

Upon his return from Paris, Roderick had received word that the investigator he'd hired had come to a blank wall. There seemed to be no way to trace the two directors who cashed the promissory notes written to the Greater London Docks Company. They'd simply disappeared without a trace. But he was certain they were merely hired accomplices. It would take a very clever person to persuade his father to invest in a nonexistent corporation.

Immediately following his wife's accident Roderick had written a letter to Gillingham, vindicating the general's defense of Lady Rugden and alerting him to the fact that someone on the Parisian staff of the Hôtel de Fontaine was a spy. Hugh had been correct; the countess was incapable of such a crime. But someone in that household had read those false reports and passed them on to the French.

"Rugden," the dowager marchioness called from the drawing room doorway as he came down the stairs. "I wonder if you'd be kind enough to help me fetch my cane. I left it under the dining room table."

"I'll be happy to get it for you, Lady Helen," he offered with a smile.

"I'll go with you," she said. "It's not often I get a handsome war hero for my escort." She placed her frail hand on his arm and walked with him into the green and white dining room.

As Roderick reached under the table and found the cane, the elderly lady sank down in one of the mahogany chairs. "Let's rest here a minute, Rugden. There's something I'd like to say to you."

Surprised, the earl nodded politely. "Of course, Lady Helen. I'm at your disposal."

The dowager looked up at him through narrowed eyes. She thwacked the gold-headed cane he'd just retrieved for her on the seat of a nearby chair. "Sit down," she said petulantly. "I can't talk to you like this. I'll get a crick in my neck that'll last a week." At her imperious gesture, Roderick sat down and waited.

She'd decided on a direct, frontal attack and launched it immediately. "Did you know Edwin Whiteham is betrothed?"

"No."

"He'll marry in the spring—a sweet, docile girl, one with whom a man like yourself would be thoroughly bored within a year's time. She'll make Ted a good wife. Christina never would have. Your spouse, on the contrary, my dear fellow, is passionate, self-willed, and stubborn to a fault."

Lady Helen paused to let him deny it. He didn't try. "Christina needs a strong man, Rugden. I thought you were that man. Now I'm not so sure. The Berringers are a fiercely loyal tribe. My granddaughter won't tolerate a husband who rambles." Her white eyebrows lifted in challenge as she waited for his reaction to her incendiary remarks.

Roderick stood and offered the meddlesome old lady his arm. "Though it's none of your concern, Lady Helen," he said in a clipped voice, "I can assure you the reputed affair with the opera dancers never progressed past the stage of casual flirtation. The absence of physical intimacy was what caused the jealousy between the two sisters. Each accused the other of what she didn't have herself."

"Ha! I thought as much." The dowager took his arm and rose. She laughed gleefully, like an obstreperous child who has succeeded in a naughty prank. "We'd hoped a match between the two of you would produce a passel of outstanding brats. But I warn you, Roderick, though the family wishes nothing so much as that this union succeed, we want it only if it continues as a loving one. Neither Christina's misery nor your own unhappiness should be the price of a dynasty built upon your marriage. Howsoever, at the rate you're going, I'll be lucky to attend a single christening before I turn up my toes." She ignored the fact that he was glowering down at her and crooked her gnarled finger at him. She poked him on the shoulder. "For God's sake, man, make your move. Seduce the gel!"

Roderick was too polite to inform the elderly lady that if the ubiquitous Berringers would just back away and give him some room, it was exactly what he planned to do.

Heading toward the stables, he passed through the abbey's magnificent fifteenth-century cloister with its fan vaulting soaring high above. Upon the visitors' midday arrival, Francis had promised Roderick a ride on a magnificent hunter he'd just purchased. As he made his way to meet his brother-in-law, the earl joyfully warbled an almost forgotten childhood ditty. Nothing, not this enforced separation from his ravishing wife, nor the desperate monetary crisis which loomed over his head, could puncture his bubble of happiness.

Christina had never betrayed him. The intimacy they'd shared that night in Paris, when he'd been so driven by jealousy and need that he'd almost taken her despite his fears, had bound her to him in a way far greater than he'd ever dreamed. She'd never known any man but him. Now all he had to do was bide his time until her convalescence was over. In the meanwhile Dr. Bowles had been correct—a little wooing was in order. Like Froggie in the nursery song his mother had taught him at her knee, Roderick would a-courting go.

After a breakfast the next morning shared with the ladies and children of the family, for the young men had left before daylight to hunt winter hares, Christina was summoned to her father's study. She found him seated on a sofa, gazing at a portrait of the late marchioness.

"Grandmother said you wanted to see me," she said nervously, aware that the long-desired interview had finally arrived.

Austin Berringer looked at his daughter, dressed in a simple rose-printed morning gown. Her honey-golden hair was pulled back and tied with a matching ribbon, much as she'd worn it as an adolescent. Today there was the artless addition of the bandage. It made her appear younger and more vulnerable than he remembered seeing her look in years.

He wisely conjured up her appearance in the sophisticated gold evening dress of the night before. She was no longer his baby girl. He patted the place beside him invitingly. "Sit down, child. We haven't discussed the letter you sent. Let's talk about it now. You wrote that you despised Rugden and accused him of carrying on adulterous relationships with at least two other women. Yet since you've been at Waldwick Abbey, I've been puzzled about what you really do want. Is it still your wish to get an annulment?"

Christina plopped down beside her father. She pleated and repleated the edge of her sling with restless fingers, torn by her conflicting desires. "I'm not certain, Father."

The marquess sighed, whether in relief or exasperation she wasn't sure. "I'd hoped," he explained patiently, "that the two of you would begin to care for each other. Contrary to what you seem to believe, I didn't marry you off to a total stranger. I've known and admired Roderick since he was a youth. But if you've developed an irrevocable animosity toward each other, then I'll support you in seeking a dissolution of the marriage."

Placing his arm around her, Waldwick pulled her closer, and she laid her head against his shoulder. After a slight pause, he continued in a voice rough with emotion, "Your mother and I loved each other deeply, poppet, as did Roderick's own parents. None of us would have wanted a loveless marriage for any of our children. Think it over carefully and don't make a hasty decision. If, when you return to London, you still wish an annulment, you'll have the loving support of every member of your family, including your grandmother. You may live with her at Waldwick Mansion or stay with Gwen while the matter is being resolved."

Christina gazed at her father with tear-filled eyes. At last she'd received the permission she'd been pursuing so desperately for three long months. Now she wasn't certain she wanted the marriage dissolved. "Oh, Father, I've never been so confused and wretched in my whole life."

"Could it be that you've fallen in love with your husband, Christy?"

Blue eyes met blue in complete understanding. "Yes," she said simply. "I love him."

"Then tell him, dear heart."

Shaking her bandaged head, Christina stood and walked over to the fireplace. She gazed into the flames, then replied in dismay, "It's not that simple, Father. His infidelity and my coldness have erected walls between us that will never be surmounted."

"If you don't try, child, you could be throwing away your one chance for real happiness in life." He rose and went over to her. He put his hand comfortingly on her shoulder and added with a smile, "You may have to eat a little crow, but it'd be worth it."

Christina hugged her father. "Gad," she said with a gurgle of laughter, "I just hope I don't choke on all the feathers!"

As his daughter turned to go, the marquess added in an afterthought, "By the by, poppet, what happened to your sweet little maid Polly Wright?"

Christina frowned. "Polly left me last June, when she married a young man from her village. That's when I hired Madame Boucher in London."

"Wherever did you find such a termagant?"

"She was recommended to me by Oliver Davenport, a personal friend of the Duke of Carlisle. Marie was his daughter's governess and had to find a new employer when the girl came of age and entered society."

"Davenport?" the marquess said thoughtfully, rubbing his chin. "The name sounds familiar, but I can't place the man."

"At any rate," Christina continued, "Marie will only be with me until we return to London. Rugden can't abide the sight of her."

Lord Waldwick chuckled. "After seeing her sourpuss face, I can't say I blame him."

Christina left her father's study so deep in thought she almost stumbled over Joanna, who was creeping along the hall rug on all fours.

"Aunt Christy," she pleaded, "help me find my kitty. She ran away."

Christina bent down and planted a kiss on the little girl's plump cheek. "That naughty Boots! Which way did she run?"

Joanna pointed to the front drawing room. "In there."

While Joanna looked behind the heavy velvet drapes, her aunt, gathering her rose-printed skirt in a bunch, knelt and awkwardly peered under the settee and upholstered chairs.

Roaming out into the hall in her quest, Joanna took it into her head to check the library curtains as well. Without a word she left Christina, who was crawling gracelessly around the salon floor, encumbered by the immobilized arm encased in its sling.

"Lost something?" a deep voice questioned from above.

The Countess of Rugden, her nose inches from the lavishly patterned Kurdistan rug as she stretched one searching hand under a sofa, recognized his leather riding boots instantly. She scooted to her knees and tipped her head up to meet his gaze.

"Yes. Boots. Joanna's kitten."

An amused smile hovered around Rugden's lips. He reached down and lifted Christina to her feet. Bluish-green needles from a Scots pine had caught on the sleeve of his brown hunting jacket, and the smell of fresh evergreen surrounded him. Though the deep tan of August had faded, he retained the robust look of an inveterate outdoors man. Tireless energy and an unabashed male virility seemed to emanate from him.

With her father's admonitions fresh in her mind, Christina looked shyly up into her husband's eyes and smiled. "How was the hunting?"

"The hunting's marvelous."

"Did you snare anything?"

"Not yet."

His strong hand cupped her chin, one finger lightly stroking her lips. He bent and kissed her tenderly on the forehead, just beside the white bandage, then kissed her closed eyelids and the tip of her nose. She could feel his cool breath caress her face. His open mouth covered hers, the firm pressure of his tongue parting her lips. The seductive kiss released a hunger inside her, and she drew in a quick, intoxicated breath. Good gad, he tasted wonderful. She couldn't get enough of him.

The now-familiar ache brought on by her husband's touch spread through her body like a wizard's enchanted potion. Christina responded, spellbound, to his sorcery. She lifted her free arm over his broad shoulder. Drawn by his magic, she slid her fingers up the back of his neck, brushing against the black ribbon that tied his dark hair.

"Mmm," she said as she quivered deliciously.

"Mmm," he responded and slipped his arm around her waist to pull her closer.

An insistent tugging on her skirt brought Christina back to reality. Through the mist of pleasure that engulfed her, she heard her niece's plaintive voice.

"Aunt Christy, you promised to help me find Boots." Joanna watched in fascination as the grownups slowly focused their attention on her. She moved to the man who towered above her and grabbed his leg. "Uncle Roderick, can I have a kiss too?"

The adults parted reluctantly. Roderick smiled ruefully down at the child and shook his head in good-natured exasperation. Then he lifted Joanna and swung her high above his head, while she squealed in mock terror. "You certainly may have a kiss!" He smacked her noisily on her cheek and then set her on his shoulders. "We'll all look for your kitty," he offered with indulgent generosity. He directed a lecherous grin at his wife before turning back to the four-year-old. "Then you can take Boots and show her to Pansy."

The trio searched the dining room together. Boots had climbed up the drapes and now sat on the curtain rod, mewling her refusal to come down. The earl lifted Joanna ceilingward. She grabbed the unhappy feline with glee and set her atop her uncle's ebony locks.

Christina's laughter rang out. "Be careful, Joanna! Don't let the kitty scratch Uncle Roderick." She stretched up with her mobile arm to grasp the animal and brought her safely down, where she cuddled against Christina's shoulder.

Unaccountably, Rugden reached out and touched his wife's lips with the tip of his forefinger. His words were soft and cajoling. "Say it again, Christina."

She looked at him and tilted her head, unsure of his meaning.

"Say my name again, sweetheart. That's only the second time you've ever used it."

With heart-stopping clarity, she remembered when she'd touched his cheek and called his name. It was the evening in Paris when she'd lain with him in her bed, bathed in the glow of his loving. She gazed searchingly into his gray eyes, outlined with their thick black lashes. Her response, soft and breathy, was hesitant, her voice unsure but filled with hope. "Roderick?"

"Joanna," came another voice, strong and clear from the hall. "Where are you?" Gwen stood in the open doorway, a look of surprise on her face. "Oh, I'm dreadfully sorry to disturb you, but Nanny was worried about her charge."

Francis came to stand behind his older sister. "Father's just challenged us all to a game of billiards," he called to the earl. "Percy wants you to help him defend the Fielding reputation."

"Blast." Rugden groaned under his breath. He lifted Joanna off his shoulder and set her on her feet. Then he took the kitten from his wife and placed it in the child's arms. At the exclamation specifically forbidden to her, the little girl buried her face in Boots's soft fur and giggled ecstatically.

"Come on, let's go," the earl said with resignation. He took Christina's hand and drew her with him toward the waiting Berringers. "There isn't a pantry in the place they wouldn't find us in, anyway."

Chapter 22

C hristina drifted into consciousness, vaguely aware
    that she felt worried and confused. She looked up at
the satin canopy above her and realized why she'd awakened so muddled. She'd been dreaming that Rugden had
come to her bed, just as he had in the Hôtel de Fontaine.
And just as on that night in Paris, when he'd kissed and
caressed her so intimately, her body had responded to the
touch of his hands and lips and tongue. Wide awake now,
she was tormented by her need for him. A need he'd purposely nurtured within her, till it raged through her limbs
like a wildfire.

For the past three days, she'd been courted. Rugden had
launched a campaign of wooing that had left her breathless. He'd juggled the members of her large family with
consummate grace while he kept her always within his
reach. He would stand with his arm about her waist as he
visited with her father. Talking to Gwen, or Francis, or
Carter, he'd hold his wife's hand and rub his thumb absently back and forth across her knuckles or caress the
nape of her neck with his long fingers.

Rugden made no attempt to hide his possessiveness. He
touched her constantly. With each passing day, she became
more vividly, more achingly aware of the tightly leashed
male power her husband embodied. He wasn't the least bit
daunted by the presence of her notable father and two
brothers. Somehow he'd even managed to contrive moments when they were alone together. And that was no
easy feat. For it soon became clear that every one of the
Berringers had heard of the infamous duel of the opera

dancers. While Carter and Francis treated Rugden with pleasant civility, on several occasions she'd caught both of her brothers watching him with cold circumspection.

And when she and Rugden were alone, he couldn't seem to keep his hands off her. Not that he made any effort to try. As they talked about the most trivial of subjects, he'd stroke her collarbone and rib cage with his fingers and brush the sides of her breasts with his palms, almost casually, yet ever heedful of her injured shoulder and her bandaged head. Right in the middle of a conversation, he'd lift the curls at the nape of her neck and place a languorous kiss on the sensitive skin behind her ear. Like a love-struck miss, she'd go all soft inside and have to reach out and grasp his arm for support. He'd smile in certain knowledge of her growing need for his touch and move even closer, till his massive thigh was pressed against her trembling one. Soon he'd aroused such a fever inside her that when he merely walked into a room she was suddenly breathless. Surrounded by her fascinated, inquisitive family and tormented by guilt and the fear that he'd discover her perfidious hoax, she had endured days of exquisite torture.

The sling and bandage had been removed the previous day. Her shoulder was completely healed, and the cut on her temple was no more than a tiny line, which would be unnoticeable in a few months. Rugden had joked about their matching scars the night before when he'd escorted her to the bedroom door and kissed her with infinite tenderness, just as he'd done every other night of their stay at the abbey. And once again on her pillow she'd found some trinket, some thoughtful token of his regard. One evening, she'd even discovered a sonnet by Shakespeare, carefully copied in Rugden's own broad scrawl. Tears had blurred her eyes when she'd thought of his callused soldier's hand painstakingly copying down the words of restrained sensuality. How could she have guessed this proud barbarian she'd married had such a flair for romantic seduction? No wonder the Ramillies sisters had tried to blow holes through each other!

But he'd made no move to enter her bedroom, and she

knew why. He'd been patiently waiting for her wounds to heal. And now it was only a matter of time.

Each caring gesture had filled her with a deeper mortification. He believed that she was recovering not only from a bad fall, but from a dangerous miscarriage as well. He'd been so worried, he'd even had the boldness to question her about the bleeding.

She'd averted her eyes and stuttered and stammered like a child. "It's ... it's ... no longer a worry. That is, I'm not ..."

He'd laughed softly at her bashfulness and pulled her to him. Kissing her temple, he murmured in her ear, the words gentle and incredibly reassuring. "Don't be embarrassed, sweetheart. Such things are a common concern to a woman's husband."

Good gad, she couldn't continue this ghastly subterfuge any longer. Yet she knew that once she admitted the truth, his gaze of tender amusement would change to one of scornful, bitter disdain. She remembered the warning that Duncan had given her when he'd told of Rugden's heroism at the battle of Quebec.

The colonel isna capable of anything dishonorable. If he has a fault, lass, it's that he imposes the same strict code on others that he does on himself. He willna tolerate deceit of any kind.

Christina knew she had to get up out of bed, though the urge to crawl beneath the coverlet and stay there for the rest of her life was nearly overwhelming. She had to face Rugden and tell him the truth. She dare not wait until he discovered her virginity for himself. She had to tell him now, knowing the look of contempt in his silvery eyes would be more than she could bear.

Then later that morning she'd meet with her father and inform him of her final decision to seek an annulment of her brief, lamentable marriage. The marquess had encouraged her to try to win Rugden's love. But her kindhearted father had no idea of the wall of lies that stood between her and her staunch, high-principled husband. She slipped out of bed, determined to get it over with before she lost what little courage she had. Changing speedily into her riding habit, she resolved to find her husband and confess the truth at once. After that she'd seek solitude outdoors, where she could nurse her broken heart undisturbed by her solicitous family.

Roderick stood before the tall window in the abbey's large library and gazed at the white lawn below. It had started to snow—light, fluffy flakes that drifted lazily to the ground—but in his abstraction he was barely aware of the changing weather. He knew that his campaign to gain Christina's love had made some small headway, but it was still far from a total victory. The fact that he'd ordered her London banker to sell Penthaven, rather than attempt a costly restoration, stood like an insurmountable rampart between them. Yet his decision had been based on hard logic, not on an emotional impracticality that placed dreams above sound judgment and reasonable foresight. He was well aware that she hadn't given up on her plan to turn the Cornwall estate into a home for indigent musicians and blamed him for its delay. Even his reasons for marrying her remained suspect in her eyes. And the godawful farce enacted by those two French doxies had just about ended his marriage before it'd begun. No, Christina wasn't about to believe any profession of love on his part. He'd have to wait till he'd proven himself with loving deeds before he uttered any words of undying devotion.

His quiet contemplation was broken by the sound of his wife's hurried footsteps on the polished oak floor. She glided through the open doorway and halted. When he started to turn, a smile of welcome on his lips, she stopped him.

"Wait, Rugden," she said, her words suffocated and hoarse. "Pray, don't turn around. There's something I must tell you, and I couldn't bear to see the look in your eyes when you hear what I have to say."

Roderick complied, recognizing the panic in her choked voice. He kept his eyes on the landscape in front of him as his heart thumped joyfully. Hope surged within him that, finally, his beautiful wife was going to tell him the complete and unvarnished truth.

"I lied," Christina admitted with bleak honesty. "I lied

and I tricked you from the very beginning. Neither Edwin Whiteham nor any other man fathered my child. I should be horsewhipped for so blackening Ted's good name in your eyes and for putting both your lives in jeopardy in the duel between you. The fall downstairs was a despicable trick in order to pretend I'd lost an unborn baby. But there never was a baby. The plain truth is"—she gulped, hurrying to get it over and done with—"I'm a virgin. And I—" Her high-pitched voice cracked, and she paused to regain control of her emotions.

Rugden waited, praying silently that she would tell him that she'd begun to care for him, if only a little. But she didn't say anything at all, and the sudden emptiness of the room engulfed him. He turned to find that his frightened, half-hysterical wife had fled.

Dashing out of the library, he flew up the stairs to throw open her bedroom door. The chamber was empty.

The dining room, where Waldwick and Sanborn still lingered over coffee, and the front salon, where Lady Helen sat reading the Bible, held no trace of his elusive wife. Gwen and Pansy looked up from their fashion plates to smile and tell him they hadn't seen her, either. Nor had Carter, Francis, or Percy, so engrossed in a game of billiards they barely glanced at him.

Rugden headed outside. A fearful recollection of another time when Christina had fled from him on horseback spurred him on. In the peaceful stables, he found a young boy brushing Mohawk's sleek black coat.

"Have you seen Lady Rugden?" the earl demanded.

The lad peeked across the stallion's mane and grinned. His freckles stood out like tiny copper coins on his pug nose. "Her ladyship's gone out ridin'," he answered. He seemed tickled to be a part of the excitement.

"Did she go alone?" Roderick thundered, angry that the fool had actually let her ride out in the falling snow.

"Nay, sir," the stable boy replied. He ducked under the great horse's neck and hurried across the stall's straw-covered floor. He took the bridle and bit and placed them on Mohawk, talking all the while. "Her ladyship refused to listen to me warnin' about a storm blowin' in. But Sergeant Duncan took out after her, swearin' in Gaelic like a red-haired madman. He told me to tell yer, soon's yer got out to the stables, that she was headin' toward the woods."

Cursing fluently under his breath, Roderick grabbed his saddle from its rack and threw it on his horse. Mohawk nickered and tossed his sleek head in happy anticipation of the coming gallop as the earl mounted and rode out of the stable.

The snowfall wasn't steady; it came in lazy little puffs. All around, the rolling hills were covered in soft, powdery drifts. Not far ahead, Roderick spotted his batman and called to him.

Duncan turned and galloped back. "The lass's just up the hill, Colonel," he said with a grin, all too happy to turn the matter over to the lady's husband. "I'll go back to the stable. I dinna think ye'll be needing me now, sir."

On the crest of a knoll, Christina sat on Sheba and watched her husband ride toward her. She made no attempt to escape. Sitting erect on the stamping mare, she waited with an air of tranquil detachment.

Roderick bit back the scathing remark on his lips about the idiocy of riding out into a storm and pulled on the reins to bring Mohawk to a halt beside her. She looked back across the open field with the calm serenity of a penitent who's just made a good confession. He turned and followed the direction of her gaze, then searched her face once more.

She kept her eyes on the sprawling abbey beneath her and spoke softly, her words barely audible in the chill air. "I was thinking how beautiful my home is, so peaceful and still in the snow."

Tearing his gaze from her delicate profile, Roderick looked down once again at the estate. Below them, Waldwick Abbey lay in quiet seclusion, surrounded by the snowy hills. The bare branches of the chestnuts and beeches in the nearby woods were black and stark against the winter whiteness.

"Your home is Rugden Court, Christina," he said gruffly. "And it will belong to our firstborn son after us."

He reached across the space that separated them and placed the tip of one finger beneath her chin. Gently, he turned her face to his, forcing her to meet his gaze. "I've some apologies to make, too, little one. I have known since your accident that you were never with child. I should have told you then, but I was hoping you'd learn to trust me enough to confide in me. It's no secret we had an unfortunate beginning. I know you believe that we're not suited for each other. And I'm well aware that I'm not the man you'd have chosen, had you been free to make that decision. For a while I even tried to convince myself it was only your fortune I desired. But it was never that, darling. Not even in the beginning. I've wanted you since the night we met."

He released her chin and gathered his reins in both hands to quiet the fretting stallion. "When you told me two days after we were married that you carried your lover's child, you unleashed the demons within me," he continued ruefully. "There was a raving lunatic inside me that wanted to smash and destroy any man who had ever touched you." Looking over at his wife, who listened in open beguilement, Roderick reached out and curved his arm around her waist to bring her toward him. "It's been a wild, crazy ride, sunshine, but I think we've outridden the storm." He kissed her hungrily. "Come to me tonight, Christina," he whispered against her sweet lips. "Come to me and let me prove how much I need you."

Almost chastely, Christina returned his kiss, the pressure feather-soft against his mouth. Her gloved hand came up to touch his cheek in a tentative gesture that betrayed her bewilderment at his unexpected disclosures.

Roderick pulled away reluctantly and saw the confusion in her eyes. "Let's go home now. Your cheeks are cold, and I don't want that pretty little nose frostbitten," he added, touching it lightly with one finger. He took her hand and brought it to his lips. "Don't look so worried, sweetheart. We have all the time in the world. I can wait until you're ready to trust me."

That evening a small blaze flickered on the hearth, casting Roderick's silhouette against the far wall of his bedchamber, where he sat in an upholstered chair and gazed into the flames. His long legs were stretched out in front of him, almost to the grate, and his head rested on the chair's high back.

The silence of the lonely room, the emptiness of his lonely arms, the desolation of his empty bed oppressed him more that night than any other since their arrival at Waldwick Abbey. Would his gorgeous little wife ever know what refined torment she'd put him through for the past three months? Was *still* putting him through.

The muffled pad of her footsteps on the thick rug was the first sound he heard. Roderick rose from his chair and turned slowly, so as not to frighten her with his wild elation. He could feel his heartbeat thundering like the roar of a cannonade against his ribs.

Christina stood framed in the open doorway. Her unbound hair fell in thick curls to her waist. She was clad in a diaphanous silk nightgown, and for a few brief seconds the candlelight from the hallway outlined her slender body through the nearly transparent material. Then she closed the door behind her and stood as still and as elusive as a wood nymph on a faded tapestry. Her blue eyes were filled with a shy anticipation; her small hands were clasped in front of her in wary uncertainty.

He waited, anchored to the spot, afraid to move lest she suspect the carnal desire that raged through every pore in his body. If she knew the effect she was having on him, as his groin grew taut and heavy with sexual need, she might disappear like the ethereal wraith she resembled.

For a long, silent moment Christina tarried. He knew she was frightened by the past misunderstandings that stretched like a chasm between them. Then, just as a trusting child takes its first tottering paces toward its parent, she moved two hesitating steps toward her husband. Roderick opened his arms wide in welcome and she flew to him.

He caught her and lifted her up, his hands encompassing her tiny waist as he twirled her round and round. Throwing his head back, he looked up at her, and his deep, joyful laugh resounded through the room. "Oh, my darling, darling wife."

Sliding her slowly, lingeringly down his hungry body until her face was directly above his own, he gazed into her enormous sapphire eyes and recognized with a thrill the glow of happiness reflected in them. He set her on her feet and cupped her lovely face in his hands. Then he covered her lips with his open mouth, his tongue thrusting inside with a fierce possession. God, he'd waited so long. Drawing her into his arms, he spread his hand across her lower back and pulled her soft hips, barely hidden beneath the thin fabric of her gown, against his hard thighs.

Christina felt his hands curve over her buttocks as he brought her closer, his touch burning through the gauze of her nightdress. He was naked beneath the gold dressing robe. She sensed it. She could feel the bulk of his muscular legs and the hardened bulge of his male arousal through the thick velvet. Whispering her name over and over, he kissed her eyelids, her cheeks, her nose, the corner of her mouth, the tender skin inside her elbow as his hands roamed up and down her bare arms and over her shoulders. Then he cupped her breasts, suddenly swollen and amazingly sensitive, and lifted them in his palms. He teased her nipples with his thumbs through the sheer silk, and she gasped in pleasure.

"Roderick," she said in a trembling whisper. It was a plea, but for what she wasn't certain.

Rugden drew her with him to the bed and sat down on the edge of the mattress, directly in front of her. Then he pulled her between his massive thighs and held her captive. "Darling," he said in a voice husky with desire, "before we go any further, I need to talk to you. Christina, do you know how a marriage is consummated?"

She met his concerned gaze and gave a startled gurgle of laughter. "Isn't it a little late to be asking me that? I mean, that night in Paris, we almost ... you nearly ..."

He chuckled deep in his throat. His hands clasped her waist to bring her even closer. Bending his head, he suckled her through the gauze of her nightgown. Spears of pleasure shot through her, hot and insistent, as his teeth gently nipped the tightening buds, and a low sigh of delight escaped her parted lips. He tipped his head back to look up at her, and she could see the sparkle of amusement in his gray eyes.

"At the time, sweetheart, I had no idea you were so inexperienced." The chiseled lines of his face grew hard with passion. "Do you know what's about to happen between us?"

"Yes." She dropped her head and lowered her lashes to hide her discomposure. "My mother told me when I was only fifteen. She was ill and wanted to be certain that she would be the one who talked to me about it."

Roderick looked up at his blushing wife, and the feverish ache of excitement surged like a flood through his veins. Above the gaping neckline of her ivory gown, a rosy glow suffused her creamy complexion. Her golden-brown lashes lay like thick brushes against her flawless skin. He recalled what Dr. Bowles had told him about the ignorance in which young girls were purposely kept and gentled his voice. "What exactly did your mother tell you at fifteen?"

She looked up, her blue eyes alight with mischief, a teasing, playful smile on her lips.

"Don't you know?"

He grinned at her saucy and evasive reply. "Yes. But I'd like to hear what you were told."

Flustered, Christina frowned in concentration. "She said that when a man cares deeply about a woman, he wants to hold her as close to him as possible. He holds her so close that part of him slips inside her." She looked at Roderick as if to verify her explanation, then added almost as an afterthought, "She said it feels wonderful, too."

His voice shook with wanting. "Your mother was a very wise woman."

Roderick slid his hands under the silken nightdress and caressed his innocent wife's bare thighs and buttocks. She trembled beneath the boldness of his touch, but made no attempt to break free. "I'm going to hold you close now, Christina. So close that the lonely, aching part of me is going to slide inside your warm, beautiful body. And it will feel very, very wonderful, I promise you. But first I'm going to touch every satiny inch of you. And you can touch me in return."

"Do you want me to?"

"Yes."

He rose, bringing the filmy material of her gown over

her head as he stood up beside her. Then he swung one arm under her knees, lifted her up, and laid her on the feather mattress.

Christina felt the warmth of a blush sweep over her as he stood by the side of the bed and looked down at her unclothed body. His gaze swept over her with such hunger, she instinctively clutched the coverlet beneath her with stiff fingers. He untied his robe and pulled it off, and she drew in a breath at the sight of his naked male beauty. His limbs were long and corded with muscles, his shoulders wide. His chest was broad and deep, the pectorals well-defined. A mat of black hair nearly covered his flat nipples, then tapered to a narrow line that ran down his hard abdomen to the thick, wiry hair at his groin. His swollen shaft surged outward with a virile energy of its own. He was fully aroused and potently male.

He seemed to sense the sudden wave of reluctance that washed over her. He quickly lay down beside her and took her in his arms, gently turning her to face him, his silvery gaze trapping hers in its fiery depths with a silent warning. This time there'd be no pulling back.

She wrapped her arms around his formidable strength and clung to him, pressing her softness against his solid frame, rubbing her chin across the hard sinew and bone of his shoulder. She'd never felt so frail and delicate and desirable. He pushed back the long strands of her tangled hair that had fallen across her cheek and trapped her face in his hands. He kissed her with a wild, fierce longing, his tongue thrusting inside her mouth in an invasion that couldn't be denied. She slid her hands up the nape of his strong neck, brushing the narrow black ribbon that tied back his hair. She loosened its knot and pulled the band away, then buried her fingers in the thick straight hair that fell to his shoulders. She caressed those powerful shoulders and the bunched muscles of his upper arms, marveling at the perfect symmetry of his physique, then ran her fingertips through the stiff hair on his chest, brushing softly over his hardened nipples and tracing the jagged scar that ran from shoulder to waist.

"That's it, baby," he urged hoarsely. "Touch every part

of me. Don't be afraid. You can't know how much I've wanted your pretty little hands on this big, ugly body."

At his cajoling words, Christina grew bolder. "You're not ugly," she murmured. "You're magnificent. Like a dark god of war, filled with thunder and lightning." She moved her hand down his hard stomach to touch the thick rod that sprang from the mat of hair at his groin. He caught his breath and groaned deep in his chest, and she jerked her fingers away, uncertain if she'd caused pleasure or pain.

"I'm sorry . . ." she apologized.

"Don't be," he said with a low, hoarse chuckle as he took her small hand in his large one and guided her back. "And don't stop. You're doing fine."

He kissed her again, and this time, as she fondled him with a knowledge as old and instinctive as mankind itself, she traced his lips with her tongue and explored the warm crevices of his mouth.

Roderick eased her on her back and crouched over her. He explored her slender body with his callused hands, running his questing fingers over the delicate curves of shoulder and hip and thigh. He suckled the rosy crests of each perfect breast as his hand sought the golden nest of curls at the juncture of her silken thighs. Parting her swollen folds, he slipped his finger inside her. He heard her sob of pleasure as he stroked the velvety flesh, building up the passion within, till she was moving her hips in concert with his intimate caresses. Then he gently lifted her knees and positioned himself between her thighs.

Cupping her buttocks in his large palms, he lifted her slim hips to meet his first, careful thrust. He inched his throbbing shaft into her tight, wet warmth, his body shaking with the effort it took to move slowly while the hunger for her roared through his veins. He met her worried eyes and read the doubt and alarm there.

"Easy, sweetheart," he crooned, knowing that if she continued to remain so tense, his entry would be all the more uncomfortable for her. He leaned over her, bracing himself on his elbows, and brushed her lips with his own. "Just let me come slow and easy."

"This isn't going to work," she said. "I'm too small. I thought you were supposed to just slip inside me."

He withdrew slightly, only to reenter deeper, harder, till he found the barrier he sought. A sheen of perspiration glistened on his bare skin from the strain of his tight control. "No," he told her, "you're not too small. You're too tense. Try to relax, darling."

Christina slid her hands along the bunched muscles of his upper arms, glowing like bronze in the candlelight and moist from the labor of his lovemaking. His scowling expression was one of intense strain, almost of apprehension. "Are *you* relaxed?" she asked with doubtful accusation.

Roderick stared at her in surprise. "Hell, no," he admitted with such rueful honesty that she started to giggle. "I've never been so goddamn tense in my life."

As the laughter shook her, her thighs opened wider, giving him greater access, and Roderick slammed through the maidenhead.

Christina gasped in surprise. Tears came to her eyes, and she blinked them away. "I thought this was supposed to feel wonderful," she whispered, trying to keep the confusion and hurt at his unexpected betrayal from her voice.

He didn't move, didn't answer, just stayed there inside her while the pain subsided and the pleasure slowly increased as her body began to accommodate the length and width of his turgid manhood. And with it came the marvelous awareness that she was filled with him. Her engorged flesh convulsed in undulating tremors around his thick, rigid staff. It was as though, with no conscious effort, her body was pulling him deeper inside her. The feeling was so tantalizing, so irresistible, all she wanted to do was move her hips against his, ever so slightly, so she could relish the exquisite sensations. But the moment Rugden felt her begin to move, he started to withdraw. A pang of disappointment shot through her.

"Wait," she begged. She wrapped her arms around his neck and clutched him tighter. "Don't leave yet. Stay inside me just a little longer."

His voice was hoarse and ragged with passion. "I'm not going anywhere, sunshine. I'm just going to give you some of that pleasure I promised."

He started slowly, with long, steady, unhurried strokes that built a spiraling pressure inside her. She gripped his shoulders and arched her hips against him, trying to hurry his rhythm. He wouldn't be rushed. He set his own pace, withdrawing and entering with a steady, gradual building of tempo that seemed to go on endlessly, till she started to plead his name over and over in a low chant of mindless eroticism. There was no one in the world but the two of them, and nothing mattered but the unimaginable pleasure he was giving her. She was panting, her heart pounding inside her, the blood racing through her veins. She teetered on the brink of ecstasy and forgot to breathe. When he braced on one arm and reached between their bodies to touch the swollen nub of her womanhood, the pleasure exploded. She plummeted over the edge only to soar upward again, like a falcon swooping down from the summit to catch the updraft and rise toward the sun. He continued to caress her, sustaining one orgasm after another, till she could endure the rapture no longer.

Roderick heard her long, final sob of fulfillment and surrendered to the all-consuming drive that roared within him. Over and over, he drove into her pulsating warmth, reaching his climax with a muffled shout of male conquest and total possession. Gasping for air, he bent his head forward and brushed her soft cheek with his own stubbled one.

"Breathe, sweetheart," he said in her ear, unable to keep the smile of victory from his voice. "I don't want you fainting on me."

Moonlight flooded the third floor room, coming boldly in through the open drapes and spilling impudently across the figures on the bed lying in each other's arms.

Roderick's gorgeous wife leaned up on one elbow and rained light kisses across his neck, shoulders, and chest. He felt her soft lips brushing across his rough, scarred, hairy body and thought he might just die of sheer, unadulterated happiness.

"Gwen was right," she mused, half to herself as she dipped the tip of her pink tongue into the hollow of his collarbone. The muscles in his groin spasmed and hardened in response to her honeyed attentions.

"Gwen?" Roderick asked, dumbfounded.

Looking up with an impish grin, she teased him. "Gwen said it would be like flying."

"Flying?" he repeated like a blockhead. He attempted unsuccessfully to follow her train of thought.

"Yes." She nodded. "Like a bird."

Comprehension dawned at last, and Roderick chuckled. He lifted her atop his hardened staff, and she bent over him with a sigh of sweet contentment. Glorying in the feel of her silken tresses as they cascaded around them like a curtain of yellow silk shimmering in the moonlight, he traced the pink aureoles above him with his fingertips in tantalizing thoroughness.

"What a lucky night that was," he teased in return.

Her face came down to his, and she gently nipped the bridge of his nose with her even white teeth. "What night?" she demanded.

"That stormy August night you were accidentally deposited at my front door."

Those weren't the words Christina longed to hear. She wanted him to tell her that he loved her. But if he considered their marriage a fortunate happenstance, she was willing to be content with that for now. Considering how she'd tricked and deceived him, she really couldn't ask for more. Lowering her lips to his, Christina softly murmured, "La, sir, what a marvelous mischance."

They mated with a near-savage intensity. Roderick expressed through the ardor of his passion all the love he felt for his beautiful wife. Certain she wasn't ready to listen to his words, he worshiped her body with his, willing her to know in her heart that he adored her. One day soon he'd tell her of the feelings locked deep inside. And someday, no matter how long it took, he vowed he'd make her love him in return.

They were newlyweds at last. Christina and Roderick ate, laughed, played, and slept together with joyful abandon, to the amazement and delight of her watching family. After two idyllic weeks in which they were inseparable, a courier arrived with orders for Roderick to leave for London immediately. He was to report to General Pickering, who'd been placed in charge of the investigation into the communications leak in Paris. It was decided that Roderick would travel in haste in the Rugden berlin, while Christina followed at a more leisurely pace with Pansy in the marquess's great traveling coach.

"When you return to London, sweetheart," Roderick informed his wife as they said their farewells, "there's something I want to tell you." He touched a honey-blond tendril that fell in front of her ear, wishing he'd expressed his love for her before the unexpected arrival of the messenger that morning and the turmoil that immediately ensued. Each day he'd yearned to tell her of his feelings, each day he'd held back, afraid it was too soon. He knew she desired him physically. He'd done his utmost to bind her to him with long winter nights of scorching passion. The memory of the way they'd warmed his cold room with their heated love play brought a grin of satisfaction. She wanted him, all right.

He took her in his arms now and kissed her good-bye, thrilling to the pressure of her sweet lips as she eagerly returned his kiss. Regretfully, they drew apart, and Christina walked with him down the front steps of Waldwick Abbey.

"I'll be coming right behind you," she said, "as fast as I can get your sister packed and in the carriage. There's something I also wish to tell you." She extended her hand and peeped up at him from beneath her long lashes. "Until we see each other in London, my lord," she said with a hesitant smile, suddenly as shy as a maiden at her first formal dance.

He took her fingers and turned them over to place a kiss on her upturned palm. His tongue lazily, suggestively traced the lifeline, exactly as he'd done on their unorthodox wedding night. His voice was filled with an ardent need he made no effort to conceal. "Till London."

In minutes the berlin was tooling down the driveway at a fast clip and soon pulled out of sight behind a wide curve. Christina was filled with a loneliness she'd never thought possible. She whirled and hurried inside, anxious to begin packing. But before she started, she sat down at the graceful French desk in her bedroom and drafted a letter to Anselm Rothenstein, urging him to proceed with the sale of Penthaven as her husband had previously directed. In the envelope, she also included a note for Jacob, informing him that she wished to put up for sale her entire collection of antique musical instruments. The proceeds were to be used to further the investigation into the Greater London Docks Company. Christina stared down at the unsealed missive, agonizingly aware of the tremendous step she was about to take.

Despite the fact that Roderick had put the Cornwall estate up for sale without her knowledge, that he'd arbitrarily sent her back to London so he could dally with not one but two Parisian opera dancers, that he used a large portion of her inheritance in a fruitless scrutinization of his father's illogical investments, she'd fallen irrevocably in love with her stubborn, single-minded, unmusical husband. If she sent the letter to Rothenstein, she'd be relinquishing all hope of turning Penthaven into a home for aged musicians so that her husband could continue his inquiry into his deceased parent's financial debacle. Roderick would never rest until he'd proven that the late Earl of Rugden hadn't left his children nearly penniless through foolish ignorance, but had been criminally swindled. Her proud husband's sense of honor and duty demanded that he free his father's name, and his, from all taint. With the sale of Penthaven and the antiques housed there, she was sacrificing her dream for the pride and self-respect of the man she loved. Her fingers trembled as she dropped hot wax on the white vellum and sealed the envelope.

Upon his arrival at Rugden House, Roderick flipped through the stack of correspondence that sat waiting on his desk, which included orders to follow General Pickering on to Brighton. He lifted another letter and recognized immediately the musky perfume and flowery script of his former mistress. Tearing the envelope open, he quickly scanned Madeline Gannet's brief note.

R.

   I have important news which cannot be set down
on paper.

M.

   Roderick shook his head in weary annoyance. It was too
late to try to see her that night. At this hour she was probably at some ball or assembly anyway, and he had far too
many things to attend to before he left for Brighton. He'd
have to stop by St. James's Square on his way out of London in the morning and find out what Madeline thought
was so all-fired important.

Chapter 23

"I've done something rather foolish, I'm afraid," Madeline said, shivering despite the warmth of the roaring blaze on the nearby hearth.

She stood in the corner of her drawing room beside a hanging Swiss birdcage and carefully turned the key at its base. The little mechanical canary on its golden swing chirped brightly to the accompaniment of a miniature organ and a revolving glass fountain.

Filled with fine French furniture, porcelain, and tapestries, her salon made an opulent showcase for Madeline's dusky beauty, and she knew it. Money had never been one of her concerns, for the deceased general had generously provided her with a town home in a fashionable part of the West End and a trust that would keep her comfortable well into her old age.

Men, not money, had always been Madeline Gannet's obsession. Men with incredible physical beauty. Men with great political power. Men with strong personal charisma. They had drawn her irresistibly to them. Her husband's wealth had made it possible for her to meet such men, even though she remained on the outer fringes of aristocratic society. But of all the countless gentlemen she'd known, the Earl of Rugden embodied in one male persona all the beauty, power, and charisma she had ever sought.

Turning away from the fanciful device, she gazed solemnly at her former lover. "You're aware, of course, that I entered into a liaison with the Duke of Carlisle despite your warning—or perhaps because of it."

At Rugden's quick scowl of disapproval, she shrugged her

shoulders defensively. "I'm sorry if I caused you any embarrassment, love. From the first I suspected that the only reason Carlisle wanted me was to parade your former mistress in front of society as his newest paramour. But I was hurt and lonely, and he was charming—in the beginning. Little by little I've come to fear Justin Somesbury more than any man I've ever known. When he watches me with those cold black eyes, I feel he can read the secrets of my soul. He hates you, Rugden, with a ferocity that terrifies me."

"There's no need for apologies, Madeline," the earl said. "But I hope you'll end your association with Carlisle for your own sake. You deserve far better than that coldhearted bastard."

Rugden was dressed for a journey in his winter uniform, the tight buff breeches tucked into high riding boots. Restlessly, he smoothed his hand across the heavy cloak folded over his arm. "You said in your note that you had important news for me. I arrived in London only yesterday and came as soon as I could."

She tugged on his scarlet sleeve with her manicured fingers and guided him to the nearby sofa. She'd been preparing to depart on a trip when he arrived and was attired for traveling in a quilted serge dress, its russet wool interlined with swansdown for added warmth.

"Yes," she replied as she took his cloak from him and placed it on the arm of the sofa. She sank down on the couch, patted the cushion beside her invitingly, and then continued as he sat down next to her. "Two weeks ago I overheard a conversation between my so-called protector and his scurrilous friend Oliver Davenport. The men didn't realize that I was listening. They were discussing the entrapment of some poor female upon whom Carlisle's fancy has descended of late. They spoke freely about forging a note in her mother's hand. At least that's what I gathered from the conversation. Davenport assured the duke that he could easily copy this lady's writing. He boasted openly of his skill in forgery. Last week Carlisle insisted that I visit his estate in Hertfordshire with him. What I thought at first was a monstrous inconvenience proved a unique opportunity for me to search Carlisle Hall for those papers. Their cowardly scheming revolted me so much, I wanted to forewarn the unfortunate damsel." She met his gaze with a wry half smile and added, "Anonymously, of course."

Knowing that Rugden's attention was now riveted upon her, Madeline propped her elbow on the back of the sofa. She rested her chin on the palm of her hand and searched his eyes for any hint of tender regard. She wondered if he would pull back, should she reach up and touch his forehead.

"There was a small group of guests at the hall over the weekend," she said, "giving me a chance to wander about by myself for short periods of time. I was able to get into Carlisle's study for a few minutes alone. In his top desk drawer—which he must have forgotten to lock—was a letter from a woman about an affair between them. Seems it had resulted in an unfortunate by-blow. Not so very strange, considering the duke," she added with a knowing lift of her brows. "No names were on any of the pages I saw. What was most peculiar was that the letter was written over and over on various sheets of paper. There must have been four or five copies of the same letter. And all in the woman's delicate and distinctive handwriting."

His gray eyes grew thoughtful. "Forgeries, of course. Did you take them?"

Madeline shook her head. "I hadn't the courage. I knew if he found those papers on me, I'd suffer dearly. Just as I returned them to the drawer and closed it, Carlisle appeared in the doorway." She put her hand to her breast, remembering her shock at the sight of him. "I told him I'd been looking for writing paper. He didn't say a word. Just walked over, opened the center drawer, pulled out a sheaf of blank pages, and handed them to me. Then he quickly escorted me out of the room. From that moment on, he watched me so closely, I thought certain he knew I'd found the duplicated letter."

Roderick rose to stride quickly across the floor and back, his head bent in concentration. "Why Carlisle would reproduce copies of a letter from a former mistress is beyond me." He looked up at her with a puzzled expression. "But I fail to see what any of this has to do with me."

"I don't think it does," she said. "Not exactly. But Carlisle's diabolical hatred should concern you. Roderick, I've seen his eyes when he speaks of you. Lud, the man's Beelzebub incarnate. I warned you once that he's threatened to kill you. Beware of him, love. He's a very dangerous enemy."

"I appreciate your warning, Madeline. But there's nothing Justin Somesbury can do to harm me." He took her hand and drew her up from the sofa. "You'll break off with him immediately?"

"I've already done so," she said with a grimace of relief. "I sent him a note yesterday, ending our relationship." She lifted her hand and touched Roderick's face, running her fingertip across the battle scar in a light caress. "Will I see you again?" she murmured, her ripe body issuing a blatant invitation as she leaned against him.

Roderick took both of her hands and clasped them firmly in his larger ones. He was very fond of his former mistress. They'd shared more than just a physical relationship, for she was intelligent and forthright and fiercely loyal. Through the years since her husband's death, she'd welcomed Roderick back each time he'd come home on leave, with open arms and an open heart. He knew she loved him, though she'd never told him in so many words. Madeline Gannet was far too wise to make vows of undying love to a man who might just shy away at the first hint of something deeper than friendship.

"If I can help you in any way," he said, "you need only ask."

A bittersweet smile curved her coral lips. "I know, my lord. You were always the most generous lover I ever had. But it isn't monetary recompense I want, my beautiful soldier." She swayed alluringly toward him. "I'd hoped the charm of your new marital state had begun to grow old. The news of the famous Parisian duel spread all over London, you know. You were the envy of every man in the city for two weeks."

"The romantic aspects of that affair of honor were greatly overestimated," he said with a sheepish grin. "Believe it or not, Madeline, you see before you a husband completely besotted with his own wife." He released her hands with a friendly squeeze. "I've been summoned by my commanding officer, who's presently relaxing in Brighton with his plump mistress. I'm on my way there now. I'll probably be gone several days. While I'm out of reach, be very careful. If Carlisle were to discover you'd met with me after giving him his congé, it could prove extremely unpleasant for you."

"Oh, lud," she said with a husky laugh, "I let him down gently. You'd never believe the flair for hypocrisy I've discovered in myself since I've been around the Duke of Carlisle." She handed Roderick his cloak and picked up her hooded traveling cape. "If you go to Brighton, I'll ride with you instead of taking my carriage. I'm leaving at once for Lambeth to visit my niece and bring a gift for her new child. It won't take you out of your way, and I can enjoy the luxury of a handsome man's conversation on the trip. I'd love to hear all about Paris."

Helping her on with her cape, Roderick nodded. "Duncan can ride up top with the coachman," he agreed. "I want to hear more about your weekend in Hertfordshire."

Joanna had fallen asleep on her Aunt Pansy's lap. She looked like an exhausted cherub, with her fair curls tousled about her flushed face and her thick lashes casting shadows on her round pink cheeks. At the last posting inn, she'd begged to be allowed to ride the final leg of the journey home in her grandfather's huge old traveling coach. She'd succeeded in twisting the grownups about her little finger, and now, after countless games and riddles with her two aunts, she reposed contentedly in the Land of Nod.

Christina sat quietly across from the two of them, exhausted after the morning spent entertaining the active four-year-old. Pansy was dozing in her corner, her dark hair spreading across the velvet squabs in lustrous waves. Covered in thick furs, the two slumbering young ladies were cozy and warm despite the cold weather. Boots, Joanna's black and white kitten, purred softly as she napped atop the furry coverlet. Christina snuggled deeper beneath a black bearskin and allowed herself the peaceful luxury of daydreaming.

The Waldwick coach rattled and bumped along the cobbled streets of London. With the increasing congestion of pedestrians, sedan chairs, and town carriages, it slowly wended its way toward Sanborn House to deposit its smallest occupant into the arms of her mother. The family had decided at their last stop to share teatime with Lady Gwendoline before Christina and Pansy went on to Rugden House.

Christina stared out the frosty windowpane, noting the familiar houses with cheerful recognition as the vehicle rumbled down Duke of York Street and entered St. James's Square. Suddenly the happy smile on her lips twisted into a tortured grimace. She rubbed the glass with her gloved fingers, unsure if it was the moisture on the pane or the mist in her eyes that blurred her vision. Her breath caught painfully in her chest at the heart-wrenching tableau she witnessed from her carriage window.

Coming down the broad steps of a red brick town home was the imposing figure of a grenadier colonel. The voluptuous Mrs. Madeline Gannet clung to his arm. The attractive couple was so deep in conversation, they didn't bother to look up as the Waldwick coach pulled into the square. When the exceptionally fine-looking officer turned to help the lovely widow into his carriage, she threw her arms around his neck and kissed him passionately on the lips. The soldier held her away from him, apparently scolding her for her unseemly behavior, then bussed her gently on the forehead. He took her hand, helped her into the waiting coach, and climbed in behind her.

Christina's heart plummeted toward her toes. Her lungs constricted so tightly, she felt as though she were suffocating. Good God, she couldn't blame the beautiful widow for such outrageous behavior on a public street! The man in question could be devastatingly, heartbreakingly, unbelievably charming when he chose to be, as she herself well knew. Few women on the face of this earth would be able to resist him for long. Oh, maybe for a month they could hold out against him. Maybe even two months, or possibly three. But they'd inevitably fall prey to his enchanting seduction.

Christina covered her trembling lips with her hand to hold back the cry of misery that welled up from her soul.

God help her.

She knew the irresistible allure of that strikingly handsome man all too well. The tall grenadier in the scarlet regimentals was none other than her deceitful, perfidious wretch of a husband, Colonel Roderick Fielding, the fifth Earl of Rugden.

She must have made an unconscious sound, perhaps only a swift intake of breath, for when she turned away from the window with its harrowing sight, Christina looked into the wide brown eyes of her husband's sister. The look of horror on Pansy's heart-shaped face made it clear that she'd recognized her oldest brother locked in the embrace of some wanton female.

Neither spoke.

Focusing her gaze quickly on the far side of the street, Christina fought back the hot tears that burned her eyes. Mercifully, Lady Penelope, for once in her exuberant life, was silent. Shocked into speechlessness, no doubt. In another minute the coach door was being opened, and the sleeping Joanna was lifted out by the liveried footman.

Christina slammed the door on her tumultuous thoughts and went through the outward motions of visiting with Lord and Lady Sanborn, who'd arrived only an hour before them. Somehow, she managed to keep up her part in the conversation, religiously avoiding the stricken eyes of her sister-in-law. Taking Christina's unspoken cue, Pansy refrained from any mention of the errant husband.

The minutes went by in agonizing slowness until Christina had returned to Rugden House and the security of her own bedchamber. There, waiting for her on the satin pillow, was a note. Her fingers shook uncontrollably as she picked up the missive and broke the seal.

My Darling Wife,

　　Our talk (which I am awaiting with increasing anticipation) must, unfortunately, be postponed. I have received further orders to report to General Pickering in Brighton immediately. I may be gone several days. Until I return to your entrancing arms I remain

Your loving husband,
R.

Liar!
Despicable, wretched liar!

You travel to Brighton with your mistress!

The note slipped from her hand. Christina knelt beside her bed and wept long, heartbroken sobs. What bitter, bitter irony. She'd held out for three long months! All that time she'd kept him at bay with her clever subterfuge. And now, only now, after she'd surrendered her body as well as her heart, did she realize the full extent of his treachery.

Suddenly she understood with horrifying insight what had happened that long-ago August night. Her husband's mistress lived directly across the street from her sister's home! She knew now whose place she'd taken in Rugden's waiting coach. He'd been expecting his curvaceous ladylove that stormy evening and received her own puny self instead.

What was it he'd said that night when he'd told her he wasn't Mr. Zachary Noyes? *Nor are you Mrs. Gannet.*

At times during her brief marriage Christina had half suspected him of planning her abduction to gain her fortune, for the note from Lady Muggleton—which wasn't from Lady Muggleton—had never been explained. But an abduction couldn't have been further from the truth. The mix-up had been an honest, simple mistake. He'd been genuinely disappointed at Christina's unexpected arrival. Why, he'd run to his doxy the moment he'd seen her at Drury Lane after the newlyweds had returned to London. He hadn't been bothered for a moment by the fact that his innocent bride was there, watching in humiliation.

Bitter, scalding tears streamed down Christina's cheeks. She pillowed her face on the yellow satin coverlet and clenched her fists in rage. He'd never explained the duel between the Ramillies sisters. Never even tried to. God, he hadn't even been faithful to his beautiful mistress while he was in Paris, let alone to his naive wife.

If only she hadn't succumbed to his seduction, it wouldn't have been so tragic. Now all hope for an annulment was gone. The clever bastard had trapped her, good and tight. If he hadn't desperately needed the use of her inheritance, he might have been more truthful. But she knew there were many men who, professing devotion to their wives, continued their lifelong liaisons with their paramours. Well, she'd never live the role of the dutiful, submissive wife, humbly accepting whatever crumbs of tenderness her philandering husband chose to throw her way. She'd seen those unfortunate women, hopelessly in love with spouses who treated them shamefully. They became old and embittered before their time. She'd rather spend her life alone, with dignity, than share her husband with another woman.

Christina got up off her knees and groped in her reticule for a handkerchief. Plopping down on the edge of the bed, she wiped her tears with stubborn determination. To have been so misled by his false kisses and his fraudulent seduction hurt her pride more than anything, she told herself. She'd never forgive his dishonesty. And he'd never give her a divorce. Blast him, she wouldn't cry. She refused to cry. It didn't matter one whit that he didn't love her. She *hated* him!

One by one, she hurled the bed's three fluffy satin pillows and watched through tear-blurred eyes as they whooshed across the room and thumped against the closed door. She hated him, she hated him, she hated him.

The next morning Christina stared numbly at the blank sheet of paper in front of her. Since an annulment was now out of the question, and Rugden would never agree to a divorce, she had to convince her father to support her decision to live apart from her husband. That wouldn't be easy. Maintaining a separate residence would be costly as well as scandalous.

She chewed on her lower lip, trying to find the right words to convince the Marquess of Waldwick that his youngest daughter's marriage was such an unbounded travesty that nothing and no one could ever put it right. She was interrupted by Madame Boucher, who brought in a letter that had been delivered to Rugden House by a liveried footman. The sealed note was addressed in an unfamiliar hand. Christina opened it with curiosity.

My dear Countess,
　I have life-threatening news which I must impart to you in person regarding a beloved member of your family.

Meet me at the Knightsbridge Inn on the Kensington Road. Come alone at one o'clock this afternoon.

Carlisle

She reread the scrawled note with skepticism. What could Justin Somesbury possibly know about any member of her family that she didn't already know herself? If the message had arrived on any other day, she'd have tossed it aside. But that morning her bruised ego and aching heart made her restless and willing to take a chance, especially if that chance might upset Rugden. Putting aside the letter to her father for a later time, she decided she'd travel to Kensington for the simple diversion of it. Just to be safe, though, she'd take the Keighlys, father and son, along for protection. With her coachman and footman close by, there'd be little the duke could do without her acquiescence. And the two servants would be certain to inform their master, when he returned from Brighton, of her sojourn into Kensington to meet the Duke of Carlisle. Of course, by then she'd be living in another household entirely.

The Knightsbridge was a delightfully quaint inn, constructed of large gray stones with half-beam timbers crisscrossing its thick walls. Inside, the large, welcoming fireplace was decorated with highly polished brass pots and cooking utensils that hung from the dark wooden beam of its mantelpiece. Christina entered the large public room warily, with Watt Keighly directly behind her.

Justin Somesbury waited in a chair by the fireside. He rose the moment he saw her. Suspiciously, Christina surveyed his erect figure, garbed in black, as he made his way to her side.

Carlisle's arrogant gaze flicked over her blue woolen traveling outfit, pausing to note its stylish white mink trim and moving up to take in the matching cossack hat. A faint smile curved his thin lips. He bowed over her hand. "Madame de Rayon de Soleil, what a pleasure to see you again. You look stunning, as ever. Did you have an enjoyable stay with your family in Wiltshire?"

Surprised at his knowledge of her movements, Christina nodded curtly. She retrieved her hand from his thin fingers and placed it within the safety of her fur muff. "You've something important to tell me, Your Grace?" she questioned.

His ebony eyes were alight with amusement. "I do indeed, *ma belle*. But first I've taken the liberty of ordering a luncheon for us. Please say you'll join me." Carlisle waved his hand around the empty room in an all-encompassing gesture. "It's quite public here. Your footman can wait in the taproom. That way we can have a private conversation while we eat."

Tapping her foot in speculation, Christina looked thoughtfully at the duke for a moment and finally shrugged. "Why not? Both my servants would come running immediately if I so much as raised my voice."

Christina ordered Watt to join his father in the room nearby and then followed the Duke of Carlisle into the corner set aside for dining.

"How charming," Christina remarked impulsively. She glanced around the cozy room. Although they were the inn's only customers, she felt quite comfortable in the homey place.

The owner, whose enormous girth was only partially covered by his bright red apron, brought them each a plate on which rested a tiny game hen stuffed with wild rice and mushrooms. He placed a tankard of ale beside the duke's elbow, poured cool, fresh milk into Christina's glass, and then retreated to the taproom to serve her two retainers.

Christina followed Carlisle's lead and chatted leisurely about the latest London gossip while they ate. Only once, after describing the society wedding of a peer, did he diverge from his witty and sometimes scathing indictments of the foibles of their mutual acquaintances to touch on a personal issue.

"You were very foolish to reject my suit, *chérie*. That clod of a colonel you married is more intrigued with your fortune than your sweet self. Even now he's in Brighton with his mistress. He'll never give Mrs. Gannet up, you know. They've loved each other for years."

She set down her fork and glared at him. Attempting an air of haughty detachment, she spoke through stiff lips.

"La, Your Grace, I'd no idea you were so familiar with my private affairs."

He reached over and took her hand. "I have enough money and power, Christina, to buy you the annulment you want so desperately. I wouldn't fail, should I seek it for you. Too many lords in Parliament owe me favors."

Tears sprang to her eyes at his softly uttered words. Shocked at his incisiveness, she stared in misery at her fingers clasped in his white, graceful hand. "I can't," she whispered.

"All you need do is come to me, *ma belle*. Spend your nights with me, that's all. Your days will be your own. I'll never say you nay. You can have anything you want, do anything you choose." He leaned closer and brought her fingertips to his lips. "Forget your paltry little inheritance. Let the fool have it, if he needs it so badly. I'll buy Penthaven for you and refurbish it completely. We'll dedicate the home for musicians in your grandfather's name together. Let me help you attain your dream, Christina. And with you by my side, I'll have mine."

"Please," she begged, "don't speak of it any further, or I'll have to leave."

"Very well, *chérie,*" he said in a tight, clipped tone as he released her hand. "As you wish." He tipped his head toward her plate. "Your food's growing cold."

At the end of the meal, Carlisle pulled out a gold snuffbox. He placed a small amount of its aromatic contents on his wrist, carried it to his thin nostrils, and politely sneezed into his lacy, perfumed handkerchief. "You enjoyed the meal, I trust?" he asked. He glanced at her empty plate with a teasing smile.

Christina had been ravenously hungry. She hadn't eaten anything since teatime at her sister's home the previous day. She nodded and admitted ruefully, "It's been a while since I've eaten."

His eyebrows lifted in puzzlement. "You weren't so upset by my invitation that you couldn't eat, *ma mie?*" His gently spoken words had a ring of sincere concern.

"No, it wasn't your note, Your Grace," she confessed. "But I admit, I am curious as to its meaning. What person in my family could possibly be threatened? The Berringers are a remarkably stable lot, despite their high spirits."

"I'd hoped I wouldn't have to share this unhappy news with you, Christina, but I'm afraid you've left me no choice. When I wrote that a member of your family was threatened, I meant your newly acquired family. I was speaking, to be precise, about your little sister-in-law."

"Lady Penelope?" Christina was incredulous. "Now I know you've brought me here on a fool's errand!"

At her hilarity, Carlisle braced his elbows on the table and pressed his long fingers together to form a steeple. "Before you make up your mind about that, Christina, let me show you a letter written to me by the girl's mother. You see, the late Countess of Rugden and I were, ah—to put it delicately—very close friends. The present earl's young sister is the result of that friendship."

"I don't believe you!" Christina swiftly gathered her gloves and muff and rose from her chair. Affronted that he could even hint at something so dreadful about Pansy, she turned to leave.

Instantly Carlisle was around the table. He caught hold of her arm to keep her beside him. "Not so fast, *ma belle,*" he said in an urgent, coaxing voice. "At least hear me out. I've the proof with me, if you'd care to look." When she gave a curt nod, he released her arm. He pulled a letter from his coat pocket and unfolded it. Holding it out in front of her, he waited in tense silence as she deciphered the flowery script on the yellowed parchment.

The contents of the letter were devastating. Written by Rugden's mother to Justin Somesbury, it revealed that Pansy's real father was the duke himself. Sabrina Fielding begged Carlisle to keep their secret, so the child wouldn't be disowned by her husband. Horrified, Christina recognized the distinctive handwriting. It was identical to the notations made on the marvelous sonata written by the deceased Countess of Rugden. Striving to keep her shock from Carlisle, Christina clenched her jaw and looked steadfastly away.

When she'd gained some measure of control over the fright and bewilderment that cartwheeled inside her, she placed her trembling hands inside her muff, straightened her shoulders, and stared dispassionately back at him. Her voice quavered, for all of her attempted nonchalance.

"So ... so what does this have to do with me, Your Grace? If it's extortion money you're after, why not apply directly to my husband? He'd pay handsomely for the letter. And I haven't a shilling of my own."

With a smile of complacence, Carlisle folded the missive and replaced it carefully in his coat pocket. "In truth, *ma mie,* it's not gold that will purchase this near-priceless epistle. There's no sum you could name that would pry it from my hands." He shrugged in an unconvincing display of compassion. "After all, the girl is my own daughter."

"Then why show it to me at all? What is it you want?"

"You," he said with silken menace. "It's as simple and uncomplicated as that, Christina. And unless I have you— totally and completely—I will see that this letter is published, if I have to print it myself. Naturally, if your husband ever discovers who's responsible, he'll challenge me." He smiled mirthlessly. "It's a risk I'm more than willing to take. I'd love to meet that prig on the field of honor. But of course, no matter what is said or done later, the chit will be ruined absolutely, and for her lifetime."

"You'd do this to your own daughter?"

"Believe it, Christina. I would. To possess you, I'd betray my own country."

Christina grabbed the back of her chair for support. "What ... what is it you would have me do?"

Taking hold of her shoulders, Carlisle pulled her toward him, and she would have tumbled over had he not caught her. His black eyes glittered as he held her up. "Come to my town home in Hanover Square tomorrow night, Christina, or I swear, by God, I'll have this tragic little love note published before the next day's over."

Christina struggled against his grasp to no avail. She kept her angry voice low, so as not to alert her nearby retainers. "This is insane! And what if I do come? Will you then give me the letter?"

Carlisle shook his head. His narrowed eyes betrayed his sudden excitement at her question. "Not immediately, *ma belle.* For I shan't tire of you in one night, I'm certain. But eventually you may pry it away from my clutches, if you do your utmost to please me. You're such a clever girl, I'm certain you'll think of something to keep my interest." He freed her and stepped back, allowing her to precede him to the door.

She hurried toward the entrance. "I'll never submit to this," she hissed. "You were crazy even to think I might."

Maddeningly, the duke grinned, completely unmoved by her scorn. "Then your little sister-in-law will be ruined. And all for your stubborn Berringer pride and your antiquated sense of virtue. Nevertheless, should you have a change of heart, I shall be waiting for you tomorrow night."

He gestured for her two servants to follow them and led her to the waiting cabriolet, where he assisted her inside with a ridiculous show of gallantry. Before he closed the door, he leaned into the coach. "By the by, Countess," he said quietly, "should you think to steal the letter from me tomorrow evening, through force or contrivance, you should know that by then it will be locked up safely once again at my country house in Hertfordshire. So don't come to Hanover Square carrying a weapon. It would only serve to annoy me. Usually I'm a gentle man, but when I'm crossed, I can become quite harsh."

Christina's voice shook with loathing. "If I come tomorrow night, Carlisle, rest assured, I'll bring a pistol—and I'll use it."

At the reckless words, he leered at her suggestively. His black eyes lit up with anticipation. "Till tomorrow night then, *chérie.* I'll look forward to giving you several lessons, only the first of which will be in the use of firearms."

Jackman's Inn at Handcross was busy that evening. Roderick leaned back in his hard wooden chair and idly watched the beefy, red-faced owner order his staff of workers to even greater industry. But the earl's thoughts were in London. Before he'd left the previous afternoon, he'd dashed off a letter to his wife's banker. He'd instructed Anselm Rothenstein to halt the sale of the Cornwall estate immediately and to place the deed of ownership in trust for an asylum for impoverished musicians.

The reconstruction of Penthaven would require an enormous portion of his ready funds. It meant giving up, at

least for the foreseeable future, the investigation into the
Greater London Docks Company and the chance to clear
his father's name from accusations of gross incompetence,
if not downright idiocy. It also meant relinquishing the
chance to retrieve his family's lost fortune through the
proof of a swindle. He would continue to support Percy
and Pansy on the rents from the various Rugden estates,
hoping that slowly, through years of careful management,
he could replenish the empty coffers he'd inherited.

In the meantime he was willing to accept the modest life
he now lived on the income of an army officer so that
Christina could fulfill her heart's desire. If four months
ago, someone had suggested that he'd make such an illogical, emotional decision, he'd have laughed in his face.
But four months ago he hadn't met the golden-haired ball
of sunshine that had transformed his gloomy life. He was
no longer the cynical, war-weary veteran who'd returned
home vowing to marry an heiress in a passionless marriage
of convenience. His marriage to Christina had proven anything but passionless, and, considering the tortured months
he'd thought her pregnant and feared to touch her, it
hadn't been very damn convenient, either.

He could hardly wait to return to his gorgeous bride and
tell her of his decision. First he'd take her to Rugden
Court, where he could have her all to himself for a while,
without their respective siblings tripping over his feet.
Then one evening he'd leave the deed to Penthaven on her
pillow, just as he'd left his tokens of love for her at
Waldwick Abbey. He smiled to himself as he thought of
her delight.

Roderick's wandering attention was pulled back to the
present by the sudden appearance of a naval officer, who
addressed him with polite formality.

"Pardon me, Colonel Fielding. I wonder if you remember me from the H.M.S. *Mediator?* Lieutenant Charles
Thompson, at your service, sir."

Roderick stood, pleased at the unexpected appearance of
an acquaintance on what had promised to be a very dull
evening spent on the road. "Of course, Lieutenant," he
said. He offered the young man his hand. "And may I convey my deepest gratitude for the safe conduct of my wife

from Paris to London. Lady Rugden told me of your concern for her welfare while she was traveling home."

Thompson's brown eyes reflected embarrassment at the praise. "It was only what any officer would do for a fellow military man, sir. I trust that Lady Rugden is well?"

"Quite. We just returned from a visit with her family in Wiltshire. Unfortunately, I was abruptly called away by orders to report to Brighton." Roderick gestured to an empty chair. "Sit down and join Sergeant Duncan and me for supper."

"I'll be honored to join you, Colonel," Thompson answered as he nodded to the little Scotsman. He slipped into the seat at the small table. "Are you on your way there now?"

"Yes. I have orders to report to General Pickering. I assume it's to receive an update on the peace negotiations. How about yourself?"

"I've just come from there, sir. If you're expecting to find Pickering in Brighton, you'll be disappointed. He left early yesterday morning and is most likely in London by now. I'm chasing right behind him. I carry important dispatches to be delivered to the general and the prime minister. However, I plan to stay the night at the inn. I've endured freezing weather the entire trip from Paris, and I'm looking forward to spending the night in a warm bed. I'll resume my journey in the morning."

Roderick frowned at the unexpected news. "If Pickering has left Brighton, then I might as well turn around and head back for London in the morning. You're welcome to ride in my coach with us. We'll leave before dawn. I'll be reporting to Whitehall myself immediately upon our arrival. Now tell me, how are the negotiations progressing in Paris?"

Thompson smiled broadly. "Confidentially, sir, I think my dispatches contain the final peace proposal. And I believe that proposal includes the transfer of the entire territory of Canada into British hands. Something, I understand, that you fought for from the beginning. You should be very happy with the final settlement, sir, and very proud of your influence on it. But perhaps you already know all this from Major General Gillingham?"

"No, I've not heard from Hugh for several weeks now."

Roderick lifted his tankard in salute. "Let's drink to the peace proposal, Lieutenant."

The naval officer raised his mug. "To the Treaty of Fontainebleau," he replied.

"Aye," Duncan added in concert. "Tae the peace."

"Percy, thank God you're up," Christina called the next morning as she followed in his valet's wake. "I was so afraid you might be still asleep." She rushed into the small salon to find her husband's brother bent over a bowl with his head covered by a large towel.

" 'Fore Gad," Percival responded ungraciously. He peeked out from under the linen cloth "Chrisdina, what are you doing here this time of day? Why it's only ten o'clock in the morning." He glanced down at his velvet dressing robe. "I ain't even decent."

"I need to talk with you, Percy. It's dreadfully important." The countess rolled her eyes toward the valet's back and then looked meaningfully at her brother-in-law.

"Odd's vish, Chrisdina!" Percy exclaimed, punctuating it with a loud sneeze. "What a start you've given me! Is it to do with that barbaric brodder of mine? Don't tell me there's been anodder duel."

Imperiously, Christina motioned for his servant to leave the room. She brought a straight-backed chair to the low table over which Percy leaned and set it down with a thump. Sitting down, she looked at her new brother with determination. "Percy, this is not about Rugden. It's about your little sister. Did you know she was illegitimate?"

Percy leaped up from the sofa. He tossed the towel wildly aside, dislodging his wig, which went flying across the room. "Stap me, Chrisdy, if you weren't a woman, I'd call you out for that! Don't ever say anyding like that again, not even in jest." His nose was bright red and his eyes were watering profusely.

"Phew!" Christina exclaimed, momentarily diverted by the horrible aroma that wafted up from the large bowl. "Whatever have you been inhaling?"

Percy grinned widely. "Awvul, ain't it? Some concoction my valet's old grandmother used to fix for him whenever he had a head co'd or a bad hangover. Works for bod of them. Wouldn't be surprised if there was a little eye of newt or a sprinkle of bee's knees in it. But it always works. Avter I inhale it for ten minutes I drink the vile stuff. Tastes like the very devil. Tomorrow I'll be right as a trivet." He retrieved his wig and plopped it unceremoniously on his head. "Now what's all this about Pansy?"

Pulled back to harsh reality, Christina grew solemn. "I thought maybe you knew, Percy. Hugh Gillingham once told me that the enmity between Rugden and Carlisle goes back to the time when both your parents were alive." She pointed her finger at the sofa and waited for him to sit back down again. "Yesterday the Duke of Carlisle showed me a letter written by your mother. In it, the late countess begged Carlisle to keep secret the fact that he is indeed Lady Penelope's father."

"That vicious, crawling vermin," Percy snarled, starting to rise again. "Why, I'll cut his tongue out for that lie!"

With a shake of her head, Christina shoved him back down. "It's no lie, Percy. I saw the letter with my own eyes. It was written by your mother. I recognized the delicate script. Carlisle's letter was penned by the same hand that wrote that beautiful sonata."

Incredulous, Percy slowly sank on the cluttered settee, absently pushing back a stack of old newspapers that threatened to slip over the edge of the cushion. "Are you certain, Chrisdina? Are you absolutely posidive of this?"

Her heart filled with sympathy at the tragic news she'd brought, Christina nodded glumly. "I'm so sorry, Percy. But I know that handwriting."

"Have you to'd Rugden? He'll cut the swine's heart out."

"No, I can't. In the first place, Rugden's out of town, and, in the second place, it's me that Carlisle wants in exchange for that letter."

"You! The fellow's a mad dog! Fiend seize him, what exacdly did he say?"

The countess stood and moved around behind her chair. She was dressed in a warm woolen traveling cape, which she hadn't bothered to remove in her excitement. Mechanically, she unfastened the braided frogs down the front as she continued. "If I don't go to Carlisle's town home in

Hanover Square tonight, he'll see to it that the letter is published and distributed throughout London by the end of the week."

"Egad! We must get the ledder from the swine! I'll go there tonight myself. He'll hand it over at the wrong end of a pair of horse pistols."

"That won't work, Percy, for the letter is locked up safely at Carlisle's estate in the country by now. He warned me specifically about trying to take the paper from him at gunpoint. But if I don't go to his town house tonight, he will most surely print it. You must help me, Percy. We have to break into Carlisle's manor in Hertfordshire and steal that letter."

A wild light appeared in Percy's eyes. "Of course! That's jus' what I'll do. I'll dress up as a common vandal and sneak into his country home tonight, while he's waiting for you here in London. Nodding could be easier."

"I'm coming with you."

Astounded, he looked at her as though she were an inmate of Bedlam. "No, you're not." Pulling an enormous handkerchief out of the pocket of his dressing robe, he blew his nose adamantly.

"Oh, yes, I am. This is my fight and I refuse to be left behind. What if you can't find the letter by yourself? I can help you search. I shan't let you take all the risks. I insist on going with you."

Percy recognized the stubborn look in her blue eyes and raised one eyebrow in consternation. "I'll tell you what," he said, suddenly grinning from ear to ear, delighted at his inspiration. "Let's enlist the aid of your brodder, Francis. I jus' left him off at his barracks a few days ago, and he said he wouldn't be on acdive assignment till next week. We'll tell him, and if I know Fran, he'll be happy to join us."

"Of course he will," Christina cried with elation. "Oh, Percy, we can do it. Hurry and get dressed! My carriage is waiting."

Chapter 24

From the window of her stylish town carriage, Christina could see Major Francis Lord Berringer hurrying down the steps of the Horse Guards at Percy's side. The guardsman clambered into the coach and sat down next to her. Scarcely waiting for his brother-in-law to climb in behind him, Francis turned to his sister, a look of astonishment on his fair features. "What's all this folderol about Pansy? Percy keeps yammering some idiocy about the Duke of Carlisle being her father."

In short order, they apprised Francis of the blot on Pansy's birthright and the threat that hung over her. He whistled through his teeth in horror at the scandal that would ruin the innocent girl.

" 'Pon rep! Of course I'll help you get the letter. Christy, you say Carlisle is expecting you at his town house tonight? Then let's get going. We'll need to get to Hertfordshire before sunset in order make a reconnaissance of Carlisle Hall."

Percival held up his thin hand and interrupted the major, trying his utmost to make his speech clear. "I to'd Lady Chrisdina that we would take care of it. There's no need for her to worry her preddy head. She had the foolish notion we'd let her come along."

"I *am* coming along," Christina said. She folded her arms across her chest and glared at them.

Indecisive, Francis looked at his sister and debated the idea. "If Carlisle is safe at his town home in Hanover Square, there's no reason why Christina can't come along. She can ride better than most men, and she can help us search, once we're inside the hall. There's nothing like a woman's nose for following a scent. With the wily duke in London, there'll be no one at the manor but a staff of unsuspecting servants. We can wait till they're asleep. It'll be safe enough."

"Thunder and turv," Percy muttered, "what a family."

"Now, we'll need some dark clothes," Francis continued thoughtfully. "And Christy, you'd best dress as a boy. You can't move quickly enough in those confounded hoops."

"Yes," Christina agreed. "You can purchase some things for me on our way out of town. I can change apparel at a posting stop."

Shaking his head, Major Berringer issued orders. "No, we won't stop at any inns until we get there. As a matter of fact, we'll not take the coach at all. Christina, you go back home. I'll get the clothes and be there as soon as possible. In the meantime, Percy, you go with her and get three good horses saddled and bridled from Rugden's stable. Christy, do you think you can ride astride? We've a lot of miles to cover in a short time."

"Don't worry about me," she declared. "I won't slow you down."

The guardsman grinned infectiously, delighted at the prospect of such a rare adventure. "We'll meet at Rugden House in one hour, then. Like the knights of old seeking the Holy Grail, we'll find that infamous letter and be back in London before daylight."

"How delightful to find you at home, my dear," the duke said in a soft, silky voice. He crossed the elegant bedchamber with the fluid grace of a predator cat. "After receiving your note, I feared you might be in Brighton with your lover."

Madeline whirled in surprise. She dropped the pitcher she held, splashing the water across the front of her green morning dress. "You . . . you startled me, Your Grace. My, but you're bold, coming into my bedroom unannounced."

Despite the teasing words, Madeline knew her eyes betrayed her horror at his sudden appearance. She swallowed the fear that rose like bile in her constricted throat. "What's this talk of a lover in Brighton? I've been visiting my niece in Lambeth. I stayed overnight, that's all, and came home yesterday afternoon." She bent and retrieved the chipped pitcher. Clutching it with shaking hands, she placed it beside the washbasin on the stand beside her bed. "What brings you here so early in the morning?"

"A innate dislike of being betrayed, my dear jade. Did you think I wouldn't learn that you've been seeing the Earl of Rugden on the sly?"

Madeline stepped quickly toward the door. She turned her head and spoke over her shoulder as she sought her escape. "I can see anyone I please, Carlisle. I'm a free woman."

The duke reached the door before her and shut it with sickening finality. He turned, leaned his shoulders against the polished wood, and stared at her. "Free? You? Gad, doxy, you're one of the most expensive whores I've ever mounted. Those trinkets I gave you didn't come cheap. And when I put out good coin for services, I expect to get what I pay for. Not some sneaking, lying slut who beds my enemy behind my back. Just exactly what did you share with Rugden, besides that overripe body of yours? Any and all information you may have picked up while you were with me?"

"I . . . I don't know what you're talking about. I gave Rugden no information." Madeline backed slowly away from the duke, who advanced upon her step by step, till she was trapped against the bed.

"Liar," he whispered savagely. He struck her full in the face with his doubled fist. "Tell me the truth, Madeline. What did you tell that bloody boor?"

"Nothing, I swear," she cried. She gripped the bedpost to keep from falling and held a shaking hand to her broken, bleeding nose. "I told him nothing!"

"What about the forged letters you found in my desk?" he asked and struck her again. "Does he know about the trap I've laid for his wife?" He pulled back his fist and smashed it against her cheekbone.

Madeline welcomed the velvety darkness that surrounded her.

"Hurry, Christy! Let's go!" Francis called as she came down the central staircase dressed in the outfit of a young gentleman. He grabbed her hand and pulled her down the last two steps. "Percy's holding the horses. We need to get on the road, if we hope to get there in time to scout the place out before nightfall. Are you certain you'll be able to keep up with us?"

"I'll keep up," she replied.

Miraculously, the boots her brother had purchased for her were a good fit, and she'd be able to ride without losing the stirrups. After throwing a long cape over her shoulders, she rakishly donned a wide-brimmed hat with a white ostrich plume. She wound a long woolen scarf around her neck. "I've always wanted to dress like a man," she confessed with a grin. "Unless you've been bound up in corsets and hoops, you'd never imagine how tiresome they can be."

Francis hooted in derision as he steered her through the front hall. "I've absolutely no intention of finding out. Now let's join Percy and be on our way." Together they flew out the high carved doors, causing a whoosh of cold air to invade the entryway.

High at the top of the landing, Marie watched them leave. She ran down the steps and into the front salon, just in time to draw back the drapes and watch the three riders turn the corner and ride up Duke of York Street. Her fingers clutched a note written in French. When she was sure that the siblings had disappeared, the abigail opened the door of Rugden House and glanced up and down the street. A young lad was coming along the paving, lazily striking the iron railings in front of the houses with a short stick.

"Here, boy! Come here!" she called. "Do you know how to find Hanover Square?"

"Cooee, ma'am. 'Course I do!"

"Here, then," she called and tossed him a coin. "Take this paper to Carlisle House and be quick about it."

"General Pickering is with the prime minister," the pimply-faced corporal announced in bored voice. "I'll let him know that you're here, sir." He turned, opened the door to the adjoining room, and disappeared.

Roderick slapped his gloves against his dusty thighs

with restless energy. He looked disinterestedly around the waiting area, empty now except for Lieutenant Charles Thompson, who'd just joined him.

"Looks like all the muckamucks are in the same meeting," Thompson said, closing the hall door behind him. "My dispatches are addressed to both Bute and Pickering. I understand they're locked in there together with Major General Gillingham."

"Hugh's back in London?" Roderick asked with surprise. "When did he get back?"

The naval lieutenant's answer was postponed by the arrival of Corporal Barber. "General Pickering will see you now, Colonel Fielding. And you're to go in also, Lieutenant Thompson. Lord Bute has been waiting for those dispatches. He left orders that he wanted to see you the minute you arrived."

Following Barber into the conference room, Roderick spotted Gillingham standing beside the large Venetian window overlooking St. James's Park. Hugh turned when he heard his friend's name announced and flashed a wide grin.

"Colonel Fielding at last," barked General Pickering, who was seated at the center of a long, narrow table. "We've been trying to reach you since yesterday afternoon. Confound it, man, you're mighty hard to trace!"

Roderick executed a quick salute. "My apologies, General. I was following your orders to report to you personally in Brighton. I didn't discover that you'd already returned to London until I reached Handcross."

"Orders?" came the mystified reply. "I never ordered you to Brighton."

John Stuart, Earl of Bute and prime minister of England, walked over to the table from the window, where he'd been standing beside General Gillingham. "Regardless, Colonel Fielding, we're glad that you arrived so opportunely. I want you to meet Captain Matthew Davies. He's attached to our intelligence operations in France."

With his stringy brown hair pulled back into a queue and his drab civilian clothes, Davies looked more like an undertaker than a secret agent. A thin, angular man, he wore no rings or fobs of any kind. His mirthless eyes were bloodshot, as though he'd gone without sleep for days. He bowed unsmilingly at Roderick, then turned to Charles Thompson. "I see you've finally arrived, Lieutenant. When you took leave of me in Paris, I would have offered to carry your dispatches for you, had I realized I, too, would be leaving immediately—and would arrive in London ahead of you."

Thompson essayed a frigid bow. "I traveled as fast as possible, Captain Davies. No one indicated that these reports were more urgent than usual. I stayed one night on the road rather than travel at night in freezing temperatures."

Davies sneered his reply. "Indeed."

Rising from his chair, General Pickering walked around the conference table. He took the letters offered by Thompson and handed them to the prime minister. "Gentlemen, I think we've all surmised the contents of these reports. I've been informed by the Duc de Nivernais that his government has agreed to our proposals as originally outlined in the preliminaries at Fontainebleau. Colonel Fielding, you'll be happy to learn that the cause you've championed so vociferously has been achieved. Canada will become part of the British Empire in February, when the treaty is signed. I want you there, sir, when that happens. You should be very proud of your part in this peace settlement."

Roderick grinned. "I'm delighted with the news, General."

The frail, bewigged prime minister scanned the dispatches and then looked up with a scowl. "Yes, well, Colonel Fielding, not all the news is so pleasant. Davies here has just completed his report to me about the suspected infiltration in Paris."

Captain Davies, his cadaverous face devoid of emotion, looked at Roderick. "Unfortunately, Fielding, my investigation has implicated a member of your own household."

With incredible speed, Roderick grabbed the intelligence officer by his dingy cravat and lifted him off his feet. "You'll take back those filthy words, you miserable worm," he growled in the man's face, "or I'll ram them right down your lying throat."

Hugh was beside them in seconds. "Easy, man, easy."

Lord Bute, peering over his glasses, raised his voice. His Scottish accent cut through the commotion in the room. "That will be quite enough heroics, Colonel Fielding. No one is accusing any member of your family."

With a gesture of disgust, Roderick released Davies. He shoved the little agent away so hard the man staggered gracelessly, barely catching his balance in time to avoid a humiliating fall in the center of the room's rug. Roderick clenched his jaw and glared around the room, openly defying anyone to question the patriotism of the Fielding family.

Bute, unmoved by the palpable aura of violence surrounding the furious colonel, readjusted his wig and sat down on a chair beside the table. "Hmph, what a fire-eater," he said under his breath. Pulling a thick dossier toward him, he reread the top page. "The report names one Marie Boucher, presently in your employ, Colonel Fielding, as the purported spy. Davies's investigation has turned up a very interesting fact—namely, that Madame Boucher is first cousin to the Duke of Carlisle on his mother's side. We know, for a certainty, that notes have continually passed between them. We have reason to believe that your wife's lady's maid, at least while in Paris, was feeding information gleaned in your household to Carlisle, who in turn passed it on to the Duc de Richelieu."

"The bloody bastard," Roderick swore softly.

"Why would someone of Carlisle's birth stoop to betraying his own government?" Hugh asked in disgust.

"His reasons appear to have been twofold," Captain Davies explained as he attempted to straighten his twisted cravat. "One was simple greed. The French paid him well for the information he passed on. The primary motivation, however, seems to have been the purpose of discrediting the Earl of Rugden. Since the acquisition of Canada had become the earl's cause célebre, Carlisle apparently hoped that by preventing it, he'd make certain Rugden received no credit for the favorable conditions of the peace treaty."

"With your permission, Colonel Fielding," Bute concluded, "we would like to question Marie Boucher and search her personal belongings."

Of course," Roderick answered. "We can go at once. I'd like to question the woman myself."

Lieutenant Thompson stepped forward. "Sir, may I accompany you?"

Roderick nodded, then turned to his friend. "Hugh?"

Flashing his gap-toothed grin, the large grenadier responded with a bellow. "I wouldn't miss this for the world!"

The instant they reached Rugden House, Roderick jumped out of the coach and took the front steps of his home at a run. He nearly overturned a small urchin who stood on the top step, deliberating to himself about ringing the brass bell pull that hung by the side of the huge doors.

"Hey, guv'na, be this the place wot belongs t' the Earl of Rugden?"

Moving the lad hastily aside, Roderick jerked on the door latch. "What is it you want, boy? I'm in a hurry."

A wide grin disclosed an empty space where two front teeth were missing. "If'n ye be the earl wot's name's on this letter, ye owe me a crown!" Handing Roderick a crumpled piece of paper with one dirty hand, he stuck out the other, palm upward to receive his pay.

Roderick tossed the boy a coin and took the note. He opened the door and entered the house. "Rawlings!" he hollered, attempting to read the poorly scrawled note at the same time. The writing was so shaky and the ink so blotted, it was nearly indecipherable.

> *Rugden,*
> *See to the safety of your wife.*
> *M.*

He crumpled the paper and stuffed it into his coat pocket as he raced up the hall stairs two at a time. "Mrs. Owens! Where's Lady Rugden?"

Passing through the sitting room he shared with his countess, Roderick entered her bedchamber. It was empty. Order prevailed, with the bed smoothly made and the clothes hanging precisely in the large mahogany armoire. Even the bottles of scent and lotions were arranged in harmony on the dressing table. Nothing in the rose-scented bower indicated that anything was wrong. The earl bent to pick up a scrap of paper that had fallen, forgotten and partially hidden by the yellow coverlet, and, glancing at it, recognized his own handwriting. It was the note he'd placed on Christina's pillow just before he left for Brighton.

Rawlings hurried into the room. "Yes, sir?"

"Where's my wife?"

"Why, I don't know, my lord. She was here in her room this morning, but I haven't seen her since. Perhaps her maid will know."

Roderick hurried out to the hallway. He glanced down at the men standing in the entry. "Come up here," he called to them from the top of the stairs. "I'm just about to interview Madame Boucher."

Marie was busily packing a large trunk when the five officers entered her tiny room unannounced. She dropped the cotton nightgown she held in her hand and took a step backward, surveying the uniforms of the British army and navy through eyes distorted in terror.

"Boucher," Roderick said in a voice as sharp and raw as broken glass, "do you know where the countess has gone?"

"The mistress does not answer to the maid," she snapped insolently. She snatched up the fallen garment and hurled it, unfolded, into the opened trunk. Turning to her narrow pallet, she lifted several black dresses and hurriedly placed them on top of the nightdress.

"Do you know where she is, Marie?" he thundered. He took a threatening step toward her, his fists clenched menacingly.

Hesitating for only a moment, she lifted her beak of a nose in the air and crowed with self-satisfaction. "Your wife has left you, my fine, foolish colonel. Even now she lies in the arms of her lover."

"You lie," Roderick said in a low, terrible voice as he reached for her.

She dodged him. Shrieking wildly, she waved her thin arms in front of her in a hopeless attempt to ward him off. "No, I tell you! She is with Justin Somesbury."

His powerful fingers encircled her scrawny neck, and he lifted her completely off the floor. "Tell me the truth, Marie, or I swear by God, I'll choke the life out of you right now. We know you've been giving British secrets to the French through that dog of a cousin of yours. You're going to hang for a spy. Now where is my wife?"

The Frenchwoman's face turned red, then purple. Helplessly, she clawed at the iron hands that held her prisoner. She kicked her feet and gurgled deep in her throat as she struggled for air.

He released her just long enough to allow a breath to go down her crushed windpipe. "The truth, Marie!" he roared. "Where is she?"

Frantically, the maid tried to nod agreement as she endeavored to pry his fingers from her throat. "Yes," came the cracked response, and he eased the pressure slightly. "I will tell you the truth," she gasped. "Your wife is at Justin's country home right now. She has been tricked into entering Carlisle Hall, believing my cousin is here in London. She has gone there to protect your bastard sister!"

"You're mad, woman. My sister is as legitimate as I am. Why would Christina think differently? Answer me!"

Seeing certain death staring at her from Rugden's pale eyes, Marie decided to confess all. "Carlisle showed her a forged letter from your mother, impugning Pansy's birth. Your wife believed it to be real. She has gone to Hertfordshire with Francis Berringer and your brother, Percy, to steal it. I warned Justin of their plans, and he lies in wait for them even now."

"Dear God!" Thompson cried, moving toward the struggling pair.

Horrified, Roderick dropped his hands, as though the touch of her burned his fingers. He stepped back and stared at her with loathing. "How could you betray an innocent young woman, who's been nothing but kind to you, into the hands of that satyr?"

Marie Boucher turned to him, her hands clasped to her flat bosom. During the scuffle, her black hair had come lose from its tight knot. It fell around her shoulders, the streak of silver tangled and twisted in its dishevelment. "Justin promised me that I would have her fortune," she wailed piercingly. "If he succeeded in entrapping her, I was to be rich at last."

"Sweet Jesus!" Hugh breathed as he came to stand between the maid and her master.

Staring at her as though she were truly the Medusa she so closely resembled, Roderick backed slowly away, fearful that if he touched her again, he would tear her limb from limb.

"You Judas," he said, drawing a ragged breath. "You were willing to turn my pure, sweet girl over to the hands of that lecher for profit? In my travels around the world, I've never met a woman so corrupt, so evil."

He turned to Matthew Davies, who'd listened astounded to the sickening confession. "She's yours for the hanging, Captain." Then he headed for the door.

Cowering beside her packed trunk, Marie screamed after him. "Don't you understand? I was to have her entire fortune. For once in my life I was to live the way I was meant to live. I am not of the canaille. I was to be *rich!*"

Lieutenant Thompson followed the earl to the door and seized his arm. "Colonel Fielding, I want to go with you. If I can be of assistance . . ."

"And I, old friend," Hugh added.

Roderick looked thankfully at the men and nodded. "Yes. I may need your help." He turned to his batman and issued orders. "Duncan, saddle two horses and bring them around front. I'll need both mounts before I'm through tonight. Then see that a fresh team is hitched to our coach and follow us in it. We'll need it to bring the countess back home."

Without a word, the little Scotsman flew out of the room.

Addressing his comrades as they moved swiftly down the stairs, Roderick outlined his plans. "Davies and two dragoons can escort Marie to Newgate. Hugh, send two men to Number 18, St. James's Square to check on the welfare of Madeline Gannet. Then Thompson and you can take horses from my stable and follow me as quickly as you can. Head for the village of Hatfield. Ask for directions to Carlisle Hall when you get there."

They were met at the foot of the stairs by Lady Penelope, who'd just returned from a visit with Gwen and the children. When she saw their grave expressions, she knew that something was terribly wrong. "What is it, Roderick?" she demanded. "What's happened?"

Roderick grasped his little sister by her slim shoulders. "It's Christina, Pansy. She's been lured to Carlisle Hall by Justin Somesbury. I want you to return to Sanborn House. Take Watt Keighly with you. Bring Lady Gwendoline back here, do you understand? I want Gwen here when I bring her sister home."

"Yes," Pansy cried. "I'll do it." She followed the men out onto the front porch and watched her brother mount up. "What else can we do?" she called, standing beside Rawlings and Mrs. Owens.

Roderick paused and looked down from Mohawk into her frightened eyes. "Pray to God that we're not too late." With the extra mount's reins in his hand, he wheeled the stallion around and galloped off.

Chapter 25

Inside the Golden Guinea, huddled together like newborn mice in a nest, two strangers to the tiny village of Hatfield sat on an oaken bench beside a rough, hand-hewn table freely carved with initials and cryptic mottoes, idling the time away over their tankards of ale in the farthest corner from the fire.

"For God's sake, keep your face down, will you?" the taller man spat in a whisper at the young gentleman beside him. "Anyone gets sighd of those b'ue peepers of yours, our disguises will be b'own in a minud."

The stripling did as his nervous companion instructed. He ducked his face beneath the wide brim of the black felt hat, allowing the enormous ostrich feather to dangle in front of his face and effectively cut off anyone's view from across the room.

Abruptly another man sat down across from them, pulled off his riding gloves, and laid them on the table. "We're all set," he said in a hushed tone as he signaled the serving girl across the room to bring him a pint. "There's been no one staying at Carlisle Hall since last week when the nefarious duke had a small house party. Everyone, including the duke and his pretty mistress, left Monday morning. As chance would have it, there's only a skeleton crew left—an old housekeeper, two footmen, and a stable boy. This is going to be easier than learning a nursery rhyme at your mother's knee. We'll wait at the inn another hour, just to be sure the household staff is bedded down for the night. It's a short ride from here. Did you order anything to eat?"

" 'Fore Gad, Francis! How can you think of eading at a time like this?" Percy scolded in hushed dismay.

"It's simple, believe me. One of the first things you learn on bivouac is to eat when there's food. You never know when you'll eat next."

"That's not a very comforting thought," Christina remarked dryly.

With a happy grin, Francis summoned the serving wench and ordered three meat pies, oblivious to the looks thrown at him by his two agitated companions. Contrary to their expectations, however, the pastries were delicious, and the crusaders devoured them with gusto.

At last it was time to go. Christina's fingers were suddenly stiff with fright as she wrapped the long woolen muffler around the lower half of her face and pulled on the thick gloves Francis had purchased for her. She straightened her shoulders, tugged on the brim of her hat, tucked her chin down to her collar, and followed them out the inn's low door.

She was riding Sheba and the spirited mare seemed delighted at the midnight prank upon which they were embarked. Setting a brisk pace, Francis led the way across the snowy tracts of open countryside. The landscape was lit by a full moon, making their journey easier over the unfamiliar ground. High above them, the northern constellations studded the night sky.

They approached Carlisle Hall from a rise. The trio of would-be knights stopped in the shelter of a small beech grove and looked down upon the gray stone country house. The manor was built in the form of an H, with two main blocks connected by a central building. High above the entry doors, three stories up on the flat roof, rose a clock tower; domes and turrets dotted the roof, and the front of the house was rich in medieval stonework and carving. Yet, despite the evidence of untold wealth, there was a brooding air of evil surrounding it.

Standing beside their horses, their breaths coming in frosty puffs in the chilly air, the three burglars studied the silent edifice and counted the lighted windows. Thankfully, there were few. A faint light glowed in an attic room—no doubt the elderly housekeeper they'd been told about. Another lantern shed its beams in the stables and then flickered out as they watched.

"We'll be cautious," Major Francis Lord Berringer said. "We'll wait until the old lady goes to sleep before we even approach the place. Then we'll enter through that cellar window on the north wing. My hunch is that it'll lead directly to the pantry area of the main kitchen. It's a chance we'll have to take."

They didn't have long to wait. In less than ten minutes, the last light went out. After forty long minutes more, they left their horses tied to low hanging branches and moved stealthily toward the sleeping house.

The snow covering the graveled driveway softened their carefully placed footsteps. No sign of carriage tracks could be seen from the front approach. Reaching the north side of the building, they crouched and headed for the predesignated cellar window. They moved silently down the brick steps leading to the low doorway and gathered in front of it.

Francis produced a small iron crowbar from the capacious pocket of his heavy cloak. He leaned next to his sister's ear under the slouch hat and spoke in a whisper. "Stay close to me, Christy. I don't want you wandering about by yourself, no matter what. Don't even think about using that pistol I gave you unless something happens to me. Just stick to me like treacle on a pancake, and for once in your life let me do the thinking."

Nodding her head vigorously, Christina pointed to the bulge under her enormous greatcoat and signed that she agreed with his commands. She had no wish even to touch the weapon he'd insisted that she carry. The thought of actually firing it made her hands clammy. She glanced at Percy. His face was white and deadly serious in the moonlight. Impishly, she grinned and gave him a mock salute.

Without another word, Francis felt along the windowsill, searching for a weak point. He found one and wedged the crowbar under the casement. There was a creak that sounded like the boom of a cannon. She held her breath and listened for the slightest response from inside the house. Amazingly, the estate was as silent as a gathering of mutes.

Her brother eased the window up inch by inch. He slipped inside and dropped deftly down to the basement floor. "Easy, Christina," he called softly. "Just fall into my arms."

After setting her on the ground, Francis aided Percy in the drop, and they were inside Carlisle Hall. They left the cellar and followed a prearranged plan. Percy waved a brief farewell and went to search the north wing. Brother and sister headed for the south, passing through the kitchen and traversing the long gallery that separated the two sections of the house.

The gallery was filled with splendid Elizabethan portraits, barely visible in the dim light. They turned the corner and entered the hall, rich with Jacobean plasterwork and carving. Touching his sister's shoulder, Francis pointed to the ornate wooden stairway, which, in the rainbow of moonlight filtering through a round stained-glass window, showed strange, grotesquely carved figures rising from every alternate post.

Bypassing the macabre staircase, they made their way along the hall in the hope of finding the library. They'd agreed earlier that it was the most likely room in which to find the letter.

Francis placed his hand on Christina's forearm. "That has to be it," he whispered, "at the end of the hall."

She nodded, and they made their way toward the arched door, pausing every few seconds to listen to the creaking sounds of the enormous, nearly empty house.

Major Francis Berringer eased the lavishly carved door open and slipped inside the room with Christina directly behind him. The library was pitch-black. Heavy drapes across the high windows barred the moonlight. Side by side, brother and sister stood quietly, just within the doorway, the only audible sound their own shallow breathing. Simultaneously they stiffened as they became aware that someone else was in the room with them.

"Do come in and close the door," a familiar voice said from across the darkened chamber.

Instinctively, Francis reached inside his cloak, but before he could touch his pistol, he felt the menacing end of a large firearm in the middle of his back. A side door opened with a creak. Oliver Davenport entered, carrying a glowing candelabrum, which he placed on a reading table. As its light spread throughout the book-filled room, the siblings saw a dark-haired man sitting at his ease in an overstuffed chair, his long legs stretched out in front of him. In his hands, he held a fine French dueling pistol with a wicked ten-inch barrel.

"Pray, do come in," the Duke of Carlisle repeated "I can see from the shock on your face that you recognize my good friend Mr. Davenport." He signaled them to step forward. "I've been expecting you for over an hour. Your overweening caution has proven exceedingly tedious, but now that you've arrived, I must admit, my ennui has disappeared completely."

Ignoring the muzzle at his back, Francis made a low growl and dove for Somesbury. Davenport intercepted him, and the two rolled on the floor at the duke's feet. Before the guardsman could land a punch, the burly servant with the firearm pushed his way past Christina and brought it down with a sickening thud on the major's head. Francis lay sprawled unconscious on the rug. Holding her gloved hand to her mouth, Christina fought back a cry of despair.

Somesbury stood over the motionless form and sneered. "Drag him out of here, Davenport. Take him down to the cellar and bind him. Then you and Swinton get Bleer and check the rest of the house to be sure they didn't bring anyone else with them. Oh, and light the fire before you leave. It's chilly in here."

The duke turned to his other captive and pointed his pistol at her head. "I'll interrogate this young marauder privately. See to it that we're not disturbed."

Her heart hammering in her chest, Christina stared in horror at Justin Somesbury. Only her eyes were visible behind the woolen muffler and big floppy hat. In mute terror, she watched as Davenport started a fire on the hearth while the two henchmen carried her brother's body out of the room. Then Davenport left, closing the door behind him.

Inexplicably, Carlisle turned and walked over to the marble fireplace with its crackling flames. He placed the dueling piece on the high ledge of the mantel. Above the mantelpiece, a magnificent set of crossed swords glittered red in the firelight.

Seeing the gun lying there, Christina remembered the heavy horse pistol hidden inside her cloak. As Somesbury came across the rug toward her, she searched clumsily for the weapon. Her stiff fingers fastened on the barrel's cold metal, and she fought the panic that always gripped her at the thought of even touching a firearm. With a sob of absolute, abject terror, she drew it out and held it up in front of her.

Carlisle stopped in mid-step. His derisive smile glittered in the candlelight. "Really, little housebreaker, would you shoot me even though I'm weaponless? Ecod, how ferocious you are! But I doubt you really have the courage to kill an unarmed man in his own home. If you were caught, the law would hang you, my pint-sized Hun. And you'd never escape my men."

A hair's breadth away from hysteria, Christina held the large pistol with trembling fingers. Gallantly, one visibly shaking hand reached up to cock it. The click-click as the safety was released and the lock pulled back sounded like a death knell in the still room.

"Don't, please," she croaked.

Ignoring the threat, Carlisle took another step forward, and Christina closed her eyes. A deafening explosion shook the room. The ball whistled past the duke, smashing a Chinese urn on the mantelpiece and making a black hole in the wall directly below the crossed dueling swords.

"Damn," he complained without rancor, "that T'ang vase was irreplaceable. That'll cost you dearly, young hoodlum. Now, let's remove that ridiculous disguise."

Moving swiftly to her, he pried the smoking weapon from her numb fingers and tossed it on the nearby chair. Then, wordlessly, he lifted the felt hat to reveal the cluster of curls piled high atop her head. Throwing the hat over the empty gun, he turned to face her again. Inch by inch, with infinite patience, he unwound the plaid wool to expose her hidden features, then let the scarf slide noiselessly to the ground.

Teardrops sparkled on her lashes. She watched him in desperation as he removed the pins from her hair one by one and allowed the captured locks to fall in tangled disarray around her shoulders.

"Why me?" Christina asked hoarsely as his long fingers reached for the buttons of her many-caped cloak.

Arrested by her question, Somesbury paused and looked hungrily into her glistening eyes. "It's always been you, *chérie*. With or without your fortune. It was my intention to have you from the moment I saw you dancing with some silly bumpkin at a tedious country ball. Had you realized the strength of my desire when I first came to court you, we might have spared ourselves all this wasted time. For the final outcome was never in doubt."

Unbuttoning the carved bone fastenings on her mantle, he continued without haste. "Perhaps it's true that the thrill is in the chase and not the capture. But, God, what a marvelous chase it's been! And I intend to savor every unhurried moment of the capture." With the assurance of a conqueror, Carlisle walked behind her to remove the outer garment.

As he lifted the heavy black cloak from her shoulders, Christina darted away. Recklessly, she raced for the mantelpiece and the loaded dueling pistol. He caught her midway and brought her down to the rug with him. They rolled between the matching settees that faced each other in front of the fireplace. There was a ripping sound, and the sleeve of her leather jacket gave way beneath the onslaught. High above her, she could see the gilded plasterwork on the ceiling and thought hysterically how beautiful the room was in which she was about to be defiled.

His hands pressed her shoulders relentlessly to the floor and held her prisoner beneath him. He panted in exhilaration and smiled down at her. Undressing her like a doll, he removed her torn jacket and threw it aside.

"Ecod, what spirit! I shan't tire of you in a hundred years, *ma mie*. I think the best plan would be to get you with child as soon as possible. How else can I bind you to me?"

His jeering words unleashed a new strength within her. She screamed and bucked, striving wildly to free herself from his grip.

Undaunted, Carlisle rolled onto the floor, keeping her within the confines of his strong arms. "For God's sake, Christina, stop it," he said in a low, terse voice. "I don't want to hurt you. If you continue to fight me, you could end up with a broken arm."

"No," she rasped, her breath coming in short gulps. "I'll never submit. If you succeed in raping me, you'll be molesting a corpse—for I'll die before I give in."

He pulled her to him. "I'll never let you go, Christina. Surrender to me, *ma belle*. Haven't I already told you the end is inevitable?"

Percy had been staring in amazement at the sheaf of letters in his hands when he heard the gunshot. Moving swiftly, he'd buried them inside his jacket and tiptoed to the closed door. He peeked out, only to discover a brawny house servant coming down the hallway. Closing the door as quietly as possible, Percy leaned against it, hoping against hope that the burly fellow would continue on his way. Just as the servant passed by, Percy felt the beginnings of a sneeze. Ruthlessly, he pinched his sore, reddened nostrils together. With his ear pressed against the wood, he listened to the sound of the heavy footsteps going down the hall carpet.

"Aaahchoo!"

The sneeze echoed around the silent bedchamber. Percy flew out of the room and raced down the corridor like a piglet darting out of its sty at a Michaelmas fair. The duke's henchman was right on his heels. Turning a corner, Percy ran straight into the muscular arms of a manservant.

"Well, what 'ave we 'ere, ya bloody rascal," the man chortled. "A fancy cove what's guilty of breakin' 'n' enterin'. We'll just lock you up whilst we look for more of yer bloomin' friends and come back later to slit yer gullet for ye."

Percival's valiant struggle was short-lived, for the servant was swiftly assisted by his cohort. The two of them shoved him into a nearby pantry and fastened it securely behind them. Pounding on the locked door, Percy bellowed curses at them. On the other side, Bleer and Swinton grinned at each other and continued on down the hall, eagerly searching for any more intruders who might have entered the house.

Outside in the moonlight, on the rise overlooking Carlisle Hall, the Earl of Rugden had discovered three horses. Recognizing Sheba and the two other mares from his stable, Roderick had patted them each in turn, reassuring the nervous animals in the frosty night.

When the muffled sound of a gunshot came from inside the manor, Roderick had remounted his exhausted stallion. He charged directly up to the front door. Jumping from the saddle, he sprinted up the broad, shallow steps, only to be met by Oliver Davenport, sword in hand, who'd opened the door to investigate the sound of the approaching hoofbeats.

Roderick untied his cloak and threw it off. He pulled his short sword from its sheath and smiled with elation as he recognized his adversary.

"Davenport! So we meet again."

The ring of steel on steel sounded as their swords met. Parrying, feinting, lunging, the earl attacked his old enemy. He immediately seized the offensive and drove him relentlessly back through the opened door and into the entryway.

A lifetime abandoned to vice had ill-prepared the portly Davenport for his inevitable meeting with a foe who'd retained his strength and agility through years of hard soldiering. Striving uselessly to keep out of Rugden's greater reach, Davenport looked into the silvery eyes of his pursuer and saw the face of death.

With a blurred thrust in quarte, Roderick drove his sword through Davenport's heart. He paused only long enough to retrieve his blade and wipe it on his fallen opponent's satin jacket. Then he turned and raced toward the sound of his wife's screams.

The library door crashed open. Carlisle released his captive and leaped to his feet. His black eyes glittered with excitement. "What an unexpected surprise, Colonel Fielding. And here I thought you were in Brighton. But I knew you'd show up eventually, once you learned that I had your wife."

Roderick turned the key in the lock and walked into the room. With a sob of humiliation, Christina struggled to her feet. She was dressed in breeches and held a man's tattered shirt to her breast. Her honey-colored hair fell in tangles around her slender shoulders.

"Are you hurt?" he asked in a tight voice.

She shook her head and moved away from the duke on wobbly legs. "I'm . . . I'm not harmed." Exhausted by her struggles, she leaned against a nearby sofa. "He . . . he has a letter which will harm Pansy," she gasped. "We can't leave without it. Francis and Percy are here with me."

"I know," Roderick answered, keeping his eyes fixed on Carlisle. "Now, Your Grace, prepare to defend yourself against someone closer to your own size."

"With pleasure." Somesbury smiled. "At last I can finish the task I began with such anticipation. When you are dying, Rugden, call to mind that today I will have it all— your enormous fortune and your exquisite lady. Nothing could please me more." He gestured toward the crossed dueling swords above the fireplace. "With your permission?" he asked in a silky tone. He moved toward the mantelpiece with the supple grace of a hunting cat.

"Rugden!" Christina cried out. "There's a gun!"

Roderick hurled his sword away and dove for Carlisle just as the duke picked up the pistol. They fell, struggling for the firearm, which dropped and spun crazily across the library rug. It discharged with a roar as it hit the wall. The men rose, facing each other. In silent agreement, they removed their coats and rolled up the lacy cuffs of their sleeves. Reaching up in synchronization, they each took a slender, feather-light small sword *par excellence* from its holder above the mantel. The sound of the blades cut through the air with a whoosh in the quiet room as they tested the balance of the steel. They shoved the twin settees out of the way with their feet. Then the two enemies turned and faced each other at last.

After the briefest of salutes, their swords engaged. Circling each other warily, each man took his opponent's measure. Though both were tall, Rugden had a slight advantage in reach. Craftily, Somesbury, a practiced swordsman, brought his rear foot stealthily forward from his on-guard position. He lunged suddenly, gaining enough ground to score a quick first hit. But Roderick had developed a sixth sense during his years of combat. He detected Carlisle's move, parried his thrust easily, and stepped out of his distance.

Carlisle recovered his on-guard position. "I see you've learned a few tricks, Rugden. But I've more surprises up my sleeve for you."

The blades engaged in sixte. Roderick dropped his point, passed it under Carlisle's blade, and engaged it in quarte. For an instant the duke's line of defense opened up, but miraculously he parried, foible on foible.

The earl smiled. "Perhaps I might show you a trick or two myself," he said, his breath even and steady.

With blurring speed Roderick engaged his opponent's sword from sixte to quarte and back to sixte. Disengaging, he passed the point of his foil into the opposite line and lunged suddenly and with deliberation. Again it seemed as though only a miracle saved the duke.

"I want that letter, Carlisle. If you agree to surrender it, I'll let you live. Be thankful. Had you harmed my wife, you'd never have left this room alive."

Pressing his attack, Roderick forced his opponent up against a sofa. Carlisle stepped on the cushion and gracefully leaped over the couch.

"It's you who won't leave this room alive, Rugden. After I cut you to ribbons, I'll have my way with your wife right beside your dead body," Carlisle goaded.

Roderick followed him over the sofa, which tipped backward under his weight. He attacked Carlisle's blade in a change-beat. It was followed by a jump lunge, and he caught the duke completely by surprise. Parrying wildly, Carlisle regained his balance, deflecting the blade that came toward him with lightning speed.

The swordsmen flew back and forth across the room. Oblivious to the world around them, not hearing the pounding on the secured door, the two men were locked in a combat to the death.

Chairs, tables, screens were overturned. The rug was littered with smashed porcelain and statuary as the two powerful antagonists crossed and recrossed its intricate patterning. The acrid smell of hate filled the air. For Christina, pressed against an outer wall beside the velvet drapes, it was the most terrifying sight she had ever witnessed. An atmosphere of cold-blooded revenge permeated the room. Two Herculean combatants, heedless of anyone or anything but themselves, each bent on destroying the other, fought with a deadly primeval instinct that would neither give, nor expect, any mercy.

With a skillful riposte, Carlisle changed tactics and took the offensive, displacing his body. He hit Rugden just above his elbow. "That's only the beginning, my dear earl," he warned, his breath coming in short, panting gasps.

With blood dripping from his extended arm, Roderick knew he could no longer wait for a surrender. From an engagement in sixte, he made a feint disengage into quarte, deceiving Carlisle's circle parry by following it around, counterclockwise. Roderick lifted his blade point and delivered the hit into the open quarte line just above Carlisle's heart. The sword dropped from the duke's hand, and he crumpled upon the library floor.

Outside the locked door, Major General Gillingham's voice could be heard bellowing. "Confound it, Rugden, unlock this door!"

Roderick flung the bloody sword aside and went over to the doorway. He turned the key with a click, and the portal was flung open.

Shoving two burly servants into the room in front of him, Hugh rushed in and glanced around at the carnage. After him came Lieutenant Charles Thompson and four Light Dragoons. Everywhere, the furniture lay on its sides. Both settees had fallen over backward. At the far end of the book-filled room, hovering in a corner by the window, the Countess of Rugden crouched on her knees. The officers watched in compassionate silence as the earl walked over to his terrified wife and tenderly lifted her to her feet.

Pale and in shock, she stared vacantly at Rugden with haunted eyes and then pulled away from him. With stiff, jerky movements, she turned to the men who'd just entered. She held out her hand and staggered toward them. "Hugh! Charles!" she cried. "Francis and Percy are somewhere in the house. Oh, please, please, find them quickly."

Lieutenant Thompson hurried to her. "Lady Rugden, let me help you," he said gently. He took off his dark blue cloak and placed it over her shoulders, covering her torn clothing. With a firm hand under her elbow, he lead her to a sofa which Hugh had uprighted for her.

Bewildered by his wife's reaction to him, Roderick followed them, at a total loss for words.

Gillingham barked orders to the four guardsmen to search the home. Going over to the fallen man, he assisted him to his feet. "You, Justin Somesbury, are under arrest. And a plague on't, you're not already dead," he added with disgust.

Carlisle stared haughtily at the invaders despite his near mortal wound. Weaving unsteadily and holding a hand to the spreading stain on his white shirtfront, he snorted in derision. "You can't arrest a man for assaulting a housebreaker."

Thompson, who was bending solicitously over the countess, looked up. "You're accused, Your Grace, of high treason, and if found guilty will be hanged, drawn, and quartered."

Somesbury turned ashen. "You've no proof."

Roderick sat down on the arm of the sofa and allowed Hugh to roll the torn shirtsleeve up above his elbow and bind a handkerchief around the bleeding wound. "We have a most important witness who is willing to swear that you turned over valuable information to the Duc de Richelieu— your cousin and fellow traitor, Marie Boucher."

A soft cry of surprise sprang from Christina's lips. "Marie!"

Two guardsmen, one on each side, guided a stunned Francis into the library. He was holding a cloth to his head but was able to walk with some assistance. "Christy!" he cried and hurried to his sister. "Thank God, you're all right!" He dropped to his knees and enclosed her in his arms.

"No thanks to you, Major Berringer," came Rugden's cold response. He rose and stepped closer to Francis, his fists clenched in rage. "How dare you bring her here in the first place."

Shamefacedly, Francis stood and turned to meet their looks of condemnation, still holding on to his sister's hand. His voice rang with relief and humiliation. "We believed that Carlisle was in London. I'd never have brought Christina here if I'd thought there was any real danger. Before God, I admit I should never have brought her at all."

Just then a shouting Percy, dressed in the most somber outfit anyone had ever seen him wear, tore into the room. He was followed by the dragoons who'd released him from the closet. "Egad, whad a pardy! Hugh, whad are you doing here? And Roddy? Who are all these people?"

Irate at his younger brother, Roderick turned on him. "Confound it, Percy," he snapped, "how could you have been a part of endangering Christina?"

"That wasn'd my idea, believe me!" his brother answered indignantly. "These Berringers insisded on having their way, though I knew you'd be mad as a hornet when you found out. But I vound what I came for," he continued with a wide grin, producing a batch of papers from inside his sober brown jacket. Triumphantly, he waved them in the air. "Look at these ledders, will you?" he cried in glee. "Here's one impugning Pansy's legidimacy—and four more jusd like it! And here's five copies in our fader's own hand of his investments in the Greater London Docks Company. Each and every one of them done by Oliver Davenport and hidden away in his bedchamber!" He threw the papers in the air and danced wildly about the room.

Roderick bent and caught a page that fluttered past his knees. He gazed at the military summons that had ordered him to report to General Pickering in Brighton.

Percy, elation shining in his eyes, scampered around his brother and kicked his heels in a Highland fling. "Thunder and turv, Roddy, we've won! The investmend's a swindle thad lined the Duke of Carlisle's pocked, and we can prove it. The Fieldings are rich again!"

Charles Thompson and Hugh Gillingham retrieved the scattered papers and read them in curiosity.

"He's right, Roderick," Hugh agreed. "They're out-and-out forgeries. When the duke is brought to trial for his crimes, you'll be a very wealthy man once more."

Sergeant Angus Duncan arrived in time to view the Scottish dancing. "Whist, mon!" He grinned as he took in the scene of chaos. "I ken verra weel ye'd no been born in the Highlands for all your fine capering."

Roderick turned to his wife, who stood in the haven of her brother's arms. "Duncan brought the carriage, darling. You can ride home in it." Addressing his brother-in-law, he continued in a sharp tone, "You'd better ride in the coach with your sister, Francis. You look a little white. You must have taken quite a thump on the head. Maybe it knocked some sense into that thick skull of yours."

Francis Berringer straightened to his full height. To the best of his ability, he ignored the searing pain that shot through his head. "It may be, Colonel Fielding, that I know my sister better than you know your wife. Christina was determined to come. She threatened to come alone if I refused to take her with me—and I know her well enough to believe she'd have tried it."

"Besides," interrupted Percy, rushing to his co-conspirator's rescue, "we thought Carlisle was safe in Hanover Square awaiding Chrisdina. We thought the break-in would be a row down the Thames on a Sabbath Day. How could we have known it was a fiendish trap set up by that son of Satan?"

The room's occupants turned as one and looked at the Duke of Carlisle, who stood with his hands bound behind his back and flanked by a dragoon on either side. Someone had placed a cloth against his wound to staunch the bleeding.

"Take him away," Gillingham ordered. "He taints the very air we breathe. And take those two worthless rascals with him," he added, pointing to Swinton and Bleer huddled together by the wall.

The brave intruders of Carlisle Hall followed the traitors out of the library. As Roderick passed through the hallway, his arm protectively around Christina's shoulder, he looked down at the body of his old enemy, Oliver Davenport—the sophisticated roué who'd despoiled the innocent Lillibeth and then abandoned her with child. Davenport's wig had been knocked off, revealing a pate as smooth and hairless as an egg. Christina shivered at the sight of the sprawled corpse, grotesque in its patched and painted maquillage, and turned her face away.

With utmost tenderness, Roderick lifted his trembling wife into the coach. Her hands were icy beneath his touch. The faraway look in her beautiful eyes tormented him, and he turned to confront Francis. Something in the cavalryman's crestfallen look deflected the earl's anger. Roderick offered his hand and his forgiveness to his abject brother-in-law. "Thank you, Francis, for what you attempted to do for Pansy's sake. It was a brave act."

Major Berringer clasped the proffered hand with a grin. " 'Fore heaven, that wife of yours is a real handful, Rugden. From now on she's your responsibility, not mine." He jumped into the berlin and sat beside the countess.

"Get in the coach, Percy," his brother commanded with a crooked smile. "I want all three of you young idiots inside where I can keep my eye on you."

Roderick shut the door and signaled for Duncan, who had tied their three horses to the back of the carriage, to let loose the four-in-hand. Behind the Rugden coach followed Lieutenant Thompson and the four guards escorting Carlisle and his cohorts, who'd been lifted onto their horses.

At the front of the cavalcade with General Gillingham, Roderick relaxed in his saddle and allowed his mount to set a more moderate pace toward home.

It was daybreak when they reached Oxford Street. Hugh reined in his bay and dismounted. "I'll be parting from you here, Roderick, for I'll be accompanying Thompson and his prisoners to the Tower. I want to be there when they interrogate Carlisle."

"Then I'll talk to you tomorrow," Roderick said as he got down from the saddle.

"Nay, I cannot. I sail with the evening tide to take our acceptance of the final proposal to France. But I expect to see you and your countess in Paris next month for the signing of the treaty. In the meantime take good care of that precious bride of yours."

"You can count on it."

"Till we meet in Paris." The comrades clasped each other's hands in unspoken fellowship.

Walking over to the carriage, Gillingham offered his hand to Christina through the opened window. "Until I see you in Paris, Lady Rugden."

Leaning out of the berlin, Christina smiled at him. "Farewell, Hugh," she whispered. Unshed tears brimmed in her eyes. "Until we meet again."

Roderick motioned for Duncan to resume the journey, and the coach slowly pulled away. The earl approached Charles Thompson, still astride his horse. "Thank you for your help, Lieutenant."

"May I assure you, sir, that no word of this night's events will cross my lips. I wouldn't have harm come to Lady Rugden for anything in the world."

Reading the unspoken truth in Thompson's brown eyes, Roderick reached up and offered his hand. "Please come to see her tomorrow. I know the countess will wish to give you her thanks, once she's regained her composure."

"I'm afraid that won't be possible," the naval officer lied as he bent and shook the earl's hand. "I've orders to leave London in the morning. Please give my regards to your lady wife."

"I will," Roderick replied with complete understanding.

Rugden House was lit by dozens of candles when the countess was brought home. Lord and Lady Sanborn were waiting on the steps before the open door as Roderick lifted his wife out of the coach and into his strong arms.

Lady Gwendoline rushed to her sister. "Thank God, thank God," she wept, clinging to his arm.

He carried Christina, still bundled in Lieutenant Thompson's warm navy cloak, up the steps and into the home. Solemnly, Francis, Percy, and Henry Sanborn trailed after them.

Inside, a tearful Pansy waited next to the Dowager Marchioness of Waldwick. Seeing Christina in her brother's arms, the girl flew to them and caught hold of Roderick's elbow on the opposite side of Gwen.

"Bring her upstairs," Grandmother Berringer said. "Only

the women, please. Now that's enough tears, Pansy. You wait down here with Percy. And dry those eyes. Weeping never changed a thing."

While the other men gathered in the front drawing room, Roderick carried his bride up the stairs and into the sitting room that adjoined her bedchamber, where he placed her on a chaise longue.

"You, too, Roderick," Lady Helen insisted emphatically. She pointed her finger toward the open door. "Out you go. This is women's business. You may come back in shortly."

The earl glanced undecidedly at his wife, whose expressionless face terrified him. "I'm coming back in ten minutes, Lady Helen, whether you agree or not."

When the door closed behind him, Gwen went to her baby sister. Taking Christina's face between her hands, she looked deep into her blank eyes. "Oh, darling, it will be all right," she whispered with heartfelt compassion. "It will be all right."

"I've not been harmed, Gwen," Christina answered dully.

Motioning for Christina to lie back on the chaise, Grandmother Berringer sat down on its edge and faced her granddaughter with matter-of-fact composure. "Were you raped, Christina?" she asked in a manner that brooked no evasion.

Christina placed her hand on top of Lady Helen's frail one and strove to ignore the tears that rolled down her cheeks. "No, Grandmother. Rugden came in time."

"In other words, you were not harmed physically?"

Nodding her head, Christina silently assented. How could she say that it was her own husband, not the Duke of Carlisle, who'd shattered her girlish dreams and broken her foolish heart?

Standing straight and tall, in spite of the need for her gold-headed cane, Grandmother Berringer stepped onto the landing and looked down at the people who stood clustered at the foot of the stairs. "You may come up now, Roderick. And so may the other members of this family."

When the entire clan had gathered in the countess's sitting room, Pansy timidly approached her sister-in-law.

"Oh, Christy," she said plaintively as she knelt in front of the chaise longue. "Whyever did you go to Carlisle Hall?"

Christina looked at the top of Pansy's chestnut curls and wondered how she could possibly explain the true reason to the innocent young girl.

"Sit down everyone," the dowager marchioness said. "There's been a great deal of confusion about the enmity between Justin Somesbury and the Fielding family. Had I spoken out previously, this near-tragic event would never have occurred. But I was bound by an oath taken many, many years ago."

Looking around at the assemblage, whose attention was fixed upon her, the dowager sat down on the edge of the chaise longue beside her granddaughter. "Very well, my dear children," she continued. "I will break the vow of secrecy I have kept for over fifteen years. I am the only living person who knows what happened that unfortunate day so long ago. But now I must break my promise to the departed. Carlisle wanted your mother, Rugden—just as he wanted Christina. And he employed foul means in the past as he did today. I know, for I was there."

"By Jove!" Lord Sanborn exclaimed, pulling Gwen closer to him, where they sat on a velvet love seat.

"Please go on," Roderick directed. He braced his hips against a side table and folded his arms across his chest.

"Your mothers, Sabrina Fielding and Joanna Berringer, were close friends. The incident happened while you were at Cambridge, Roderick. One afternoon, we three ladies were traveling by coach to London when we were accosted by two masked highwaymen. They didn't demand our money or our jewels. It was Sabrina they wanted. The taller brigand dragged her, terrified, from the coach, while the other held a blunderbuss on our coachman and footman. Despite our pleas for mercy, she was thrown up in front of the leader's saddle, and they started off."

Allowing time for the murmurs of concern and compassion to die down, Grandmother Berringer glanced around the room. Percy, a look of dread on his stricken features, was perched on the arm of the love seat close to Gwen and her husband. Francis had plopped down on the floor beside the small sofa. Pansy knelt in front of the chaise longue at the dowager's feet.

"Quiet, please!" Roderick said. "Let Lady Helen go on with her story."

The dowager marchioness nodded her elegantly powdered coiffure and resumed her tale. "By chance, a solitary officer of the Fifteenth Foot was coming down the London road. He heard our cries for help and quickly realized what had happened. He raised his pistol and took careful aim. The rider fell from his horse, taking Sabrina to the ground with him. The officer galloped over, quickly disarmed the man, and freed Sabrina."

Cheers errupted briefly, and then all was quiet again.

"Overjoyed, we ran to her, while the second man rode away free. Our brave rescuer introduced himself as Captain Thurlow. We then turned to the fallen villain. Imagine our shock to discover that the highwayman, once unmasked, was none other than the Duke of Carlisle. Envision our consternation, if you will. Were we to turn such a high-ranking peer over to the law, all would be made public, and Sabrina would have to appear in court. Despite the facts to the contrary, we knew her unblemished reputation would be besmirched."

"Thunder and turv," shouted Percy. He snatched off his wig and threw it across the room. "I would have shod the vermin!"

Ignoring the interruption, Lady Helen added with emphasis, "And there was one other concern. Sabrina had that day confided her joyous news that she was with child. Would she lose the baby because of the fall? To subject her to a court trial would be to further risk the life of the unborn child. So we three women cajoled Captain Thurlow into allowing Carlisle his freedom. We claimed we knew the man, and that it was all a terrible prank gone astray. Luckily, he believed us. The only other person ever to know what had happened that day was Sabrina's husband, the Earl of Rugden. Not even my son, the Marquess of Waldwick, learned about it."

The elderly woman took her granddaughter's hand. "Had you not wisely refused Somesbury's offer of marriage, Christina, I was prepared to break my long silence.

No doubt he'd forgotten that I was even in the coach with the two younger women and believed he had a clear field, since both of them were now dead. But your common sense in refusing him made my intervention unnecessary."

Facing her spellbound audience once again, the dowager took Pansy's small hand. "The serious wound that Carlisle sustained precluded any immediate challenge from the late Earl of Rugden. After being taken to a nearby inn by the solicitous Captain Thurlow, he recovered and fled to Paris, where he stayed for several years—long after your mother's death, Pansy. Your father remained his most bitter enemy. He always held Carlisle responsible for the birth complications that finally took your mother's life."

Roderick shook his head in amazement at the incredible tale. "So that was the reason behind the deep hatred between them."

"Odds my life," added Percy, leaping up in his excitement, "what a dasdardly rogue. Had I known all this, I might never have had the courage to break into his house."

"The three of you were very brave," Roderick admitted. He smiled tenderly at his wife. "But the next time you find yourself in trouble, come to me."

"Well, I like that," Percy exploded. "How could we, when you were galloping off lickedy-split to Brighdon?"

His eyes on his lovely wife, Roderick saw the look of disdain she turned on him before the rest of the gathering demanded her attention.

Then everyone, it seemed, was talking at once.

Chapter 26

Seated at the breakfast table the next morning, Roderick listened indulgently to his young sister review the thrilling events of the previous evening.

"Why is it that I always miss the excitement?" Pansy complained in a martyred tone. "I could have gone along with them. I'd have carried a gun, and when Christy missed the evil duke, I'd have shot him right through his gizzard!"

Roderick laughed and shook his head in reproach. "Lady Penelope, where did you learn that vulgar expression?"

Before she could answer Christina entered the dining room, and he stood and laid his napkin beside his plate. He went over to his lovely wife and led her to the table, where he pulled out a chair for her. "I thought you were supposed to be teaching this hoyden some graces," he chided her softly. "Instead you've given her ideas about dressing up like a man and challenging everyone she knows to a duel. A fine model of deportment you've been."

Christina smiled wanly at his teasing. She recalled with dejection the way her husband had thanked her in front of everyone for her heroic attempt to save Pansy from ruin. After Lady Helen's startling revelations, they'd all been talking at once about the forgeries, the sword fight, and the treasonous crimes of the Duke of Carlisle and his cousin Marie Boucher. Pleading exhaustion, she'd slipped away to her bedroom, determined to hide her misery from all those joyous people rather than ruin their celebration.

"I've not been the best duenna, I'll admit," she said in a flat, spiritless tone. "Pansy would have been better under Gwen's tutelage."

"No, I wouldn't have," Pansy exclaimed indignantly. "I'd never want anyone but you to be my chaperone."

Tears filled Christina's eyes. She blinked them away and looked down at the plate Rawlings placed in front of her. She was determined to hide her feeling of absolute desolation. How could she admit to anyone that she'd given her heart irrevocably to a man who kept a mistress—or two—or three? A man who one minute could be so tender and gentle, so brave and courageous, and then turn around the next moment and openly consort with a bird of paradise or two Parisian doxies.

"May I add, my lady," the butler said as he bent to serve her, "that all of the staff are very grateful that the master brought you home safe and unharmed."

Afraid to lift her face for fear the tears would be seen, Christina kept her gaze upon the scrambled eggs and toast in front of her. "Thank you, Rawlings. Please express to the others how touched I am by their kindness." Gaining control of her quavering voice, she glanced at Rugden. "It's so hard to believe that Marie is really the Duke of Carlisle's cousin and that she was in league with him all this time. I would never have suspected her of such horrible duplicity."

The earl leaned back in his chair to allow Rawlings to refill his coffeecup. "I read a copy of the forged note that was supposed to have been written by Lady Muggleton," he said. "It was composed, along with all the other fake documents, by Oliver Davenport. Boucher admitted that she'd abetted Carlisle in his scheme to abduct you that evening. She'd pretended to be too ill to accompany you in order to ensure that you left Sanborn House alone. She was to acquire your fortune in return for her complicity. That's also why she passed on the information to her cousin."

"And Carlisle?" she asked. "What was his reason for betraying his own country?"

"Greed could have played some part. But the primary

motivation behind selling our secrets was the intent to undermine my efforts at the negotiating table."

Subdued, Christina pondered the far-reaching, complicated scheme that Justin Somesbury had set into motion after she'd refused his offer of marriage last spring. Had she not entered the wrong coach that late August afternoon, she might now be the Duchess of Carlisle. What her life would have been like, had that happened, was too frightening to explore. She bit her trembling lower lip. "It appears that I've caused you quite a lot of trouble."

"Just a smile from those beautiful lips would make it all worthwhile, sunshine." The timbre of his quiet voice betrayed his worry.

From the corner of her eye, Christina could see Pansy swerve her head to stare at Rugden. "I didn't get a chance to congratulate you on the success of the negotiations," Christina told her husband. "I understand that every point for which you strove has been incorporated into the final document."

Reaching across the table, Rugden took her hand. "We shall return to Paris next month for the signing of the treaty. You never had a chance to visit Septimanie's chateau in the Loire Valley. I'll take you there myself. From France, we'll go on to Italy for the wedding trip we never had."

Christina reclaimed her captured hand on the pretext of reaching for her cup. She lowered her lashes and sipped the coffee before she answered quietly, "A month is too far away to make any definite plans."

"Roderick says we'll leave for Rugden Court as soon as we're packed," Pansy contributed brightly. "Duncan has already gone with Mohawk and Sheba. I haven't been home since I left the academy. Aren't you excited about spending Christmas in Buckinghamshire?"

"I don't think I'll be going, dear," Christina replied. "I'll probably make other plans for the holidays." She toyed with the food on the lovely Sèvres china and then laid down her fork, unable to eat. Her heart felt like a frozen lump inside her chest.

At long last Rugden would agree to a legal separation, she realized. Now that the Greater London Docks Company had been proven to be nothing more than a piece of paper forged by Carlisle, the enormous funds swindled from the Fielding family would be returned from the duke's vast wealth. Her husband no longer needed the use of her small fortune. A separation would free him to chase those high-flying demireps for which he seemed to have such a passion, unhindered by the embarrassment of a clinging, long-faced wife. She'd be all the better for it, she argued to herself. No more scandalous duels to humiliate her—that would certainly be one positive aspect. He could court *both* the Ramillies sisters for all she'd care and keep his dark-haired mistress on the side as well.

Rugden reached over and took her hand. He brought her cold fingers to his warm lips. "Are you feeling ill, darling?" he asked with utmost tenderness. "I didn't mean to upset you with my teasing. You must know that I trust you completely with Pansy. After what you risked for her, how could I not?" Retaining hold of her hand, he looked into her eyes, his troubled gray ones filled with concern. "If you're overtired, sweetheart, we'll wait for a few days and give you some time to rest before we leave for Rugden Court."

Unable to bear his meaningless endearments a moment longer, Christina snatched her hand away. She rose from her chair and rushed from the room without a word of explanation.

Roderick started to follow her. After such a terrifying ordeal, it would be natural for her to be disoriented and confused, even angry.

Pansy stood up, plopped her hands on her hips, and scowled fiercely. "How can you be such a hypocrite?" she asked the brother she'd always idolized. "Don't pretend you care about her. We know better!"

Shocked at her words, Roderick accosted his sister. "What are you talking about?"

"We know," she said. "We saw you with that—that *woman* the day we came back to London from Waldwick Abbey. You were standing right out on Duke of York Street, kissing her."

"Pansy," he said, enunciating each word as though he were speaking to a very small child, "the lady you saw me with is a friend. A very loyal one, whom I've just learned this morning was severely beaten by the Duke of Carlisle because she'd warned me about him. I owe Madeline Gannet a great deal, and she will certainly have my friendship throughout my lifetime. But she does not have my protection as a lover. Nor does any lady except the one I'm married to."

"Oh, Roderick," Pansy croaked, "I thought the most awful things about you." She put her slim arms around his waist and laid her head on his chest. "I should have known you were not a . . . a philanderer."

"Is that what Christina thinks?"

"I don't know what she thinks. She didn't say a word that morning. She only looked the other way and pretended not to have seen you. I wondered how you could treat her so badly when she's been so wonderful to us all. Even if you didn't love her, I knew that Percy and I did."

"Pansy," Roderick stated in a voice that demanded obedience, "I want you to spend a few days with Lady Gwendoline. Christina and I need to have some time by ourselves."

"Not again," Lady Penelope said wrathfully as she pulled away from him. "I'm always being left behind. I thought we were all going to Buckinghamshire."

"We will, little one, I promise. We'll all be together at Rugden Court for Christmas next week. You can ride with the Sanborns and help Lady Gwen entertain Joanna and Alexander on the trip." He kissed her on the forehead. "But not one word of this to Christina, understand?"

Pansy nodded. Her brown eyes glowed with delight at being a part of her brother's secret.

"Now go and write a note to Lady Sanborn." Smiling, he placed one finger in front of his lips. "And shh!"

As Pansy and Roderick left the room and entered the hallway, Christina was coming down the stairs. The delighted fifteen-year-old scampered up the steps and threw her arms around the countess. "I'm so happy you're my sister," she said with a giggle. "I'll talk to you later. I have a letter that must be written immediately." Not waiting for a reply, Pansy bounded up the staircase, her laughter ringing out above their heads.

"What was that all about?" Christina asked as she came to a halt on the bottom stair.

"She's happy that everyone's safe," Roderick told his wife. He surveyed the quilted blue coat she wore and the large bandbox held tightly in one hand. "Are you really feeling well enough to pay calls this morning?"

"I'm going to visit Gwen," she announced with determination.

He propped his booted foot on the bottom step, braced one hand on the newel post, and blocked her exit. "It looks as though you plan to stay with your sister for some time. I think there are a few things we need to discuss before you leave."

"I'm in a dreadful hurry." Nearly eye level with her husband, she stared at him as though he were some wretched, long-legged aphid crawling over a newly budded rose.

He took the bandbox from her and strode down the hall. "I promise not to take too much of your precious time."

Christina followed her husband into his study, her head high. The box he placed beside the narrow library table contained a nightdress and slippers. She debated his reaction should she disclose the truth. Although evasion had seemed the safer course when she'd decided upon it earlier that morning, she couldn't bring herself to act in such an underhanded way.

"I'm planning on staying with Gwen tonight," she said, then blurted out with scrupulous honesty, "and every night in the foreseeable future." She straightened her shoulders and met his gaze while she tried to ignore the cold tentacle of despair that wrapped itself around her heart.

His deep voice was quiet and gentle. "Without telling me?"

"There's a note for you on my pillow," she answered. She tried to read the thoughts hidden behind his shuttered gray eyes.

He leaned against the table and braced his palms on its edge. "I see," he said conversationally. "And what does the note say?"

"That I'm leaving you." She swallowed the sobs that

clogged her aching throat and forced herself to continue. "I'm going to seek a legal separation."

Roderick fought the urge to sweep her into his arms and tell her how much he adored her. He wanted to cover her sweet lips with his own, to take possession of her beautiful body as he surrendered his heart and his soul to her keeping. But he knew if he took one step toward her, she'd bolt for the door. At that moment she probably believed that she hated him.

"And nothing I can say will change your mind?" he asked reasonably.

"Nothing."

"Not even after what happened between us at Waldwick Abbey?" Despite his attempt to remain coolly unemotional, his words sounded harsh and urgent to his own ears.

Her blue eyes were dark pools of stalwart resolution. She lifted her stubborn chin. "What happened at my father's home was the result of mere physical attraction, nothing more." She drew a long, ragged breath, turned, and walked to the fireplace. Bracing her hand on the mantelpiece, she stared down into the flames for several minutes before she continued. "When it comes to building a lifetime together, you and I are entirely unsuitable. We have absolutely nothing in common."

"I don't agree," Roderick said as he followed her across the room. He placed his hand on her shoulder, and she trembled beneath his touch. "We have many things in common."

Her head snapped up. "Name one."

"Love of family," he answered, gentling his voice. "Both of us know how important family ties are, and both of us are willing to fight to protect our loved ones. Our home will be the center of our life, Christina, not our wealth, or our estates, or even your valuable collection of antiques in Cornwall. Our children will be our priceless treasures." He paused, waiting for her to reply. She remained perfectly still, as though hoping he'd have his say and then leave her in peace.

Lightly, Roderick traced the graceful line of her shoulder with one forefinger. "If by unsuitable you're referring to your incredible gift for music and my lack of any musical talent whatsoever, I promise, I'll never interfere with the pursuit of your interests. You've my permission to begin the restoration of Penthaven immediately. Surely that change of heart is a measure of my sincere intentions in this marriage?"

"Your sudden generosity is scarcely impressive," she scoffed, "when one considers that you no longer need my fortune for your own purposes. You were right when you said that had I been given a choice, I'd never have chosen you for my husband." Christina made no attempt to keep the biting sarcasm from her voice. "You're not the kind of man I want at all."

His words were a soft breath in her ear. "I was hoping that you'd come to feel some measure of affection for me." He caressed the base of her throat with his strong fingers, and Christina felt the flame of desire ignite inside her. That was exactly why she'd decided to leave him a written message, instead of confronting him in person. Every time he touched her, he aroused the relentless yearning that only his lips, his arms, his body could fulfill.

He bent to place a soft kiss on her temple, and she shrugged free of his touch. She turned to face him and spoke in a scathing tone. "You may have misinterpreted my violent disapproval of your affair with the Ramillies sisters. Or is it affairs? I'm not quite sure. If you thought I acted from jealousy over your *ménage a trois,* you were mistaken. It was simply the notoriety that upset me. My pride, not my heart, was bruised by your scandalous behavior."

Quirking his scarred eyebrow, Rugden shook his head ruefully. "The so-called affair with the opera dancers was no more than an innocent flirtation brought about by my temporary insanity while in Paris." His gaze dropped to her lips, and the trace of a smile flickered over his rugged features. "I used to think you were a witch, so trapped was I in your spell. So hopelessly obsessed that I actually became convinced that you were involved with Carlisle in spying for the French."

Incredulous, Christina laughed in his face. "You thought

I was a spy? Me? Patriotic Christina Berringer? I can't believe it!"

"You. Patriotic Christina Fielding. Believe it, darling. It's but a measure of how bewitched I was. And still am."

"Is that why you sent me home from Paris?" she demanded. "You thought I was spying for the French?"

He gently traced the line of her upper lip with the tip of his finger. His touch was unbearably seductive. His words were a hoarse whisper of enticement. "I was a raving lunatic, wasn't I?" He bent down to kiss her.

She pushed against his wide shoulders and moved resolutely away. "I thought you sent me home because you wanted to be free to be with those—"

Roderick followed her retreat and interrupted her without compunction. "Since the day I met you, Christina, I've not bedded, or even wanted, another woman."

"Ha!"

He decided to breach all the walls of her defenses at once. "Has anyone ever spoken to you about Madeline Gannet?"

Christina's chin jerked up as though he'd just struck her. "No," she replied with obvious evasion. "The woman attended the Duchess of Olwood's soiree in the company of Justin Somesbury. What else is there to know?"

"Madeline is an old friend of mine. Lately she'd been under the protection of the Duke of Carlisle. She became convinced that he was my deadly enemy. While in his home, she attempted, at the risk of her own safety, to discover information which might help me."

"She must be a very good friend indeed," Christina said stiffly.

"Loyal enough that she almost died for it," Rugden affirmed. "Yesterday morning Madeline was savagely beaten for passing that information on to me. Despite the injuries she sustained, she sent word of what she'd learned from Somesbury during that brutal punishment—the warning that you were in grave danger."

"Then I owe her my life," Christina said humbly, "for I was determined that I would never submit to Carlisle. How fortunate for us both that you have such a loyal friend."

"That's all she is, Christina. Just a friend. Nothing more."

Roderick captured her face in his hand. He bent his head and covered her mouth with his own. His lips clung to hers, persuading, imploring, demanding she return his kiss. He caressed her shoulders and slid his hands down her back to bring her hips against his taut thighs, molding her soft curves to his hard, hungry body. He could feel her fighting against his seduction as she drew strength from somewhere deep inside her to withstand his passionate onslaught. She was allowing him to kiss her. Nothing more.

He drew back slightly and read the confusion in her tormented eyes as she tried to dissect all the information he'd thrown at her like a wily barrister pleading before the bar. Taking her hands, he brought them to his lips and nibbled her fingertips in sensuous, purposeful beguilement.

"Darling, believe me," he whispered.

Tortured by doubts and afraid to hope, Christina saw once again the picture of her husband in Madeline Gannet's arms. An ache of desolation engulfed her. "I . . . I don't know what to believe," she said. "Or if I dare ever to trust you again."

"Don't leave now," he urged, "not today. At least wait until the holidays are over. Your family is planning on joining us in the country next week. Don't spoil Christmas for everyone, including the children."

Christina knew he was bargaining for time. He was cleverly using her weakness for her loved ones against her. She was also aware that staying even a week with her strong-willed husband could destroy all her steadfast resolutions. His ardent courtship at Waldwick Abbey had proven devastating. There was no reason to suppose he wouldn't launch another such erotic offensive at Rugden Court. If she succumbed to his charm once again, she'd risk the chance that he might get her with child. Then she'd be trapped for a lifetime, hopelessly in love with a man who didn't love her—at least, not any more than he loved his brave and beautiful mistress.

She exhaled a long, shaky breath and shook her head with unswerving fortitude. "I don't think it would be wise for me to go to Rugden Court with you."

"Christina—"

He was interrupted by a tap on the door.

"Yes?" came Rugden's sharp reply, and Rawlings entered hesitantly, holding a calling card on a small silver tray.

"Mr. Jacob Rothenstein begs permission to see you, my lord."

"Jacob?" Christina cried. Dismayed, she clasped her hands tightly in front of her. In the turmoil that had begun with the sight of her husband in the arms of his mistress and ended with her rescue at Carlisle Hall, she'd completely forgotten that she'd written to Jacob, instructing him to dispose of her antiques collection and proceed in all haste with the sale of Penthaven. If her shrewd husband found out what she'd done, he would know without a doubt that she'd fallen head over heels in love with him. There'd be no other plausible explanation for her actions.

"Tell him I'm very busy right now," Roderick said to the butler with obvious irritation.

"Very well, sir. But Mr. Rothenstein said it was extremely important. He said he'd be happy to wait until you were free."

Roderick remembered the stack of unopened letters sitting on his desk nearby. He hadn't had a chance to read any correspondence in the last three whirlwind days, but he knew that at least two of the envelopes were from the elderly merchant and financier. "Very well," he said with a sigh. "He may wait, if he wishes."

"No, no," cried Christina in a breathless voice. "Tell him to come back another day."

Roderick turned to study his wife in amazement. Her suddenly callous attitude toward someone she cared for so deeply didn't make any sense. A flush stained her lovely complexion. Her wide eyes betrayed her panic.

"Surely we can spare a few minutes to see your old friend," he said.

"There's no need to take up your valuable time," she countered. "You must be very busy this morning. I can visit with Jacob in the front salon."

Roderick met his butler's fascinated gaze. "Show Mr.

Rothenstein in," he instructed. "We'll see the gentleman right now."

Christina rushed forward the moment Jacob appeared in the doorway. Putting her arm about his stooped shoulders, she guided him into the room. "My dear friend," she said with a nervous smile, "how good of you to pay us a visit."

The two men shook hands before the countess led Jacob to a soft chair by the fire and sat down on the ottoman at his feet.

"I didn't come to gossip, child," he said as he fondly patted her smooth hand with his gnarled one. "I'm afraid I've come to Rugden House on business once again." He looked up at Roderick, who stood with one elbow resting on the marble mantelpiece. "I'm sorry to bother you in your own home, my lord, but I felt it was important to get this tangled coil straightened out immediately."

"Of course," the earl said with a polite inclination of his head. "Go on."

"Would you like some tea?" Christina nearly shouted.

Jacob shook his snowy head, and the long curls that dangled in front of his ears swayed slightly. "I breakfasted just before I came this morning." He returned his gaze to Rugden. "I'm here in regard to the messages I sent to you over the last several days. I need to know how you wish me to handle the contradictory instructions I've received."

Roderick frowned. "I'm not sure I understand what the problem is, Mr. Rothenstein. I haven't had time to open any of my correspondence lately. I do know, however, that I've received several letters from you."

"Three, to be exact, sir," the merchant said. He smoothed his long white beard in the unhurried manner of the very old. "The first was in regard to the Greater London Docks Company. I launched an inquiry of my own through my numerous connections along the waterfront. I was able to trace the two men who posed as the directors of that fraudulent corporation. Their real names were Swinton and Bleer. They used aliases, however, to collect the promissory notes supposedly pledged by your father and submitted to his bank on the very morning of his death only hours after his sudden demise."

"Damn," Roderick swore, "how could they have known? Unless they were with him when he died?"

"Unfortunately, my lord, we must deduct that the late earl's fall from his horse may not have been an accident. The Duke of Carlisle's own servants were probably responsible for your father's death, though we may never know for certain."

Roderick met Jacob's solemn gaze. "I appreciate your efforts on my behalf, sir. And what was in the other two letters?"

Christina jumped to her feet. Rothenstein, leaning on his cane, started to rise politely, and she plopped back down on the hassock. "I think I'd like some tea, myself," she said with an over-bright smile. "I didn't have much breakfast." She turned to her husband. "Why don't you ring for a maid?"

"Why don't we let Jacob finish what he's trying to say?" Roderick interposed. "Then we can order an entire dinner, if you're still hungry." He motioned for the businessman to be seated once again. "Now, if you'll continue, sir. What was in the second letter?"

Jacob sank back down on the wing chair. His dark eyes twinkled with merriment. "The second was in response to Lady Christina's instructions for me to place her entire collection of musical instruments up for auction and to expedite immediately the sale of your estate at Penthaven."

"What?" Roderick exclaimed. He moved away from the fireplace and stared in astonishment at Christina. She was sitting on the low stool as stiff and straight as a musket barrel, a look of utter mortification flushing her delicate features.

"Yes," Rothenstein continued, unperturbed by her obvious agitation. "Christina asked that all funds from these sales be used to further the exploration into your late father's ill-favored investment."

"Did she, by God?" Roderick said in exultation. The full meaning of the wealthy financier's statement came with a bolt of glorious comprehension. Christina hadn't only risked her life to search for the incriminating evidence against Pansy. She'd also relinquished her most cherished dream to aid Roderick in his fight for his family's lost wealth. She'd been willing to give up her precious antiques and her grandfather's vision to save the Rugden fortune and honor. There was only one explanation for such a heart-stopping sacrifice. His wife was in love with him. More in love than she knew. More in love than he dared hope was possible. He grinned in triumph.

Christina refused to meet his gaze. With a frown wrinkling her clear brow, she stared down in fierce concentration at the tips of her fingers as though studying a difficult treatise in Latin.

"But, of course, I was completely stymied by those exceedingly specific instructions," Jacob explained. "For on the very next day I received the message from you, my lord, telling me to cease all attempts to continue the probe into the Greater London Docks Company and begin, instead, the renovations in Cornwall necessary to the establishment of an asylum for elderly musicians. And to use the rest of Lady Christina's inheritance to add to the already fine collection housed at Penthaven." He looked from one to the other and shook his head in wry amusement. "Hence, the reason for the third letter. I'd simply like to know whose instructions to follow, since I can't possibly accommodate you both."

Christina rose slowly to her feet, her gaze fastened on her tall husband. "Dear God in heaven," she whispered. Tears sprang to her eyes, clouding the vision of his beloved face. "You were willing to give up all chance of clearing your father's name? Of restoring your family's wealth? You were going to do this so I could pursue my grandfather's dream?" A joy she never imagined possible swelled within her. He loved her. She could no longer doubt it. He loved her with such a deep, abiding love that he was willing to sacrifice everything he held dear—honor, duty, pride—for her sake.

He took a step toward her, and she hurried to meet him. She reached up to touch his face and felt the wet warmth of tears on his cheeks.

"Roderick," she whispered, "my own true love." Her husband drew her tenderly into his arms, and she nestled her head against his broad chest.

Behind her, Jacob rose from his chair and, with a hint

of smothered laughter, cleared his throat. "I take it this means you don't wish to sell Penthaven or the collection of antiquities, either one, my lord?"

Roderick brushed the top of his wife's curls with his chin and grinned at the venerable patriarch. "You have it correct, sir."

Jacob moved to the door, then paused to look back at them. "By the way, my lord, do you remember selling three useless old musical instruments that you found in your attic at Rugden Court last August to a traveling peddler?"

Roderick frowned. "Vaguely."

"They happened to be a flute, a timbrel, and a zither from the fourteenth century, all in excellent condition and of the highest quality. A trader named Colley Moss bought them from that peddler and brought them to me. I, in turn, showed them to Lady Christina."

Roderick's wife turned in his arms, a look of amazement on her face. "Jacob, you don't mean ... ?"

"Exactly," he replied. "Colley said to tell you that he'd be happy to return the money that Lord Rugden paid for the purchase of his own antiques. However, there is a modest fee for some information he ferreted out for me. You see, Mr. Moss is the one who identified the two directors of the Greater London Docks Company as Abstrupus Swinton and Jasper Bleer. And he will be happy to so testify in court."

"How much do I owe Mr. Moss for all his help?" Roderick asked with a curious smile.

Jacob opened the door and saluted farewell with his cane before answering. "Precisely nine thousand pounds, my lord."

The door closed behind him, and husband and wife looked into each other's startled gazes. Then they broke into gales of happy laughter.

"Tell me, Roderick," his wife coaxed. Sated and content, they lay side by side in his enormous bed at Rugden Court. She ran her languorous fingers through the mat of hair on his chest and traced the battle scar that crossed it. Playfully, she tweaked his ear and touched it with her tongue in blatant seduction. Then she nibbled his earlobe insistently.

Thrilling to her touch, Roderick turned, rested his head on one hand, and gazed at her. He reached beneath his pillow and brought out a scarlet box. "First open your Christmas gift," he said with a smile.

Christina scooted up against the fluffy pillow. "But it's not Christmas yet," she protested. She lifted the present with undisguised curiosity. Attached to its wide gold bow was a small tag with an inscription in his broad scrawl.

To My Lady Sunshine,
Because no one as beautiful as you should
ever feel destitute or homeless.

"In a few more days Rugden Court is going to be swarming with Berringers," he said, "not to mention my brother and sister. We'll have relatives hanging from the rafters. I'm not waiting for an audience. Go ahead," he coaxed, "unwrap it now."

With a smile curving her lips, she did as he asked. He watched the glow of pleasure suffuse her creamy complexion as she removed the red wrapping and opened the lid of the velvet-covered case. Inside lay a magnificent necklace of diamonds and sapphires. She caught her breath at the sight, then slowly picked it up. The near-priceless jewels were set in an intricate pattern of gold filigree, so cunningly wrought, they seemed to move and shimmer of their own accord in the candlelight.

Her hushed voice was filled with awe. "It's breathtaking, Roderick. I've never seen such a beautiful piece." She lifted her long lashes to meet his gaze in surprise. "The stones match my ring perfectly."

"They belonged to my mother," he told her. "They were in a necklace given to her by my father on their wedding day along with her ring. But the chain was heavy and old-fashioned. I had them reset in a more fragile design that would complement your slender figure."

He sat up and took the necklace from her hand. She turned to allow him to hook the clasp behind her neck, then lay back against the pillow.

"How does it look?" she asked. A blush spread across her satiny skin.

He bent his head and placed a kiss on her soft lips. "The sapphires match your beautiful eyes," he murmured.

Christina buried her fingers in his straight black hair. Earlier she'd removed the narrow ribbon that tied his queue, and his shiny locks fell to grace his powerful shoulders.

"Thank you," she said softly. Overwhelmed by his generosity, she wondered when he'd ordered the jewels reset. It must have been before she'd tumbled down the stairs. At any moment during their tumultuous marriage, he could have sold the precious stones and used the money as he wished. Instead he'd kept the diamonds and sapphires as a gift for his reluctant and untruthful bride.

"There's more in the box, sweetheart."

She looked down to discover a parchment, rolled into a narrow cylinder and tied with a gold thread, resting on the case's satin lining. Curious, she lifted the document and untied the string. She glanced again at her husband, opened the scroll, and stared at the paper before her. Tears misted her eyes as she read the letters inscribed in fancy calligraphy. There in front of her, as a bride's settlement, was the deed to Penthaven in her own name. She met his loving gaze, unable to express her feelings. She lifted her hand to his cheek and brushed her thumb across his lips.

"You've given me the memories of my childhood wrapped up in a gold thread," she said in a voice shaking with emotion. She rested her head back against the pillow, and Rugden moved over her. "Now will you tell me?" she persisted.

"I can't say when I fell in love with you, darling." He stroked her bare flesh with increasing intimacy. "It could have been that night when I helped you undress for your bath. Or the next day, when I heard you playing my mother's haunting sonata. Or sometime in between, when you carried that ridiculous horse pistol about the house threatening to shoot me. After we were married and you told me you were pregnant, I tried to convince myself that what I felt was only lust." He grinned and leered at her suggestively. "Every time I was near you," he said, "I was hot and hard and wild with desire. But I was afraid to touch you, lest I harm the child. So I fought back, lashing out at you in my own self-imposed frustration."

He cupped her face in his hands and met her gaze with a look of rueful honesty. "Only after I became convinced that you'd betrayed not only me, but our country as well, did I have to admit to myself that I loved you. I couldn't face the thought of living my life without you, lost in an abyss of loneliness and never daring to hope you'd grow to love me in return."

"You were mistaken about several things," she told him with a throaty laugh.

"Mmm," he said as he traced the shell of her ear with his tongue, "what were they?"

"First, my tempestuous, hardheaded husband, I loved you in return."

"What else?"

"And second, when you said you had no musical talent whatsoever, you couldn't have been more wrong. You have a perfect sense of tempo, a genius for lyrical movement, and exquisite, faultless timing."

He flashed his devastating grin and pulled her down to lie beside him. "Merry Christmas, darling," he said.

"Merry Christmas," she answered.

They came together, a meeting of bodies, a meeting of souls, as they pledged their love to each other, a love that would last through a lifetime and beyond. On that snowy winter night, Roderick bestowed on his wife a gift far lovelier than mere diamonds or sapphires, a treasure far greater than any paltry deed to a manor house. He gave her a child. And before the next Christmastide, she would present him with an heir.

Dr. Bowles and the Honorable Percival Fielding had been absolutely right.

Before very long there would be lots of little Fieldings.